THE BABY

*I thought that if I showed him all of my worst traits, bit by bit,
then one day I would have shown them all, would be free of
them, and I could allow myself to be the romantic partner in
love that I felt was my real nature.*

THE BABY

A VIDEO NOVEL BY

VIVA

ALFRED A. KNOPF · NEW YORK · 1975

THIS IS A BORZOI BOOK
PUBLISHED BY ALFRED A. KNOPF, INC.

Grateful acknowledgment is made to the following for permission to reprint
previously published material:

American Broadcasting Music, Inc.: Title "California Dreamin'" by John Phillips
and Michelle Gilliam, Copyright © 1965, American Broadcasting Music, Inc. Used by
permission only. All rights reserved.

Chappell & Co., Inc.: One line of lyrics from "Summertime". Copyright © 1935 by
Gershwin Publishing Corp. Copyright renewed. All rights reserved.
Used by permission.

Harper & Row Publishers, Inc.: Brief excerpt from *Infant and Child in the Culture of
Today* by Arnold Gessell and Frances L. Ilg. (1943 edition).

Penguin Books Ltd.: Two brief excerpts from *The Politics of Experience* by
R. D. Laing (pages 32, 50). Copyright © 1967 by R. D. Laing.

Random House, Inc.: Brief excerpt from *Remembrance of Things Past* by Marcel
Proust, translated by C. K. Scott Moncrief. Copyright 1934, renewed 1962 by
Random House, Inc.

Routledge & Kegan Paul Ltd.: Brief excerpt from *Maori Symbolism* by Ettie Rout.
Copyright 1926 by Ettie Rout.

Viking Press, Inc.: Brief excerpt from *Pregnancy, Birth & Family Planning* by Alan
F. Guttmacher, M.D. Copyright 1937, © 1973 by Alan F. Guttmacher.
All rights reserved.

Library of Congress Cataloging in Publication Data
Viva, [Date]   The baby.   I. Title.
PZ4.V84Bab   [PS3572.I83]   813'.5'4   74-21332
ISBN 0-394-49198-X

Manufactured in the United States of America
First Edition

I dedicate this book to
my mother

CONTENTS

I thank for their help:
Regina Ryan
Michel Auder
Lindy Hess

All stills are excerpts from
Journals of Alexandra Toporoff: A Video Novel, by Michel Auder

Part	One	Mother, father, and friends before her birth and The Birth. (1 hour 30 min.)
Part	Two	Mother, father, friends and her first four years. (1 hour 30 min.)
Part	Three	In progress . . .

Photography printed by Jack Voorzanger.

THE BABY

CHAPTER I

Thim and Thur One

. . . "didn't you ever hear that story?" mother asked me when the baby was a year old and I was still complaining of exhaustion. "No," I told her, "what was it about?"

"On the feast of the Holy Family," she began, "Mr. and Mrs. Murphy took their nine children to mass. All through the sermon the children were fighting and talking and fidgeting. The parents, sitting in a pew behind their children, kept poking them and nudging them and whispering 'shhh,' while the priest gave them dirty looks between sentences. After the mass was over, Mrs. Murphy's neighbor, Mrs. Reilly, came up to Mrs. Murphy on the churchsteps and said, 'Wasn't that a lovely sermon that father Shanahan gave, about the Holy Family?'"

"Hmmmmph," Mrs. Murphy sneered, "thim and thur ONE!"

"Tu est très belle!" Marie-Claude cried, hoarsely, because she had the flu. "Your breasts look fantastic! You've *got* to 'ave the baby!" Then she sneezed just as she was reaching for the Kleenex on her bedside table, sending a spray of fine moisture through the air; some of it landed on my

3

plump, sore breasts half-exposed under a wraparound cotton dress. I was taking advantage of finally being able to wear a décolleté neckline.

Abortion had just become legal and I was going to get mine the next day. I had severe doubts about it, but Frederick and I were completely broke and everyone knows it's foolish to have a baby when you don't have any money. It was a "bad time" for movies (that's what everyone says when you complain about not having a job or a producer) and my husband was a filmmaker. Compounding his frustration was the fact that he had just spent six months making a film called *Cleopatra* but when the backers saw the rushes they confiscated the film and sued him for a million dollars. He was not only "mocking history" they said, by having Cleopatra consult an oracle at a court orgy, but his humor was "too sophisticated" for a "modern audience."

Frederick's occasional producer, Gunter von Habsburg, was nodding over his guitar, playing it with that air of cool self-possession endemic to either the very talented or the very rich. In Gunter's case it was the latter virtue that was responsible for his confidence.

Gunter comes from a German family who, unlike the rest of their compatriots, realized early in the thirties that not only was Berlin no longer the artistic center it had been ten years before, but that Hitler was about to plunge the country into ruin as well, and had, before the Second World War, established a beachhead in America. No dummies, they went straight to Florida, where they immediately discovered several oil wells before launching an attack, a generation later, on both the intellectual life of the local community and the artistic life of the nation at large. They built a university in Miami and an art collection in New York.

Gunter, at twenty-nine years of age, was following his parents' footsteps into the avant-garde. This position necessitated an appearance, at least, of being hip—a condition that caused his vast wealth to appear to him as more a burden than a blessing. His friends were all brilliant but poor, a category he himself would have liked to belong to. But, alas, it was too late for a von Habsburg to play Horatio Alger.

If Gunter had stuck to the rich for his social, intellectual, and sexual intercourse a lot of his paranoia would never have surfaced, but as it was he found himself judging every friendship he had in terms of: "How much money will I have to give him or her?" For the very wealthy have to give money to their less fortunate friends just as they have to give to charity; the trick is finding just the right amount to give without losing the secrecy that surrounds wealth. Too much, and the recipients will get a glimmering of just how vast the fortune is; too little, and they will harbor resentment. The lessons of the French Revolution weren't lost on the von Habsburgs; in fact, the architecture of their houses recalled that of the Renaissance in Italy; stark and dull on the outside, to confound the peasants, sumptuous on the inside. It's only the nouveau riche who make the same mistake that caused the downfall of Louis the Sixteenth: ostentation.

Frederick and I were in East Hampton in a house patterned after Le Petit Trianon, which Gunter had rented for us, his cameraman, himself, and his latest girlfriend, Marie-Claude, a very pretty French actress. The four of them were passing the white powder around again. I nodded my head when Frederick passed the piece of cardboard to me. He then handed me the rolled-up dollar bill and I sniffed as much as I could up both nostrils. Two full lines. I had already had some cocaine. I was feeling miserable because Marie-Claude was right. I did look beautiful, for I was three months pregnant and as much as I disliked the idea of being pregnant I disliked even more the idea of losing my newfound beauty.

For the first time I got high on the white powder. I hated it. I lay down and the room spun around; I couldn't walk without weaving and stumbling. I had no control. Frederick got into bed with me and put his arms around me. His beard pricked my chin because he hadn't shaved in two days; the pregnancy problem was just as disturbing to him as it was to me. When I went to the hospital to make my abortion appointment, the first thing I saw was a photograph of a three-month fetus in an open book on the doctor's desk. The location of the heart, brain, eyes, fingers, and toes were pointed out. Later, on the examining table he took my hand and placed it just above my pelvic bone saying, "There, feel the head?" I burst into tears and was still sobbing when, five minutes later, the telephone rang. It was Frederick, asking the doctor when I could join him for dinner in The Russian Tea Room. The doctor carried on a whispered conversation with him, hung up, went to a cabinet and took out a bottle. Coming toward me with two big white pills on his open palm he said, "Here's two tranquillizers; you take one, and give your husband the other." That night, just as this night, we couldn't make up our minds.

I come from such a large family that throughout my childhood and adolescence my mother was always pregnant. This was taken as a matter of course in our neighborhood (everyone was Irish Catholic). A pregnant woman was regarded in the same light as a feudal queen (provided she was married); that is to say, her position in the sphere of things was due to Divine Right, and no one, least of all the woman herself, would have thought of questioning it.

On the block where we lived if a woman didn't have at least six children the family was considered "small." Some of my mother's friends were practically martyrs to reproduction, their wounds rivaling those of St. Sebastian, St. Agatha, or, in the case of Mrs. Ryan, Job himself.

Out of Mrs. Ryan's brood of fourteen only five or six were to survive, and Mrs. Ryan herself was usually in bed with hemorrhages, a prolapsed uterus, an infected bladder, rotting kidneys, or a mental collapse. Since she usually enjoyed her mystical visions of the bleeding heart of Jesus during her various illnesses, it never occurred to her to discontinue breeding her line of the species. It was an unspoken certainty that the more children she had, the more visions of Christ and the Blessed Mother she would enjoy.

To the right of Mrs. Ryan lived the Nicolson family. Tootsie Nicolson, a peroxide blonde with only two sons, had the distinction of being the most often quoted woman on the block. Her lament, *I went through the valley of the shadow of death twice and I'll never do it again*, was so often and so scornfully quoted by mother and her friends (their undertone of humor didn't fool me) that I understood at an early age the one thing that could brand a woman a fool: cowardice in the delivery room. It didn't matter that Tootsie was a professor; her skimpy family was as severe an indictment against her as her peroxided hair.

To the left of the Ryans lived the Doughertys—a family of five children. Babs Dougherty was no friend of Mrs. Ryan, being of the opinion that both Mrs. Ryan's filthy housekeeping and her religious fervor were equally subversive to the neighborhood children (meaning her own), and I knew she wasn't as shocked as she pretended to be the day she opened the freezer door.

She was called to their house by one of the Ryan children, as their mother had suffered a stroke. I think it was curiosity rather than a neighborly impulse to cook dinner that led her to open that door, and I never learned what she found there, but I still remember the look on her face and the sound of her voice as she looked down into the freezer and said, "My God, I don't know what she *feeds* those children!"

It wasn't long afterwards that the moving van pulled up at the Ryan house to the accompaniment of the voices at my mother's kitchen table, fellow-breeders all, lamenting the persecution of Mrs. Ryan by Mrs. Dougherty. "*A saint, that's what she is, a saint!*" my mother kept repeating. Mrs. Ryan, in the years to come, carted her brood from one small town to the next in upstate New York, and my mother paid visits to her as religious in their regularity as her visits to the parish church on Fridays to say the Stations of the Cross.

And then, one day, her husband dead and her children all either dead or gone away, save for one or two, Mrs. Ryan confounded Babs Dougherty by moving back to Watertown, to a street only two blocks away from her original house, though miles away in social prestige (the prestige in Mrs. Ryan's favor). She was clothed in the latest designer fashions and her new house was as elegant, as well kept, and as cluttered with expensive bric-a-brac as anything in *Vogue* Magazine. On top of this unlikely turnabout Mrs. Ryan made several trips each year to Europe, visited the Pope regularly, ran her dead husband's business, which meant supervising twenty younger men, and had a circle of international friends so soigné that Mrs. Dougherty moved away from the neighborhood altogether, unable to stand the evidence right under her nose, each day, of her own bad judgment and provincial existence.

However, despite the change in Mrs. Ryan's life style, her visions and mental collapses remained constant, further humiliating Mrs. Dougherty by proving that Mrs. Ryan's favor under the Lord would always be the same; and, that once she was chosen, neither slovenly housekeeping nor running with the jet set was likely to diminish it. We all knew that Mrs. Ryan's original call to saintliness was due to her never-empty womb.

It was with this background of steady, relentless reproduction, blessed by the bleeding heart of Jesus, that I confronted my own pregnancy.

Now, the fake Empress Josephine bedroom in our expensive East Hampton commune spinning around me, I was waiting for Frederick to make the decision about the baby. Instead, he looked at me closely, examined my face in detail, and told me that I reminded him of his sister, Minette. Minette was a year older than I was, making her thirty-one. I had always suspected that Frederick married me out of suppressed incestuous desires, since he was five years younger than me.

"Tell me the truth," I was asking him. "Are you in love with your sister?"

"You want to know the truth, dummy?"

"Of course."

"Zere is no truth, don't you know that?"

"Don't give me that Cartesian reasoning again," I snapped at him. "Otherwise, why bother to talk at all?"

"Right!" he laughed, "why bother to talk at all, you're finally getting the point!

I wormed the confession out of him, finally that indeed he had not only been in love with but had actually consummated his passion for his sister, many years before; however it was his younger sister, Tatania (who resembled me even more), and not, as I had supposed, his older sister, Minette. Instead of being shocked by this discovery I found that the idea excited me. I moved closer to him and put my hand between his legs.

The next morning we both threw up for hours. There was no question of making it to the hospital. Frederick called them and canceled the abortion.

My husband, Frederick Marat, is the last of a dying breed—the romantic Frenchman. When I met him it was just as de rigueur for a Frenchman to have an "American Experience" as the contrary had been for the past fifty years or so. Most of his French friends, as well as the German, Gunter von Habsburg, who claims to have acquired the style in Vero Beach, Florida, affected cowboy boots, Stetson hats, bleached-out bluejeans, and Navajo jewelry. Not Frederick. He remained true to his heritage, dying though it was supposed to have been, and dressed only in silk shirts and scarves, cashmere sweaters and jackets, and Italian shoes. His literary heroes were Balzac, the Marquis de Sade, especially *Philosophie dans le Boudoir* (*"You'll see, people will recognize him as the political genius he was, in fifty years' time"*), and Antonin Artaud, who said, *"All writing is pigshit and all writers are pigs."*

His one concession to American culture went to films; he admired Andy Warhol. While his cowboy-booted contemporaries talked about Godard and Truffaut, Frederick sniffed, secure in the knowledge that he, unlike them, had picked up on the only true form of originality in America—films.

Unfortunately for him, falling in love with me ground all of his romantic ideas into powder. It was his predilection toward "experimental" American films that predisposed him to fall in love with me, for if I was anything, I was a product of my age. Even though I had been a dreamer as a child, spoon-fed by Mrs. Ryan with the heady stuff of mysticism, I learned soon after leaving home to scoff at romanticism and embrace practicality.

I knew that when I interrupted Frederick's lovemaking with a statement not at all in keeping with his romantic mood, he felt betrayed and wondered what had ever possessed him to fall in love with me. I hated myself for those mundane interruptions, dictated really, by self-consciousness and not as I pretended then, by modern American sophistication. Yet even then I knew that those interruptions weren't endemic to my nature but, rather, that they were some obsession I had to break a mood, to throw a pall of "reality" over everything, as though to force Frederick into proving that he loved me despite the middle-class stamp on my soul.

I thought that if I showed him all of my worst traits, bit by bit, then one day I would have shown them all, would be free of them, and I could allow myself to be the romantic partner in love that I felt was my real self.

If one substitutes the word "raunchy" for "mundane" and eliminates the word "self-consciousness," Marie-Claude, the troublesome "fiancée" (as they say in Paris) of Gunter von Habsburg, possesses a lot of the same traits I have just described. Surprising in a Parisian woman, she has a real barnyard humor, loves to talk to her lovers about the sexual peculiarities of her former lovers, and never makes any attempts at "femininity" and mystery beyond her make-up, perfume, and wardrobe. Her passive presentation is fashionable, elegant, modest, and malleable—the perfect nineteenth-century drawing-room decoration; actively, however, she's like something out of a William Burroughs novel.

I have never seen Marie-Claude happier than she was the morning she woke me up to tell me that both Gunter and his cameraman had made love to her the night before (simultaneously) in the fake Napoleon Bonaparte bedroom. *"Comme nous avons dechirè!"* she laughed. *"Tous les deux etaient formidable!"*

"Dr. Schwartz says that if you don't have the baby now, at thirty, you might as well forget it. You'll always find a reason why you shouldn't do it. There'll always be an assignment, or not enough money, or something that's unfinished."

Frederick had just come from Dr. Schwartz's, where he had gone to have his cock checked out. It was burning because he had made love to a whore two days before.

I agreed that it was about time I had a baby if I was going to have one at all. Then I went into the rose bushes and vomited again. The trouble with the house Gunter was renting was that every time I leaned down to throw up in the gardens, my olfactory organs, sensitized by pregnancy, could smell the DDT. Nobody would believe me that there was all that DDT around. They said it was my imagination. I recognize DDT. It smells like oil and a chemical at the same time.

Marijuana drove me nuts too. The smell. I stayed in my bedroom while Frederick and his friends got stoned all night. I was hating him more and more.

Three and a half months pregnant. I really hate my husband now. I hate the way he eats, the way he brushes his teeth, the way he dries his hair (rubbing his scalp with his hands and shaking his head in front of the mirror), and the way he speaks French. What especially irritates me is the way he keeps saying, *"Tu vois?"*

I told him that I couldn't stand it—the way he speaks his own language. So whenever he had the chance, if there were French people around, he told them that his wife hates to hear him speak French. I began feeling guiltier and guiltier. I couldn't understand what had possessed me to tell him that. So what if it were true? Why did I have to tell him? I remembered all the times I used to say things about him, or about us, or about something he had said to me, only in the company of our friends, as though I were too inhibited to bring up the subject without witnesses. Now here he was, doing the same thing. I loved him again, because he had this quirk, just like me.

For Christmas we went to Marian Levine's house in Mexico, where her husband, Brian, stayed in bed the whole time, watching pro football on television and ordering Marian to bring him grape juice and soda water. He said he was sick.

Jack Kirby, another movie director, was there too.

"Listen, Augustine," he kept telling me, "why don't you rub some Johnson's Baby Cream on Frederick's cock and then lower yourself gently down on it? I know what you're going through . . . poor baby . . . and that's the only thing that'll work." We never tried it. I was seven months pregnant and Frederick and I hadn't made love in four months.

Concurrently with the advice Jack was giving us on our non-existent sex life, he felt obligated as a friend to give Frederick some professional advice. Being totally American in artistic orientation—that is, apparently never having heard of the drug habits of Rimbaud, Baudelaire, Verlaine, Lautreamont, Genêt, or Cocteau—he told Frederick that if he wanted to become a success he'd have to stop smoking pot. Frederick parried with one of his sardonic smiles, saying nothing.

Back in New York, Marie-Claude and Gunter are living in his brownstone, uptown. Every time I go over there, Marie-Claude shows me the new antique clothes she's just bought.

"He won't give me enough money," she complains. "I want to buy this fantastic velvet cape I just found on Third Avenue; what should I do?"

"Tell him you need it for the movie," I tell her (Gunter has decided to write, direct, produce, and star in his own movie). "He has plenty of money."

Marie-Claude comes from a family of tailors and, although she smokes a liberal amount of marijuana and sniffs almost anything she can get her Gallic profile into, her mind is still basically on her clothes.

Running neck-and-neck with her clothing obsession is an equally strong preoccupation with her hair. While acting in a film in Morocco a few years before, she hennaed her brunette hair, not only inspired by the native women but also in competition with the star of the film ("*When I saw Sylvinna standing in the sunlight, her hair a blazing red, I rushed to the henna pot*"). Upon her return to France, disgusted by the red, she cut off her hair. Once it grew back to its natural color she bleached it blond, only to be further disgusted by the color and to cut it off a second time.

She has a beautiful face, yet there's a certain nuance of vulgarity about it. It's something about the features; they're too perfectly sculpted. Her nose and mouth are those of a statue, made by an artist who, not content with the three-dimensional aspect of the sculpture, drew over it with an instrument that gave out liquid marble, a sort of magic marker, outlining the shapes, making them graphic as well. Even her eyes are too perfect. Slanted, with dark lashes (an inheritance from her Vietnamese father), they always look as though she's wearing eye make-up on them.

Marie-Claude has just finished telling me that she wants a baby too. She's sick of having abortions, she says.

Alone, in the bedroom. I developed a fear of the window. I repeatedly saw myself sailing down into the parking lot. The summer over, we were back in the Metro, a hotel on Twenty-first Street whose good reputation was a relic of the past. The present-day hotel was a dingy mess full of dust, shredding upholstery, and missing mosaic tiles. Below, seen from our bedroom window, lay a parking lot.

My fear of the window became an obsession. Finally, at night, before going to bed I closed the shutters and latched them. I was afraid of jumping out in my sleep. I told myself this was a crazy idea but reasoning didn't help at all. I changed my tactics. Each day I walked over to the window whenever I thought of it, looked down, and leaned out as far as I could. I still saw myself sailing out. I decided to open the window only a few inches during the daytime. Finally it occurred to me to open the window from the top.

I telephoned Jack Kirby's wife, Jeannie, in California. She told me my reaction was normal. That's why I telephoned her. I knew she would tell me that, although I did think I was placing an unfair burden on her, since she had spent so many hours on the telephone long distance trying to convince me to have an abortion when I was three months pregnant.

"I don't understand, Jeannie," I had said to her. "Why do you think I shouldn't have this baby?"

"Because I'm afraid that Frederick will leave you if you have a baby at this stage of your relationship."

"But why should he?"

"Well, I didn't have a baby until I was married for five years!"

The thing is Jeannie was always so well organized that I'm sure she planned it all out in advance and that everything worked out according to schedule. I can't plan anything. In fact, if I plan to get up at a certain hour in the morning then I can't sleep all night, just knowing I have to get up early.

> "Don't ask me to pick you up for the airport at ten o'clock because if I know that I have to get up at nine thirty in the morning then I can't sleep all night. Rather, let me do it this way; I'll say that if I wake up I'll drive you to the airport and if I don't wake up then you'll take a later plane."
>
> J. J. SCHUHL, PARIS, FEBRUARY 1973

"You can have a baby in five years, or in two years; it doesn't matter; you're not going into menopause after all," Jeannie had continued that day on the phone. "Wait until Frederick makes it; until he has some money; don't put this burden on him so soon."

I told her she was right. "I know it, you're right," I said over the phone, "but I can't afford an abortion."

She loaned me the money. We met at Downey's Steak House when she flew to New York two days later and she handed me three hundred dollars. I got the rest from Malcolm, a dealer, living on the sixth floor of the Metro Hotel. I still haven't paid them back and the baby is three years old.

Gunter von Habsburg is beside himself with frustration because Marie-Claude's former lover is here from Paris and Marie-Claude has not only decided to take a room in the Metro Hotel, but she's also charging it to Gunter. She says it ought to come out of the movie budget; after all, he could give some thought to keeping the star of the production happy.

Gunter slept in his car all night, last night—a white Citroën with a Maserati engine, which he had parked right in front of Marie-Claude's window at the hotel.

Tonight he came in to see me and sat for three hours in a chair next to my bed without speaking. I was knitting. My next-door neighbor had given me some hideous pink wool and two knitting needles. He wanted me to call the baby "Rose." He said it was going to be a girl. I didn't know what I was knitting, but I remembered how to knit one, purl two, and how to make stripes. (Now that the baby is three the knitting is still on the needles. I didn't know how to cast off.)

Gunter said he was depressed. Finally he asked me what he should do. He was wearing his cowboy hat from Vero Beach and his Navajo jewelry. I told him that it was ridiculous to mope over Marie-Claude like that when she was right downstairs fucking her other lover. I was the one who ought to be depressed, I said; Frederick had taken to staying away entire nights now that I was eight and a half months pregnant. What did Gunter have to be depressed about? At least he wasn't pregnant.

CHAPTER II

The Greatest Reward Life Holds

The ambition of Maori men was to grow big and fine and handsome, strong and healthy. Thus only could they be sure of gaining the greatest rewards life held; to be classed by the elders as among those fit to reproduce the next generation, to be selected by the finest women as their mates; and to take rank among the elders and their leaders. The ambition of the Maori women was similar; they desired to be physically fine, healthy and strong, fit to be mothers of rulers, nobles, and warriors. Deformed women were not usually allowed to become mothers, although they were not barred from love relationships.

ETTIE ROUT, *Maori Symbolism*, FROM THE
EVIDENCE OF HOHEPA TE RAKE (AN ARAWA NOBLE)

During the birth of our baby Frederick was stoned on heroin. Giving him the benefit of the doubt, I presumed that was why the videotapes of the event concentrated mainly on the ceiling, the walls, and the sink in the delivery room. He did manage to keep the videcon tube steadily focused on my crotch in time for the emergence of the head, however, so I decided to look at it in the most charitable light possible; that is, that he was simply building up the suspense, like Hitchcock. All those quick passes to the

15

crotch, speedily averted to focus on a ceiling beam, gave to the spectator a vast feeling of relief when the head finally made its appearance. Anyway

that view was easier for me to bear than the idea that he found my distended vagina actually too repulsive to look at.

I myself couldn't bear to look at it in the mirror. It looked like a drum with something corrugated, hairy, and wrinkled pressing against its skin; already splitting it a little.

Later, after I had seen the tape many times over, I saw that I had expected Frederick to be less squeamish than me. Apparently that was one of my most common failings—to expect more of him than I was capable of myself. But, after all, he was a man and I had always looked up to men. I used to beg him for advice, even when he didn't want to give it.

When I went into labor Frederick disappeared into one of the dealers' rooms. Calling Malcolm to look for him, I learned that he wasn't there. Rather than try all the other rooms in the hotel (Frederick would never tell me who the dealers were; he said I would forget and talk about it in the elevator some day), I took advantage of Malcolm's presence on the phone to ask him to come up and clean the place. Then I phoned a bellman to come up and put two Swanson's turkey T.V. dinners in the oven. He said he'd come back in twenty minutes to take them out. I couldn't move off the couch.

Just as the bellman arrived for the second time, to take the dinners out of the oven, Malcolm showed up with a woman friend of his (probably a client). She was tall and brunette and Amazonish. He picked up the clothes on the floor and made the bed while she cleaned the kitchen.

As I jabbed my fork into the mashed potatoes, Malcolm (a health-food addict), turned up his nose, sniffed, and said that I couldn't expect much energy from that. I didn't care. All those puddles of gravy and potatoes and that stringy, dried-out turkey were the only things I wanted —other than, of course, my mother.

When the dishes were finished the Amazon came in and sat down on the couch next to me. The greatest moment of my life and I have to rely on a total stranger for comfort. I couldn't believe it.

She told me I should move around a bit. "When I had my baby in

Spain I just kept walking around the house, in and out of the courtyard, holding my stomach, and screaming, 'Goddammit son-of-a-bitch.' All the Spanish women in the neighborhood were laughing at me," she told me as I breathed in and out from the chest.

"Then what happened?" I was ravenous for more detail.

"Jesus, it was fabulous. I had the kid right in the house." I made a mental note of what a bastard Frederick was not to want me to have the baby at home.

"I had taken so much acid during the pregnancy that I was really into it. I did all the breathing exercises, ate the right foods, and it was the greatest experience of my life."

"Where's the baby now?"

"Dead. He died a few hours after it was born. It was really weird. They wouldn't let me look at it until just before it died. A woman stayed with me, and she watched over it until it died. We put a candle and a tuberose in the room and waited. When she thought it was about to die she brought it to me. He was purple and had pointed ears. He looked into my eyes and *he knew* and I *knew*. He was like a Buddha. His eyes were green. You see, his intestines were all on the outside when he was born; they knew he wouldn't live. But *he knew*. I saw God when I looked into his eyes."

I went into the bedroom, holding my stomach and breathing fast, picked up the telephone, and begged Mrs. Murray, the switchboard operator, to find Frederick. She always knew where everybody was. Within a minute Frederick called back.

"Get right up here, Frederick," I whispered, "and get these people out of the house." I thought that story was a rather stiff price to pay for cleanliness.

Following the rules of the Lamaze handbook I waited until the pain was unbearable before calling the doctor. Frederick kept asking me when I was going to call him as he rushed around, putting a new tape in the deck. Or, rather, the tape he had just borrowed from Magda MacDonald, our penthouse neighbor—the only person in the hotel I could really have a conversation with and the only Irish Colleen I'd ever seen who looked like a Kabuki dancer. Tiny and dark and the mother of a twenty-eight year old daughter, she has slanted eyes and wears her hair in a knot at the nape of her neck. Like me, she's always complaining. Magda had gone from being an avant-garde filmmaker to an avant-garde videoist. (She hated the term "videofreak" and insisted on being called a "videoist" though later she decided definitively on the term "video artist," saying that once the sixties were over she realized the word "artist" could be used again.) Frederick had used up the tapes he was saving for the birth three days before by filming two of the hotel's guests as they were shooting up.

Vietnam was on television, bombs bursting in the air and all, and Frederick alternated the lens between the casualties on the battlefield and me on the telephone. Ever since he had been in America the televised war had fascinated him.

"Look at this spectacular!" he kept saying. "Nixon is the greatest movie producer in the world. Do you realize how big the budget is?" (Later, when we moved to California, I met a woman who was convinced that the war was being shot in a Hollywood studio.)

I breathed and rubbed and rocked to the rhythm of "American Pie" on the radio while making arrangements for our arrival at the hospital. Frederick always played the television and the radio at the same time. It wasn't easy keeping the right rhythm with the war noises going on behind me, but I managed by switching to the Grantly Dick-Read method of deep diaphragm breathing.

While waiting for the taxi in the lobby I got down on the floor under the sculpture of a pregnant Pompidou, with Jasper Johns's American flag painting on my right, and massaged my stomach while groaning. (The owner of the hotel, Sidney Renard, often accepted "art" in lieu of rent money. This he did to encourage artists to live there, hoping to upgrade the tone of the place, swarming as it was with pimps, hookers, dealers, and junkies like the rest of New York City in latter-day America.) The usual crowd of lobby loiterers thought I was putting on a show for the videotape, but it was my impression that I was exercising remarkable self-control. If this was "painless" childbirth I couldn't imagine surviving the other kind.

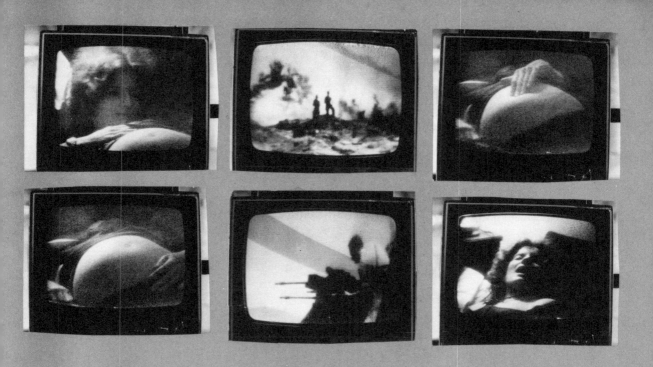

*Frederick alternated the lens between the casualties on the battlefield
and me on the telephone.*

*In the lobby I got down on the floor. . . . If this was "painless" childbirth, I couldn't
imagine surviving the other kind.*

The big sign on the door they were wheeling me through, stating "Labor Room," gave me the feeling I was entering either a concentration camp or a jail.

We had two enormous suitcases with us. One was filled with clothes and the other was filled with equipment. The nurse asked us why we were bringing all those bags. I was so embarrassed by my own packing that I never opened the clothes bag the whole time I was there. I kept the blue-and-white striped hospital gown on all the time while the other mothers pranced down the hall from their rooms to the nursery in frilly fuchsia nylon nightgowns. I've always freaked out before going on a trip and usually take the whole house with me, but this time we were only going five blocks and Frederick wasn't even spending the night.

It gets me very nervous, moving from one place to another; I usually wait until the last minute to pack and then I take all the wrong things. On the way to an airport I'm a nervous wreck trying to remember what I've left behind. Even if I haven't left anything behind I'm still worrying. Then I always somehow take all the clothes that I never wear anyway in New York, thinking that I'll wear them wherever I'm going. For the past two years I've been carrying an old sock full of broken jewelry all over the world with me, planning on having the pieces fixed in Paris, in London, or wherever. Needless to say, all the jewelry is still in the sock, broken. At least I didn't take that to the hospital. Frederick and I always have a struggle of wills before every trip. He says, "Don't bring that and that and that," and I say, "Okay," and then I secretly squirrel the things away in a suitcase until he finds them and we start to argue all over again. I can't stand traveling.

The private labor room was supposed to be a real luxury, but through the cardboard walls I was hearing nothing but the piercing shrieks of another woman in labor. They started with a low quivering murmur, built up to an electronic wail, and subsided with a catlike mewing. I asked one of the midwives in my room if the laboring mother was doing the Lamaze method.

"No, honey, she's on drugs."

The thought that I would be going through the same experience any hour now made me want to postpone the whole thing. Every time she screamed I began to cry just thinking about the pain she was in. Were the drugs making it harder for her? If the drugs were making it easier then just think of how horrible it was going to be for me without them. The mind boggles. (I use the word "boggles" because ever since the birth of the baby I've reverted back to the Forties and Fifties, when I was growing up. I've become just like my mother; I even use her vocabulary now.)

"I think I'd be more comfortable on the floor, Ida," I told the fat midwife. (She had a nameplate pinned to her bosom.)

"Okay, honey, anything you want. I'll get you some blankets."

"What those blankets doin' on the floah?" the thin midwife was demanding. (Incredibly her name was Dora. The two of them had the same names as both of my grandmothers.)

"She says she wants to labor on the floah," Ida told her.

"I always practiced on the floor at home," I said.

"Ain't nothin' like yoah own floah, honey," Dora replied.

Ida, the fat midwife, with the forename of my fat maternal grandmother, helped me off the bed and onto the floor. Just as I got myself into a squatting position another contraction came. Fixed into the squat for what seemed to be forever, I just couldn't find the right position. What I didn't know then was that there *was* no right position.

"I think I'd be happier on the bed."

"Dr. Fabin's patients kin do whatever makes 'em feel most comfortable."

"What about the chair? The chair with the hole in it?" (The first reason I went to Dr. Fabin was because he said he'd let us videotape. The second was the chair he invented with the hole in it for labor.)

"Honey, you don't want that chair now. That's only for the transition stage." (Apparently the hole is there for the doctors to stick their fingers through, to see how dilated your cervix is; I had naïvely supposed that the baby would come through the hole.)

"What stage am I in?"

"Oh, you got a long way to go. A loooooooong way; doesn't she, Dora?"

"Honey, you gonna be heah foah hours!" Dora kindly informed me. "Ain't nothin' to it, honey," I expected them to say any minute.

"You wanna sit up, honey? Okay, we'll sit ya up."

Frederick had taped my picture of St. Michael on the wall. It was the only picture I could find around the house when we left for the hospital. A grateful teacher had sent it as a postcard after Frederick and I showed some rushes from *Cleopatra* to the students at Marymount College. The painting I had practiced in front of at home was too big to take to the hospital. (Lamaze counsels you to have a picture nearby to focus on; it's supposed to take your mind off the pain.)

I tried to focus my eyes on St. Michael but found that Frederick was focusing his lens on the sink. Curious about his sudden love for porcelain, I investigated the room. The bare walls were apple green, the sink had its plumbing exposed, and the light bulb was missing its shade. Bottles of medicine and ointments were lined up under the mirror over the sink, like a display counter in a pharmacy; and the bed was an adult-sized iron crib. It was all very depressing.

I went back to the picture of St. Michael. He went in and out of focus, changed colors, acquired a brilliant diamond overlay made of light, and the details of the art nouveau border alternately manifested and obliterated themselves. I attributed this gratuitous hallucinogenic experience to the effects of hyperventilation.

A female doctor came in and gave me the finger examination. "Only one centimeter dilation," she told the Haitian wizards. They called a speedy conference in the hallway and made a telephone call. That was the part I resented the most. I thought I ought to be told what was going on. Otherwise why not just dope me up? It was like being twelve years old and going to the doctor. He examines you and then tells your mother what he's found.

"Do you want to go home? We called Dr. Fabin and he said maybe you should go home and come back later." I asked them if they were kidding.

"No; Dr. Fabin's patients usually wait a while longer before admitting themselves."

I hated being such an imposition on their time, but I informed them, between breaths, that I couldn't possibly imagine getting in and out of any more taxis, not to mention the long wait for the hotel elevator. I looked at Frederick, who was focusing out in the hall.

"Listen, Freddy, if you're bored, why don't you go home and come back later? I'm not moving."

"You crazy? I stay with you. I'm fine!"

I felt better. A proof that he really did love me. A desperate woman will grasp at anything.

When they decided to give me an enema I remembered the Lamaze handbook telling the "expectant mother" to do it herself at home, before she left for the hospital; but of course I hadn't done it, having been too preoccupied with the taping. *Anything for art.*

They made me walk to the toilet. I closed the door and sat down, expecting a little pain. Nothing in life had prepared me for the experience of shitting out an enema, popping the water sac, and having labor contractions simultaneously. Combined with the wails from the next room I was afraid that maybe this was hell. Maybe I had already died. I wanted Frederick in there with his machine, but every time I tried to make it to the door a contraction forced me to the floor. I decided to investigate the popping noise I had heard, thinking maybe it wasn't the water sac bursting after all. I searched the walls, ceiling, and floor for "the telltale plug of blood" (Lamaze handbook), but the place was spotless. Finally I located it in the toilet.

Relieved, I tried again to make it to the door, but had to stop, hang on to the sink, bend over, and once again stifle the impulse to scream and shout and call the whole thing off.

The indignity of it all! Here I was, performing the noble time-honored rite of childbirth, and instead of being ministered to in a softly lit room, family at my side, the women holding my hands and the men playing the guitar, incense burning and prayers being offered to the gods, I was alone, moaning, in one of the three standard-brand white-tiled antiseptic toilets manufactured in Geneva, New York.

Back in the bed (i.e., back in camera range) Frederick tried to sponge off my forehead with the sponge I had bought at Lamston's, obediently following my Bible, the Lamaze handbook. How I worried that that sponge wouldn't get into the luggage in time. It was a hideous, giant-sized nylon sponge; I had planned on buying a real sponge, or at least a silk sponge later, in the pharmacy, but later never came. Like the letters I never sent, always planning on mailing them "later." Besides, I owed the pharmacy money. The touch of the sponge drove me wild with irritation, and as sorry as I felt for Frederick, wishing he could do something to relieve me, I had to shout, "No, don't *touch* me!" I settled on holding his hand. I really wanted my mother.

All of a sudden the Haitian wizards realized that I was doing something wrong.

"Oh no, honey, don' rub yoah tummy that hard; yoah just makin' things worse foah yourself. That just stimulates the contractions. They strong enough, ain't they, as they is?"

I couldn't believe that all my hours of practice at home, underneath my abstract, hard-edge painting of a pink cunt (the only thing left from my earlier life as a painter), had been wrong. And why didn't my private Lamaze tutor say anything?

"What shall I do?"

"Jes don' touch yoah tummy. Fold yoah hands in yoah lap or somethin'."

I couldn't do it, so I settled for using my hands to orchestrate the pain, like Leonard Bernstein. The Haitians laughed.

Two more hours went by and Frederick kept forgetting to keep track of the timing. I begged for drugs.

"You doin' so fine, so nice, you don' wanna quit now, do ya? It'd be a shame, you comin' this far without anything."

Frederick was at my side. "Breathe, breathe, breathe," he kept insisting. I settled for a breathing groan. The woman in the next room was totally hysterical. I started crying for her again but Frederick made me breathe. I lay on my side, rubbing my feet together, forcing myself not to scream, furious that Frederick was filming my feet instead of my face. I wanted him to film my face so that I could remind myself afterwards how awful it had been and to never go through it again. I tried to direct him but couldn't speak; I knew if I stopped breathing I wouldn't be able to stand the pain. They kept telling me to relax between contractions and I tried to tell them that there wasn't any "between." They didn't believe me. I wasn't dilated enough to be in transition, they said. The last time I was examined was about three and a half hours ago. How did they know I wasn't dilated enough?

All of a sudden all of my insides were pushing downwards and I let out an involuntary, hideous, animal grunt. Very loud.

"I'm shitting in the bed!" Nobody heard me. They were all out in the hall, on the telephone.

It happened again. Dora rushed in. "Ida! Ida! She's pushing! Stop pushing!"

Now they were both beside me, exhorting me to blow instead of push. I hadn't known that I was pushing; I remain convinced, to this day, that it was totally involuntary. ("The urge to push," Lamaze calls it.) I decided to try blowing anyway, for the hell of it, and miraculously, there I was, blowing away. I had to cross my legs and groan at the same time, but nevertheless I was still blowing. They were so elated that it was like getting a gold star in the first grade. (Do they still give them out?) It occurred to me that the whole process was terribly artificial.

Upon reflection it appeared that the midwives were exhorting me to blow instead of push because the doctor hadn't yet arrived. How could I give birth without one? Better, it seemed, to let the child, who was struggling to be born, for god's sake, suffer the agony and possible brain damage of being held back under the pretense that I, who hadn't been examined in hours, wasn't "dilated" enough and therefore couldn't really be giving birth already.

"Well, well, it looks like you're going to have a baby!" Dr. Fabin's voice boomed over my feet. "Now I'm going to examine you. Just breathe hard and blow while I do it." The thought of a hand going up me while I was suffering the pangs of crucifixion was unbearable but I took a deep breath and gritted my teeth. For once the book was right. It didn't hurt.

"There's the head. You can push now, Augustine. Just put your feet against my shoulders and push." For the first time in four hours I was free of pain.

"Look, Frederick, you can see the head!" Dr. Fabin called to him.

"My god! The head!" Frederick was impressed.

I wondered where the head was but I coudn't stop breathing to ask. Actually, whenever I wondered about anything I couldn't ask it out loud; the pain had me so abstracted from myself that I couldn't speak.

"Push again, Augustine." This time when I pushed I knew I was going to break in two. I stopped pushing just before the break and then regretted my cowardice. "The next time," I decided, "I'm going to push right through it."

"*Here it comes again*," I heard myself scream.

"Get your video unit, Frederick, and I'll give you a cap and gown in the delivery room."

When I heard that I wondered who was going to pay any attention to me on the next contraction. They were all so concerned with the video-tape unit.

"How am *I* going to get to the delivery room?" ("God," I thought, "why didn't we come to the hospital ahead of time to check it out, the way Lamaze counsels you to?")

"We're just going to wheel you in, Augustine, don't worry about a thing!"

The procession began into the delivery room. I had my eyes closed for some reason (fright probably), yet I felt that everybody was either ahead of me or behind me. When I felt another contraction I yelled, "What do I do now?" Nobody answered; they were too busy with the unit and the caps and gowns. I pushed as hard as I could and felt the thing that was about to break give way. Now the bed with wheels I was on was parallel to the delivery table. Another contraction. I held my breath and drifted onto a beach with the blue water lapping against the shore. I could see my first lover on the beach. What was he doing there? Nevertheless it was so pleasant I couldn't expel the breath. I knew that would end the sight.

From far away I heard Dr. Fabin's voice ordering me to take another breath. As I took it they lifted me onto the table and I could feel the head between my legs. I was afraid it was going to fall out onto the floor before I could get to the table. Now I was on the table and the head was still inside.

"Blow, Augustine, don't push!" Dr. Fabin was at the sink washing his hands.

"Got the unit, Frederick?" I asked.

"Everything's here, don't worry. My god, the head!"

I looked up and found a mirror. My vaginal entrance was stretched tight between my thighs and in the opening I could see a wrinkled piece of flesh with wet hair growing on it. To me it looked like an umbilical cord but I couldn't understand why it was growing hair. Again, it didn't occur to me to ask.

"Get it out, doctor, get it out!" I was sure the head would never make it through that little hole.

"I can't get it out right away unless I cut!"

"Then go ahead and cut," I heard myself say. I couldn't believe I was violating one of my own principles. (All the underground newspapers say an episiotomy is unnecessary, performed just because all doctors are butchers at heart.)

"It may not be necessary if we wait for a few minutes," Dr. Fabin said. (During my pregnancy the doctor had told me that only two of his patients hadn't required episiotomies and both had "snapped right back into shape," but that was because they were both dancers.) I agreed to wait.

"Nope, Augustine, it's going to tear," he said on the next push. "I'm going to give you a little local anesthesia before I make this cut. Tell me if it hurts."

"It hurts!" I was afraid to look in the mirror. I turned my head away.

"Push again, Augustine, push!" I looked into the mirror and saw bright-red blood gushing out around the baby's head. I heard a terrible yell, the same one I had dreamed about two months before. There was a big shiny schmoo with a pregnant belly who flew from a tree to a rock. The rock had a hole in the center just like the top of the mountain in Positano, the village in Southern Italy where Frederick and I had spent our honeymoon. At the time of the dream I hadn't been able to decide if this was a true Jungian dream or if the dream had been inspired by Joni Smith.

Joni had told me that before she gave birth her mother warned her that she was going to let out a dreadful scream at the last minute, no matter how well she controlled herself during the labor. "Everyone does, Joni," her mother told her.

Although Joni restrained herself completely throughout the labor, as a modern woman should, at the last moment she let out that yell.

While I was ruminating on the possibilities I looked into the mirror again. The baby's head was cradled in the doctor's hands and the umbilical cord was tightly wrapped around its neck (probably because the birth had been retarded while we waited for the doctor to arrive). The head was absolutely white with a blue tinge. It looked like rubber.

"Dead," I said to myself as the doctor took a pair of scissors and, as I watched in the mirror, slid his index finger under the cord against the baby's neck and neatly snipped the cord in two; "dead," after all this work, "dead."

The cord cut, the baby let out a cry. "Sounds like a boy!" Frederick laughed. "Is it a boy?"

"Wait'll I see the other end," the doctor counseled him. I pushed again and felt the warm wet body slide out of my vagina. Dr. Fabin lifted the baby up by its feet into the air and said, "Hello, Miss Marat!"

As I watched it all I felt a certain detachment, as though the baby belonged to someone else. Handing her to me, Dr. Fabin said, "It's a girl baby!" and I laughed and held out my arms to gather my daughter to my bosom. But before the magical touch of skin to skin, the midwife slipped a paper towel under her in an action as swift and as deft as that of my cousin Sally, from Marin County, who, the first time I came to visit her there in her newly built Spanish-style house, had whipped a paper coaster under my drink before the glass could touch the polished oak of her living room table. (The paper coasters were stacked up neatly in a box that sat permanently on the table, like a Buddha.) Out of the womb only ten seconds and already warned to keep the place clean.

While I was waiting for the flood of motherly love to wash over me the baby washed my breasts with a little arched fountain of urine. Then she opened her eyes and took a shit on my arm.

Once again Frederick asked if it was a boy, apparently too excited to see the evidence before his eyes. When I told him that it was a girl, a certain edge to my voice, annoyed that he was asking again, he asked if I was disappointed that she wasn't a boy.

"Of course not," I lied, "are you?"

"I told you I prefer a girl."

While Frederick kept marveling over the fact that she was a girl ("*A little girl, a little girl*"), the doctor walked up to her and began examining her fingers.

"What's the matter?" I wanted to know, terrified that she had a deformity only he could spot.

"Nothing, nothing," he reassured me, "only checking to make sure she has all her fingers and toes."

"It was a six-pound fetus, doctor," Ida breezily announced coming back into the room from the door through which she had departed minutes before to assist at an abortion.

"I thought I held the record with a three pounder. [You'd think we were on a fishing expedition.] I'm glad I don't hold it any more," Dr. Fabin laughed while stitching me up, pleased with his joke. Stoically bearing the stitching up until now, I winced at the words. As I lay there captive under the needle, I wondered whether they were so hardened to doing abortions by now that it didn't even occur to them that their conversation might be indelicate, to put it mildly, to the ears of a new mother, her first baby not yet dry from its passage; or whether they were unconsciously trying to shock me with their casual attitude toward life and death. To my mind a six-pound fetus was a six-pound baby. Was there no delicacy in the medical profession? I had to speak.

"Do you do abortions, doctor?"

"Oh sure, but I'm going to turn them over to someone else; I don't have time for them any more. Too many births."

There should be a law against that, I thought, the same person aborting and delivering. It seemed to me like a curse; a curse on the baby. An abortionist's hands the first to touch her body. I decided not to pay the bill.

The baby started crying. The midwife picked her up and took her footprints. She screamed louder. I couldn't bear it. I was shivering so badly

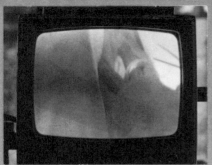 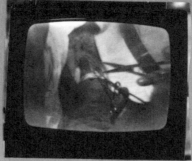 

He did manage to keep the videcon tube steadily focused on my crotch in time for the emergence of the head.

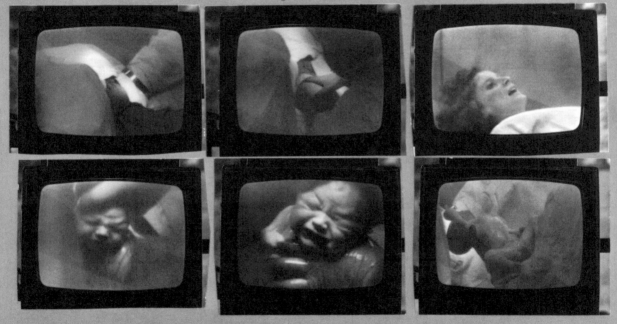

The umbilical cord was tightly wrapped around its neck (probably because the birth had been retarded while we waited for the doctor to arrive).

 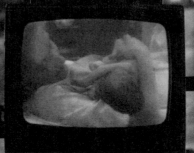 

The midwife picked her up and took her footprints. She screamed louder.

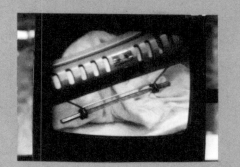

Then they put her in a glass cage.

I took the videcon tube from Frederick and began taping my husband....

that my teeth were making a racket. They weighed the baby. When her naked little body touched the cold metal scales she screamed again. They gave her back to me but then they took her away once more because I was shivering so they were afraid I'd drop her. Then they put her in a glass cage.

"Isn't there a danger that she'll suffocate in there?"

"Honey, this crib is ventilated."

"Let us worry about the baby. You relax."

I took the videcon tube from Frederick and began taping my husband and the doctor.

"We used to give 'em a drug called scopolamine" (beloved by Carlos Castaneda) Dr. Fabin was telling Frederick; "made 'em forget everything. Trouble was they'd be married to Harry, say, and they'd be yellin', *George, don't you ever touch me again!* Meanwhile Harry'd be in the room. That's why they had to get rid of the husbands. Too embarrassing. One woman, she had the kid hanging out of her, its head was hanging down between her legs and she was on scopolamine, climbing up the wall; actually trying to climb up the wall in the delivery room, screaming with pain, yelling, *'I can't stand it, I can't stand it!'* "

Meanwhile Emma was still crying in her cage. I didn't know what to do. I focused the lens on her long body, short legs, and big nose, thinking, "Shit, she's going to look just like me," and then they wheeled her out of the delivery room. They told me they'd bring her to me in three hours so I could begin breastfeeding her. I didn't know why I couldn't begin right away, especially since suckling expels the placenta, but I was too ignorant to insist. *No one told me.*

CHAPTER III

The Moment of Triumph

After one or two hours, depending on hospital routine, the mother is wheeled in her bed to one of the post-partum floors. Hers is a victorious march; if a woman is ever a queen it is at this TRIUMPHANT MOMENT OF HER LIFE.

ALAN F. GUTTMACHER, M.D., *Pregnancy and Birth*

Back in the room Frederick collapsed on my bed saying he was exhausted from videotaping, and he fell immediately asleep. He was taking up nearly the whole bed so I squeezed myself along the edge near the telephone and called one of my sisters, the only one who had also given birth. Her husband answered the phone.

"When was the baby born? A half hour ago and you're on the phone?" ("*You delivered her like an experienced mother of five,*" Dr. Fabin had told me. I was really puffed up with pride. I wanted everybody to know all the details immediately.) "My god," he continued, "Antoinette didn't even talk until forty-eight hours after Gunnar was born!"

Antoinette got on the phone and told me about how they had doped her up three months before in California. I gave her a blow by blow account of Emma's birth, and then I called my mother. "You know," she said, "I just *knew* you were in labor last night. I was on the toilet all night with cramps, for no apparent reason, and then, in the middle of the night, while I was still groaning on the toilet, Andrea (one of my sisters) walked in, moaning. She said she had been at a bar with her boyfriend and suddenly was attacked with such cramps that he had to carry her to the car and bring her home."

In the middle of mother's description of Andrea's cramps a nurse walked in.

"You'll have to get him off that bed."

"Why?"

"It's against hospital regulations."

"He's asleep. He's exhausted from childbirth."

"Well, wake him up!"

I promised to wake him up and resumed my conversation. He slept for hours. Then he left before they brought Emma in to be nursed. He needed another snort I supposed.

When I looked at the placenta, after it was laboriously pushed out without the aid of a nursing baby, the doctor told me that a friend of his had written a book about why mothers should eat the placenta. It looked like anemic steak tartare without the seasonings. I looked at it and knew I should eat it, but I couldn't. I reasoned later that that was probably why I was so tired for weeks after Emma was born—because I couldn't bring myself to eat the placenta. For the first three days afterwards, though, I was so high that I couldn't sleep. When they first brought her in to me, after Frederick had left, I lay in bed for a while and looked at her through the glass of her crib. She was on her side and her hair had been washed. It glinted in the sunlight, a reddish blond, and her little chin was visible above the swaddling clothes, square, like her father's.

I got out of bed, walked over to the glass crib, and looked down at her—I blush to say that what I felt could only be described as "fulfillment." Then I phoned Frederick to tell him that his daughter looked just like him.

Awake, Emma was fascinated by the light coming from the window. She focused her enormous blue, badly crossed eyes directly at the windows from the first moment I held her in my arms. As I was comparing her, poetically (in spite of the crossed left eye), to a sparrow, a nurse walked in.

"She can't see anything yet. Don't bother showing her the window."

I finished breastfeeding her and gave her a bottle of water. A nurse walked in.

"Don't hold her away from you like that. Hold her close. Cuddle her. They like to be cuddled." Emma was stretched out along my arms, her head in my hand, drinking her water, certainly looking very happy. I began to feel testy.

Marie-Claude called. "Oh, you should see the baby," I raved, "she looks just like Frederick!"

"I can't wait to see her! When can I come?"

"Oh, shit! I forgot, they don't let anybody in the room except the father when the baby's in here. Do you know that if I had other kids they wouldn't even let them in here?"

"You should have gone to Santa Fe the way Joni Smith did. She had the baby in her own house. The doctor actually came to the house. I think it's the only place in America where you can have a baby at home."

"Outside of Appalachia."

"Where I'm sure you can't even get a midwife. You probably have to have a sister or a mother."

"Can you believe that an ancestor of mine, in Scotland, developed chloroform [my grandmother talked about him all the time—her only claim to fame] and was the first doctor to give anesthesia to mothers? Queen Victoria had one of her kids on chloroform with one of his disciples; my ancestor's name was Simpson, and it was a big scandal until the Queen did it. Considered to be going against the will of God? He was knighted for it."

"And here you are, trying to turn back the clock."

"Yeah, progress."

"Well, I guess I'll just have to wait to see the baby until you come home."

"Oh, I forgot. You can go to the nursery and look at her through the glass wall."

"Describe her to me so I'll know what to look for."

"Oh, she looks like Frederick. Curly reddish-blond hair, big blue eyes, and a long square chin."

A few hours later Marie-Claude came bursting into my room. "What do you mean?" she cried, "curly reddish-blond hair and a long square chin? There's nobody in there like that!"

"My god! What happened to her?"

"You'd better come with me down to the nursery."

I went down to the nursery in my pin-striped robe to look for my baby.

In the middle of the room was a Puerto Rican baby boy, lying on his back and screaming. His face was strained and red and his penis was standing straight up, a piece of blood-soaked white gauze tied around it. He had just been circumcized. Next to him was Emma, easy to find, since she was the only white baby there, but, my god, she was nowhere near my earlier description of her. Somewhere between the morning and the afternoon her hair had turned brown; she had lost half of it (in contrast to the others, all with thick black silky mops); her chin was unremarkable, and you could barely see her eyes, let alone discern the color of them, since the flesh around them was so puffed up from her crying.

"There she is, Marie-Claude. See!"

Three days later when the milk was supposed to come in I asked the nurse, "Will it bother me if I don't nurse the baby tonight? I think my milk is coming in but I want some sleep." (They always woke me up an hour before I was due to nurse her to give me a glass of apple juice, making the hours of sleep so few as to be almost nonexistent.)

"Oh no, it won't hurt you. We'll give her a bottle in the nursery."

At two in the morning I woke up in agony. My breasts were like rocks and the pain was running down my arms and sides. I jammed my finger down savagely on the call button and demanded the baby.

"You should have told us earlier. We've already given her a bottle."

"Well bring her in anyway. She can eat twice."

"Oh no, we can't do that."

I burst into tears. Finally someone came in and told me to sit on a chair in front of the sink. "I can't sit down. My stitches hurt too much."

She made a ring of towels on the seat of the chair, leaving a hole in the middle, and asked me to sit down again. Her lips were set in a tight grimace as she systematically soaked more towels in hot water and held them against my breasts while hand pumping the milk out of them. She was very annoyed—the nurse, that is. Very annoyed. I cried throughout the process. It was worse than the birth.

Eleven o'clock at night. I had taken two sleeping pills earlier. Nothing. I walked down to the nursery. Emma was squalling.

"Please let me nurse her. She's hungry."

"What are you doing out of bed? I just gave you two sleeping pills. Ida! Get her back in her room!"

"I'm all right. I just can't sleep. Please, let me have my baby."

"You get back in your room before you fall down." I let myself be led back to bed.

The next day I called my mother.

"You'd better stay in the hospital until after the fifth day. On the fifth day you get very, uh, testy, I think is the word."

"Really, Mother, why?"

"Well, I don't know why, but I was that way after each child was born. Always on the fifth day. It's better to be in the hospital, where they can take care of you. You might get too depressed at home."

"But Frederick wants me to stay here for ten days!"

"I always stayed two weeks. I loved it. It was the only time I had a vacation."

"A vacation! Mother! They're horrible here! I had to clean my own room the very day I gave birth!"

"Now, Augustine, you know how you exaggerate!"

"No, really, Mother, I had to clean my own room. The head nurse came in and said, 'What a mess! I can't let a newborn baby into this room in that condition,' and there wasn't anybody around to do it. Christ, the nurse who picks up the tray won't even wipe the crumbs off the table, union rules. Just like the Metro Hotel. It's against the union rules to dust the rooms. Just to shut them up I cleaned it myself. I got out of bed, in agony from the stitches, just to clean up the room. They made me go to the toilet the minute I got into the room after she was born. Hell, I could hardly *walk* from the stitches!"

"I always had a bedpan."

"I guess times have changed."

"I hope you're not one of those demanding women. Whenever I was in the hospital there was always one of those on the floor. Pushing the call button constantly, complaining all the time, making the nurses' lives just hell."

"Mother, it's more expensive than the Plaza here. Why should they ignore me? I just gave birth. Why should I clean my room at eighty dollars a day?"

"But do they wipe your ass at the Plaza?"

"My god! Wipe your ass! They don't even wipe off the table! You don't believe me? Come down here and see for yourself."

"Your father can't get away and you know I can't go anyplace without him."

"Why not?"

"Well, I never have!"

I said goodbye and hung up, depressed. It was bad enough, Frederick passing out on my bed, but my own mother not coming to see me and those goddam nurses, always complaining instead of patting me on the back and saying, "Well done!"

"When are you going to get out of here?" It was Dr. Fabin.

"I wish I knew," I told him, "but I don't have anybody back at the hotel to help me."

"You'd better get out soon or you'll go batty!"

The stitches are really killing me. I search my mind for a simple practical apparatus that will relieve the pain. Something to sit on. It occurs to me that an innertube would be just the thing. I ask for one.

"Where do you think you are? Atlantic City?"

I don't get it. The pain has erased my sense of humor. By the time I realize that she's trying to be funny she's left the room again. The fact that someone could connect the request for an innertube with a vision of someone floating blissfully offshore when my mind connects it only to that hammerlock of pain that used to be my vagina totally mystifies me. I hit the call button again ("one of those demanding women," I suppose) and this time I explain about the innertube.

"You have to have your doctor's permission for that," the first voice says.

"We can't even give out an aspirin without your doctor's permission," a second voice adds.

"I didn't ask for an aspirin."

"You'll have to wait."

"Get me the head nurse!"

The head nurse gets on the telephone. "Oh, we can give you that," she says, "but we can't give you any aspirin."

"Dammit, I didn't ask for aspirin. I've been asking for an innertube all day."

"Don't talk to me that way, Mrs. Marat, we're doing all we can here."

"You get that innertube in here right away or I'm moving to the Plaza. They have room service there and it's cheaper." I knew from past experience that at the Plaza all you had to do was pick up that white princess telephone and you could have an aspirin, an innertube, or a masseur, as long as you paid for it. Even at the Metro Hotel, whose service I had been complaining about for years, you could always get two of the above. Was this eighty-dollar-a-day flophouse being run by Zero Population Growth?

Ten minutes later my room was filled with nurses and orderlies all arguing about the innertube. The phone rang while I was packing my bags.

"What's wrong?" It was Dr. Fabin. Apparently the head nurse had called him to complain about me. I explained the situation to him.

"I told you you'd go batty in that hospital."

"Well, you recommended it!"

"Why don't you go home?"

"My husband won't let me. I'm moving to the Plaza."

"Listen, don't go to the Plaza. Your insurance doesn't cover it. I'll fix everything. They'll bring you the innertube and then you get on that telephone and hire some help so you can go home, okay?" I meekly agreed, kicked everyone out of my room, and went to sleep.

When they woke me up two hours later for the goddam apple juice again I asked them for rooming-in—a system where the baby stays in the mother's room all day. I thought that at least if I had Emma in the room with me then they'd leave me alone. When they brought her to me she was asleep. I let her sleep until she woke up and then I fed her. One of the nurses walked in, horrified that I had fed her so late.

"Her next feeding is scheduled for an hour from now. Why did you wait so long?"

"She was asleep."

"You should have wakened her."

"Why?"

"Because she's supposed to eat every four hours. She had her two o'clock feeding at five and now she's supposed to be fed again at six. You can't do that. It ruins our whole schedule!"

All those overheard stories elaborately narrated by my mother's friends (Agnes McCarthy, Helen Dick, Tootsie Nicolson, Mrs. Ryan, Marian Carey, Ann Keser, Grace Slattery, Jean Hennesy, Babs Dougherty) of childbirth in the Forties, which I had poo-poohed as feminine exaggerations or their way of competing with their husbands' battle stories of the war (the Second World War) suddenly made a great deal of sense. Those women had not exaggerated one little bit. Why is it that when a woman tells a terrible story no one, not even her own mother, believes her?

"And there I was, hemorrhaging because the placenta wasn't all out and no one knew it. I was screaming for a nurse. 'You're okay,' they all said, patting my hair, until one of them spotted a puddle of blood on the floor under my bed."

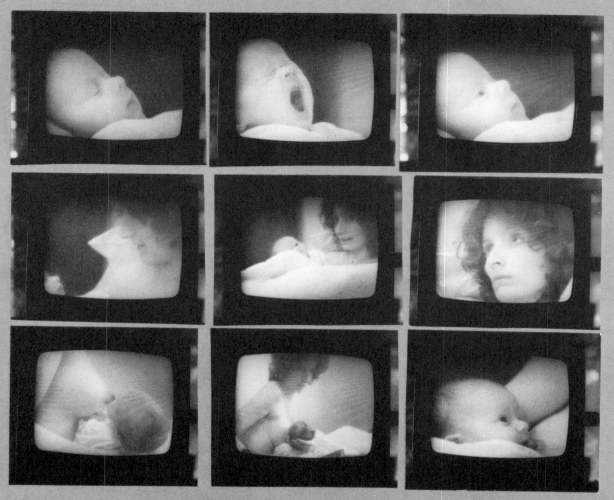

"You can't do that. It ruins our whole schedule!"

"It was a difficult delivery. When they pulled her out with forceps they damaged her arm. As soon as I came out of the anesthesia they told me she'd never be normal. I wanted to throw her out the window. Look at her! Eight years old and there isn't a thing wrong with her!"

"As the ether took effect I could hear people dancing in the street outside and I thought the war must have ended. When I woke up I was told that we had just dropped the bomb on Hiroshima. In their excitement they had left a suture clamp in me but I didn't discover that until I developed peritonitis a month later."

My favorite story was the one told to me by Joni Smith. A friend of hers had given birth to a black baby and, when she tried to make love six weeks later, she discovered that the doctor had sewn up her vagina.

Frederick came in. Finally. After not having shown up for two days. I supposed he was having an affair with the girl across the hall. She didn't have any kids. Emma started crying and I couldn't stop her. Afraid to nurse her for more than four minutes at a time according to Doctor's Orders (any more, was the supposition, and your nipples would crack), I didn't realize that she wanted the tit until I saw the videotapes months later—that sucking movement of her mouth; I asked myself how I could have been so stupid as not to have known enough to ignore the rules. After videotaping her crying Frederick said he couldn't stand it any more and left. No, he didn't leave; I sent her back to the nursery. My maternal instincts weren't fully developed enough to transfer them from the husband to the child.

Every night the other husbands would come to see their wives and newborns. I would put on my make-up, brush my hair, and wait. He only came once at night.

The fifth day. My nerves were killing me. I called one of my mother's nannies now living in Baltimore. She had taken care of one of my younger brothers when I was twelve.

"Why didn't you call me before? I told you I would come any time you needed me."

"I didn't realize how difficult it would be."

She said she'd be able to come up to New York in two days. She had a butcher shop in Baltimore and had to hire another butcher to work for her while she was away.

One of the young nurses came in and said, "Let me know when you're leaving and I'll dress the baby for you."

"Oh?" I was surprised. "How come you dress the babies? Do you do it because you like to or what?"

"Well, if it's an ugly baby and has ugly clothes I don't like to do it; but if it's a beautiful baby and it has cute clothes I love to do it."

After she left I called Frederick.

"You've got to find Emma's hand-knit blue sweater, and that blue-and-white gingham dress—you know, the one I got in Spain—and her little white bonnet. Look in the middle drawer." Afraid that the nurse would label Emma's clothes ugly (it never occurred to me that she would label Emma herself ugly) and confident that Frederick wouldn't bother to look for the pretty clothes, I spent the morning rummaging through what clothes I had brought for Emma in one of the two giant suitcases.

Trying to leave the hospital was hell. When Frederick arrived we immediately began fighting. I ended up sitting in a chair, sobbing, while a black nurse dressed the baby. The young nurse who liked pretty babies came in to say goodbye but didn't mention dressing Emma herself. I was so tired I could hardly move and Frederick acted as though he was suffering from heroin withdrawal. Finally I had learned to recognize the symptoms.

Driving back to the hotel in the limousine he had rented—rented so that we would look rich on the videotape—he concentrated on filming the streets. When I asked him why he wasn't filming the baby he told me that he was doing an ethnological study for her, of the streets, at the time she was born. I was reconvinced of his genius. I never would have thought of that myself. When we reached the hotel I paid the chauffeur, went upstairs, and got into bed. Frederick left.

I telephoned Magda, telling her how exhausted I was and asked her to come down and make me some eggs. My mother's nanny, Rosemary, called, and said she'd had a change of heart and she'd be there in five hours. While I ate, Frederick came in and out of the apartment to play the baby's music box for her and videotape her.

"Get back in bed!" Magda kept yelling at me. Naked, with my Kotex belt around me, I was filming Frederick and the baby. He loved her so much. He kept playing with her and staring at her. He was so sweet to her. I guess he had managed to score some dope on one of his forays into the halls.

CHAPTER IV

"The First One Is Always the Hardest"

A popular international cliché

I lay there in my bed, the baby in her bassinette, imagining her flying out the window. I even saw myself throwing her out. I telephoned Jeannie again to discuss it. She referred me to the latest book by a psychologist. I can never remember their names.

"He says it's a natural reaction to the fear that something will happen to the baby. You know, for the first few weeks it's very crucial, whether the baby will live or die."

I telephoned Marian in Mexico. She had two children. "Listen," she told me, "I used to see their heads being split open with the machete. Right down the middle! The things I could tell you!"

When Frederick and I were there, in Zihuatanejo, a sea coast village about 150 miles north of Acapulco, the machete was kept stuck, blade down, in the grass near the kitchen door. Sometimes her four-year-old son would swing it around out on the patio. I was always taking it away from him, asking his father, "Where do you keep the machete?" They kept it in the grass near the kitchen.

"Marian," I confessed, "I've seen Emma's head, split open, on the bathroom tiles, the black-and-white tiles of the Metro Hotel."

Tonight I took Emma out of the bathtub and, holding her in my arms, reached up on the rack that used to be above her bathinette, before I moved it, for a towel.

A shriek, a clash on the black and white tiles, hysterical sobbing. I looked down. An enormous long-bladed pair of scissors lay open, on the tiles at my feet. The handle had struck the baby's shoulder.

"The maid!" I screamed. "How could she have put the scissors there?" Then I remembered that I had done it myself one night, while Emma lay on her bathinette after I used them to cut the mittens off her nightgown sleeves. And I remembered telling myself that it was a foolish place to put the scissors.

Now that we're home I can see why she cried so much in the hospital. That four-hour nursing schedule was ridiculous, just as I thought it was. She wants the tit every three hours, like clockwork. She never sleeps for more than three hours at a time and then she wakes up, crying, her mouth open like a baby robin, making pecking motions toward my breast. As her mouth clamps down she makes cooing noises and I can hear the milk pouring down her throat and landing with a splash in her stomach.

Duñel, the Haitian maid for the ninth floor of the hotel (they're all Haitians here, just like the midwives in the hospital) told me that in Haiti the mothers drink a teaspoon of their own milk as soon as it "comes in" to prevent the baby from ever getting pimples. The logic of it escaped me but since I didn't want to hurt Duñel's feelings, I tried it. (Besides, Duñel has promised to give me a voodoo bath in banana peels to bring me money.) I had a cocktail party right here in my bedroom and gave all my visitors a shotglass full of milk. Everyone drank it and exclaimed on its taste but I'm sure they were all too polite to refuse. Curious about how it would taste straight from the tit, I asked Frederick to try it. "It's so much better warm," he said. "*You* ought to try it."

It took me a while to get my nipple to my mouth, but I finally did it. The jets of milk hit the back of my throat like moist sugary air and seemed to disappear before they reached my stomach. The gymnastics of it were so difficult that I couldn't get enough to fill my mouth. The taste was between cotton candy and that fine Italian pastry they sell in Little Italy that melts in your mouth.

That night I dreamed that I was a baby again, at my mother's breast. Her nipples were rosy and moist and I could smell the milk and feel it on my cheek as some of it escaped my mouth and trickled down my face. As I began to get sleepy and stopped sucking so hard it tapered off to a trickle—just enough to keep my throat wet as I breathed through my nose. She held me for a long time after that, her arms around my back, one hand stroking my hair, her perfume drifting into my nose. I looked up into her eyes; they were moist and blue and I could see reflections in them that were always different. In the morning when the blinds were drawn the blue was dark, almost black. I would look for a reflection but could see only a pool of dark, surrounded by the clear white of her eyes. So I would close my eyes again and just breathe in the smell of her armpit, musty and hot, like a drug. Then, my stomach full, I would fall asleep.

Sometimes she left the blinds open and I could see the orange sun dancing in her eyes. She smiled as I looked for those little orange suns and, as she moved, they moved, from one side of her eye to the other. In the early afternoon I could see a tiny face in there and I always wondered who it was, that other baby in my mother's eyes.

Right now Rosemary is sitting in a chair at the foot of my bed, staring at us, Emma and me, while I nurse her. It makes me so uneasy. She told me that she never nursed her children; so she can't advise me on that. I don't need her advice on "that," but I wouldn't dream of telling her.

"I got married because I wanted children," she told me, "but we didn't stay married very long and I don't think I'll ever try it again."

"That won't happen to me," I'm thinking, "I got married for love."

"Remember that day when you pulled me out of the river?" she reminds me. I can remember; I was about twelve years old and Rosemary had just rescued my younger brother, who had locked himself in a room on the second floor. She put up a ladder, opened the window from the outside, and carried him down the ladder. I don't know why she didn't just climb into the room, unlock the door, and carry him down the stairs; but we were all inspired by the dramatic scene she made (and, besides, Daddy was filming it). Then she jumped into the river to cool off, but it was over her head and she couldn't swim. I dove in after her and dragged her to the cement retaining wall.

"Why can't Rosemary swim in the pool at the Club?" we asked Mother. "They don't allow the 'help' to swim in the pool," Mother had answered. "But how will they know that she's 'help'?" we wanted to know.

Rosemary is black, but we thought that if we just told the management that she was part of the family they would let her swim in the pool. We didn't know the difference.

Now Rosemary is giving me a bath. She ordered some mint-flavored alcohol from the drugstore and is giving me a backrub in the tub. I'm complaining that it stings too much. "I always did this for your mother," she tells me. "I was the only one she would ever allow to see her naked." (*"In the twenty years I've been married to your father, he's never seen me undress in front of him."*)

"Your mother told me a lot of things," Rosemary continues when I express my amazement. "She had confidence in me."

Rosemary sleeps on a cot in the living room, gets up in the middle of the night with the baby, and does all the shopping and cooking. She worries that Frederick isn't eating enough. She does the cleaning, since the maid, Duñel, does nothing (it's against union rules to move anything off a surface to dust it, to move furniture, or to vacuum and wash dishes), and takes care of me as though I were a baby too, which I've felt like ever since I had Emma. In a week she'll have to go back to her butcher shop and I'm frantic wondering how I'll get along without her.

The baby is two weeks old. Frederick videotaped her first crawl. She crawled from the foot of her bassinette to the head of it. Rosemary and I watched it in the living room on the T.V. set as she was doing it. Rosemary says that means she'll be very fast. (*"I'll be able to tell whether she's fast or slow within the next two weeks."*) Actually, she had done it when she was two days old but I had forgotten to write it down. Frederick has rented another room downstairs for his "office." Unless I telephone

Unless I telephone before I visit him he makes a remark. I've never felt more persecuted.

before I visit him he makes a remark. I've never felt more persecuted. However, I'm too tired to do anything about it.

Mother, Dad, and Mother's sister came to see me (for the first time) and told me that no wonder I'm so tired; I never go out. They persuaded me to go next door with them to a restaurant; I had refused to leave the block. Before they finished eating I had to go back to the baby. I couldn't stand being away from her. Mother wanted me to wear a brassiere under my sweater. Now that I've taken the ethnological viewpoint on all of it I don't get too upset. I just take notes.

Frederick asked them if they would like to see the videotape of the baby's birth. Daddy said no.

"Don't worry, dear, she's all covered up with white sheets; you won't see anything," mother told him.

"Yes," I agreed, "don't worry, you won't see anything."

None of us could persuade him to look at it. Mother came down to the office, however, and we all cried while watching it—that is, until the doctor asks me if I want to be sewed up small, medium, or large. Then Mother steals a look at her youngest son (Rosemary's former charge) who's also sitting there, watching, with his girlfriend. ("Unlike his usual following, a lady to her fingertips," Mother described her.) "Don't worry about a thing like that, Mother," I want to tell her. "Your son is fully acquainted with female anatomy." However, I said nothing. Motherhood has stamped out my rebel instincts. It's too exhausting to create ferment.

Back upstairs, Mother told Daddy that it was the most beautiful thing she had ever seen, and he was really missing something by not seeing it. He steadfastly refused.

"Didn't you ever go into the delivery room with Mother, Daddy?" I asked.

"The delivery room!" she answered for him. "He wouldn't even stay in the labor room. He was always out hunting when I had my babies!" Mother was showing the familiar signs of repressed anger, her eyes blazing, her mouth tight, remembering all those childbirth scenes, with him out there in the woods stalking deer (*and nobody even liked the taste of it*). I, of course, felt that I had found a superior man. I managed to forget all my reproaches against Frederick. How could I have complained that he didn't even keep the lens focused on my vagina during the birth? Apparently the sight of it was too much for the average man to bear at all, if my father was any example. What do I mean "man"? Coco Chanel said that she found it so messy and disgusting that she didn't know how a man could ever make love again to a woman he had witnessed giving birth. I guess that's why my mother had ten; if only she had managed a surprise birth right at home in bed, before my father could escape (using hospital regulations as an excuse), then she would have been spared further ordeals.

Daddy loves the results of the process, however; right now he's cooing and ahhing and making all those strange sounds people make in the presence of anyone under four years of age. Emma is nestled on his shoulder in a pair of pink terrycloth stretch pajamas.

"She's a beautiful baby," he said, "beautiful!"

"But she has a crossed left eye," I told him.

"What!" he bellowed, "what are you talking about? There isn't a *thing* wrong with her! You should get down on your knees every night and thank God for giving you such a perfect baby!"

Before she left Mother told me I really should wean the baby. After all, at three weeks of age she's already gotten all the immunities out of my milk; why should I suffer with aching breasts and leaking tits any longer?

Remembering my dream, I wondered what Mother's attitude had really been when she was nursing me. I once heard a story about American Indians yanking their sons away from their mothers' breasts periodically, in order to make them angry enough to become good warriors; I wondered if that was the cause of all of my "violence." Was I a modern female warrior? Should I change my image of myself from neurotic to tribal?

Mother would never tell me the truth. She always said that she couldn't remember things you especially wanted to know—like the exact time of your birth, what was your first word, etc. In fact, her favorite monologue was: "I didn't have any *idea* that I would get *pregnant* when I got married! That was the farthest thing from my mind."

"Did you know, Mother, that sexual intercourse produces babies?" my sisters and I would ask her.

"Well, of course!" she would say, with true Irish Catholic ingenuousness, "but *pregnancy*! I just never thought about it!" This particular conversation always took place while my sisters and I were discussing contraception.

"And as for contraception! Why, I didn't even know what it *was*!"

I decided to ask her about the weaning anyway.

"Well, I got a breast infection when you were four or five or six months old, I can't remember which. I was pregnant with Alexandra, and I *had* to stop nursing!" I wasn't learning anything new.

"Nowadays," I told her, "they tell you that you don't have to stop nursing if you have an infection. You just nurse on the other side."

"My doctor said, 'Stop immediately.' "

"Don't you know that doctors don't know anything? Frederick counted twenty-one traumas delivered to Emma before she even left the delivery room."

"He had time to count?"

"He discovered them when he looked at the videotape."

"That videotape machine," my father butted in. "I don't know why you bought it. It's a waste of money!"

"Now, Henry," from my mother, "let them do what they want. They're old enough!"

It was time for my aunt to speak up. "Augustine, your mother went through hell. I remember walking you and walking you because you were crying so hard one night when she was out, and I was frantic; I didn't know what was wrong. You refused the bottle; you weren't hungry, you weren't wet, you wouldn't sleep. I was so relieved when your mother came home. I was crying myself I felt so sorry for you. You immediately stopped crying as soon as your mother took you in her arms."

"What was wrong with me?" I was sure she was telling this story apropos of my abrupt weaning.

"You were teething."

It was obvious to me that I was crying because I missed my mother. Why didn't they get it? Social conditioning and Dr. Spock I supposed.

Finally Mother got back on the track. "I remember one day," she reminisced, "when I was nursing you and the pain was so intense and my nerves were so raw that I screamed at your father to stop making so much noise. He was using a putty knife on the window pane, repairing it, and just the sound of the knife against the glass drove me insane."

"My god," I thought, "I don't even have a breast infection and I feel that way all the time." Right before Rosemary went back to her butcher shop (when Emma was two weeks old) my editor came to see me with her boyfriend. Jeannie Kirby's mother was there too; she had stopped by to give me a baby quilt she had been saving for thirty years. It had belonged to one of her sons. The three of them were just sitting there in the living room, talking quietly to me, and suddenly I couldn't stand the sound of their voices. My eardrums felt like raw nerves, their voices like files, shaving away the nerves, bit by bit.

"I have to go to the toilet," I told them (actually, it was true) and I fled the room. When I came out of the bathroom, Rosemary pulled down the covers on my bed and said to get in.

"I have to at least say goodbye to them," I told her. "They've all brought presents for the baby."

"You get in this bed," she said. "I don't want to have to tell you again."

I got in between the clean cool sheets, grateful to her for making the decision for me.

Since Emma and I left the hospital, all my reactions have undergone a rapid change. I don't want anyone to touch the baby. I don't want any "strangers" to so much as look at her. Jealously I stand guard over my treasure, trying to totally control the environment. If anything even slightly disturbs her I can feel it myself. Before she herself knows that she's going to stiffen her body and cry, I know it. My hands are always ready to reach out and grab her away from any "stranger" who is holding her at the moment.

CHAPTER V

Incest Is Best

"Many new mothers, afraid of the sensuous pleasure they feel upon nursing the baby, stop nursing. Some even report experiencing orgasm."

TWO SENTENCES OUT OF EVERY BOOK I'VE EVER
READ ON PREGNANCY AND CHILDBIRTH

"Oh you'll love making love after you have the baby. It's much better after children are born. There's something so nitty-gritty about it."

A MANHATTAN ACTRESS

"You're as tight as a sixteen-year-old virgin."

DR. FABIN, DURING A CHECK-UP

None of the above applied to me. I experienced no pleasure of the sensuous variety in nursing unless you count the time that I was stoned and we lay in bed, naked, body to body, Emma and I, while she nursed herself to sleep and I experienced the most exquisite sensations (I wasn't organized enough ever to get the joint and the baby together again at the same time). The only one I wanted to make love to was the baby, and

54

rather than being a sixteen-year-old virgin I was a thirty-year-old mother whose cunt had been sewn up so tight that it hurt to make love.

Dr. Fabin had brainwashed me during my pregnancy to ask him at the crucial moment to sew me up "small." Even though Frederick had said, "I don't care, darling," when I asked him what he preferred—small, medium, or large—during the stitching of the episiotomy, I, like a good subject, had said, "You might as well make it small."

Further evidence against my strength of mind was the fact that Dr. Fabin was the fourth doctor who attended me (the others all refused, when the crunch came, to allow us to videotape) and I hadn't found him until I was in my eighth month. Hardly a lot of time to brainwash someone.

Every visit I made to him after Emma's birth was the same. I would tell him that my vagina hurt too much to make love and he would say, "Don't worry, it'll stretch with use."

"But it isn't getting any use!" I would wail and he would ask me, "Is Frederick on dope?"

It was flattering to think that Dr. Fabin would think that the only reason my husband wouldn't make love to me was because he was impotent on account of his heroin habit, but the truth was that I didn't care. I didn't know whether or not Frederick was still taking heroin (like my mother, he would never tell me what I wanted most to know) and I didn't care that much about fucking. What obsessed me, especially at night, was the fantasy that I would have another baby in the wilderness and my cunt would be too tight to let it out without a doctor around who had a pair of scissors on him.

I'm not exaggerating. The fact that, at the rate I was going, I wouldn't be able to conceive another baby, let alone deliver one, didn't occur to me at all. The image was persistent—I was lying on a jungle trail, writhing in agony, a baby's head straining and straining to get out of my sixteen-year-old virgin vagina.

I kept thinking about the perversity of the medical profession, how antagonistic they were to nature. It was natural, I believed, for the first baby to be difficult—after all, that passage had never been used before—but the ones following that should be easier and easier. With the episiotomy and tightening-up obsession of the doctors, every woman had to go through the agonies of a first "crowning" again with each child. I thrashed around in bed every night, stewing over that one.

When I say that the only person I wanted to make love to was the baby it's true. Something I had never thought about before (except in nightmares) began obsessing me—incest. I asked everyone about it. Later, after Marie-Claude gave birth, I asked her about it. She was the only one who gave me a straight answer.

"Oh," she told me without hesitating, "I lick my daughter's pussy for a while whenever she gets nervous." I wondered what Marie-Claude's criterion for "nervousness" was but instead I asked her how many minutes she did it.

"Ten minutes usually. Only when she's nervous and can't sleep." I kept wondering what would happen if we had little boys.

"I know that they masturbate little boys in Africa when they cry," I told her, "but I don't know anything about little girls."

"No wonder, they're so male chauvinist that they cut off the baby girls' clitorises anyway." (Marie-Claude, since I had last seen her, had become a champion of womens' rights in France. There were always photographs of her in the papers, going to demonstrations, sit-ins, hunger strikes, always with her daughter, Carry-Nation, on her back in an American backpack.)

"But that's only a few agricultural tribes and not until they're twelve or thirteen, no?"

"I should think that would be worse," Marie-Claude said. "By that time they know what they'll be missing."

I've been thinking about animals; dogs and cats especially. They lick their newborn for months afterwards. Especially the genitals. I think it's like eating the placenta, something we used to do but don't any more because we can't remember having done it in our collective unconscious. Marie-Claude, however, is unconcerned. How nice to be so instinctive and guiltless. I wonder if it's a French trait, or if, in Marie-Claude's case, it's a political statement.

Frederick told me that whenever he sleeps with Emma she massages his cock between her feet very delicately until he gets a hard-on. When they take a bath together she picks up his foreskin between her fingertips and giggles. He says she's the most sensitive woman he's ever known.

I try to sublimate my incestuous desires by giving her massages. I rub her back first while she cranes her still nearly bald head around and smiles at me, and then I turn her over and rub her front. I'm a good masseuse. I rub all the way down to the fingertips and toenails. Emma coos and gurgles.

When she was born I thought her pubis seemed large for her body. My friends with daughters told me that all baby girls are like that. However, Rosemary brought it up, saying that she thought the same thing, but was afraid to say anything in the beginning. (Would anyone think that a baby boy's penis was too large?) As a result of Rosemary's misgivings I've been examining all the baby girls I know. Amazing how you can see all those shapes so clearly, since there's no pubic hair. They're all different: most of them are high and narrow; some of them, like Emma's, are low-slung and plump (large?), begging, like a child's plump rosy cheek, to be affectionately pinched. The majority of them seem to be tightly sealed, their slender lips never opening; some, however, usually the plump ones, open like a summer rose whenever their owners make a movement. All are infinitely erotic. I keep wondering if you're born with the same size cunt you'll have at adulthood, like your eyes. I remember when my youngest brother was born; his eyes were so big, and Mother said that your eyes always stay the same size that they were when you were born.

CHAPTER VI

The Servant Problem

During the betrothal period it was the sacred duty of both parties to acquire a practical knowledge of maternity, so that when they undertook parenthood they should be proficient in midwifery and child-rearing. Pregnant women and nursing mothers were not permitted to work, and a husband and father who neglected to save his wife from family tasks during these times would be despised and condemned.

ETTIE ROUT, *Maori Symbolism*

Frederick sat at the control booth day and night, editing videotapes. He had put two tables in front of the bay window and between the window and the bedroom door. "Why do you have to work right here?" Magda kept asking him whenever she had to go to the toilet. The bathroom could only be reached by going through the bedroom, and in order to get into the bedroom you had to climb over Frederick and his cables. He had three monitors going. That was the only area in the apartment that was relatively neat. Wherever Frederick worked there was always order. Yet there would be a snowstorm in hell, as my father would say, before Frederick would put his hands into a kitchen sink. Duñel would do it if I gave her a big tip. Yet she came only once a day for fifteen minutes unless I bribed her to stay longer. Despite the fact that every time I called Sidney Renard to complain about the mess he told me that the maids were supposed to stay a half hour in each room, they only stayed fifteen minutes. The routine was to make the bed, use a carpet sweeper on the rug (vacuuming was against union rules—could only be done by a man), and run a filthy mop, saturated with ammonia, over the bathroom and kitchen floors. That was it. I could never bring myself to ask Duñel to do anything else. Chained as I was to the baby, who was always nursing, I would sit on the couch, helplessly watching the mess pile up around me.

When I was a small girl, I thought there was something lacking in Mother because she couldn't seem to bring herself to give orders to "the girl who helped Mother." My sisters and I would talk incessantly about the problem. (We had to say "the girl who helps Mother"; we weren't allowed to say "the maid.") Now that I was the victim of my own inability to give the simplest order I had to reorganize my conception of Mother. Or perhaps I was the way I was because of my genes? More likely it was a case of imprinting. I was totally incapable of asking an employee (I once had a secretary) to do anything. Maybe, I thought, on the other hand, it was because I was a Leo. "A Leo personality has trouble delegating authority; they think they can do everything better themselves," the books always said.

Rosemary was gone and I couldn't even bring myself to hire a babysitter. I wanted to be with Emma all the time. The only other person I really trusted with her was Frederick; if I left her with him she didn't cry as soon as I reached the doorknob.

Duñel finally suggested that I hire her cousin, Helga. Helga had been in New York for a couple of weeks and needed a job so that she could send for her six children, who were still living in Haiti. "Where is Helga living now?" I asked Duñel. "She live in my house. I rent her a room," Duñel told me. Upon prodding, I learned that Duñel owned a brownstone in Brooklyn that she rented out. It seemed that Duñel had quite a bit of money.

Helga arrived with a pair of pajamas in a paper bag. We had negotiated an incredible salary that was to pay her for five days a week and two nights.

Her duties were supposed to be taking care of Emma when I had to

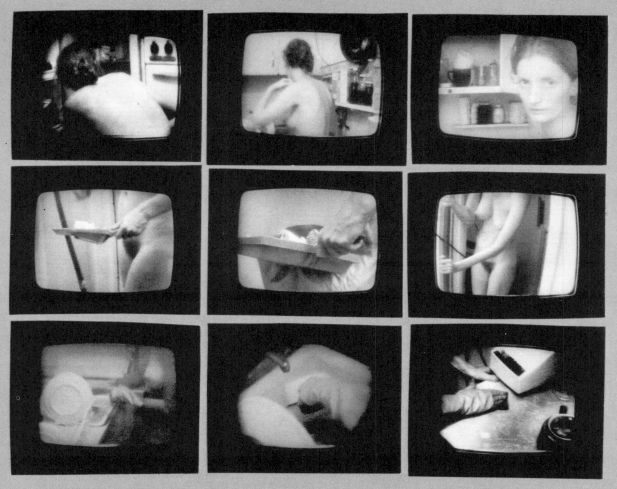

*Yet there would be a snowstorm in hell, as my father used to say, before Frederick
would put his hands into a kitchen sink.*

 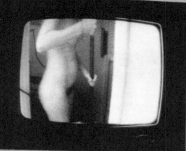 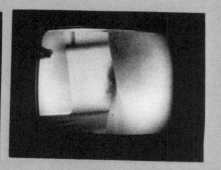

work or go out, but she insisted on cooking and cleaning too. "Don't tell Duñel that I'm doing this," she would say to me as she dusted the furniture. By this time Duñel and I had made an arrangement about the dusting. She would do it for another five dollars' tip a week. I was now paying her cousin one hundred and twenty dollars in cash and Duñel was getting fifteen dollars a week in tips. I had tried to suspend the maid service and thus pay less rent but Sidney wouldn't hear of it. He insisted that I keep Duñel so that he wouldn't have to lower the rent. I found out from Duñel that he told the maids to do the exact opposite from what he told me he was telling them. "Divide and Conquer" seemed to be the modus operandi of the Metro Hotel.

I kept quiet about Helga's dusting technique, principally because she did a better job than Duñel, and I continued paying Duñel extra to clean. Now when she came into the apartment, since there was nothing left for her to do she just sat down and rapped with her cousin.

There was a conflict between the cousins about Catholicism and voodoo. Helga was an ardent convert to Catholicism and Duñel practiced voodoo. When Magda and I were arrested for filming in the streets Duñel put a curse on the arresting officer that consisted of a new, clear drinking glass, a candle, and a white handkerchief, all ceremoniously given to her by me. Helga, on the other hand, read every day a frightful passage from the Bible that had to do with smiting thine enemies' children, tearing out their eyeballs, burning down their houses, destroying their wives and live-stock, and rending them impotent. Like a novena, it had to be read aloud for nine days in order to produce these calamities. I was amazed at the vindictiveness of the passage, never having seen it before. Yet when Mother and Daddy came to visit again they were very pleased that I had a Catholic nanny who read the Bible. Helga had the same Bible that Mother had; it was an illustrated version. I guess Mother had only read the New Testament, though, for two reasons: the nude painting of Bath-sheba in the Old Testament (my favorite illustration as a child), which she considered pornographic, and the fact that her favorite quote was strictly revisionist—"Turn the other cheek."

There was one major problem with Helga. She never took Emma outdoors. I realized the significance of this when Emma took to crying religiously for three hours every day—from six to nine p.m. Unluckily for me, it was after Helga had gone home—but was it because she missed

Helga? At the time that possibility didn't occur to me. The only place she didn't cry was on her bathinette. I would lay her there on her back and crouch up against her, one tit lying alongside her mouth, trying to get her to suck—my first reaction always being that she must be hungry. Once I gave an interview that way—suckling Emma on the bathinette. The woman who was interviewing me felt so sorry for me that she called me the next day to ask if Emma was still crying.

During Emma's first month on earth Frederick eagerly jumped out of bed in the middle of the night the minute he heard her whimper, to change her diaper and hand her to me to nurse, so that I wouldn't have to get up. So solicitous was he that Jeannie, visiting one day, remarked, "Frederick, you're so wonderful with the baby; I never thought you'd be like this! I'm so impressed!" After that first month he began disappearing during the daily three-hour cry, a reaction I should have anticipated that day in the hospital when I so unsuccessfully tried "rooming-in."

One evening, after he disappeared, I did something I never would have thought myself capable of: I put her in her bassinette and closed the bedroom door and the living room door, shut myself up in the kitchen and tried to eat something, alone. Her sobs pierced both doors, faintly but audibly, a form of Muzak ringing in my ears as I pushed rice and vegetables into my mouth.

"What shall I do?"

I was on the phone, talking to a La Leche counselor (Nursing Mothers, they were actually called).

"How often does she cry like this?" the Mother asked me (Emma was in my arms, screaming into the receiver).

"Every day between six and nine."

"Does she get plenty of love?"

"She's either in my arms, in my husband's arms, or the nanny's arms all the time."

"That's the way it should be, plenty of loving arms around her all the time," the Nursing Mother cooed in a sugary voice that really irritated me. Not that I was against love, but I recognized her phrase as coming right out of the La Leche manual, verbatim.

"Stop it, Tommy! Yes, Carol can have another cookie. Now, stop it or you won't be allowed to have another one! My children," she explained to me, "they're allowed to have two cookies if they've been good all day and today they've been very good. Now, let's see, what else? Oh, yes! I almost forgot! Have you tried burping her?"

"Frederick used to be great at burping," I explained, eager to prove we were a loving family, that the crying had nothing to do with us, "he used to burp her all the time, but now I'm doing the burping and maybe I'm burping wrong."

"Do you put her with her stomach pressing into your shoulder?"

"I never thought of that."

"Try it. Wait a minute . . . I just thought of something. Do you take her out every day?"

I explained that I had a Haitian woman helping me who was afraid to go out in the streets. The Nursing Mother asked me then, how old the baby was. When I said, "Five weeks," and she replied, horror-stricken, "Five weeks! And she's never been out?" I was so embarrassed that, to pretend I didn't realize the significance of fresh air, I explained that I had taken her to the doctor's once (it wasn't as though she had *never* been out). The Mother charitably overlooked my pathetic attempt to acquit myself and asked me if I had a Happy Baby Carrier. I explained that Emma hated it.

"Once you get her in it," the Mother said, "and out in the air, she'll go to sleep. Bundle yourself up in a warm coat and wrap the coat around her while she's in the carrier."

"She won't nurse, either."

"If you take her out I guarantee you she'll fall asleep and when she wakes up she'll nurse."

The Mother told me, "Good luck and if you have any problems don't hesitate to call," and then I did as she recommended. As soon as I hit the penthouse roof Emma went to sleep. I picked up Magda and we went to the supermarket. All the way Magda reminisced about her experiences with her daughter Leni, when she was a baby.

"I refused to nurse her," Magda laughed, "I said, 'What do you think I am, a cow?' I must say that you're making a remarkable attempt at being a mother. I was the worst mother in the world, but I had money so I had a baby nurse do the whole thing. I never washed a diaper in my life."

Emma slept through the entire shopping expedition, and when

Magda showed me a park, in the middle of the grounds of an Episcopalian seminary, we went in, walked the grounds, and stopped in the lobby because Emma had awakened and was making signs that she wanted to nurse. While we sat in the lobby on a yellow plastic couch, surrounded by fake walnut wallboard and paintings of dead bishops Emma nursed herself right back to sleep. As we walked back to the hotel I realized that it had never occurred to me to take Emma out after dark (let alone before dark). I remembered from my childhood that babies were always home in bed as soon as the sun set—an old custom, I decided, apparently left over from the cave days.

I still had the weekend ahead of me, the nannyless weekend. I remembered Marian Levine telling me that whenever the weekends came up she went crazy without any help. In fact, her own mother, when Marian was a baby, hired two nannies; the second replaced the first on weekends. Just the thought of the Saturday and Sunday ahead was exhausting me, as I rode upstairs on the elevator with Magda.

On Saturday, to break the monotony, I pushed the carriage down to the Village. I had decided to spend the afternoon with my publisher and his wife. While Emma slept, he put the carriage out on his tiny corner terrace, twenty floors up. Just looking at it there, teetering above the traffic on Sixth Avenue, the Empire State Building's tower swaying in the background, made me tremble with paranoia. Each time I got up to move the carriage back inside he told me, "Don't be silly, the air will make her sleep. What do you think is going to happen? Do you think the terrace is going to collapse suddenly?" Finally I couldn't stand it any longer, watching that navy-blue carriage vibrate with the wind, twenty stories up, and I rushed out through the glass doors, dragging the baby back inside.

That Monday I tried to outline the new hygiene program to Helga, but she was so busy talking to her cousin Duñel about the latest political coup in Haiti that she wouldn't listen to me.

"You know," Duñel told me, as I tried to explain about fresh air, "Helga ha maids in Haiti. Her husban—he make lotta money, down there —he sell used cars. Helga—her maids iron her nightgowns. She go bed every night wi the sheets turned down and a clean nightgown layin on the bed. She rich woman."

"Why in the world," I asked Helga, "did you ever leave?"

"I watched my friends' sons being shot right in the street," she said in French, by Papa Doc's soldiers. You think I want my sons to be shot?" She said she was going to save enough money to bring her two sons from Haiti to New York by next year. I returned to the subject of fresh air. She looked at me uncomprehendingly, so I asked Frederick to translate. He refused, saying that if she didn't understand me it was because she didn't want to; my French was fine, he said. Besides, why did I want Emma to go out? All I had to do was bundle her up in warm blankets and put the carriage in front of an open window; it was much less polluted nine stories up anyway. However, the Moroccan unwed mother, living just above us in the hotel, had given me a French book on baby-raising and in it I learned that a baby not only ought to see "the pageant of the sun filtering through the green leaves above his little pram, to hear the joyful noises of children playing in the park, the cheerful sight of colorful birds hopping from branch to branch," but ought to see these things daily, from the same route, *as he really loves habit.*

The next day I got the carriage ready and set out for the seminary park with Jasmina, the unwed mother, her baby, Emma, and Helga, who, as I ought to have anticipated, was completely unhappy about the whole expedition. On her wide, benign, maternal face a disapproving look was set (you'd almost think we were going to a blue movie) and she got into the elevator like a condemned murderer into the electric chair. Duñel had told me that Helga wasn't used to taking orders, so maybe that was it; yet I would think that working for me at a hundred and twenty dollars a week was a lot easier than working in a perfume factory (her former job) at eighty dollars a week and taking orders from a foreman.

Before we even got out of the lobby I discovered that Helga hadn't dressed Emma warmly enough (probably forgetting that she wasn't in Haiti any more) and, since I was suffering from a hypoglycemia attack (having forgotten to eat any breakfast) this oversight affected me more strongly than it ought to have.

Sighing like a martyr I told Helga that I would go back to the tenth floor to get some sweaters for Emma, who, meanwhile was soaking wet. Helga had forgotten the rubber panties.

When I returned to the lobby Helga and I got into a heated argument about who was going to change Emma's diaper. Helga wasn't moving fast enough for me; in fact she was acting like a sleepwalker. In a rage I told her I would do it and, clenching my teeth, I took Emma out of the carriage and put her up on the desk next to the cash register, where I jabbed the pins into her diaper so savagely that I bloodied my finger. Emma, who had been sleeping peacefully in her English pram, woke up under this rough treatment and began screaming. I sat down on a bench under the Jasper Johns painting and began to nurse her, finally aware of what had stopped me from taking her out before this. In the freezing temperatures of a New York winter it was just too much trouble.

The unwed mother calmed me down and, the nursing finished, we proceeded out the door and up Twenty-first Street, Helga trailing despondently behind, shivering with the cold.

"Why don't you go back to the hotel and put on one of my coats?" I asked her, but she refused to answer me.

Once I had everyone settled near the swings in the seminary park I left to buy a sandwich at Walgreens, hoping to raise my blood sugar level and lower my temper.

I hurried up Ninth Avenue as though I were really pressed for time and raced through my egg salad and lettuce sandwich despite the fact that I had a one hundred and twenty dollar a week mother surrogate watching over my one and only child back there in the seminary park. When I returned, Jasmina had a strange story to tell.

"As soon as you left," she told me, "Helga moved Emma's carriage over to where I was sitting, moved her pocketbook over, and then sat down next to it on a bench, all huddled up, as though she were afraid someone was going to mug her. Then suddenly she stood up, and, stamping her feet on the ground, she shouted that she wasn't going to be anybody's slave. She kept repeating that. *'Je ne suis pas esclave à personne,'* she kept saying. I don't know whether she was talking about being a slave to you or to her own children."

We left the park, Helga pouting and silent, bringing up the rear, while Jasmina and I pushed the prams ahead of us, up Ninth Avenue, across Twentieth Street, up Eighth Avenue, past the Puerto Rican shops full of witchcraft artifacts and statues of Jesus Christ, gay tinkling Spanish music softly issuing from the loudspeakers above the shop doors; soft because the loudspeakers were so old that you could hear the music only as you passed the storefronts themselves.

Back at the hotel Helga went into the bathroom, sat down on the edge of the tub, and resumed her favorite occupation—the one I had so roughly torn her away from to "get some air"—that is, washing the baby's clothes in the bathroom sink. That was the way she had always insisted on doing it—in the sink. Like Rosemary before her, when I had tried to persuade her to drop the clothes off at the laundromat she had insisted that it was too full of "microbes." "*Mais les microbes!*" she had cried, "*les microbes!*" I think they were both trying to blackmail me into having the laundry done at a "hand laundry," where everything would come back freshly ironed and sweetly smelling; in Rosemary's case it was nostalgia for the South, and in Helga's nostalgia for her days as a "rich woman" in Haiti, whose maid had turned down the corners of her bedsheets and laid upon them a freshly ironed nightgown every night. My way of life, I was certain, they found utterly repulsive.

While she was washing the clothes Helga kept wailing something over and over, in a singsong voice, a chant almost, addressing itself to God it appeared, for the only words I could make out were: "*Mon Dieu, ah, mon Dieu!*" The wail began to take on a distinct personality of its own; it rose with a quaver, warbling into high gear, sending sound waves through the old nineteenth-century redwood doors, on and on it went, right into my eardrums. I couldn't stand it another minute. Grabbing Emma out of her carriage, where she was still sleeping, I ran out of the apartment and up the stairs to Jasmina's room. From there I telephoned Frederick, five floors below, in the "office," begging him to go up to our apartment and fire her. After unsuccessfully pleading incompetence in such matters, he finally agreed, but only on the condition that I meet him there. We arranged to rendezvous in the kitchenette.

Once there, Frederick told me he couldn't do it. He tried; got as far as the fireplace in the living room, but at that moment another wail rose from the bathroom sink: "*Mon Dieuuuuuuuu . . .*" it pealed on and on, "*Mon Dieuuuuuuuu . . .*" Frederick beat a hasty retreat.

After perhaps fifteen minutes more of procrastination (I read all the labels on the Spice Islands bottles) I myself went as far as the fireplace, cut off a *"Mon Dieu"* in midstream, and called to Helga to come out of the bathroom. Out she came, hands dripping wet, face sorrowful and pained.

"You're obviously not happy here," I told her, "I think you ought to leave."

"Not happy! Not happy!" She was astonished. "How can you say that?"

"You seem to be . . . troubled."

"Troubled! When I arrive here in the morning I leave my troubles at the door, just as I leave my paper bag in the closet, and I come in . . . smiling."

"That's not true. Anyway, I can't afford you any longer. I'm almost out of money."

"I don't care. You can pay me when you make some more."

"I may not make any more," I told her, "for a long time."

"That doesn't matter." Helga was very calm, casual almost. "I can wait."

"What if I never make any more money?"

"I'll work for nothing."

"What about your children in Haiti?"

"They can wait."

I hardened my heart and insisted. All I wanted at that moment was for her to leave my house forever. I had to restrain myself from picking her up and carrying her out. That happens to me with a lot with people. Suddenly I can't bear another minute of them. I always wonder if anyone has ever felt that way about me. "You have to leave," I told her. She walked into the bedroom and a minute later came out with her paper bag and some dry laundry from the day before in her hands.

"Look!" she shouted, "I was going to leave anyway! I had planned on leaving since I arrived this morning! Look!" She indicated her paper bag. "I've had my things packed since this morning!" Then she threw the pile of dry laundry down on the couch next to me, took her coat from the closet, and slammed out the door. I never saw her again.

Helga's departure was the catalyst Frederick needed. He crawled out of his office the next day and delved into the ingenuity so uniquely his own and so frustratingly withheld from me in the past to come up with a solution to Emma's nighttime crying. We had discovered that a car ride was, to her, the equivalent of a sleeping pill; the motion knocked her out painlessly, without tears (although her pediatrician prescribed phenobarbitol, and my obstetrician prescribed whiskey—for her, not me), so Frederick began, that night, the custom of hiring a taxi and driving around the block with her, over and over, until she fell asleep. It cost a fortune.

Yet without Helga's organizational capacities the indoor chaos built up to unendurable proportions. The drawers were filled with pencil stubs, addresses on scraps of paper, buttons, old brassieres, bits of tubing and electric cords, old pieces of cloth, and, as Magda called it, "half-assed odds and ends of make-up."

As a child I was always obsessed with mother's lack of organization and general untidiness. I couldn't bear to open one of her drawers. They were filled with old family photographs, manila files that belonged to my father, make-up, old perfume bottles, mateless socks, and old plastic combs, their teeth filled with clumps of hair and sprinklings of dandruff.

How I suffered when I went to visit my friends and saw their bed-rooms. Frilly pink dressing table skirts, holding up shiny glass tabletops laden with shiny clean pink glass bottles of lotions and perfumes. Drawers piled neatly with socks: white, blue, pink, and yellow, all in separate piles. Ironed underwear and piles of lace panties. Books stacked neatly in book-cases instead of being mixed with baby bottles, pencils, notebooks, toys, and bottles of holy water from Lourdes without the tops. Beds with ruffles on the edges of the bedspreads, skirted innersprings, stuffed animals art-fully arranged on delicately slipcovered pillows.

In short, I wanted my mother to be like every other mother; she wasn't middle class enough for me. And my father! I wanted him to be like all the liberal, progressive, psychologically oriented fathers of my friends.

I judged my mother strictly, the poor thing, with her herd of children and her husband, who, when he came home from the office only wanted his dinner promptly on the table at six, and then, fork in hand, to retire behind the newspaper in silence. He was jolted from his deep study of the evening news only by the hand of one of his children, who, having left his place at the table, would walk over to Daddy and wrench his chin around, thus literally forcing him to pay attention to that particular off-spring.

To question the way of life in that house was to betray Mother. "I'll bet *she* doesn't have seven children!" (or five children, or nine children, whatever the case was at the moment) Mother would snort, contemptuously whenever one of us made a comparison between our friends' mothers and her. Even the question of writing thank you notes became a betrayal. I once visited Edna, the maternal aunt of my cousin Sally, for three days in Homer, New York (perfect early American farmhouse; period intact), and when I was describing to Mother the wonders of the house, she turned on me, furious, with the inevitable "I'll bet she doesn't have six children!" I felt so embarrassed that I couldn't bring myself to write Edna a thank you note.

In Mother's eyes, to praise another woman's housekeeping was to criticize her own. That idea was so imprinted on me that to this day when I meet a perfect housekeeper I search immediately for the hidden flaw in her character.

It was the same with the nuns. No matter what they told us, Mother would snort, "Hump! Easy for *her* to talk! She doesn't have seven children!"

"But it isn't sister's fault," we would whine each time, "it isn't her fault that she doesn't have babies; God didn't give her any!"

Now as I look into my hideously unkempt bureau drawers I remember all this, and a truly fearful thought won't go away. Am I doomed to repeat everything about my mother that drove me crazy as a child? The worse thing of all is that I don't have five, seven, eight, nine, or ten children as an excuse. I have no excuse.

As a child I tried to detour my fate; periodically I would throw everything out of my drawers at least once a month, where it mounted into a pile in the middle of the floor. Mother used to say to me, "Augustine, you always clean out all your drawers but you leave everything in the middle of the floor for days and then I have to pick it up!" I always told her that by the time I had the drawers emptied I was too tired to put the stuff back in. Then, as now, the simplest domestic chore totally exhausted me.

It was only the girls who had to clean their rooms, wash the dishes

("Girls! Girls! Dishes!"), vacuum, dust, change diapers, dust (I always liked dusting), give bottles to babies, and set the table (I hated that the most). This dreadful memory only makes me more antagonistic to Frederick. He becomes one of my privileged lazy brothers, who had only to take out the trash and feed the dogs. And we don't even have a dog.

I suppose that it goes without saying that Emma is doomed to envying all of her friends' mothers for their meticulous housekeeping. For there isn't one mother I know, of my own age, who isn't a paragon of middle-class values. Even the wife of the drug dealer downstairs keeps her plants watered, her drawers neat, her dishes done, and the clothes ironed. And they have a baby and live in one room with no help.

I can't go through the effort of looking for another woman to help me. I hate to make phone calls; looking through the Classified section of the newspaper reminds me of that awful period when I first arrived in New York, penniless; and my nerves can't stand another stranger in the house. Thank god the French government has sent us a round-trip ticket to Paris. They want Frederick to show his tapes at the Malraux Center for Global Understanding. Although I'm immediately suspicious of anything with a name like that I hate to look a gift horse in the mouth.

The night before leaving we argued about whose videotapes they were. I didn't think Frederick should take full credit; after all, *I* insisted that he buy the machine (after being brainwashed by Magda). Then *I* had to insist on the taping of Emma's birth; he didn't really want to do it. Frederick was very odd about the whole thing (we videotaped the argument). He didn't seem to want me to have anything to do with the exhibition. Everyone on the ninth floor said that it was a case of professional jealousy.

CHAPTER VII

European Style

Poor little thing; there she lay, screaming and sobbing, her face red from the exertion of it all, driving me crazy. (Frederick had left me alone three hours before, claiming he would be back in twenty minutes. He went to buy some of his precious Russian vodka now that we were in the promised land, Paris.) Nursing didn't help; nothing helped. I decided to take her out to the park, even if she didn't want to go. The primeval instinct to "give the baby some air" had taken over, even though there wasn't any air, only carbon monoxide.

I screamed at her. "Shuddup!" I screamed. She cried louder. I hated myself but I couldn't stop. Watching my actions from above, like the classical schizophrenic, I grabbed the blue knitted sweater (the one from Spain) and shoved her tiny arm into the right sleeve as roughly as I could without actually injuring her. She stopped crying for a moment, looked at me with big startled blue eyes, and, taking a deep breath, set off into an even louder series of sobs. Unmoved, I grabbed her other arm and gave it the same treatment. God, how I hated myself. I wanted to take her in my arms and cry over the blasphemy I was perpetrating, but the part of me that was in control for the moment stood firm and rapidly bundled her into the rest of her clothes as nastily as possible. Then I strapped on the Happy Baby Carrier, shoved her into it, and slammed out the door.

Once out in the street, I realized that I didn't know where the nearest park was, but by this time my anger, if you could call it that, had crystallized into a hard knot somewhere in the part of the brain that controls the larynx. I just couldn't bring myself to ask anyone where a park was.

I marched in long strides, from Rue Bertrand, past l'Hôpital des Enfants Malades, exhausted before I started, in the general direction north. As soon as we hit the air Emma had fallen asleep. I thought she was getting sleepy back in the apartment, but in my firm determination to take her to a park I had ignored the signals. At that point any normal person would have turned back and gone to bed if they were as exhausted as I was, but, instead, I quickened my stride.

At the first metro station I studied a map. The nearest park was quite far away. The sensible thing to have done, given my inability to return to the apartment, would have been to take a taxi to the park, but deep in my masochistic state I took a perverse pleasure in walking the three or four miles through the screaming streets of Paris, across infernal boulevards full of carbon monoxide and various other unpleasant industrial odors. Passing a bakery, I inhaled the heavenly perfume of bread, realized how hungry I was, and continued on my spiteful way with an empty stomach. Who was I so angry at? Myself, the baby, or Frederick? I didn't even ask that question, but I think, looking back, that I was angry at Frederick for putting us in his brother's one-room apartment. It seemed to me he could have gotten the Malraux Center for Global Understanding to pay for at least a second-class hotel.

Finally in the park, I sat down on the nearest bench that had a view of green grass and pigeons. Every plot of that beautifully pure green grass was bordered by tiny iron arches, and nestling poisonously in the breast of each one was a sign commanding me not to step on it. Determined that Emma should enjoy this scenic beauty, for which Paris was so famous, I actually woke her up. I must say that she took it well. Didn't even cry. Perched on my knees, dazed with sleep, she stared ahead, eyes hypnotically fixed on a fat, glisteningly clean gray pigeon who was nibbling on some grain an old woman had just strewn about. Suddenly he swooped up and flew in a diagonal line just above our heads. Startled, Emma jumped. "There!" I said to her, "see! That was a pigeon!" (Oh, what an ass I was.)

"Look, Emma, look at all the other babies!" The other babies were all, every one of them, heavily snuggled into white crocheted sweaters, bonnets, booties, mittens, and blankets. They all peered out from under white piqué ruffles, coyly sewn into their navy-blue carriage hoods. Next to each one sat a plump navy-blue coated lady, gossiping with a similarly dressed lady next to her. They were all wearing white shoes. The placidity of these dressed-up babies was amazing, considering their condition of confinement on this bright, sunny day.

This revelation of Parisian baby life completely unhinged the knot in my brain. Now I had a new reason for living through the next three hours (I couldn't think ahead for more than three hours those days). I would show these awful nannies the American Way of Life. In my leather pants and turtle-necked sweater, the Happy Baby Carrier dangling from my chest and Emma perched now on my shoulders, I pranced through the forest of navy-blue carriages, a veritable Amazon, calling the rest to battle. No one even so much as glanced at us.

Optimistic, I strode on, convinced that some one, somewhere, in that training ground for future office workers would notice us and say silently, "What a marvelous mother she is! Look at her! So strong!"

Finally, along the edge of the park, sitting on a wooden bench in front of the iron fence tipped with golden spears, a little old man looked up.

"Heavy, isn't she?" he asked.

"Oh no, not really, I've been carrying her like this since she was born," I told him. (When Emma was older, Marian came to New York and begged me to let her carry Emma in the backpack. *The only reason she likes to have children,* her husband, Brian, said, *is to carry them around in that backpack!*)

He took his pipe out of his mouth, ready to talk, happy to have found a listener, and gestured with it toward the Happy Baby Carrier, asking me what it was and where I'd bought it. When I told him he said that he had thought I was Scandinavian. At last someone had gotten the message and saw me as the strapping Scandinavian Amazon I thought I was. I tried to engage him in a conversation about the "other" babies in the park and how unfortunate they were not to have a mother like me but he didn't seem to understand that I considered myself to be a paragon of maternal virtues.

I pointed out some more fountains to Emma, making sure that her two-month-old eyes saw them, and took her into a twenty-five-cent photo booth with me to take some pictures. My fit of masochism dissapated, I then found a taxi and took her back to our one-room bachelor apartment.

I found my sister-in-law, Minette, there ahead of me, washing out Emma's clothes and hanging them on the balcony to dry. The apartment was on a busy boulevard and the balcony was in the front, over the street, an iron balustrade surrounding it. The building was new; cheap American modern.

"Oh, Minette, you shouldn't be doing that. I can do it myself."

"But *chérie*, if it were me with a new baby, you'd do the same for me, wouldn't you?" she inquired, looking into my eyes with a giggle.

"I really hope so," I told her, thinking that I'd never be that generous, "but I don't know if I'd have the energy."

"Oh, you would, you would," she insisted.

I scrutinized her face, trying to find a clue as to what made her the fantastic housewife and mother that she was. I had never seen her do anything but smile. She was indefatigable: her house was always clean; the refrigerator always had just what you wanted; she gave a dinner party every night with at least five wines; she was always laughing; and she never lost her temper.

Her three children, ages eight, ten, and twelve, always had clean clothes; her husband's shirts were always pressed; the dining room table always had on it a starched white cloth; and whenever I came to Paris she devoted herself to me completely, taking me shopping, telling me what perfume to buy, making lunch for me every day. And now that I had Emma, she bought me baby clothes, cereal, powdered milk, and medicine, took me to doctors, and put Emma to sleep when I was too exhausted to move. At the same time, Minette's kidneys were nearly extinct; she lived on painkillers and antibiotics, spent at least two months of each year in the hospital, and was always having gallstones removed.

Today I noticed that the two parallel lines between her eyes had deepened; and the family trademark, three horizontal lines across the forehead from constantly raising the eyebrows, had also deepened. The line just under the corner of her mouth had increased the perimeter of its curve and a second line was beginning next to it. Yet her skin was still bisque-colored and glowing, her figure was perfect, and her long, blond hair still glittered over her shoulders in a straight stream of gold. I kept comparing myself unfavorably to her, wondering what sick force inside me made me think I had to write books when I couldn't even handle my most important job: that of a mother. I wondered: Did she ever get tired, bored, depressed? Did she have moments of rebellion, doubt? Did she ever want to run away?

"Did you see the review in *Le Monde* of your book?" she was asking me. I mumbled something about it being a gross misunderstanding of my work, but all the time I was thinking of the way that Frederick, while kissing me (obviously far in the past), had suddenly stopped and whispered, "My god, you look just like my sister!"

"You know," she continued, "I had written a lot of questions in the margin on that book, intending to ask you the answers, but then I lost the book or I loaned it to somebody. I wanted to know who was who, and then, Mama had some questions too." I was thinking about all the questions I had, such as, did Tatania enjoy her affair with Frederick and who was Mama's lover?

While I tried to think up a reason for not answering Minette's questions, feeling that the family would be too shocked if they found out the answers, someone began pounding on the door.

"Let me in! Let me in!" a masculine voice was shouting.

"Just a minute, we can hear you," Minette yelled, "there's no need to shout. There's a sleeping baby in here!" She went to the door and opened it a crack. A big hand wearing a couple of gold rings pushed the door further open and in stepped our downstairs neighbor. He was neatly dressed, wearing a shirt, tie, and jacket, hair recently cut, not exactly white-walled like a G.I.'s but close to it, and he had the face of a *petit bourgeois* who thought of himself as an International Playboy. The kind of face that says the same things to each of his girlfriends, always drinks a certain brand of wine, smokes the same kind of cigar all the time, and, most important to this type, his bathroom shelf always contains at least five bottles of lotions and sprays. He had the surprised look of a man who can't get over the fact that the years are passing. You could just see him anxiously massaging cream into the corners of his eyes every night behind closed doors.

Today his face was just slightly red from what I mistakenly thought to be the effects of a sunlamp. Instead, it turned out to be the effect of suppressed rage.

"I have friends coming over here today," he shouted, "and I don't want them to think I live in an HLM!"

"What's an HLM?" I asked him.

"Oh, sort of cheap government housing," Minette giggled.

"What are you talking about?" I wanted to know.

"That, that, that *laundry!*" he sputtered, "hanging out on the balcony! *Get it down!*"

"But Madame has a three-month-old baby," Minette tried to explain to him, "and she's living in one room. She's American, she doesn't know where the laundromat is. She's tired, she's a working mother."

"I don't care," he screamed, "I'll get the police over here if I have to. I'll call the landlord. Get that laundry off that balcony right now!"

My rage instinct took over. There I was, for the second time in one day, a persecuted mother. The fact that Minette had done all the washing only made it worse. How dare he, the lazy good-for-nothing *petit bourgeois* playboy, who had nothing to do all day but go to the office and then get his clothes out of the cleaners so he could impress his girlfriends with how middle class he was?

"*Fuck off!*" I screamed at him. "Get out of here, you little pimp! Cocksucker!" I flew at him (knowing that the French can't stand to hear a woman use dirty language), fists flying. Off guard, he began to head for the door, changed his mind, and tried to fight back. Minette rushed at him, pushing him toward the door. We both shoved at him with all of our strength and got him out the door, save for a foot and a hand. The foot was holding the door open at the bottom, and the gold-ringed hand at the top. He was screaming as Minette stamped on his foot while I pounded his fingers with my fists. After ten seconds he let go and we bolted the door from inside and sat down on the bed, next to the still sleeping Emma, and laughed and laughed. I wondered if Minette would have had an experience like that without me. It always seemed to me that other people never got into half the ridiculous scenes that I did.

The table was set with five bottles of wine, all from different châteaux, *pâté de foie gras* with truffles, sausage, cheese, and bread. I couldn't believe how much everybody was eating because I knew that waiting in the kitchen was a platter of noodles and roast beef, gravy, and a bowl of salad. Emma was in my arms, howling. I had just spent one hour trying to nurse her to sleep, lying in a corner of the divan in the tiny room off the dining room, against a pile of pillows, listening to Frederick, his two sisters, his brother and their friends, all talking at once.

I struggled to my feet, blankets trailing on the floor behind me (the houses in Paris are so cold in the winter), Emma a mess in my arms, red from crying, and appeared in the dining room door. Minette rushed right over to me, took Emma from me, and within ten minutes had put her to sleep.

"I don't know what's wrong with me," I complained to her, "I'm so exhausted that I can't stand it."

"But *chérie*, it's normal!"

"What do you mean it's normal? Look at you."

"It's not the same thing. My children are all grown up. Besides, I didn't breastfeed them. When Sacha was a baby do you know what happened?"

"What?"

"She nearly died," Minette said while I followed her into the kitchen for the noodles and roast beef. "Pierre was in Switzerland working, and I was supposed to go there with Sacha, to live with him. She had diarrhea. Everytime I fed her it came right out. I wasn't nursing her, as you know; I was giving her a bottle. They told me not to have any children because of my kidneys, and then, when I did anyway, they forbade me to nurse them."

"How could nursing have hurt your kidneys?" I asked her while we ladled out the noodles to the crowd.

"I don't remember." Minette had the simple faith in the medical profession so characteristic of the good French housewife. "Anyway, the doctor told me to feed her almost plain water. Period. I was to put only the smallest amount of powdered milk in it. She kept crying and crying. I used to sit, holding her in my lap, listening to her cry day and night. I didn't get any sleep. My heart was breaking, listening to her, and at the same time I was having a nervous breakdown from lack of sleep."

"What did you do?"

"Mama would come over sometimes and take her, so I could sleep. Finally I went to Switzerland anyway with her, sick as she was. You can't imagine the paraphernalia. In those days you sterilized the bottles, the nipples, and the formula. At the train station I was carrying, besides Sacha, a big satchel with the sterilizer, another with the bottles, another with the powdered milk and mineral water, plus the clothes and the diapers. We didn't have paper diapers; I had to carry the cloth diapers and a special bucket for the dirty diapers, since we didn't have plastic bags then either. On top of it all I was exhausted from not having had any sleep for weeks.

"When I got to Geneva, Pierre took one look at the baby and went pale. We rushed her to a Swiss doctor, who examined her and asked me what I was feeding her. When I told him he said, 'Madame, you've been starving this baby to death. She has the most terrible case of malnutrition that I've seen outside of the Second World War orphans. That's why she's crying. She's hungry all the time.'"

"How did it turn out?" I asked Minette. She pointed to Sacha, a husky, tall, muscular ten-year-old. "Well, there she is, ten years old now, and hasn't been sick a day since."

Frederick has now taken over the duties of supervising Emma's diet. He allows her one half jar of carrot purée, convinced that if she eats the whole thing she'll be sick. Between the Lamaze handbook, which states unequivocally that the baby shouldn't have anything other than breast milk or juice for the first four months, my sister-in-law, Minette (Tatania is always mysteriously absent), who keeps taking me to the pharmacy across the street to show me the different kinds of cereal, her sister-in-law, who keeps asking, "How do you know you've got enough milk?", and

Emma herself (enormously fat), who keeps sticking out her tongue and panting for the other half of the carrot purée, I've been reduced to the state of a mental defective.

The entire family and all their friends stand in front of me and stare as I nurse Emma. (*Tu donnes le sein à ton bébé? Incroyable! Es-tu sûr que tu a assez du lait?*) Their concern over her nutritional requirements has me as brainwashed as I was when I made the mistake of giving birth to her in a hospital instead of at home. Although I have no intention of weaning her yet I allowed Minette to buy me two bottles yesterday *for cereal, chérie, and maybe a little supplement of powdered milk.* The nipples have a slit in them, which, according to the way you place the slit in the baby's mouth, gives forth either very thin liquid, medium-thick liquid, or gruel. To give her plain milk, which is really water and powdered milk, you put the slit vertically in her mouth by pointing an arrow on the nipple holder directly under her nose. For medium consistency the arrow goes to the left of her nose, making the slit diagonal in her mouth, and for thick gruel the slit is placed horizontally. It's awful to feed her in the dark, because then you don't see the arrow. Minette explained the whole arrow system to me thoroughly and very seriously, delighted to be buying bottles again.

Underneath Emma's four chins, I discovered, while examining her in the car as Frederick drove, a band of dirt encircling her neck. It was the first time I had examined her in outdoor light. I supposed the dirt had accumulated after Helga left, because it had eaten a fine, red, scaly line into her skin. Searching further, I discovered the same condition behind her ears, under her arms, and in the deep folds between her thighs and her pelvis. And to think that I refused bathing instructions at the hospital saying that I was the oldest of ten! When I told her about it later, my mother-in-law said, "In these modern times that such a thing could happen! And, to an American mother *en plus!*" We're traveling through the Midi with sixty-five plastic bottles of Evian Water on the floor in the back of the car that rattle every time we make a turn, a case containing three different kinds of cereal, two baby bottles with a modified shape (three flat sides) so that they won't roll (another French invention), some extra slitted nipples, one jar of powdered milk, and four jars of carrot purée. Whenever Emma so much as glances at my right breast she stiffens her body and refuses to suck on it, screaming and turning red in the face. As a result of this caprice of hers, my right breast aches and is as hard as a rock, filled up as it is with all that stagnant milk. The peasants I consult tell me it's because the heart is on the left side and the baby wants to hear the heartbeat while she sucks. *It's very common*, they say, yet I don't know where they get their knowledge since I've yet to see a breastfeeding baby here. They all take bottles.

I partly resolve the baby's bias against my right breast by buying a French breast pump (*tire-lait*), which I'm happy to discover is a lot more attractive than the American version, being made of glass instead of plastic, and delicately shaped so that it looks almost hand-blown. When the right breast fills up I laboriously pump it out, no mean feat, since it takes much longer to empty that way than it does via a baby's mouth. You have to massage the breast, pushing the milk toward the nipple at the same time that you squeeze on the rubber bulb of the *tire-lait;* the massaging makes for a speedier flow but the whole process is painful. All this is done while driving in the car.

Then I pour the precious nutrients into the bottle with the three sides and the slitted nipple and try to get Emma to drink it that way, still unbrainwashed enough to know that my own milk is superior to Guigoz artificially sweetened powdered milk combined with Evian mineral water. My relatives objected to my nursing her not only on the grounds that I couldn't be sure that she was getting enough milk, but also on the grounds that she was crying because my milk was probably giving her colic. (As far as I can see, the term *colic*, like the term *consumption* in another era, is used to cover any unknown ailment.) During the trip, however, I've discovered that she only cries when she's bored. A walk through the woods, a little bird-watching, some flower-sniffing, or the sight of a new face shuts her up instantly. She isn't any different from me, having an insatiable need for both variety and a constant flow of new information.

I partly resolve the baby's bias against my right breast by buying a French breast pump (tire-lait) . . .

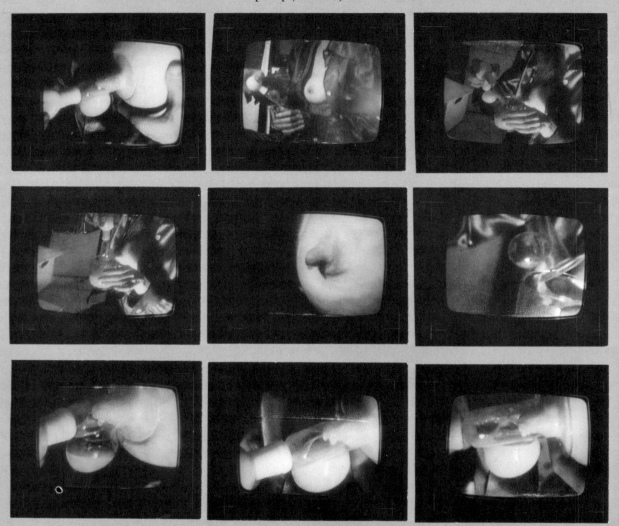

a lot more attractive than the American version, being made of glass instead of plastic, and delicately shaped so that it looks almost hand-blown.

Each time we stop in a new town, Frederick goes into the pharmacy to see what kind of baby food they have. At the moment he's discovered purée of eggplant and apricot pudding. We can't use canned orange juice (monosodium glutamate), so Frederick squeezes fresh oranges and strains the juice through a handkerchief. Today he rediscovered the French method of grating apples by using a spoon and scraping the flesh from as close to the skin as possible. That way the baby gets all the pectin, which, as we all know, is the only cure for diarrhea. Does she have diarrhea? Well, Frederick thought that her "stool" was a bit loose when he examined the last diaper. I only wish he had been as solicitous at the Metro Hotel. But I guess he has nothing else to do, closed up in a car with his wife and baby—no rooms to visit, no new dealers just arrived, no fresh girls in the elevator. And since the Malraux Center has given him more money for taping the French countryside and the habits of the peasants, he needs me to run the camera. The baby sits on his lap while he drives, sucking on a finger he's placed in her mouth, and I stand up and videotape through the hole in the car roof. We argue as much about what I should shoot as we do about the Pampers.

Before we left New York I had bought dozens of Pampers, taken them out of their boxes, and stuffed them into a big suitcase. Frederick went out of his mind, said that I was crazy, all that overweight (meanwhile he had three hundred pounds of overweight on equipment alone), and didn't I know that Europe was modern now and of course they would have Pampers in Paris. Dutifully, I unpacked the Pampers and left them on the living room couch. Now my mind keeps going back to that heavenly pile of Pampers on that couch. How I wish they were here! The only kind of paper diaper to be found here is a hideous-looking thing like a giant Kotex that you're supposed to stuff inside a plastic panty. That, and a paper diaper with a long plastic outer covering that has to be wrapped around the baby like swaddling clothes and that I'm unable to figure out unless Minette is there to do it for me. I've forgotten the brand name too and nobody seems to have heard of it in the provinces. Every day I change the diaper situation either by trying out a different brand or by buying a different-sized plastic panty. The poor little thing, no matter what I do, has a hideous thick wad of plastic and gauze or paper and panty jutting between her legs like an over-sized codpiece. I'm afraid she'll be bow-legged the rest of her life. She wants to walk all the time, with one of us supporting her under the arms; she makes running movements with her legs, and that horrible bulge between them causes her to spread her legs like the wishbone of a chicken. I decided to put cloth diapers on her and wash them myself. Unfortunately, the house we're staying in has no running water.

We're in the town of Pommiers, in the Cévennes Mountains, pop. 10. Decades of washing with hot water have blinded me to the fact that it can be done with cold water, so each morning I rise at six, go to the pump, and laboriously pump out gallons of water, which I heat up on the gas burner and carry out to the back garden to wash the diapers. I'm too dumb even to rinse them in cold water. It takes me about twenty gallons of heated water to do one load of diapers. Frederick says it's good for my muscle development. He takes care of Emma, playing with her in her newly bought canvas garden chair and feeding her eggplant purée and mashed apples in the garden while I virtually sterilize all the diapers. I decide to wash all her clothes at the same time, having all that hot water at my disposal, feeling for all the world like a true peasant woman. Little did I know the peasant women would have laughed at me.

Last night I came downstairs at about three in the morning to prepare another slitted bottle and found a huge log, which had just popped out of the fireplace, burning on the floor next to the woodpile. (We had no heat, so Frederick and I went up the mountain to gather fallen logs and chop down trees.) Hysterical, I rushed upstairs to rout Frederick out of bed. He managed to shove the log back in before we all went up in flames. Getting back into bed alone (Frederick and I slept on different floors because the double bed was shaped like a sled, sinking in the middle and rising at the ends, so that it was impossible to sleep two in it), between the now-icy sheets, I noticed that the main beam over the bed, which supported the ceiling, was nearly hollow, having been eaten by termites, and was dangerously cracked right above my head.

Deep in my heart I know that Frederick is glad for the excuse of a lousy bed so that he can sleep in another room. He can't stand me.

In the main square, across from the cemetery, lives the largest family in town. In fact, it's really the only family, since the other inhabitants are either single or old couples, their children living down in the valleys in the cities, where they can get jobs in factories.

This largest family in town consists of the mother, her five sons, all grown and working in the fields, the father, and one of the grandchildren. The grandchild is six months old. His grandmother keeps him in a carriage, strapped into a harness, twenty-four hours a day.

"*Quelle drôle de manière de porter un enfant!*" she exclaimed to me as I walked past her house with Emma in the Happy Baby Carrier.

"It's called a Happy Baby Carrier."

"Isn't it tiring?"

"Sometimes my back hurts, but I always had trouble with my back anyway. How else can you carry a baby around here? There's no place for a baby carriage." The town was built into the mountain, and all the paths were narrow, rocky, and steep.

"I always leave my grandson in the house in his carriage."

"Doesn't he cry?"

"When he cries I put him in another room and close the door. I don't even hear it."

We went into the house. The baby, when he saw Emma, tried pathetically to reach up, his harness straining against his little body, his pale face smiling. He finally gave up and sank back into his carriage, resigned. Emma was laughing and cooing at him, waving her short little arms up and down, trying to touch him.

"Do you ever take him out?" I asked her.

She told me that she takes him out when she feeds him; that she has so much to do around the farm that she can't occupy herself with him. When I asked her what happened to the baby's mother she told me that the mother had four other children.

"I took care of him while she was sick, a few months ago, and then we decided, when she was well again, to leave the baby here until he can walk."

"I wonder how he'll ever learn to walk, strapped down like that."

The big stout healthy peasant woman told me that he'd learn to walk all right, just as her own children did.

Frederick came in and before we left the house we both avidly examined her shelves to discover what brand of cereal she used. It was the same brand Minette had bought for Emma.

In a remote restaurant in the mountains, known for it's *cèpe omelettes* (*cèpes* are delicious large mushrooms that grow only in certain regions at certain times), we discovered a whole family consisting of four generations. There was a baby there, and about three other small children. When I took out my breast to give it to Emma all the children gathered around me to watch. To those who were in another room the grandmother called out, "Come here, come here, and watch this!" Turning to me, she told me that they'd never seen a woman breastfeed before. So much for my theories about peasants.

After ten days of this idyllic country life we drove back to Paris, too exhausted to continue.

"But why didn't you use your money to hire a maid?" wondered Minette.

"I can't believe I never thought of that," I told her.

"It's awful to have someone living in the house with you, awful," Frederick answered. "What do you want a maid for? You don't realize how lucky you are."

CHAPTER VIII

The Happiness of the Community

As an ancient proverb put it: "A man's happiness is in the happiness of the community and the happiness of the community is in the happiness of each individual." Thus whatever led to Joy was regarded as right and innocent; anything which led to needless pain and suffering was wrong and sinful. Individual suffering was, of course, inevitable in the natural course of life; but when the sufferer was fortified by the knowledge that through his pain the community was benefitted, he accepted it gladly and regarded it as an honour and a privilege. The sufferings of the mother in childbirth and the warrior in battle were equally entitled to honour; the two things were described by one word, and were classified as socially identical. The mother was a heroine, the warrior a hero.

ETTIE ROUT, *Maori Symbolism*

I feel I must closely chronicle the events of today, because they are so typical of New York City.

First of all, as I was pushing the baby carriage across Eighth Avenue a car, with the Marine Corps logo on it, deliberately speeded up on a red light and nearly hit the baby carriage. Insane with fury and fright, I screamed at him, only to have the driver give me the "fuck you" sign and shout some obscenities. (No wonder Helga wouldn't go out; she must have known.) Just after that incident I tried to get into Walgreen's with the carriage, and a man leaving the store slammed the door against the carriage hood, forcing me to maneuver the carriage and myself inside unaided.

Later, having had a fight with Frederick (I had asked him to hold the baby and he answered with, "Who do you think I am, the maid?"), I took Emma, wearing a wool dress, in my arms and walked for about three miles with her. (I had been too angry to look for the Happy Baby Carrier.) Finally exhausted, without a penny in my pocket, I sat down on a bench in Union Square with the intention of nursing her. A local drunk sat down next to me and leered down the front of my dress, asking me if I were free later on. I got up, worn out, and tried to sit down on the windowsill of the bank on the corner of Fifth and Twenty-third. There were metal spikes on the ledge. So I walked on, ready to collapse, only to have a fat, gray-haired woman hiss at me as she passed, "What's the matter with you? It's cold! You ought to put warmer clothes on that baby!"

By this time I felt psychotic. How dare another stranger interfere in my motherhood? "Go home and drink some more milkshakes, you disgusting pig," I screamed at her, "and put on some more fat!"

I was literally leaning over, knees bent, with the effort of screaming, my mouth wide open. I continued shouting a while, even though I was peripherally aware that everyone in the street had come to a dead stop and was standing there, agape.

"How dare you tell me what to do, you old witch," I continued, and then, inspired by that remark, I continued shouting, "Witch! witch! witch . . ." Emma slept through the whole thing, but when I got home I was still trembling with rage.

Later that night my father arrived. He wanted, of course, to see Emma, who was in the bedroom, asleep.

"You'd better not wake her up," he kept saying while pacing to and fro in front of the bedroom door, anxiously trying to peer through the crack.

"Well, if you want me to, I will," I told him, knowing that he would keep on saying, "Oh no, I wouldn't *think* of letting you wake her up," while all the while hoping I would. I felt badly that he had come all that way just to see her (although he did have to be in New York on business) and would have to leave without so much as a peep at his grand-daughter, yet I couldn't bear to disturb her. The telephone rang, interrupting our polite discussion. It was Frederick, calling from his office.

"Oh, Frederick," I began, "I'm so *tired*! Do you know what happened today?"

"I can just imagine," Frederick laughed.

"A terrible woman . . ." I continued, but my father interrupted me with, "Stop it! Don't start complaining to him!" I put my hand over the phone briefly to listen to Daddy and then continued, ignoring him, to catalogue to Frederick the horrors of the day.

"What's the matter with you?" my father muttered. "If you don't stop that he'll leave you! He doesn't want to hear that!"

After I hung up, Daddy told me that all I had was one child, that when my mother was my age she had six, and if I thought I had a lot of work I didn't know what work was, etc. Then he inquired, "Where was Frederick?"

"Down in his office."

"What does he *do* down there?"

"He edits his tapes."

"Goddam tapes, cost a fortune!" he muttered, taking another slug of his Manhattan. "What is he going to *do* with them, anyway?"

2 p.m. August 23, 1972, Grenadier Island:
"Put some clothes on her!"

"But, Daddy, it's hot! It's summer!"

"Well, put some diapers on her at least; what if somebody comes?"

"Daddy! She's only six months old and she's so fat! Think how hot those diapers must be!"

Although Emma was still fat, her face had by now caught up with her nose, which was turning out to be very tiny and delicate. Examining it for the thousandth time, I breathed a sigh of relief; she wasn't going to look like me after all, thank god. We were sitting on Daddy's dock, Emma and I. He was afraid somebody would come by in a boat and see his granddaughter naked. Actually, I knew that he wasn't really afraid of that; he was afraid to look at her cunt. I still remembered his refusal to look at the videotape of her birth. He wasn't a male chauvinist on this issue; I knew that from the time he told my brother to cover himself when he found him naked on his bed. He was just afraid to look at anybody's sexual organ.

Emma took a pee between the wooden slats. Then I recognized the grunt on her face; a shit was coming, so I rushed her into the woods. Luckily Daddy didn't notice.

I looked through the bushes while she was shitting and saw Daddy pouring a pail of water over the boards through which she had just taken a piss.

Mother made her late afternoon appearance on the dock, wearing a royal-blue one-piece bathing suit with attached skirt and carrying the morning newspaper. She saw us coming out of the woods and asked, "Why don't you put some diapers on Emma?"

"Mother," I whined, "at home she always goes around naked. She pees on the rug all the time. Why shouldn't she pee in the river? It's biodegradable."

"Don't talk to me about biodegradable! I was going all the way to Watertown to buy that biodegradable detergent until I saw on television where housewives should be careful; nonphosphate detergent can blind you, it said. I'm going right back to Tide!" I looked over at the space between the boathouse and the toolshed and, sure enough, the washing machine drain was pumping out a steady stream of soapsuds. "Anyway, I don't care about her peeing in the river. It's your father; you know he doesn't like to see her naked. I don't know why you always want to aggravate him; anyway, I think it's disgusting that you let her pee on your rugs."

"Why should I care? It's a hotel. Anyway, they charge us too much rent to begin with, you know that."

"It's your life. You're old enough to know what you're doing. Why don't you put her in a playpen?"

Emma was on my lap, fondling my right nipple, which she had just dragged out of my bikini top. I told mother that I couldn't afford a playpen.

"Now make sure her life preserver is buckled Augustine, one big wave and she could be thrown out of the boat, you know!"

Emma and I were sitting on a deck chair in the back of the cruiser. My arms were tightly wrapped around her and it would have taken a hurricane to dislodge us, but I obediently buckled her life preserver and settled down, resigned to listening to another twenty minutes of safety precautions from Daddy. We were on our way to Clayton to buy Emma a crib, playpen, pacifier, and backpack. I had consented to the first three items on the list provided I would be able to buy the fourth.

"You'll see," mother had said, "how much easier life will be once you have a playpen." She had come into the bedroom that afternoon as I was nursing Emma to sleep, lying down with her on the bed.

"Augustine," she told me, "you shouldn't do that, you know. You should force yourself to nurse her sitting up so you won't go to sleep with her. You'll be sorry later if you do that now. Here," she reached under my shoulder, "let me help you up. Come on now, let's go and sit in that rocking chair."

I was so used to sleeping with Emma—in fact, I looked forward to it, since her sucking put me to sleep like a tranquillizer—that I didn't even realize what Mother was talking about. I just nodded my head, exhausted, and let her lead me to the rocking chair, wondering why she was doing that. As soon as she left the room I got back in bed. After I woke up I remembered reading in Dr. Spock:

> . . . he is apt to cling to the security of his parents' bed, and there is the devil to pay getting him back out again. So *always* bring him promptly and firmly back to his own bed. I think it's a sensible rule not to take a child into the parents' bed for any reason (even as a a treat when the father is away on a business trip).
> INDEXED AS *"Out of Parents' Bed"*

> . . . another trouble is that the young child may be upset by the parents' intercourse, which he misunderstands and which frightens him . . .

I wished we had that problem. We hadn't had any "intercourse" to speak of since I got pregnant.

In the Metro Hotel I had thrown out Emma's crib after reading *The Primal Scream*. It wasn't much use anyway, because I couldn't put her in it until she was really soundly asleep. I used to nurse her to sleep and then try to lay her down there. She was beautifully unconscious until

her cheek hit the mattress and then it was a constant howl until I got her back to sleep in our bed, back at the tit.

However, I let Mother talk me into letting Daddy buy her a crib, a playpen, and a pacifier. It was only money, and they had plenty of it. After they saw how useless these items were maybe they'd shut up about them. Anyway, I was sure that Emma's cousin could use them.

We set the playpen up on the dock.

"Oh, what a beautiful playpen!" Mother raved. "They didn't have playpens like that when you kids were little." (Instead of wooden bars it had a fishnet around it.) "How much did it cost? I hope you thanked your father for it. You see how generous he is?"

We put Emma in the playpen. She immediately began crying. I rushed to the pen and pulled her out of it.

"Now you see, you did that too quickly," Mother counseled me. "Wait ten minutes. Just leave her in there for ten minutes and I guarantee you she'll get used to it. You can stand to hear her cry for ten minutes, can't you?"

"Okay, Mother, I'll try it." The same thing. I let her cry this time for about three and a half minutes and then I pulled her out again. Mother shook her head sadly, eyelids lowered, mouth tight, telling me that I'd be sorry later and that I wouldn't be able to do this if I had other children to take care of. I put Emma in her new green backpack and headed for the woods; she was smiling and craning her neck around to get a good look at the barn swallows, who were swooping into the boathouse to feed their young nested in the grooves of the metal runners that held the iron hooks and chains used to pull the boats out of the water for dry-dock.

The next day Mother told me to take a nap by myself and she'd "keep an eye on" Emma, who was then asleep in her carriage on the front porch. Our room was right above the porch and I went upstairs, pulled down the pink chenille bedspread, and fell asleep. An hour later Emma's sobs woke me up. I rushed down to the porch, wondering where everybody had gone. As I reached the living room I could see them through the picture window that looked out onto the porch. Mother, one of my brothers, and the cook were all sitting on a porch couch, the carriage directly in front of them, silently watching Emma scream, her face red from the exertion. Mother was tapping her foot on the rug, her arms grimly folded over her chest, waiting I supposed, for ten minutes to elapse.

I was so mad that my breath felt like fire pouring out of my nostrils. I rushed to the carriage, yanked her out of it, saying, "I can't believe that three adults are sitting here, watching this baby cry. Couldn't one of you have picked her up?" No one answered me.

On the dock I ran into Mrs. Quinn, a houseguest who had been a childhood friend of Mother's from Buckeye, Arizona, and indignantly told her the story. She says that I'm too hard on Mother, that that's the way they handled babies when Mother was younger; it was the "social climate" and I should just be happy that Emma was born thirty years later.

That's just what *I* had said to one of Dr. Janov's staff when she moaned about how she had "destroyed her children." While I was on a promotion tour I had gone to the Primal Institute after Dr. Janov had called me. He had seen me talk about babies on television. He told me that he wanted to see me because I "made sense" when I said that the baby regards the mother in the same manner that a young girl regards her first lover.

In the conference room he held Emma up in the air for his staff to see and said, "This is the first Primal Baby." (That was before Dr. Leboyer and "nonviolent" birth became the avant-garde of obstetrics.)

During our visit, as I was nursing Emma and simultaneously rocking her in my arms, the doctor said, "Good! See that! Rocking! That's right!" Just then one of his staff entered the room and cried, "Oh, Augustine, I wasn't going to come in here today, but when I heard you were coming I decided to come anyway, and I'm so glad I did! Seeing you with little Emma like that just brings my pain right up to *here* (she motioned to her throat) and I'm going to go into that session today and I'm going to let it all out!"

I asked her why she was in pain and that's when she told me that she had destroyed her children. "Not only did I give them *bottles!*" she sobbed, "but I'm ashamed to say that I even *propped the bottles up* in their cribs!"

"How old are they now?" I asked her.

"Eighteen and twenty-one."

"You shouldn't blame yourself," I told her, "it was the social climate at the time." Then one of the other staff members walked over to the sobbing mother and laid her head on her shoulder, squeezing her and saying, "But the point is she still *feels* it! The *pain!* She *hurts!*"

Mrs. Quinn has just celebrated her third marriage to the same man. Both Catholics and both newly divorced when they met, they nevertheless flouted the laws of the Church by marrying each other. The first issue of their illicit union was Jimmy, a Mongoloid. Certain that Jimmy was God's punishment inflicted on them for breaking one of His Laws (the discovery that a thirty-nine-year-old womb is a "totally inedaquate environment" hadn't yet been made), they were remarried a year later by the bishop of Phoenix (secretly) under the stipulation that they live together as "brother and sister."

Now, in their late sixties, with both former spouses dead they were remarried again, this time with all the Rights and Privileges of The Blessed State; after twenty-five years of abstinence they are permitted carnal knowledge of each other.

"Don't do that at the table. You know it bothers your father!"

"But, Mother, I haven't finished eating myself and I'm hungry."

"Well, take your plate upstairs then, or go out in the kitchen. You know that bothers your father."

I was nursing Emma at the dinner table. I wasn't sure whether Mother was talking about Daddy or herself. Yet there was that time I was arrested with Magda MacDonald for filming a collapsed building on Seventh Avenue and Twenty-sixth Street, and we were in court, with Daddy, awaiting our turn to come before the judge. Emma began crying, so I pulled up my sweater and gave her my breast. Simultaneously the judge bellowed, "Shut that baby up or take it out of here!"

"She's just hungry, your honor," I shouted back, "and I'm feeding her!" At that moment a black policewoman spotted me and called out, pointing at me, "You can't do that in here; get out of here!" Daddy looked down and saw for the first time what I was doing. "I don't want to be in this courthouse anyway," I was yelling at the woman, "I didn't ask to be arrested for doing something that wasn't illegal. I told them when they arrested me that I was a nursing mother and I couldn't go to jail because I had to feed my baby, but they pretended not to hear me!"

"What's the matter with you?" Daddy was whispering furiously in my ear. "I'm trying to get this case dismissed. Go out in the hall and *do that* with your back to the corridor. Face the corner!"

"Did you get that?" I whispered to Magda on my way out of the pew; she had a tape recorder hidden in her purse, having been forbidden to bring the video machine into the courthouse. We had brought it as far as the lobby, documenting at least that much. We had already gotten the arrest on video and we wanted to record the whole saga. Magda and Frederick had been competing for the documentary video of the year, since the day Frederick videoed me getting thrown out of a hotel in London by the police for breastfeeding in the restaurant.

In retrospect, I realize that Emma's three-hour crying spells that first month began the day I was arrested, handcuffed, and smashed against a waiting squad car, making it impossible for me to be home for the evening nursing hour. Rosemary reported at the time that Emma had screamed in her arms as she paced the floor with her (trying to get her to take a bottle) for the last three hours I was in jail.

Mother repeated her request. I decided to ignore it. Besides, my sisters were all on my side and she hated to alienate Alexandra, who, unlike me, had made a "good match." She had married a South American aristocrat who dressed for dinner. In fact, since they had arrived everyone except Frederick dressed for dinner. Poor Frederick—all he owned was two pairs of pants and three shirts. His one pair of boots were full of holes and somewhere en route he had lost his swimming trunks. Daddy had given him a pair he found in the boathouse. They were white denim with blue stripes along the sides and in the corner was a blue ship's wheel. Around the wheel were the words "Grenadier Golf Club." They were too big.

Frederick got up from the table. He couldn't stand another scene. I couldn't understand his dislike of the family fights, because I loved them.

My third sister, Mary-Agnes, had left for Paris the day before because she said that Mother and Daddy were ruining her personality. She had to be careful about everything she said, she complained; and her mind, as a result, was getting rusty. She was afraid that if she stayed she would go completely to pieces and would be unable, in the future, to shine in international circles the way she was accustomed to. It was too bad, because she loved the St. Lawrence River. I was just as mystified by her departure as I was by Frederick's withdrawal from the dinner table. Since Andrea, one of my younger sisters, had demonstrated to me, the year before, how to truly enjoy the family dinners, I awaited them with eager anticipation. "Get stoned," she advised me. "Smoke a joint before you go downstairs and you'll just die with exhaustion from laughing at Daddy. Everything he says is a joke. He's really a scream." Andrea and I went down that night, loaded. I never laughed so hard in my life. Everything Daddy said was a put-on. The problem was that Mother never got it. Like me with Frederick. I never got it. To be fair, I also had the problem of the language barrier. It was hard to assimilate a foreign culture even if you spoke the language; in fact it was totally impossible. We would never really know each other, Frederick and I. We would go through life and die without ever really knowing what the other one was talking about. It didn't bother me, though; I figured that that was the only way we could have married each other. Otherwise we would have found plenty of reasons not to do it. We were both perfectionists.

I perked up my ears. Alexandra was complaining. This was rare. Antoinette's son, Gunnar, was on my lap, with Emma; they were both eating ice cream. Daddy had mourned the fact that his vanilla-colored rugs were full of vanilla ice cream and Antoinette's twin brother, Angus, was down on his knees, cleaning it up. Poor Angus, he always had to do the dirty work. Probably because he was a Vietnam vet. For some reason vets can always put up with anything. They're so glad to be out of the army, out of the war, out of prison, that anything else seems like paradise, Magda had told me when I once complained to her about Frederick's refusal to get a job.

If he would just get a job, I had complained to her, then maybe our marriage would have a chance. She told me that I couldn't ever expect him to get a job because he was a veteran and vets can't ever accept authority. Frederick was in Algeria, given the job of filming the war because he said he didn't want to fight. His mother's Corsican lover, who was then assistant to the War Minister, got him that assignment. But when Frederick bought liquor for the troops every Saturday night, getting them drunk instead of using the money to buy film as he was supposed to, they threw him in jail. He refused to perform his jail chores so they put him in solitary confinement where he tried to commit suicide by slitting his wrists, hoping to be discovered in time, saved, and sent to the psychiatric ward. Everything went according to schedule until the resident psychiatrist noticed that the wrist wounds were in the wrong place, across the vein instead of along the vein. Just as well, Frederick said, because he hadn't realized that the psychiatric ward would be worse than solitary confinement. His mother's lover, Raphael, again came to the rescue, using his influence with the War Minister to get Frederick transferred back to France.

"We've gotten you a much better jail; now please stop embarrassing us and behave this time!" his mother warned him.

In the better jail Frederick was given the job of washing the walls.

"It was the lowest job they had, the job for cretins," he said. "I was considered too stupid to even wash out the latrines, thank God."

Frederick managed to maintain his posture of passive resistance even there, by sitting on the floor in the corridor all day until the inspecting lieutenant came around to check on his walls. When he heard the lieutenant's footsteps he would pick up the pail and fling the water against the wall, making it look as though he had just washed it.

"Good job, Marat!" the lieutenant would say, patting him on the shoulder, "glad to see you're obeying orders now!"

"In Montevideo," Alexandra was complaining, "the children always eat before the adults, in the kitchen. I don't see why those children aren't in bed right now."

"Who's going to feed them in the kitchen, Alexandra?" Mother wanted to know. "You, Alexandra?"

"I'll feed them in the kitchen, Alexandra," I told her, "I'll be happy

Emma managed to get out of the hospital with her paganism intact, but getting out of her grandfather's household with it was another matter.

to. In fact Frederick and I will both feed them in the kitchen." (I was happy to find an excuse for Frederick to avoid the dinner scenes.) I called out to Frederick, sprawled in front of the television in the sun room, "We'll both feed them in the kitchen, won't we, Frederick?"

"You know what Mabel says, Augustine," Mother responded (Mabel was the cook who never washed the dishes, too much work), "there's no sense running a good horse to death!"

Frederick, sauntering into the dining room, told Mother, "Your daughter has killed a lot of horses."

They baptized Emma today. I had always wondered if, like the ex-Catholic heroine I had read about in a novel once, I would secretly creep to the sink in my hospital room to baptize my babies. Emma managed to get out of the hospital with her paganism intact, but getting out of her grandfather's household with it was another matter. The only person who mentioned it was my aunt, who also doubled as my godmother, and she was so afraid to bring up the subject that she waited until we were in the boat to ask me, shouting above the sound of the motor to disguise her nervousness.

I told her that if she wanted to be the godmother, making her great-aunt and great-godmother, I didn't care, but she'd have to make all the arrangements herself; I wasn't going to lift a finger.

When the great day came, not only did Frederick and I refuse to get out of bed, but also Angus, the prospective godfather, had forgotten all about it and was out in the woods on horseback. So that is how Jimmy Quinn, one of God's innocents and probably the most sensitive member of his family (he had always proved to be my best critic in the days when I painted), came to be Emma's godfather; he was the only man around. Since in Catholic mythology the godparents are responsible for a child's spiritual development, in the event of the parents' negligence or death, I was reassured that with Jimmy Quinn as her godfather she had at least half a chance.

"You should have seen her," Mother said to us after the ceremony. "She was so adorable! She wanted more salt on her tongue . . . you know they usually hate it. She laughed, she tried to grab Father Meehan's cossack, she tried to read the Bible. Father said she was the most aware baby he'd ever baptized."

I pointed out to Mother that that was probably because she was the oldest baby he had ever baptized.

"Can I bring the baby in here and try it on her tomorrow?"

"No. We don't do that here."

"Why not?"

"Because we don't have the room."

"The room! She's only thirty inches long!"

"I said no! We don't have the room. We don't do that. That's our policy." I was in a snowsuit store for babies in the Village, trying to buy a snowsuit for Emma, arguing with the saleswoman, a middle-aged, bleached blonde, red-lipsticked harridan. I wondered if she had any children at home.

"Let's go uptown," Harriet Vanderlip half-whispered in my ear, her black eyes shining with that special urgency she owes to frequent self-administered amphetamine injections. "I know a place. My mother always took us there to buy clothes when we were kids." Harriet described herself as a three-hundred-pound canary. She was the fat but pretty actress daughter of a munitions king and a society girl who said, when Harriet raved to her about my perfect motherhood, "You children were brought up with the best of care! You were never left alone for a second! You had all the best nannies and your pee-pees were always cleaned out with Q-tips!"

On the way out of the store I shouted that we'd never set foot in that place again. It was November and for the past three days I had been obsessed with the idea of buying a snowsuit for Emma. Since I never went into a store to buy anything but food or typing paper, the purchase of a snowsuit looms large, still, in my mind. I can't stand stores. They're as bad as office buildings. The lack of windows that open gives me a head-ache; the saleswomen are always bitchy to me because I never look rich, and I can never make a decision on what to buy because everything looks so trashy. How can you decide between a pink acrylic snowsuit with fake fur trim and a white acrylic snowsuit with red acetate piping?

We went to Harriet's store, Ingebord Kupinger's, only to find that she didn't carry snowsuits, only hand-knit caps and sweaters and dresses right out of *Heidi*. Still, I managed to spend one hundred dollars. Then we went to Bloomingdale's, and found that their baby department had become a triumph of modern psychology. Resting on top of the bootie counter was a color videotape monitor constantly replaying the same tape. A baby lay in his crib, playing with a cribmobile that hung in reach of his fingers and toes. A voice reminiscent of a radio ad for whipped butter (those voices advertising creamy things always sounded to me, since I was a child, as though they were made of cream or butter) explained each object. One was for stretching the muscles, one for coordinating eye movement, one for stretching toes, one for fingers, and so on. The infant dutifully obeyed the voice. Anything to prevent the mother or father from having to go over to the crib and actually pick up the child and entertain it themselves.

My headache got worse. Harriet kept pretending to find snowsuits that she just loved, in an effort to get me to buy something. This was our fourth store.

Back at the hotel, white acrylic snowsuit clutched in my hands, I timidly held it up for Frederick's inspection. If I put the final burden of choice on his shoulders then I never worried about whether or not I made the right one. The strange thing was if Frederick made the wrong choice that never worried me. Whereas if it were me who made that choice, then I suffered and suffered about it.

"This, this is hideous," he said.

"Well, there was a pink one with nice soft lining, but I know how you hate pink."

"It must have been better. The lining is the most important thing." Frederick was approaching fabric now the way he had carrot purée a few months before. Anything that touched the baby's skin had to be soft. He had been asking me to buy her a cashmere sweater for weeks. They didn't make them for babies.

I couldn't stop thinking about the lining in the pink snowsuit. I tossed and turned in bed that night, comparing snowsuits in my mind. The next day I went back to Bloomingdale's and bought the pink snowsuit without returning the white one. At home, Frederick and I compared the two. "The pink," he decided.

Getting Emma into the snowsuit was another matter. She screamed and kicked whenever I came near her with it. In fact, she even tried to escape me by crawling as fast as she could away from me. The first few days I solved the problem by cornering her between the fireplace and a chair, and, using the leverage of the side of the fireplace (the one with the missing mosaic tiles), I pushed first one arm into it and then the other. By the time her arms were in she gave up, so that the legs were less of a problem. Actually I think it was an arm and a leg diagonally, and then another arm.

By January I was even tireder. Every day I would stick my arm out of the window, hoping that, miraculously, the weather would be warm somehow, and I wouldn't have to fight the battle of the snowsuit that day. I begged Frederick to take us away to a warm climate. He was willing to go but we didn't have any money.

Our relationship to money was simple. When we had it we spent it and when we didn't have any more we didn't spend any. The idea of a budget was as foreign to us as the idea of making investments. As for something tangible, like buying land, or a house, that had never occurred to us. We spent so much on videotapes and machines and airplane tickets (we had to have something exotic to videotape) that we didn't even have enough left over to buy clothes. That's why Frederick had those holes in his boots.

Finally a check came through from Germany—a big advance for my last book. It sat in the bank waiting; we couldn't decide where to go.

One morning in the middle of January I went berserk. Not being able to wedge Emma into her snowsuit, I had decided to cook breakfast. The kitchen was a mess from the night before and Frederick told me that he wasn't the "help" when I asked him why he never did the dishes.

"You're a little Hitler, Augustine," he said. "You're a fascist. Of course it is hard to take care of a baby and write at the same time. You need help. Why don't you get help? I told you I wasn't going to be the help."

Since living in the Metro Hotel, with steam heat, my skin had become terribly dry. Every morning, when I woke up, my face felt as though it had dried eggwhite all over it. If I didn't get into the bathroom to wash it then I felt lousy until I did get there, but when I washed it it felt even drier five minutes later. Therefore an elaborate system of oils and creams had to be followed or my disposition would be awful that day.

This particular morning I hadn't made it to the bathroom. Emma had wakened me, crying, wanting to be nursed right away and, one thing leading to another, I had neglected my toilette. This may appear to be a frivolous reason for going berserk, but I can't explain it.

In this mood I surveyed the mess in the kitchen: every inch of the table covered with bottles and jars, half filled butter dishes, and other unesthetic objects; the sink filled with dirty dishes; and all the cupboard doors open, revealing a thin layer of mouse shit on the bottom shelves. Running over the grid of plastic crockery was a family of cockroaches.

As I say, I went berserk. I swept everything off the counters and table with my arm, smashed the expensive juice extractor and a blender onto the floor, and threw an opened jar of honey against the wall. Then I went into the bedroom and did the same thing.

After I left, Emma was sitting in her stroller, her eyes wide, not making a sound, and Frederick told her, "Emma, your mother is crazy. See what she did?" I know he said that to her because I saw it on the videotape later.

I let Emma sit in the sink while I washed some clothes. She always wanted to do that. She was wearing a pair of gold satin embroidered Chinese pajamas I had found for her in Chinatown, and they were, of course, ruined. But I felt that she deserved some fun after the terrible scene she had witnessed. Frederick couldn't understand why I was deliberately ruining her pajamas.

That afternoon Lydia Anderson had come to town. Lydia was a friend of Malcolm's the dealer who lived on the sixth floor, and she had often invited us to her house in La Jolla. We had never gone there, as I always thought it was too much trouble to go all the way to California for a weekend and she only invited us for weekends.

I went to lunch with her and told her the long tale of my exploitation as a wife and mother. As her eyes danced, lighting up her usually unexpressive, depressive face, I realized that she was the kind of person

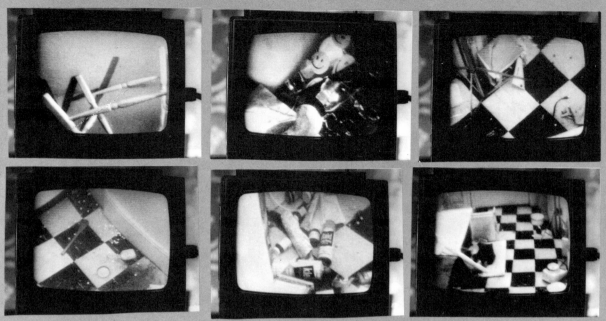

As I say, I went berserk. I swept everything off the counters and table with my arm .

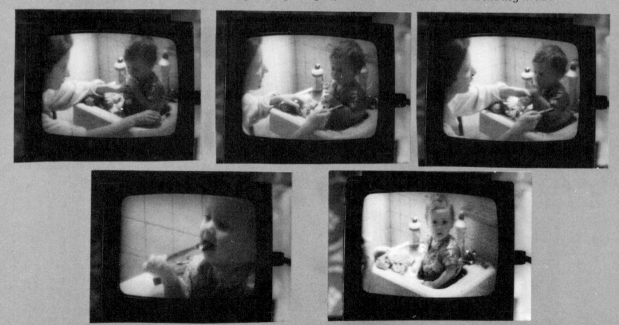

I felt that she deserved some fun after the terrible scene she had witnessed.

who just loves tragedy; so I piled it on, making longer and longer my list of grievances against Frederick. She invited me to La Jolla, telling me I could stay as long as I wanted. Before we had finished our coffee there were tears welling up in her eyes, she was so sympathetic.

When I let myself back into the apartment Frederick was poring over a map of the world with Malcolm.

"Forget about the kitchen," he told me, "let's just leave everything where it is." Pointing to a spot on the map in Nepal, he said that's where we were going. It was the Himalayas.

"But it's freezing in the Himalayas right now; it's January!" I told him.

"It will be beautiful, though. We can go south where it's warmer." I was afraid that he just wanted to go on a sight-seeing trip and was exaggerating the climate of the foothills so I'd say yes. I said no. Finally he told me that there was another choice, Morocco.

I remembered how I had hated Morocco when, five months pregnant, I went there with Mary-Agnes. And I knew that the winter in Morocco was cold and rainy. Frederick poo-poohed my misgivings and told me that we would go south. Looking at the map, I realized that the country was so small that going south was like going to Washington, D.C., from New York City. However, I repressed that knowledge, so eager was I to avoid the Himalayas. I should have realized that Frederick's geographical choices were solely based on the availability of marijuana in those particular countries.

Gunter von Habsburg agreed to drive us to the airport. He was alone. Marie-Claude had finally left him to return to her Parisian lover. While they all had been in the desert together, making the movie that Gunter wrote, produced, directed, and starred in, he had sort of fallen in love with an actress from Iceland, Elkse Boserup. Elkse had been living with him since the departure of Marie-Claude, I thought, but I wasn't sure. I hated to ask him anything; he was the type who would call it "prying." I was sure he regretted those nights he spent at my bedside, depressed over Marie-Claude. He was the type who, if he confided anything to you, would regret it later. Secretive, I suppose you call it.

From the minute I got into the white Citroën with the Maserati engine, I was distracted, trying to think if I'd left anything behind. Finally I remembered it—the black patent-leather hatbox that Magda had given me, filled with all my cosmetics, creams, hairbrush, shampoo, Emma's two warm jumpsuits made of velour imported from Switzerland, and Frederick's razor. I was so depressed at that realization I wanted to go back and get them. Mentally I was figuring out how much money we'd have to spend to replace everything. Frederick was furious at me for being so bourgeois. Gunter thought I was crazy. Of course we couldn't go back. If we did we'd miss the plane. And it was so hard to get ready to go with a baby. Now that we were finally ready—the bottles and Pampers in their place—no one wanted to postpone the departure. I was so upset I couldn't talk to any of them all the way out to Kennedy. I just sat there, staring out the window, adding up figures in my head. By the time we reached the airport I was up to seventy-three dollars.

PART TWO

THE WOMEN

CHAPTER IX

If You Can Get Through the First Year, You're Okay

Another popular international cliché

Emma reached out her hand to take mine, and I let her lead me up the stairs, her lower lip jutting out and closed over her upper lip. She appeared very determined. With a few grunts she led me through the master bedroom, through the green-and-white dressing room, and on to the dressing table. "Ma, ma, da! Uh!" she grunted, pointing to the stool; so I got up on it and pulled her up into my lap.

Then she pointed to several different things on the table and I told her what they were for. She was satisfied and let me put them back. We had a little trouble when we came to the liquid mascara, because I showed her that it was for eyelashes and she wanted it on hers, but I told her that it was dangerous by using the sound I had devised for "hot," which is a sucking in of air while saying "oooo oooo." I told her it would make her eyes burn if it got into them. She seemed satisfied and let me put it away. Finally she settled for a plastic tube of protein nail conditioner and put it in her right hand, letting herself down on the floor with her

109

other hand. Then she led me into Chrissy's room, and picked up a small yellow-green plastic ball and a bright-green plastic building block with little spurs sticking out all over it. She handed them to me. "Thank you," I said.

Next she picked up a little blue wicker basket with a furry dog nestled in it and, carrying the basket in one hand and the plastic tube of nail conditioner in the other, she slid down the stairs backwards until she came to the landing. She let me hold her under the arms while she tried to run down the rest of the staircase. Then she led me to the television set, where Lydia and her boyfriend Gino Mussante were sitting, glowering at me, waiting for me to go out to dinner with them.

The dog's mouth was red enamel and painted on the enamel were little white teeth. He squeaked whenever you pried his mouth open. Emma and I were playing with the plastic ball and the dog, lazily and happily. At least that was the expression I was trying to maintain for her. At the back of my head I could feel the lovers' eyes on me, impatient, almost angry. They had been waiting for an hour. I knew I was going against all established protocol and social morality, keeping two adults waiting (my hostess!) while I let my one-year-old lead me around by the nose, but the truth was I'd much rather have stayed home to play with Emma.

We were in La Jolla, Emma and I, on a street where the houses were close together but fortified against each other by lush, green shrubbery.

Harriet was right when she said, "Why are you going to Morocco? Why don't you just go to California? It's closer." (She didn't want to be too far away from Emma.) Our Moroccan odyssey was a fiasco. Frederick, however, is still there. After battling the elements—the cold, the rain, the wind—for a month, we got into a terrible fight outside of Agadir and I jumped out of the car with Emma, our passports, the travelers' checks, and three diapers. I walked through the chaparral to the airport.

"Da, da!" Emma had pointed to the lipstick in Lydia's room. "Lipix!" I put some on her. Her over-sized marble-like blue-and-white eyes staring into mine, she giggled and grinned, the dimple in her right cheek deepening. "The little rascal!" I thought, "she knows I'm going out and she's trying to charm me into staying." It usually takes me about two puffs of marijuana to penetrate the trickery of her mind, and Tony had passed me a joint upon arriving in the house. If I had gone beyond a second puff I'd never have made it back down the stairs; I would just have stayed there with Emma, trying on one "lipix" tube after another.

It was a fight over diapers and baby food we had, back there in Agadir. We had left our house in Tiznit to go to the dentist, and, afterwards, Frederick had stopped in front of a drugstore, telling me not to buy any paper diapers if they had hexachlorophene in them. Before leaving N.Y. we had read in *The New York Times* that some brands of paper diapers contain hexachlorophene. The salesgirl was quite nasty about the hexachlorophene problem. I explained to her that hexachlorophene destroys the brain cells; I told her all about the monkeys, but she pretended not to understand my French.

"*The New York Times*, monkeys, brain damage," I said to her.

"These are all we have, Madame."

Emma headed for the bottom shelf and pulled all the bottles of baby food down on the floor, one by one. I was so furious at the salesgirl for looking at me as though I were a demented hippy that I didn't interfere; I let Emma empty the shelf. This always drives the clerks crazy, even though everything that's put on bottom shelves is put there expressly to attract the marauding hands of a child so that the mother's attention will be riveted to the spot and she'll feel compelled to buy something. I was no exception. I bought two jars of strained liver, imported from France, at $2.50 a jar.

Back in the car, Frederick flipped out, predictably (he had just bought her some rubber panties and when I said, "I think they're too big," he had furiously said, "Either they're too big or they're not too big! Try them on her!"), and made me return the jars. He was so contemptuous of me for having spent five dollars for two ounces of strained liver that my cheeks burned with humiliation and anger. We exchanged insults and blows; I was kicking him as he leaned over the back seat, aiming his blows at my head. Emma was in my lap, since I had taken her off the lap of our twelve-year-old houseboy, Attique, when I got back into the car. Emma and Attique were both screaming.

I was horribly aware that Emma was being traumatized yet I couldn't stop; neither could Frederick; we had both gone through the cerebral partition that encloses the little chamber for will power. The Arab men in the street were watching us with open glee. One of them, in a black and white striped djellabah, poked his companion in the ribs, pointing to us and giggling, just like the Italians in Rome who had stood by and giggled in the airport while Frederick and I fought with each other on the floor, years before. (We were fighting then because I was nervous, not having eaten anything for over six hours which is way past my limit of endurance.)

Throughout the battle I was watching those djellabah-clad bastards out of the corner of my eye, mentally skewering them. How I would have liked to see them roast: brochettes over their own braziers.

Attique succeeded in preventing us from killing each other and Frederick started the car. By the time we reached the outskirts of Agadir, Frederick was muttering insults at me again. I bit my tongue and tried to keep my mouth shut. *"Can't you ever learn to keep your mouth shut?"* my mother used to beg me, when I got into fights with my father. *"Can't you learn to keep your mouth shut?"* There in Morocco, where a woman never opened her mouth to begin with, it should have been easier to comply. The only thing they ever opened was their legs, it seemed, judging from the amount of children hanging off their backs and clinging to their skirts, whereas I, in contrast, hadn't even been asked to open mine in months.

"You have an old pussy," Frederick was shouting, "and you're just mad because I don't fuck you!" Now I knew why I hadn't been asked in months; my pussy was too old.

"That's right, you son-of-a-bitch!" I shouted back, "it aged from having your child!" I was mortally wounded by that last remark of his, and while attempting to sound flip I was trying to remember exactly what my pussy did look like, before and after. It was so cold in our house in Tiznit that we hadn't been able to bathe for weeks, months even, including the amount of time we had spent in cold tubless hotels. In fact, the only part of my body I could remember from my neck to my ankles were my breasts, due to Emma's constant sucking, fingering, and toeing of them. (If both of her hands were occupied she would pull off a shoe and sock and absentmindedly massage one nipple with a foot while sucking on the other.) Since they were still in relatively good shape, I thought he was asking too much to expect me to be perfect, like a new car.

"Oh, I wouldn't let that bother me if I were you, Frederick," I sneered, "since you're so middle class you can just trade me in for a new model!"

Apparently I had gone too far; enraged, he flew at me, the back of his hand just missing my head as I ducked to the floor of the car. While he screeched it to a halt along the side of the road I prepared my exit. My hand already on the doorknob, my straw bag with passports, travelers' checks, and diapers ready, looped over my other arm, Emma held firm against my still-presentable breasts, I pushed the door open as the car ground to a halt in the sand. Before the tires had completely stopped revolving I rolled out of the car, into the ditch, straw bag, baby, and all.

Frederick, my husband, jumped out of his side of the car, rushed over to me, and tried to grab the baby. I was still lying on the ground and we silently struggled with each other, there in the sandy ditch, for possession of the baby. A crowd of bicycling Arabs had gathered at the scene.

"Elle est folle!" Frederick kept shouting to them. *"Appellez les gendarmes!"* Between each call for the police to them, he muttered to me with a manic smile on his face, "This is Morocco! There's no women's liberation here! I can have you put away in a nuthouse. All I have to do is say the word!"

This was the one thing that really frightened me, the image of being shut away in an Arab mental institution. I was certain that Bellevue Hospital's psychopathic ward would be paradise compared with whatever the Muslims had dreamed up for recalcitrant women. I made a brilliant wrestler's move and evaded his next pass at me, and running across the highway I escaped into the chaparral. Like most mothers in a custody case, I had won.

Frederick got back into the car and drove down the road, tires screeching, toward Tiznit. When the car disappeared I crept back to the highway and tried to hitchhike to Agadir. I scanned the occupants of each car and only put out my thumb for cars containing middle-aged white couples. After those incidents in front of the drugstore and in the ditch I was leery of any man who carried in his genes so much as a drop of Arab blood.

Presently Frederick's car loomed into my line of vision. He had come back. Pulling up alongside me he bellowed, tears streaming down his face, "Get into this car!" I ran across the highway again. Like a novice matador he circled me in the car, while I ran back and forth, from one side of the highway to the other. "You just want to get fucked by an Arab," he was yelling. "Get into this car or I'll never speak to you again!"

Attique, sitting next to him, was also crying. Adding to Attique's dismay was the fact that, just before the hexachlorophene–strained-liver incident I had taken him to a dentist in Agadir and made an appointment to have his last rear right molar extracted. The pit in it had been killing him (I often found him crying, his fist against his jaw) and since I had the travelers' checks in my straw bag, he knew he'd never see the dentist again. I was leaving Frederick penniless save for the thousand-dollar check Magda had given him before we left New York, for the purpose of buying land for her in Pommiers. I didn't think he'd be so unethical as to cash it.

It turned out that Attique had been so disturbed by this display of Western marital disagreement that he took the car that same night, without a license (he was only twelve) and crashed into another car in one of the tiny village squares. The authorities put him in prison for six months. While in prison he sent for his possessions left behind in our house: a plastic comb, a leather belt, a mirror with a magazine photograph of Elizabeth Taylor pasted on the back, and the thin flannel blanket he used as a bed in the five cents a night communal hall for the homeless where he used to sleep before he met us.

After Frederick's tenth pass, circling me on the highway and threatening all kinds of retribution if I didn't get back into the car with his daughter, he gave up for the second time and drove away.

An airplane engine roared overhead, sounding as though it were coming in for a landing. I stood there on the side of the road, trying to locate the direction of the landing strip. Two little Berber girls, dressed in semi-rags, every square inch of exposed skin smeared with dirt, came out of a rotting adobe shack right there on the edge of the highway. Since the Agadir earthquake in 1962, after which the city had to be rebuilt, none of the houses seemed substantial; either they were already falling apart or they would be any day, being made in the American Bauhaus style of reinforced plywood.

In that earthquake Attique's parents were both killed. "I remember it," he said, "two balls of fire came out of the sky and plunged into the ocean. Then the sidewalk trembled. After that the whole street began to roll and pitch like the deck of a ship and I fell down, rolling with the pavement, trees, bricks, and planks of wood whistling past me, and then boulders falling from what used to be flat streets and were now like mountains to me. I was only two years old."

The two little girls stared at Emma and me; both of them had their fingers shoved deep into their mouths. I tried French with them to no avail, so, not speaking Arabic, I gestured with my hands, imitating an airplane and pointing toward the sound of the engine. Grinning with excitement at the idea that they could understand me, they motioned for me to follow them. After we had picked our way through the chaparral for a few hundred yards they pointed out the proper direction and left us, running back to their shack.

Emma, who had been staring at me all this time bewildered, kept slipping down toward my knees and I kept hitching her up, hooking her hip over mine. (They say that carrying babies on your hip both develops their own hips and imparts to them a graceful motion later in life.) Her backpack had been left in the back of the car.

A quarter of a mile ahead, a narrow strip of macadam sliced through the sand. I reached it and as I started walking toward the building in the distance with its wind sock floating on the roof, a taxi stopped beside me and I got in. It was the usual 1957 Cadillac, just as was every other taxi in the area. At the airport the driver refused to take a single dirham from me, distressed as he was by my obvious state of agitation. Inside the building, at the end of a long line of American and English tourists, the airline clerk refused a single penny. "We don't take travelers' checks," he announced coldly. After several fruitless attempts to get him to change his mind, I went to a bench against the far wall (the only one that was unoccupied) and wept, copiously. The clerk, probably not because of my distress but because Emma had begun sobbing in sympathy with me, or more likely because the American and English tourists were shocked that "one of theirs" should be reduced to such misery, left his station to rush over to me (sitting on the bench with my head in my hands and my daughter trying to lift my chin, crying all the while with me) and tell me that he had decided to make an exception in my case. (Many are the times, since then, that I have wished he hadn't been so nice, had utterly refused to cash the checks, thus forcing me to go back home to Tiznit and make more videotapes. Frederick's turned out so well.)

In a Casablanca hotel Emma celebrated her first birthday, and on the Casablanca–Paris plane she suffered terribly from diarrhea. I had taken off her diaper to change it, not expecting anything like the horrendous odor that immediately wafted throughout the cabin, causing a low murmur, sounds of shifting asses, and several discreet coughs to rise up from the tourist class seats. I was mortified. The smell had a vaguely familiar ring to it, though I couldn't put my finger on it until she filled the second diaper. Then I remembered—the outhouses on the beach at Lake Ontario. However, at the same time, I was sure that the distinctiveness of the odor came from the crude green Moroccan olive oil, something that the bathers at Lake Ontario had never even seen, let alone mal-digested. To this day I haven't been able to reconcile those two elements—Moroccan olive oil and Lake Ontario outhouses.

Meanwhile down the aisle, like a priest at benediction with censer swaying to and fro, sending smoky clouds of sandlewood ahead to announce the proximity of the Sacred Host, came the steward, sending ahead of him a spray of "Realemon-scented Odoro-No," whose button he held down with one hand while with the other he held his nose. Just as the deodorant hissed as it left the nozzle, so his words hissed as they left his pursed lips: "Go into the toilet with her, Madame!"

"But it's too small!"

"No it isn't!"

"I can hardly fit in there myself; how can I change a baby in there?"

"It's entirely possible!"

Seeing that I remained unmoved by his plea for better hygiene, he shoved several towels down between my elbow and the side of the plane, dropped several packets of "wipe-ups" into my lap, and deodorized again the immediate area with his aerosol can. Then, continuing down the aisle, tall and thin, head high, shoulders painfully drawn back, bony chest thrusting forward (as though showing the passengers that he was *still* proud of his calling and of his plane, a sort of lieutenant of the airways, a true patriot, an official loyal government apologist for unjust wars), he let forth torrents of lemon-scented mist among the now-gagging tourists. No one dared to really look at me, to meet my eyes, to turn around.

By the time we had left the third stop on the voyage, Nice, having already come and gone from Barcelona, and I had told my story to one of the stewardesses, the steward had completely done an aboutface and began thrusting a series of "Care" packages into my lap, where the "wipe-ups" had originally rested. Plastic bags full of various combinations of Vichy water, canned milk, French bread, packets of cheese (La Vache Qui Rit), and apples piled up on my lap and the seat beside me; they were threatening to engulf the baby when I assured the steward that he had given me enough, that neither I nor Emma would starve, and that, in any case, I had both money in my pocket and relatives in Paris.

At the "relatives in Paris" disclosure, both the steward and the two stewardesses, who were by now also bearing gifts, raised their collective eyebrows in surprise; apparently their image of me was that of someone so hopelessly American that not only couldn't she get from one country to the next without a lot of help (actually this was true; once I had gotten on what I thought was a direct seven-hour flight from New York to Rome; fourteen hours later, after having landed in Lisbon, Barcelona, Nice, and Paris, I reached my destination) but she was also friendless and familyless outside of her native turf. Unwilling, even then, to believe what they had just heard, they asked, Didn't I need a ride to Paris, did I have some-place to stay, and was anyone meeting me? I told them that once on the ground my troubles would be over, a statement that turned out to be false optimism, because once on the ground I couldn't raise a soul by telephone.

In the driving sleet, Emma asleep in my arms, I waited in a line of people outside the terminal, for a taxi. Twenty minutes later, inside one of the taxis, rain dripping off us into a puddle at my feet I directed the driver to take me to Minette's apartment on Rue Jules Chaplain. This was after a skirmish inside the terminal similar to the one on the airplane. I ran into a boyfriend of Mary-Agnes's, a Greek advertising executive.

"Do you have enough money?" he asked me. "I'm going to London but only for four hours, and I'll be back this evening."

"Oh yes," I assured him, as he took several hundred-franc notes out of his billfold. "Don't bother, I have plenty!"

"Oh," he insisted, "please! Let me help you out! I'm so sorry that I have to go to London; otherwise I'd drive you into Paris; please let me give you some money."

I insisted that I didn't need any; he insisted that I take some, for what seemed to be a good fifteen minutes. Finally, to end the discussion, as Emma had wakened and begun to scream and smell at the same time (more diarrhea) I agreed to take his francs. He put two hundred francs into my hand, without withdrawing his hand from the money, then said, "But! I forgot! What will I do for money when I arrive in London?"

"Jesus Christ!" I said to him, releasing my palm from underneath the two bills, whereupon he immediately tightened his fingers over them, "I never wanted to take the goddam money in the first place!" As I headed for the taxi line I reflected that it was a strange coincidence indeed that two males in one day had undergone complete mental reversals concerning me.

Once safely inside Minette's apartment, I finally met my mother-in-law's Corsican lover, Raphael, who was now a plainclothesman. "They are either in the Mafia or the police," Frederick had said, "the Corsicans; they are the toughest French; they are like the Sicilians."

"Meet your grandfather," my mother-in-law said to Emma, when the tall, elegant Corsican who resembled Ramon Novarro appeared from the kitchen. Minette was behind him, the ever-present platter of roast beef and noodles in one hand, the other hand over her mouth, trying to stifle a case of nervous giggles. Of course, Raphael wasn't really Emma's grandfather— that is, according to the story my mother-in-law had told me the last time I'd been in Paris (a happier occasion, when the three of us were on our way to Morocco).

When she was forty years old, and the mother of four children, ranging in age from the one-year-old Tatania to her fifteen-year-old brother André, my mother-in-law was on a train traveling to Paris, from Gif-sur-Yvette, her home. Standing on the quai, at Massy-Palaiseau, was a twenty-year-old man, who, seeing her face through the coach window, determined right then and there that he wanted to be with her until he died. He jumped aboard (even though he was going in the opposite direction) and sat down next to my mother-in-law, drinking in the elegant bone structure of her face, the smooth, soft, baby-fine skin that covered those bones ("*I owe my complexion to Guerlain's Creme Réductrice*"), her benevolent and amused gray-blue eyes, and her thick, heavy chestnut hair.

Professing his love, he told her that he would like to move right in with her but that it was, alas, impossible, because he had a young wife and a three-month-old daughter. If he had only his wife, he explained, he would jump ship without hesitation, but he just couldn't do a thing like that to his beautiful, sweet baby daughter, who, at three months, already manifested all of the qualities that he had been so disappointed at not finding in his wife.

My mother-in-law, as equally enchanted by this dashing young Corsican as he was by her, told him that not only was she too old for him, (*"I could be your mother!"*) but she also had a very young son and daughter still at home, as well as two teenagers away at school and that their father came home only on Sundays. (Until Frederick's father died, two months before Emma was born, and Frederick found a photograph of a woman and child, circa the late Forties, in his wallet, my husband had believed the story that his father had to work in the provinces all week and was able to come home only on Sundays, when he came loaded down with vodka, caviar, and dill pickles, a taste he had acquired from his Russian mother-in-law, to hold a neighborhood feast and to criticize Frederick's report card.)

My mother-in-law and her new suitor resolved the obstacles to their happiness by meeting in Paris hotels. I had heard from Frederick about a mysterious man who frequented the garden, never coming inside the house (the house being next door to that of Frederick's grandmother).

"I don't think Frederick knows about him," she said to me, "I've never told him."

"He told me about a man in the garden."

"Oh yes, he always stayed in the garden. I would never let Raphael into the house because of Frederick!"

Three days later, after serving Emma and me a sumptuous lunch in her apartment ("*Look at what a little lady she is! Such wonderful table manners!*" they said of Emma, sitting solemnly at table, a white linen napkin tucked into her dress), my mother-in-law and her lover drove us to the airport, where they put us on a plane for New York. During the ride discreet inquiries were made as to the cause of her son's rupture with me.

"He's nothing but a lazy junkie," I told her, "and what's worse, he never fucks me!"

"How long did you know each other before you married?" she asked me, seemingly unperturbed by stories of his addiction and unnatural sex practices.

"We knew each other for two months," I responded.

"Then," she said, triumphantly, "that's the reason! You made the same mistake I did with his father!"

"Why? How long did you know him?"

"Two weeks."

On the way to New York I tried seriously to analyze the reasons for our sudden bursts of anger and violence. Convinced by Frederick that he had never been either argumentative or violent until he met me, I isolated the blame on myself. Forgetting my mother-in-law's discovery about the two months, because I didn't believe it made any difference (my lifelong problems with men and violence began with my father), I tried out and discarded many theories, the primary one being the sirocco, a wind that, like the full moon, is supposed to drive both women and livestock crazy. It had been blowing for the past three weeks, from the Sahara Desert to Spain, yet my troubles certainly dated from a pre-siroccan period, as the sirocco had never been known to make it to New York State (although my mother blamed "the northeasterly blow" on many of her own nervous troubles).

I also tried to blame them on a lack of dopamine, a vital chemical in the brain, which caused irritability and irrational anger when its level was low. This was a genetic defect I had read about in *The New York Times* similar to the genetic defects Frederick was sure to have passed on to Emma as a result of the radiation poisoning inherited from his grandparents who were radium experimenters, and acquired in a secondhand fashion by playing constantly as a child in the radioactive laboratory ruins which weren't to be deradioactivated by the laggard French government until 1971.

Then I could blame my troubles on social and economic conditions (i.e., Frederick)—having a husband who refused to get a job, who, like the Baltimore Cathechism description of God the Father ("always was, always is, and always will be"), had told me many times, "I never had a job, I don't have a job now, and I never will have a job." Worse, he had catted around the hotel, picking up girls on the elevator, while I stayed in the apartment for one solid year, cooking, breastfeeding, and trying to write.

Although he changed his attitude and became a doting father as

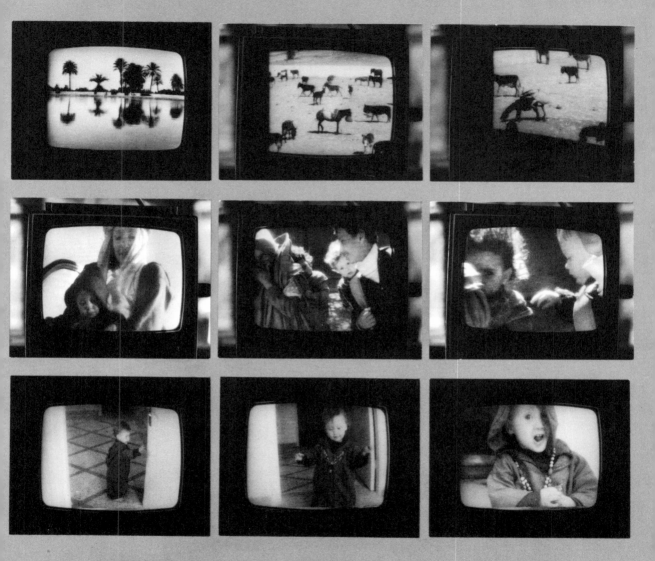

He changed his attitude and became a doting father as soon as Emma learned to walk.

soon as Emma learned to walk (smiling broadly as he watched her in the Marrakech marketplace—the D'jem el fna—standing with her head down between her legs to look backwards and laugh at the Arabs while they asked, "How much do you want for her?"), I hadn't had enough time to assimilate his changed behavior into my emotional response patterns. I still blamed him for everything; I even blamed him when we ran out of hot water.

Coming to a dead end in my self-analysis, and deciding finally that explanations of violence are merely a literary convention, I turned my attention to where we would go next, my traumatized daughter and I. It didn't take too much thought, since I was still longing for some warm weather. I decided to telephone Lydia Anderson, knowing that if I related my tale to her of violence in the Sahara, she would be eager to have me at her house in La Jolla as a guest, if only to gather more details about the tragic happening.

CHAPTER X

"California Dreamin'"

A song by John Phillips

In front of Lydia's television set her four-year-old daughter, Chrissy, came charging at me with an improvised sword. "Grrrr," she growled, "you're a lion!" As I ducked under the dining room table, I could see Lydia and Gino pretending to be absorbed in "The Price Is Right." Gino was wearing a pair of royal-blue crocodile Gucci loafers, the color approximating that of the bags under his eyes. The bags really stood out, since the color of the rest of his face was a sort of gray-white. He was rumored to be the head of a big East Coast cocaine ring. In actuality, he was the manufacturer of a noiseless lawnmower, which he had also designed. The problem with the lawnmower, however, was that all the things that could get into it had to be removed before mowing the lawn. The tiniest piece of twig could wreck the motor. Understandably, business was falling off. Too many complaints. Those in the know said that the business was just a front anyway, the latest in a long series.

His best front, actually, if the rumors were true about his real occupation, was Lydia. She was the founder of a "progressive" nursery school, loosely based on the theories of Piaget, a French child psychologist who was enjoying a vogue in Miami Beach, Florida; Atlanta, Georgia; and Southern California. Her library was filled with books on child development. The books overflowed onto the staircases, the top of the refrigerator, bedside tables, and the backs of toilets.

At any rate, Lydia's occupation, combined with her upper-middle-class pink stucco-Spanish tiled house and her Mainbocher wardrobe, certainly would lead neither the neighbors nor the police to believe that she was housing a major criminal.

The criminal, Gino Mussante, was the type of man who affected a sort of camaraderie with the children; a camaraderie that lasted for a preordained amount of time, something to fill in a gap in his schedule; it certainly was not meant to delay any previously made dinner plans. He was childless.

Still playing with Emma I told him I'd stay with the kids. "Why don't you and Lydia go out without me?" I asked him. "It doesn't matter."

Hurt, Lydia asked, "Why? Don't you want to eat with us?"

Lydia was a woman of such naked vulnerability that it would take an unfeeling monster to deliberately hurt her. Generous almost to a fault (it seemed as though the entire New York–La Jolla drug-dealing contingent had taken advantage of her hospitality to make her home their headquarters—rather bold of them I thought, as she herself wasn't a dealer), she dispensed her fortune with a largesse unequaled in my experience: "Charge anything you want at the Gourmet Mart," she told me, "and take any of my clothes you want out of my drawers. I don't need half of them." She seemed to want to rid herself of any excess money she had, as though her money was partly responsible for her unhappiness. Her sallow skin was always covered with a thin layer of perspiration, a patina of the depression that seemed deep within her guts, and that was allowed to escape only through her pores. I sometimes thought, looking at that veil of sweat on her face, that if she could take a really good shit she would be relieved of most of her unhappiness. In a way, I loved her.

One of Lydia's houseguests, another man with a dappled past and uncertain present, had told me, "There are two things that Lydia likes in life; one of them is food and the other is fucking. I supply her with the first." He said this while experimentally running his hand down my naked back, crouched next to me on the floor in my bedroom in the dark while I was nursing Emma. I had just come in from the swimming pool with him, having let him persuade me to take a moonlight dip. While I had been lazily doing the sidestroke in the heated water he had stood above me, on the tiled edge of the pool, telling me that "a good pimp never lets his old lady have his cock; that's the secret of his success." I remember that I was puzzled as to why he had told me this, out of the blue. Paranoid on one puff of the joint he had passed me, I was sure that he was talking about Frederick, that someone had told him we weren't fucking. I was furious at him for intimating that Frederick could be classed with a pimp. When he had tried later, in the bedroom, to excite me, I had expressed utter shock that he could even think of such a thing while I was nursing my daughter.

"Why don't you nurse her now and put her to sleep?" Lydia asked. "Then we can all go out in peace."

I took Emma to her room and put on her diapers and pajamas, which she let me do without complaining (she hated wearing anything on her ass), and then she started playing tricks on Deedee and me. Deedee was a twenty-five-year-old ex-waitress whom I had brought with me to help with Emma. The idea was that I would finish my book while Deedee watched Emma.

Emma put a piece of a cheap necklace into her mouth, letting it hang out at either end, jutted her chin forward into Deedee's face, giggled, waited until Deedee's hand was within one inch of grabbing the chain out of her mouth, and then spun on her heel, ran into the closet, and hid, laughing. Earlier Deedee had expressed acute anxiety whenever Emma put anything into her mouth; she used to run after her and struggle with her for the offending object. "Relax, Deedee," I had counseled, "she won't swallow it."

Emma repeated her new trick, her eyes snapping, her giggle deep in her throat, like a man, mocking Deedee with glee whenever she tried to extricate the jewelry. I was amazed at this display of inventiveness. I kept staring at Emma, hypnotized as effectively as if she were a magician.

Finally Emma let the piece of chain just dangle between her two lower teeth and, taking me by the hand, led me back to the television room, where she released me and settled down, seemingly content, to play with Chrissy.

"Why don't you sneak out the back door, so she won't know you're leaving," Lydia suggested, "and meet us in the driveway?"

"I can hear her screaming," I said to Lydia from the back seat of the car.

"That's not because you left, it's because we left," Lydia said, letting herself out of the car to go back in the house to get her sweater.

When she returned I restrained myself from asking if Emma was still crying; I felt embarrassed about showing my feelings, the same feeling I used to have as a young girl when kissing a boy in public, aware that all the older people in the street were disgusted. I was afraid that Lydia and Gino would think I was an emotional exhibitionist. When I was younger, childless, I tried to remember: did I feel that way myself when I used to watch mothers cooing over their babies? I couldn't remember. I did remember, though, how Mother and Daddy used to laugh at any display of affection, publicly, between parents and children, giving us the idea, never really articulated, that the children were spoiled and coddled and, somehow, "sissies," even the girls. My sisters and I used to ridicule any child who was seen to get a lot of parental attention.

In the car I could hear Emma still screaming and I could see her face, all red, her mouth drawn down, her six-and-a-half teeth showing, and tears streaming down her face as she held out her hands and strained to get out of Deedee's arms. A song was playing on the car radio—"we've got to liiiiiiive together," a rock voice was chanting, "we've got to liiiii . . . iiiiive together, baaaaaaby . . ." I totally identified, tears welling up behind my eyes; that singer was me, singing to my baby, Emma. I was sure now, as we drove farther and farther from the house, that something dreadful was going to happen to her. If my intuition was so strong, I reasoned, how could I be wrong? I debated with myself whether or not to ask Gino to turn around and go back to the house. I tortured myself with the question. Over the sound of "I'll always looove you" I could still hear Emma crying. We were in a closed car, at least five miles away from the house, in a long stream of traffic, on a major highway, with the air conditioner running. How could I possibly hear anybody cry, let alone Emma? I was convinced I was experiencing a psychic phenomenon.

If I mentioned it to Gino and Lydia I knew what they would say: "Oh, don't be silly, you're imagining things, she's stopped crying by now!" Before the radio song was over I had arrived at the theory that this evening was set up by cosmic forces to show me that in real, adult life, I had social obligations, and I had better get used to them. I couldn't ruin everybody's dinner just because I had a baby.

By the time we reached the restaurant I had a migraine headache. I sat glumly all through the enchiladas and tacos, trying not to move my neck, while the lovers made desultory conversation on either side of me. I was a fine example of singing for your supper. Here they were, expecting streams of wit to issue from my much publicized mouth, and all they were getting was a series of winces. The cashier took pity on me and rubbed some Tiger Balm, an ancient Oriental medicinal paste, on my forehead. Being Chinese, she understood.

It had been so cold in Tiznit that I had had to leave Emma's pink snowsuit on her all the time, even for sleeping; especially for sleeping. Now, in La Jolla, in one of the parks, she was running around wearing only her panties. We tried to get them off her in time for her to pee, since the diapers were too hot and she hated them. If she took a shit in the panties I just surreptitiously washed them out in a drinking fountain and put the spare pair on her that I kept in the stroller. In Morocco Frederick would only wash shit out of a diaper if he could do it in a desert pool or, better yet, on a beach. He especially liked the pools where the water was red, from the clay; he had made a ritual out of washing the diapers, probably because I was filming him, so he could say, later, "You see, I always washed out her diapers, you cunt!"

I had sent her out the day before with Deedee, naked; but upon their return Deedee told me that all the other children were fully clothed and maybe we'd better put panties on her. I decided to go myself and take a look at the native habits.

The playground was a study in role reversal. The little girls, three years and up, were all wearing brightly colored pantyhose, polyester double-knit separates, from Bullocks, and shoes with two-inch heels, just as their mothers had worn in the mid-Sixties.

The little boys were attired as miniature men, all wearing creased trousers, white shirts, ties, socks, undershirts, and oxfords.

Some of the children were accompanied by their Chicano nannies, who were uniformly dressed in standard white nylon. Others were accompanied by one or both parents, but rarely by a father. The mothers dressed as little girls, in tiny shorts and halters, or in thin, very short smocked dresses, embroidered with pink, yellow, and blue flowers. The fathers were all wearing small boys' rough-and-tumble attire—shorts, dungarees, and tee-shirts. Both mothers and fathers were wearing sandals or going barefoot. Only their children were heavily overburdened with clothing. The temperature was in the nineties.

The mothers all wore the same expression—bored, sullen, and determined. They followed their children closely, supervising every step. The fathers, by contrast, affected a cheerful, hearty manner, voices loud, exhorting their sons to greater feats of climbing, running, and ball-playing. The women's complexions were all the same, deeply tanned and thick from overexposure to the sun.

One day a naked little boy, about two years old, appeared on the monkey bars.

"Oh! Oh! Look! It's a boy, it's a boy! He's got a pe-nis!" the children began shouting and screaming, pointing at him as he hung up there on the bars, upside down, his little tassel of a penis hanging down perpendicular to his body.

I wanted to help him climb down, since I was sure he was being embarrassed by the other children; but no, he wasn't; he was happy to be getting all this attention, and in the glow of it was performing astounding acrobatic feats, considering his age.

A woman walked toward me, calling to him, "Timmy! Timmy! That's a great baby; show 'em where it's at!" Unlike the other mothers, she was dressed in a see-through antique chiffon dress, nothing on underneath.

Her feet were bare and her blond hair hung down in lank strands nearly to her waist. I suddenly realized who it was—Rayanne Quackenbush, our

neighbor.

I had met her a week before when her husband, wearing nothing but bathing shorts and a beard, had walked into Lydia's house, pushing one of their children in a stroller. That child had been Timmy; I recognized him now that I heard Rayanne calling to him.

"Why don't you go over and pay my wife a visit?" he had asked me. "She's a great fan of yours; she's read everything that you've ever written."

She had met me at the door, wearing a transparent lace dress with nothing on underneath. Her face was shining with good will and, I learned later, a liberal dose of LSD. The yard was littered with toys and dogs, and over the door of the veranda was a rather primitive rendition, in enamel, of the Rolling Stones. The only way it could be recognized as a painting of the Rolling Stones was the black, rhinestone-encrusted jumpsuit on the figure in the foreground, topped by a floor-length crimson scarf wrapped several times around his neck. Children were running in and out of the house and the first floor was littered with debris. Like a stage set, one of the rooms had been stripped of its floor to ceiling windows and lay open on three sides, dead autumn leaves from the previous year rustling across the white linoleum. A purple velvet chair stood in the middle of the floor, the only piece of furniture in the room. To the left of this surreal setting, outside the nonexistent walls, was a kidney-shaped swimming pool that hadn't been cleaned in weeks. A layer of moss, dead insects, and newly sprouted acacia blossoms covered the surface of the brackish water, and a broken surfboard floated on the scum.

The ecstatic-faced mother of six hugged me, breathed huskily into my ear, "At last!", and then led me into the kitchen, where her husband was washing the dishes.

"I'm giving her a vacation," he told me, a 1940s white apron covering the front of his nude body. "She hasn't had a rest since Timmy was born two years ago, and she's a little stoned."

"She was taking a vacation," I told Lydia afterwards. "She was on acid."

"A vacation!" Lydia pretended horror. "Her whole life is a vacation; she's been on acid every day since I met her three years ago!"

Rayanne then led me up the stairs to a very clean, neat Spanish-style bedroom and sat me down on the bed. Her face still radiant, she pointed to the wall over the bureau, where dozens of old photographs were tacked. Eighty percent of them were photographs of me that she had cut out of newspapers and magazines. The other twenty percent were of Tim Leary and his then wife, Rosemary. "Our heroes!" she smiled. Then she asked me about Frederick.

"Do you want him back?" she asked me.

"I don't know."

"Do you? You do, don't you?"

"I left . . ."

"I know, but do you want him back?"

"Yes."

"You know what to do?" She was staring intently into my eyes, high on acid, boring into my face. I felt extremely uncomfortable.

"What?" I asked.

"Become," she said, "not a *cocksucker*," giving the word a snarling, obscene delivery, "but a *cahksuckha!*" She had opened her eyes wide on the last delivery of "cocksucker," and drew the word out, like honey, with a smile on her still-beatified face.

"I suck David's cock so good he'll do anything for me. He says, 'Ahhhh, baby, that's good, baby, so good, keep sucking.' He'll cook the dinner, wash the dishes, take care of the kids, and bring me breakfast in bed!" she finished triumphantly.

I was looking out of the bedroom window and concentrating on the clouds in the blue California sky. They didn't budge an inch.

"I find it boring," I said, finally.

"Do you love him?"

"Yes."

"Then you can get to looooove it!"

Then she told me to wait there and she'd bring me up some lunch. "Relax, honey," she told me, "everything's cool. I'll rock Emma in my arms if she cries. I'll hold her on my hip while I make you some lunch. Everything's cooooool."

I told her that I'd keep Emma—who was asleep on the sleeve of my kimono—with me; and then I fell asleep sitting up, watching the clouds, which remained stationary. About an hour later she woke me up with a plate of chicken salad and some sliced tomatoes. My fork hit something hard. The chicken was still partially frozen.

As I gingerly took off my kimono, so as not to awaken Emma, Rayanne said, "That reminds me of the story of the Chinese emperor whose lover, a beautiful young boy, was asleep on the sleeve of the emperor's priceless silk kimono. Then he was called to an important conference. Rather than wake up the boy he cut off his own sleeve." "Thank God," I told her, "I thought you were going to say he cut off his own arm!" Laughing, Rayanne picked up a bottle of brandy and slugged down about an ounce while I walked over to the window and looked down at the swimming pool.

"I took all the screens out downstairs," she said, "I was sick of looking through them."

Now she was howling with laughter, tickled pink, watching Timmy on the monkey bars. I had borrowed a videotape machine that day and was trying to tape him, but just as I focused in on his penis I ran out of tape. As I rewound, intending to recycle some of my previous shots, I could hear the other mothers complaining. They were aghast.

"It isn't a question of hygiene," one of them was explaining to Lydia, "nor of religion. It's a question of morals! I want you to tell that to Rayanne Quackenbush."

On the way home Lydia told me that the mother was a member of the committee of her nursery school and that she liked her a lot. "She's very religious," said Lydia, "she was just converted to something or other, I forget the name."

Lydia and Rayanne didn't really approve of each other. Lydia was a hypocrite, Rayanne thought, because she filled her library with books on child development and ran a nursery school yet hardly ever saw her own daughter. "I even think," Rayanne mused, "that Chrissy thinks that Sally is her real mother. One day when I was over there Lydia was trying to get Chrissy to go someplace with her and Chrissy kept saying 'no' and hanging on to Sally's skirts."

On Lydia's side, she hated the way Rayanne dressed, usually nude on top, her sagging breasts swaying, the nipples sunken in from having nursed her six children for a year apiece. "You'd think," Lydia would complain, "that she'd at least have the sense to cover her tits. Why does she always wear those Pucci stretch underpants when there's nothing wrong with her cunt? She ought to put the pants over her tits instead." I would study Rayanne's tits morbidly, wondering and fearing that mine would turn out the same way after I weaned Emma.

Another thing about Rayanne that really bothered Lydia was Rayanne's constant ingestion of LSD. Besides being highly unfashionable in 1973 (*"I mean, really! Even the college kids don't do it any more!"*), acid, to Lydia, was a messy drug that accordingly messed up one's mind.

"Look at Rayanne, Augustine," she would constantly nag at me, "slobbering all over you, telling you how much she loves you; it's types like that that end up stabbing you in the back. You wait and see. She's really unstable emotionally. You know what we used to call her?"

"No, what?"

"Wreckanne."

Rayanne, or Wreckanne, was out by the pool, Lydia's pool (Lydia was away; only then would Rayanne and entourage visit the house), her breasts naked, wearing a pair of synthetic lace stretch bikini panties. She didn't look like the same woman who had embraced me at her front door; today she was thick, sluggish, older looking than I remembered. One of her houseguests, a five-year-old, came up to her and said that the other children had told her she was ugly and they wouldn't let her play with them. The little girl was actually quite pretty, though constantly pouting.

"Go on out now, honey," Rayanne told her, "and do your own thing. We're busy." The little girl bit her lower lip and went into the house, leaving the dining room door open behind her. David came through it. Looking over his shoulder at the child, who was beginning to sob, he said, "She gets too much attention; she always wants more."

"Wasn't Rosanna like that at five, honey?" Rayanne asked him, while doing a backstroke, her breasts trailing after her in the pool like half inflated waterwings. I watched them, fascinated, wondering once again if this was a premonition of my future.

"Hell," David answered, "I don't remember."

"It's the age," Rayanne decided, "it's the age."

I was up in my "studio," a circular room above the pool, looking down, listening. I had been watching Deedee with Emma, trying to determine whether her gestures were natural or whether she was forcing herself to play with Emma. I had been following her every movement, comparing them with my own, asking myself if she was being a little bit manic. "I should be working," I thought, while listening to Rayanne and David.

Instead, I went down to the pool. David handed me a joint. Gino was looking at a lizard crawling along the edge of the garden wall, saying, "A *brujo*, like women; all women are *brujos*. This lizard is probably a woman."

"Oh, god," I asked him, "you aren't reading Carlos Castaneda are you?"

"Yeah. Why don't you like him?"

"Snobbism. I can't stand anybody popular."

"Seriously, why?"

"I went through that phase ten years ago."

"No, really, why?"

"Okay, baby, I'll give it to ya, straight. I hate him because I'm a woman and I'm jealous of his superior advantages."

"What does being a woman have to do with it?"

"Listen, a mother barely has time to write three or four hours a day. Can you see me, out in New Mexico or wherever the hell it is, coming in off the mesa every three hours, interrupting my visions of cockroaches, to give a kid the tit?"

"I don't think that's a valid reason for putting him down."

"Gino, you just lost the argument by using the word 'valid' with me. That was a grievous mistake."

"Say, you really are a snob, aren't you?"

"Yep," I said and went back upstairs just as they started a conversation about how the whole world is hooked on sugar.

I tried to work but I could hear them discussing sugar and Coca-Cola. I went to the window again. The voices were all around me; the tower seemed to be floating in a sea of people. The walls were so thin, almost nonexistent; it was as if I were floating on top of them, invisible, behind a pane of one-way glass. I watched Emma in Deedee's arms, swimming after a red plastic ball, catching it over and over again. I tried to relax, to get rid of that surreal feeling that had been attacking me lately whenever I smoked. I told myself that this was the best possible position that I could be in, and that I would realize it if only I weren't so neurotic. A room of my own, the baby safe, within eyesight, being cared for by a girl who loved her. No problems. Someone to cook the meals; all I had to do was write. Like a man.

"Men," I thought, "have the best possible position." I imagined myself as a man, with a wife down there, caring for my child, cooking dinner. All I had to do was work; and when I came to a dead end I could go down there, listen to them talk, smoke a little dope, and go back upstairs with some more ideas. I wrote a long conversation about sugar and Coca-Cola. I missed Frederick—that was it, that was why I couldn't relax, as I imagined a man would have been able to; I needed to feel the presence of my husband behind me as I worked.

"Half the world is hooked on sugar," he said. "You should go to Greece, Turkey, it gets worse from country to country."

"I just started on sugar, this chocolate; it's only lately, before I never used sugar, except . . . yes, once I was hooked on one thing, and that was . . ."

"Coca-Cola," he interrupted.

"How did you know?"

"Because half the world is hooked on Coca-Cola. A brujo, that's what they are; almost all women are brujos."

"Look, there's no difference between men and women. What's wrong with men is equally wrong with women."

Looking either for a new kick or for a natural source of sugar, David began to discuss with me the erotic possibilities of mother's milk. "I'll give you fifty dollars an ounce for it," he said, "but I'll have to suck it out."

"How will you measure it if you suck it out?"

"We'll line up for it," Gino added.

"But," I repeated, "how will you measure it?"

"You can charge by the minute," David decided. "Fifty dollars a minute!"

Timmy came into the kitchen and grabbed one of Emma's new Playtex nurser nipples. I took it away from him. Under the new regime, under Lydia's directions, we were trying to wean Emma, and one of the things that was most important, according to Lydia, was that the hole in the nipple remain small. She'd have to have a new nipple every day, and I was afraid that Timmy would lose the nipple. Timmy burst into sobs.

"Mean ole white woman," David mocked, "she won't let you have a bottle."

"A bottle!" I exploded with anger. "He wants to suck on a bottle? Fine, I thought he wanted to play with it. Of course he can have a bottle; I'll go get the lining. At his age . . . a bottle . . . I didn't know . . . what do you mean anyway by 'mean ole white woman'? You're not exactly black, and just how many black women do you know, anyway?"

"Ah was raised by a black woman."

"Oh," I said, "look at the pretty lizard on the wall."

"A *brujo*," Gino began again. "That's what they are, almost all women are *brujos*."

"Oh, come on, Gino, don't give me that Carlos Castaneda shit again."

He looked up from underneath his sun-bleached eyebrows, the lines under his eyes and wrinkles in his forehead giving him a satyrish expression, and fixed me with a look from his yellowish eyes. I went back upstairs and locked the door to my studio. I couldn't really lock them out, because I could still see and hear them, down there around the pool, knotted together; Gino lying on a chaise longue on his stomach—his black nylon bikini pulled down over the cleft of his buttocks, as though he were trying to entice the little boy swimming near him—the others squatting or sitting around him, earnestly talking. Now, when I went to the window, one of them always looked up toward me. A baby was crying for his mother, but she didn't pay any attention, waiting for someone else to pick him up. I wondered if I would feel better in Chrissy's room, where there were four walls. The circular bank of windows now made me feel as though everyone was reading over my shoulder. It was their voices, though, that bothered me the most. I kept wanting to go over to the window and listen.

"Rayanne," I said that evening in the kitchen, "Gino and David think I should charge people for sucking out my mother's milk. At first they thought I should charge fifty dollars an ounce, but when they realized that there would be no way to measure it they decided on fifty dollars a minute."

"Have you looked in the mirror lately, honey?" she asked and, before noticing my expression, added, "and ah say that out of love, love, honey . . . it comes straight from the heart."

"Rayanne," I said, not understanding whether she was "stabbing me in the back" or whether I was misinterpreting her, "I'm not going to do it, I was just talking about it."

"Ya gotta be young, honey, young . . . and then you can get away with anything; you're protected. There's nothing like innocence."

Rayanne used to be a whore, here in La Jolla. She had come down from Los Angeles, her earlier center of operations. Sometimes she took a special flight to Las Vegas and, along with several other whores, spent weekends there with New York businessmen. One of them had taken her to La Jolla and that's where she met David. He was already married and he had four children. When he told his family he was going to marry Rayanne they were shocked. He was a big successful psychiatrist at the time.

"I was a rip-off artist," he said, "that's why I made so much money. Now, I don't care about money, I have Rayanne. I only take the patients that interest me."

He drove an old Hispano-Suiza with fake jewels soldered onto it. It was painted gold and was set up so that when a gas station attendant lifted the hood, rock music blared out of the radiator. The engine was painted with psychedelic swirls and encrusted with rhinestones.

"If you took on some more patients," I told him, "you could have enough money to hire someone to clean out the swimming pool."

We were in the gold Hispano-Suiza, on our way to Los Angeles. David had to meet with a lawyer about a patient who had been arrested for drugs. Timmy, Emma, Rosanna, Rayanne, David, the dog, and I were all in the car together. Rayanne sifted through a paper bag and pulled out an amyl nitrate popper. The car filled up with the smell of ammonia.

"Open the window! My headache!" I lied, knowing that if I objected to the drug on account of Emma they'd tell me that Rosanna and Timmy and Coralee and David Junior had all been turned on at the age of seven months and look at them.

Always eager to add to her growing anthology of Tim Leary stories, Rayanne asked me for the tenth time what he was really like.

"Oh, he was always talking about the lace-curtain Irish," I said.

"Lace-curtain Irish?" Rayanne was puzzled. "What does that mean?"

"You mean you've never heard that phrase?"

"No. What does it mean?"

"It's a popular expression in Boston, especially. Paul Morissey used to use it a lot too. It means that the type of Irish who put lace curtains on their windows, usually immigrants or first generation immigrants, are usually . . . " I broke off, unable to think of the right description.

"Are usually what?" Rayanne persisted.

"Are usually . . . the type who put lace curtains on their windows," I finished lamely.

Rayanne was even more puzzled now, because to her lace curtains where the chicest, hippest things that could possibly dress a window. She had started the fad in La Jolla.

We passed the Beverly Hills Hotel on Sunset Boulevard and Rayanne began reminiscing about her days as a whore. "Right there," she told David, pointing at the hotel, "right there in one of the cabanas, that's where I had that trick who was impotent, that seventy-year-old guy, that millionaire from Texas. He pulled his pants down and asked me to . . ."

"Yes? Go on . . ." David was pleading.

" 'Get it hard, baby, get it hard,' he told me, and I said, 'Maybe if you stand up . . .' "

"Stand up?" David asked, his voice low. I looked at him, in the front seat, driving; his tongue was hanging, slowly licking his lower lip back and forth, like a satisfied cat.

"Yeah, honey," Rayanne said impatiently, "I *told* you about that one!"

"I don't remember. Tell me again."

Rayanne giggled, crawled next to her husband, and whispered something in his ear. David was having trouble concentrating on the road. For my part I found it hard to believe that this acid guru of the Sixties was turning into a Havelock Ellis specimen right before my eyes. The car accelerated.

"Red light!" I shouted.

"My god, almost missed it," David laughed, the rubber peeling off the tires as he slammed the brakes down, just missing a white Porsche, coming from Alpine Street. I resolved never to set foot in the gold Hispano-Suiza again.

David dropped us off at Venice Beach. He had finished his business in Hollywood and had to go and see the patient, who was in a "holding tank" on Venice Boulevard. Rayanne spread a sheet on the sand, right near the parking area filled with people, bicycles, and cars.

"Look, honey," Rayanne squealed, "look at those rich old men. Both of them for fifty dollars apiece. All we have to do is jerk them off fast!" Then she pulled out the picnic lunch David had just bought at a nearby delicatessen. A young boy, his dog trailing after him, cycled past and asked us if the noise didn't bother us.

"Go with the flow, honey," Rayanne told him. "It's all music to us!" She leaned over to me. "He doesn't look very rich," she whispered in my ear. Now he was halfway across the parking lot, threading his way among the crowd; a couple in their sixties were passing him, coming toward us on their way to the beach, the woman very white-skinned, white-haired, a black parasol opened over her head. "Hey," Rayanne called out to the boy, a hysterical gleam in her eyes, "is that dog a lace-curtain Irish wolfhound with his thing between his legs?"

"It's Russian, Ray," I told her.

CHAPTER XI

The Order
of the Heavenly Host

When a man is asleep he has in a circle around him the chain of the hours, the sequence of the years, the order of the heavenly host. Instinctively, when he awakes, he looks to these, and in an instant reads off his own position on the earth's surface and the amount of time that has elapsed during his slumbers; but this ordered procession is apt to grow confused and to break its ranks.

PROUST

All sleep is vulnerable . . . he (the child) is especially likely to show disturbances of sleep behavior during transitional periods of disequilibrium, when growth changes are most actively taking place . . . Some of the apparent disturbances may actually have a positive usefulness in the economy of development.

Infant and Child in the Culture of Today,
ARNOLD GESSELL, M.D., AND FRANCES L. ILG, M.D., 1943
(From Lydia Anderson's Library, La Jolla, California, March, 1973)

"There's no reason why she doesn't sleep through the night, at her age," Lydia had insisted, that first morning over coffee. "I know," I agreed, "that's what everyone tells me. But she's never once slept through the night, not since she was born."

139

"You should be able to put her to bed at six in the evening and she should sleep until six or seven the next morning."

"Six in the evening! She'd be up for the day at four the next morning!"

"Look, I have friends who put their kid in his crib at six. The kid plays alone in the crib until seven when he goes to sleep. He wakes up at six in the morning and she puts a cracker in his crib and he eats the cracker and plays alone until nine in the morning."

"They're like my father. He says that a child needs a lot of sleep or it will get a heart condition. He was always trying to get me to put Emma in bed all the time. Once I took her to a bar with me and came back at two in the morning. My father nearly threw me out of the house."

"Do you ever let her cry when she wakes up?"

"No. Do you think I should?"

"No. It's horrible, just horrible; but the truth of the matter is that it does work. It really does."

"Maybe we only sleep so much because our parents trained us to. Maybe it's normal to wake up for something to eat or drink every three or four hours. Look at people like Alexander Graham Bell and Albert Einstein. They never slept. I remember," I told Lydia, "lying awake at night listening to my father and his cronies downstairs in the living room, telling dirty jokes. I was never able to go to sleep for hours after they put me to bed. They called me a night owl."

"Yeah, that was a popular expression in the Forties. They just try to get you out of sight so they can yak with their friends. They wouldn't dare talk about the same things in front of the kids."

"Who's doing it to whom, who's cock is bigger, what deal they just pulled off with the judge . . ."

"How many times does she wake up at night?"

"Always two. Sometimes three or four or five."

"That's insane."

"I think it is too. She likes nursing so much that she won't eat; all she wants is milk, and I don't have that much anymore. But what can I do?"

"Stop nursing her."

"You're right."

"No, that doesn't mean I'm right. I just think that if you stopped nursing her she wouldn't wake up so much because she wouldn't be thinking about that tit and then you could get some sleep."

Lydia, intense and determined, was concentrating on the instructions that came with the Playtex nurser set. She blew up the liner bags one after the other with the apparatus that came with the set, and fitted them onto the plastic nipple holders. (Liner bags are transparent plastic bags into which the milk is poured, on the assumption that as the baby empties the bag it contracts, as the interior of the breast does, rather than fill up with air, which is supposed to give the baby a case of colic. Advertised as "the nearest thing to mother's breast.") One, two, three, four, five, six; they were all lined up in a straight row on top of the television set, nipples on, ready to go. She had taken me to the drugstore an hour before and bought me the whole kit, along with two cartons of Enfamil. She was just as excited about the whole ritual as Minette had been, three months before, in Paris. I was deep into my role again of helpless, passive mother, too worn out to do anything but accept, gratefully, any help that any woman deigned to give me. I wondered if there were any other women like me around; I hadn't met any. All the mothers I met were highly efficient. Yet, "You're the best mother we know," my own mother had said, "in fact we think you're overdoing it." She, like Andy Warhol, used the term "we" whenever she meant "I." Frederick thought they were both referring to God. On a videotape, one of the tapes we made in Pommiers, an old peasant who had gotten into the car with us to go to the village had said, "On va vous dit au revoir."

"Did you hear that?" Frederick asked me, delighted, "the way she says 'on'? I guess she means God, like Andy Warhol and your mother." For my part (no matter what Queen Victoria thought), I was sure that the use of "we" or "on" was simply a clever way of avoiding personal responsibility for whatever idea was being expressed.

"We'll let Emma sleep with Deedee," Lydia was saying, "and the first time she wakes up Deedee will bring her to you and the second time Deedee will give her a Playtex nurser filled with Enfamil. Is that all right with you, Deedee?"

"Oh," Deedee replied, "sorry, terribly sorry, really, but I didn't catch what you were saying."

"Deedee," I snapped at her, "I've told you a thousand times not to say 'I'm sorry' all the time. There's nothing to be sorry for. Frederick always says that you should never apologize for anything." My new "nanny" was the type who apologized for a bottle of spilled milk even if someone else had spilled it. As much as she loved Emma, this habit of saying "I'm sorry" all the time drove me wild.

Lydia repeated the night schedule for Deedee and she happily agreed. Anything to help me out.

The night schedule isn't working. Deedee says that no matter how hard she tries, Emma refuses the Playtex nurser. Each time she wakes up, Deedee brings her to me, saying, "It doesn't work." We are giving up the night schedule; Lydia has gone away again, to visit Tony in San Francisco, so we won't have to account for our actions until she returns. By that time I hope to be in Zihuatanejo with Marian Levine. The over-all fascist environment of La Jolla is beginning to get to me. Even here, in the drug dealers' paradise of the Western Hemisphere, the atmosphere isn't right. I hate to go out of the grounds. Yesterday a policeman tried to arrest me in Lydia's own driveway for wearing a crocheted sweater without a bra.

"You cut youah hair again, didn't you all? Ah know, you all cut youah hair even shorter this time, you did. And what's that smudge undahneath youah left eye? You look really tired, really tired." Rayanne was persecuting Deedee tonight. Pouring her Southern accent on as thick as she could (she came from Mississippi). One of Deedee's boyfriends had come from Los Angeles to see her and he was sitting there, in front of the T.V. set, waiting for us.

"Why don't you come with us?" Deedee had asked me. "Let Sally watch Emma; come with us."

I was trying to decide what to do. I could leave her there, take her with us, nurse her to sleep before I left, or stay home with her. Deedee was pressuring me to make up my mind, which was bad enough, but I had a headache on top of that and I was starving. She was sitting there, in the dining room, in a long dress, her mouth clamped shut, her bare tanned shoulders jutting forward, muscles rippling, as she tapped out one cigarette in the ashtray and struck matches for the next.

"What are you doing, Deedee?" Rayanne continued, for some inexplicable reason of her own, to persecute my babysitter.

"I'm waiting," Deedee grimaced between tight lips, "to see what's happening. I'm climbing the walls. I have to get out of here."

I was furious. I wanted to scream at Deedee for her selfishness. (I wanted to get out of there too!)

In the car, her boyfriend driving, I told her that she ought to give up smoking cigarettes. The way she smoked them showed so much hostility, I told her, that I couldn't stand it; I knew it was directed against me. Again, in the restaurant, I brought it up. I knew I would be losing myself another good babysitter but I couldn't help it.

"You ought to see yourself, Deedee," I said to her, "the way you smoke. You jam the cigarette into your mouth and blow it into the face of the person next to you, and with such a vengeance!" I showed her. I imitated her smoking. I took a cigarette, my mouth tight, jammed it in, puffed the smoke out in short, angry bursts, into Deedee's face. On our way out of the restaurant she told me she was leaving with her boyfriend.

In the morning she vacillated. She came into my room (the first time she'd ever gotten up before me) and told me how depressed she was. The reason she couldn't get up in the mornings, she said, was that she was so depressed. She had been "horny" for weeks, and now that Sven was here, she was feeling a little better; yet California made her depressed.

"Everybody is depressed in the mornings, Deedee," I told her. "Did you know that Picasso is so depressed in the mornings that his wives have to bring him coffee in bed and sit there, waiting for him to drink it up, telling him all the while what a genius he is? In the mornings he thinks he can't paint at all!"

"He can't," Deedee solemnly whispered.

"I'm willing to do that for you, Deedee. I'll make coffee for you in the mornings if you'll stay and I'll tell you how wonderful you are if that will put you in a better mood."

"No, no," Deedee insisted, "tomorrow morning I'll get up the minute Emma is awake and I'll take care of her all day so you can get some work done; I promise."

Later in the day I decided to tell Deedee that if she really was that depressed then she could leave, I could get along without her. I never did it, though; I was too afraid of her actually doing it, and leaving me alone with Emma. In the end, though, after about three more days Deedee did leave. She left with her boyfriend, reluctantly, guiltily. I assured her that I didn't mind at all.

"Isn't it great when they finally go down?" Rayanne grinned, jumping around in her Spanish bedroom, clapping her hands, like a kid. "Go down," I thought to myself. "What a strange expression to use, it sounds obscene, I wonder if it's endemic to California."

"When you finally get them down in the crib I mean . . . now listen, you hear Timmy crying? Well, he'll stop in a minute. Do you wanna put Emma down? No? She can go down with Timmy."

"I never put her down until she's asleep, Rayanne; she's in the habit of nursing herself to sleep," I said, apologetically, embarrassed that I was coddling my only child ("*You couldn't do that, if you had more than one child*," I remembered my mother saying), and wishing that Rayanne would go back into Timmy's room and get him. I had a headache and his crying was driving me crazy; what it was doing to him was probably even worse. I had just taken him for a walk around the block. He ran and ran, skimming around each corner, knowing exactly where he was going, refusing to make the turn to his house, and instead, running to Lydia's, where I followed him. Then David came and took him home, insisting that I come along too.

I looked closely at Rayanne. She was a mess. Her eyes were wild, red-rimmed, black circles under them. She'd been on acid since I first met her. I didn't know how long she could keep this up. I thought about Marie-Claude.

Marie-Claude, opening the door of her mother's apartment to me when I had arrived in Paris after leaving Frederick in Agadir. Marie-Claude, looking like a Ukrainian Easter egg, pink and white and ebony, nestled in artificial pink-and-white American Easter basket grass. That's what her mother's apartment had looked like, an American Easter basket. Marie-Claude was pregnant. Pregnant by her French lover, not by Gunter von Habsburg. Pregnant by Louis-François.

Louis-François had been a great, much admired film star. Now he refused to work. Said that all directors were pigs and that he was going to become a musician, at his age, thirty-eight. He refused all movie work, and he didn't have a cent. He stood around in different rooms, morose, heavy, his big, square bull-like head hanging over his guitar, his hair hanging almost into the strings as he plucked, always strumming the same rhythm, totally monotonous. It was my opinion that he was going crazy.

"Look, look at my stomach," Marie-Claude squealed. "Does it show yet? No? Not even a little? The doctors gave me all these pills, I've been so sick. I can't leave the house. Louis doesn't have a penny to give me, the pig, the bastard. I 'ate 'im. I can't live with 'im. Oh, look at Emma. She's so beautiful. You're so lucky. Why did you leave Frederick? You must be crazy. You're so lucky to 'ave a man 'ho cares about you, 'ho lives with you, 'ho takes care of the baby. You don't know 'ow lucky you are."

She led me through the rooms of her mother's apartment. It was in a new, American-type high-rise apartment house, on the edge of Neuilly. Pink and white and gold; blond antiqued furniture everywhere, like Hollywood in the Forties. Heavy satin quilted bedspreads, pink satin quilted headboards, a kitchen full of frills and flounces, knick-knacks everywhere; it was an atmosphere to get sick in and stay sick. There was so much furniture that I felt weighed down, laden, oppressed. The apartment itself was pregnant, every corner was pregnant, even the bathroom was pregnant. Overheated, with fluffy pink rugs on the floor, pink and white jars and bottles everywhere, weighing scales (the French, always a good ten years behind the Americans, were still obsessed with a pregnant woman's weight gain), a pink douche bag, its tube running down to the pink rubber mat on the bathtub floor like an umbilical cord to the placenta; a giant womb.

"Who cares about her?" Louis-François had said. "She is a pig. She come from a family of tailors. Bourgeois tailors. She's crazy, like her whole family. I 'ate 'er."

Marie-Claude had cut her hair again. It lay about her perfect skull like a black velvet cap. Her skin was blue-white, not a blemish, not a pore visible. When she smiled the skin under her narrow nostrils creased upwards, into a thin curve, framing them. There was something solid about her face, I decided, not vulgar at all; she could almost have been a boy. Louis-François had been living with her there, at her mother's, she told me, but they had fought constantly and so he left. (" 'e was nevair here, Augustine, 'e used to stay out all night. I nevair knew where 'e was.") She didn't care, she said, she was glad. She was "waiting for the baby."

"What will it be like?" she asked me. "Tell me, what will it be like?"

Rayanne and David are trying to suffocate me with attention. They arrived at Lydia's last night with some honeydew melon and prosciutto, because I had told them I missed Italy, because of the melon and prosciutto. "Anything you want," they told me, "just ask us. We love you."

"I'd like to get Emma to sleep," I told them, "and I don't have a car. The only way I can seem to do it lately is to take her for a ride; then she'll pass out while we're driving." (I had forgotten about my resolution not to step into the Hispano-Suiza again.) "Sure honey," Rayanne told me, "let's go out and get in the car. David will drive us, won't you, David?" David agreed. We headed for the beach.

"Honey," Rayanne said to me as we passed the Scripps Institute of Oceanography, "you can be part of David's harem. He wants to *do* you. It's okay with me, I love you. He'll take care of Emma, he'll do whatever you want. We'll get Frederick back and then we'll all live together, huh? Wouldn't you like it?"

I smiled, thinking all the time about Marie-Claude—her clothes, her scarves, her necklaces, her heavy Moroccan silver bracelets that a witch in the mountains had traded her for her own jewelry. I was thinking about her reserve, her harmony, and, oddly enough, her politeness. She was so discreet. She always said the right thing.

"Who else is in the harem?" I asked.

"We've shown our love to a lot of people," Rayanne said sadly, uncomprehendingly, "and they've all disappeared." Then, turning the conversation to a cheerier subject, a subject that seemed inspired by drives in the Hispano, she said, "I was driving along here when I was fifteen and I said to my friend Sol, 'Sol, *everything* is sex!' and I believe it to this day. It's still true."

"Yup," David agreed, "it's still true."

"I don't know about that," I demurred. "I passed through that phase in 1966."

"Loving kindness," David added, "that's the only important thing in life."

"I'll tell you what's important, David," I said. "First get a telephone so you won't have to keep using Lydia's (David hadn't paid the phone bill in so long they cut off his phone; after that he said he liked it better that way, no calls, but still he spent an inordinate amount of time, only when Lydia wasn't there, on her phone), then hire a maid, then reopen your office, make some money, and have the swimming pool cleaned out. After that throw out the LSD in your house and send your wife to a nutrition specialist."

David looked at me disapprovingly, shocked, as though I had betrayed him. "I can only talk to people who have taken acid and who are no more than three or four years older or younger than me," he said.

"Well, I don't know if I qualify, David, I've only taken acid five times. Anyway, you should forget about that and reopen your office if you want to keep your family together."

"I can't talk to anyone who doesn't agree with me," he stated flatly.

"Clean out the swimming pool," I repeated, ignoring his personal ground rules for conversation. "If one of the kids falls in they'll die of blood poisoning."

Rayanne was looking at me strangely. Finally she opened her mouth. "I didn't know you'd taken acid only five times!" she breathed, her astonishment coming out in a long sigh, a diver coming up for air, after having mistaken a shark for a porpoise.

The next day Rayanne came over to see me, alone. She wanted to know why I hadn't invited them into Lydia's house after they had driven me home the night before (Lydia was away again). I remained evasive.

"What's wrong?" she kept insisting, "you don't like David any more? What are these 'changes' between you? You think he's terrible, don't you?"

"Yes," I answered, "I think he's terrible."

Rayanne was stricken. Her face hardened, her eyes narrowed; she was about to say something nasty to me, I knew it.

"No, Rayanne," I told her, "I was just kidding. It's just that I think the two of you should stop taking so much LSD."

"Why?"

"Brain damage," I told her, solemn. "How long have you been taking it?"

"Since 1965."

"Well, oh . . . never mind . . ."

"No! Don't say, 'Oh, never mind'; tell me!"

"All right, I'll tell you. I'm sick of hearing about LSD and love. I find the two of them really boring subjects."

"Okay, that's all right. You should have told me. I understand. Why don't you come over to my house? I want to show you something."

"Here, come to the closet; you're taller than I am. I want to show you David's writing."

I pulled down a light-blue plastic air travel bag full of school tablets covered with ballpoint pen writing.

"Here's some of David's. He's really good."

Timmy came upstairs with a bottle of milk.

"Oh, Timmy, you found your milk. Good boy!" Rayanne picked him up and put him, screaming, into his crib and closed the door. "Now, let me read a line from David's writing, okay?" She pulled out a piece of paper and began reading.

Dreams of sex, and kings, and LSD and fishes in the sea. The love for you the love for me and LSD Lsd Lsd.

While she read and Timmy wailed, I went through some of her own writing.

"Listen, Rayanne, I like yours better. Can I take it?"

"Oh, of course, honey, but it's nothing."

"Do you think Timmy would like a bottle with fresh milk in it?"

"Yeah. His is probably sour. Are you sure you don't want to read any of David's?"

"Maybe later. But are you sure you don't want me to get some fresh milk for Timmy?"

"No, no. He'll go down in a minute."

I took Rayanne's writing and let myself out through the verandah door, under the painting of the Rolling Stones, went back to Lydia's, and wrote a letter to Frederick's mother, telling her that I felt like Ruth in the alien corn.

Then I telephoned Marian Levine in Zihuatanejo, asking her if I could come down with Emma. Brian, her husband, had died of cancer a few months before. (It had turned out that he really was sick.) Marian was delighted to hear from me and told me not to worry about money; she would buy me a plane ticket to Acapulco and from there she would also prepay a ticket on the hydroplane to the beach, Playa La Ropa, where she lived in Zihuatanejo.

"How long do you think you'll want to stay?" she asked.

"Oh, I don't know, I guess about a week," I told her, hoping that she'd say, "Oh, don't be silly, stay as long as you want!"

"Instead she said, "Good, I'm going to move out of there and I'll be packing all week; I have some other guests too and we should all be out of there in a week anyway."

CHAPTER XII

Sisters Under the Skin

The hydroplane skidded up to the beach called Playa La Ropa. It had become in the past year a popular refuge for the growing class of abandoned American mothers, victims of the drug and sex revolution, and their tiny offspring. We could see some of them in the distance, playing in the gentle surf. The children all seemed to be blond, tanned, and male. In the foreground, coming to meet us, was Marian Levine with her two children in tow, and another woman who was big, blond, deeply tanned, and naked. A set of triplets, two boys and a girl, about three years old, were scampering around her legs, running in and out. She was laughing and pinching the naked bottom of the little girl, saying, "Oooh, what a cute little tushie you've got! Mama loves you sooo much!" The little girl, with her long blond curls swinging down to her waist, was adorable; she looked like a miniature Lolita.

I put Emma down on the sand and stared at the nude mother, wondering who she was; she looked very familiar to me. By this time Marian had reached us and was leading us in the direction of an adobe house, on the beach, between the surf and the jungle. I suddenly realized who the other woman was. Over the sound of the hydroplane's engine (it was taking off again) I shouted, "Roberta! My god, what are *you* doing here?"

"You won't believe it, Augustine, but Bill left me for that red-headed nurse he had, remember? And Marian said I could come down here with the kids and try to get my head together again. It's been hell."

"Bill? Bill Taylor? You married him?"

"Not exactly. We had a sort of Indian ceremony in Santa Fe, with the local chief officiating; I mean, I don't think it's really legal, according to the courts and all, a Zuñi ceremony, but . . ."

"Can you get alimony?"

"He gave me some money . . ."

"Roberta! That's ridiculous! You have three children to support!"

"I know, I know, but my father is helping me out and I'm still hoping that Bill will ask us to come back; he really loves the children . . ."

"Oh, Ventura!" Marian was calling to a tall good-looking Mexican coming out onto the terrace, "put the *huachinago* right here, and then go back in the house for the wine." The Mexican set down the bowl of hot red snapper on a metal and glass table and then went back into the house saying, "Yes sir!"

"He keeps calling me 'sir' ever since Brian died," Marian whispered, "I think he's going to quit. He never liked me anyway. He would do anything for Brian, but not for me. Anyway, I'm leaving this place. Gregory is helping me pack up. I'm sick of it here. They're building another hotel on the beach, I can't even take a walk without seeing those goddam glass towers, blocking out the sun. There have been so many murders here you wouldn't believe it; last week one of the natives came home to find his sixteen-year-old daughter in bed, making love with a girlfriend. He shot and killed them both. Then just the other day I was talking to this American guy, a dealer. He told me—he has a wooden leg—he told me that his donkey is in such perfect communication with him that he doesn't even have to tie it up. He doesn't even have to call him, he said, because the donkey can read his mind. When the guy wants to go to town the donkey just knows it, and appears at the door. Well, after he told me this he picked up the donkey's rope to lead him away and the donkey insisted on going in the opposite direction. The donkey pulled on him and dragged him in the dirt, the guy cursing and swearing at the donkey . . . finally the wooden leg got stuck in the mud and came off, so there's the guy, hopping on one foot, swearing at the donkey, who's still dragging him by the rope, until finally the guy drops the rope, goes back, pulls his wooden leg out of the mud and throws it at the donkey. Well, the point of the story is that the guy was trying to be so hip, he did so much talking about the drug business . . . the natives have a really big business going on up in the mountains. They grow tons of marijuana . . . he went up into the mountains and came back down again, bragging about how much dope he was going to buy . . . and then the next day he was found right up there in the mountains, dead. His head was cut off . . . ugh, can you imagine? He was wearing this cowboy hat and the hat was still on his head when they found it . . . the head I mean, wedged into a ciruela tree. No, Noonoo, no! Don't throw sand on the terrace, we're going to eat. Get her, Roberta! She's going to throw sand into the *huachinago!*"

"Where'd they find his wooden leg?" Roberta asked as she grabbed her three-year-old daughter, pried open her fist, and made her drop the sand she was about to fling into the fish. Noonoo set up a howl, and was immediately joined in the chorus not only by several parrots perched in the nearby trees but by Manuel as well—a former salesman from Mexico City who had come to Zihuatanejo for a week three years before, and had been there ever since, living in the giant nest he constructed at the top of a Banyon tree.

Roberta Haussman was a woman who had been a make-up expert in New York, from 1960 to 1967. She was in charge of making up all the models for the editorial pages of *Vogue, Harper's Bazaar* and *Mademoiselle* magazines and had invented the "doe-eye" look. In 1967 she disappeared and later turned up in New Mexico, the mother of triplets. The triplets' father was Bill Taylor, a former ski bum and heir to the Blue Stamp fortune. He had moved from Utah to Santa Fe, where he was principally concerned with building himself a new house and running for mayor.

His mayoralty campaign was based on three planks: legalizing marijuana, abolishing prisons, and reforming the marriage laws. He wanted to give women a fair shake, he said. He lost the campaign.

Noonoo's brother, Ned, careened onto the terrace in a Big Wheel, the popular plastic replacement for the tricycle, and narrowly missed Emma, who began to cry, pulled on my leg and reached up for me to take her. I picked her up and she dove down the front of my shirt for a breast; pulling it out, she began to suck on it.

"You're still nursing her; I think that's great," Roberta told me. "I want to hear all about your life. Let's go down to the bar after lunch with the kids and let Ingrid watch them while we talk. Did you meet Ingrid? No? There she comes. She's my babysitter. I brought her out from New Mexico. She's great. I'd be lost without her."

Ingrid strode into view, wearing a patchwork bikini. She was tall, a natural platinum blonde, beautiful, about twenty-two years old and she wore a perpetual smile.

"Ingrid, this is Augustine. You've heard me talk about her. I've talked about you a lot, Augustine. I've kept track of you all these years. I knew you were going to do something great some day. I saved all the clippings about you, didn't I, Ingrid? Ingrid will tell you, won't you, Ingrid? Remember that photo I put on the wall in the den? The woman with the red hair, all frizzed out, and the eye make-up? Didn't I say she looked like Colette? You don't wear eye make-up any more, Augustine? I stopped wearing eye liner myself. What a relief not to have to carry that little bottle and that brush around with me, always worrying about the line, that it was disappearing or smudging or something. Always going into someone's bathroom to check on it. It took me two years to make the decision. Now I just wear mascara. You know what forced me to make up my mind? I was sitting down to dinner in Santa Fe with this model and Bill, and the boyfriend of this model.

" 'Look at her eyes,' Bill said to me. 'Why do they look so open and wide-awake, and yours look so closed down?' It was the eye liner. I went into the bathroom and looked; and then I looked closely at her. She wasn't wearing eye liner. That was it. She was only wearing eye shadow and mascara."

"You really should wear mascara, Augustine. You're so beautiful and nobody would know it. Your eyes look bald right now. Here, take my mascara and go into the bathroom and try it. Wait until the first layer dries and then put on two more. Don't worry, Emma can sit on my lap. Can't you, Emma? You're so pretty, Emma. Come here, that's it, sit on my lap, Aunt Roberta's lap. Mama Roberta. Isn't that funny, Augustine, the way Emma calls all the women mama? And the breast! The way she calls the breast mama too? I think that's great. Come here, darling, to Mama Roberta. Ingrid, get ahold of Noonoo. She's going to spill that drink."

Ingrid moved in slow motion toward Noonoo and scooped her off the bar, murmuring something in her ear. I was on my way to the toilet, Roberta's mascara in my hand, wondering why I was so docilely obeying her. Probably to get her off the subject of mascara.

"*I don't know why she keeps Ingrid around,*" Marian said to me while we were clearing off the lunch table. "*She's so beautiful and so young. I told her she was crazy. I'd never hire somebody who looked like that. And do you know what she told me?*"

"*What did she say?*"

"*She actually told me that that was the reason she hired her, so that the men they met would be attracted to Ingrid and keep away from her. I can't understand it.*"

After telling me that was better, the mascara, now you could see my eyes, now I looked like I used to look, Roberta said, "Ingrid loves those kids. That's why I hired her. She treats them the same way I do. She saved my life back there in Santa Fe. She was always there when I needed her."

Ingrid had disappeared down the beach with the four children scampering after her. "Don't worry," Roberta told me, "she's great with the kids. Mine have their water wings, they won't drown. She'll hang onto Emma. We'll get Emma some wings tomorrow. Listen, tell me, what are you doing here?"

I told her about Morocco, about the cold, Emma sleeping in her snowsuit, the fight, how I hated Morocco.

"Clean sheets!" Roberta emphatically pronounced, "clean sheets and pillowcases and hot water and a nice bathroom. I don't care what anybody says. That's how we were brought up. Our mothers were right. If you've got heat, and clean sheets, and a nice bathroom with plenty of hot water and clean towels that's all you need. Face it, Augustine, that's how we were brought up and it wasn't so bad, was it? Actually, Mexico is like Morocco. The scorpions, the food; when you have children it isn't easy. You have to be on the lookout all the time for scorpions. A child gets one bite and that's it! Did you bring any serum? That's okay, we have plenty. And the sand in the beds! And the fireplaces, all the time, worrying about wood. It isn't easy."

"How's Marian been?"

"Look, you and I, we know. I've been watching you with Emma. I can tell right away that you're a good mother, like me. When I quit working and had the triplets I said to myself, 'That's all I'm gonna do from now on, I'm gonna be a mama. And you know what a mama is, it's a slave. But I'll never work again. Wild horses couldn't drag me into it. I don't care who I have to beg for money. I've taken a vow that I'll never have another job. But Marian! That's another story. I don't know whether it's because of Brian's death, or what, but I can't stand the way she's bringing up those kids. We're just from two different schools of thought, that's all. I hate to say anything to her; we're on bad enough terms as it is. Boy, am I glad you came down here. I spend every afternoon at this bar with the kids. You know why? Because the vibes down at that house are so bad that I can't even stay around."

"Why don't you go back to Santa Fe then?"

"I can't. That woman is there. I'd go to New York and visit my family, but I hate New York. And Marian's leaving and I'm trying to rent her house for two more months. She wants me to leave before she goes, says she wants a couple of days alone with the kids, but hell, I'll move into the guest house and I'll feed the kids at the hotel. You know Philip? Marian's youngest boy? Well, he's become so insecure it breaks my heart. Marian's got this boyfriend, Gregory Waldon, she met him at some rally in L.A. He's from some videotape guerrilla commune in Atlanta, Georgia; he videos strikes and demonstrations and things like that. Well, since he's been here, Philip is really a mess . . ."

Norman, one of the triplets, returned, crying. "Oh, Normie baby, what's the matter? You didn't get bitten, did you? Where's Ingrid? Oh, there she is, come on, baby, come to Mama, I love you so much . . . and anyway," she said, pulling her son onto her lap and taking another sip of her rum collins, "Philip is a mess. Marian just ignores him. Teddy, on the other hand, well, she gave him so much love when he was a baby that he's cool. And he's got Brian's charm, he'll be okay. She says that she spent all her time with Teddy when he was a baby. I remember; I was here then, she was always playing with him, on the beach; but Philip! He's a real pain in the neck. You'll see, though, when you give him any attention at all he'll want to stay with you, he'll hang onto your hand. He becomes a different person entirely. And that nanny she's got now, a new one, from England, Bonnie, did you meet her? Well, Marian hates Bonnie, so in retaliation Bonnie hides in her room, pretending she has cramps. Listen, let's take *all* the kids with us tomorrow. We'll take them to the swimming pool."

"I don't know why she hired Ingrid," Marian was complaining, "she never leaves the kids with her. She's always with them herself. They're driving her crazy. What's wrong with her? Do you know what she told me? That she's never spent a day without them since they were born. Not one day! Now, don't tell me that isn't insane!"

"Brian always wanted the kids in bed by seven thirty. We couldn't eat dinner with them. We had to eat later, after they were in bed. He entertained so much that I had to do it that way; he would have a fit if they came downstairs after seven o'clock. That's why they sleep upstairs with Bonnie. The room upstairs is better, we should have used it ourselves. But that's the way I had to do it. I had to put them all upstairs, the three of them. Remember Lillian? The other English girl? Well, she fell in love with a Mexican cop. She used to meet him on the beach. I didn't know anything about it. And then she got pregnant. I had to send her back. This one, she's about to go. I can feel it. I don't like her and she doesn't like me. It's awful having somebody live under your roof whom you don't like. I can't even talk to her. Last week she said she was sick. I tried to get her to see a doctor. I hope she isn't pregnant. She spent four days in bed. She refused to see a doctor; I hope she isn't pregnant. I think she was faking but I have no way of finding out. Now I'll have to go back to London to find another one, dammit!"

We had just finished dinner. Marian was wearing a loose caftan, with red and yellow embroidery. She said it was a Mexican wedding dress, that the women spend a year embroidering their wedding dresses and then, after the ceremony, they bury them. "Probably," Marian thought, "to bury the memory of the worst day of their lives."

Gregory had gone into the bedroom, where he spent most of his time. No one knew what he did in there; maybe he was writing.

"I don't know how I did it," Marian continued. "I used to come in off the beach in my bikini, go out into that dark, hot kitchen, and cook these elaborate dinners, over the wood stove, for Brian's friends. He was always scheming out some business deal with them. I didn't really mind; I mean they were my friends, too; but Brian would say, if I didn't change into a long dress, 'Marian, why are you still wearing your bikini?' I'd look down and say, 'Oh, you're right, I'm sorry. I'll go into the bedroom and change.' And I always did! I always changed my clothes; I was his slave; I did whatever he told me. I never realized that he was being impossible. I just took it for granted that I should be wearing a long dress. I'd be so tired; all I'd want to do was go to sleep, and I'd have to shower and fix my hair and change my clothes . . . after spending hours in that awful kitchen."

"What about Ventura? He did a good job with the lunch."

"Oh Ventura!" Marian sighed, "he'll only do *certain* things. I was lucky to even *see* him yesterday. Ventura was Brian's man. He would take orders only from Brian. And Brian said that he couldn't ask him to stay here that late. You know what I did the whole time Brian was sick? I brought him grape juice and soda water. Everybody had to stay away from the cabinet where he kept his soda water. Noise bothered him, but he watched television all day. And gave orders. You know what he wanted in the hospital? You remember. Frederick was there, videotaping him. He wanted to be filmed with all his famous friends before he died. It was ghoulish. I couldn't stand it. Remember that day he called Frederick and told him to get right over there, that Charlie Mingus was coming? And how he tortured everybody? How he tried to make everybody uptight because he was dying and they weren't? He always knew just where their Achilles' heels were and he'd get them. And that girlfriend of his? That Barbara Mierson? Did you know that he always wanted me on one side of the bed and Barbara on the other, each one of us holding his hands? All the time. He tortured us both. He wouldn't let me leave and he wouldn't let her leave."

Marian's eyes were filling with tears. She had never looked more beautiful. I went over to her side of the table, stood behind her, and put my arms around her neck. She pushed me away.

Frederick had loved Brian. He thought the way Brian had driven everyone crazy while he was dying was brilliant. Frederick had wanted to drill a hole in the wall above Brian's bed and videotape him from the adjoining room, so that none of Brian's visitors would know that the camera was there. Brian loved the idea but the doctors and administrators of the hospital wouldn't hear of it, even though Brian offered them a large sum of money for the damage to the wall. The reason Frederick wanted the hole to be just over Brian's head was that when the visitors arrived, Frederick said, and approached Brian's bed trying to be cheerful, Brian would say something to each one of them guaranteed to make their expressions change. "You know," he told his lawyer, "I'm going to die any day."

"Nonsense, Brian," his lawyer said, "you'll lick it; look at John Wayne." (Brian had terminal cancer.)

"John Wayne had only one lung removed. Do you know that when they opened me up yesterday I was so rotten inside that they closed me right back up again? You should ask Frederick to show you the tape he made last week in the cobalt treatment chamber, underground. It's really grotesque. You'd love it. Show him, Frederick, thread it up on the machine."

Brian spared his more famous friends, though; he didn't want to scare them away; he said he needed them at their best on the tapes, because he wanted the tapes played at his wake. He made Frederick promise to tape the funeral, but when the time came Brian's relatives and in-laws wouldn't allow it. They said it would be in the worst possible taste.

"At least the rabbi didn't say what a wonderful father and husband Brian had been," Marian told us. "I warned him that if he said anything like that at the funeral I'd get up and walk out. So, instead, he just said that Brian had been a very unusual man, a catalyst of the Sixties; it took only three minutes."

CHAPTER XIII

Two Women Under One Roof

Seven o'clock in the morning, April 12, 1973. The sun has just risen over the Sierra Madres and Roberta Haussman is in the kitchen, as is her habit, making pancakes for her triplets, who are having a furious fight in the living room over a piece of driftwood. Upstairs Marian's children are supposed to be quietly playing, restrained by Bonnie, waiting for the magic hour of eight thirty to come downstairs. By then, hopefully, their mother will be up. However, Emma and I have just walked into the living room, having passed Philip on the way, sneaking down the stairs to his mother's bedroom.

Two minutes later: Marian has just appeared at her door, looking like a witch, her thick long dark-brown hair tumbled all over her head, her eyes half closed; she throws a screaming Philip out in the hallway and slams the door behind her. Roberta shoots me a meaningful look.

April 12, 1973, afternoon: Roberta and Marian are arguing. "You know what I said, Roberta. I told you I don't want any children in that room until eight thirty or nine o'clock. Bonnie has always kept my children upstairs and I don't see why you can't do the same thing. My bedroom is right next to the living room. You know that!" Marian is wearing black leotards, having just come from her yoga class, which meets farther down on the beach.

Roberta is naked, as Ingrid, the children, and I usually are most of the time now, fulfilling the twofold purpose of saving laundry (the old manual machine is broken) and saving our vaginas from another episiotomy in the case of further childbirths. (Dr. Bradley, Leboyer disciple and proponent of "husband-coached childbirth," said in *Playgirl* Magazine that civilized women tear in childbirth because they have "chapped lips"; according to him, chapped lips are caused by never getting any "sun on the bottom" and by wearing panties; a sunless bottom loses its elasticity and panties collect vaginal moisture.)

Roberta counters Marian with: "What can I say, Marian? The kids are up with the sun and I've always made them pancakes. It's my favorite time of day. I'll be happy to make pancakes for your children too; I can take care of them all, Ingrid and Augustine and I. We've been taking care of them all week anyway."

"This is my house. Can't I give orders in my own house? This is getting to be ridiculous. It's like a play I once saw on Broadway, *The Caretaker* it was called. The caretaker drove the owners out of their own house, by sheer intimidation. Listen, six more people are coming today. Where are they going to sleep?"

"Put them in my room. I don't mind. I'll sleep in the basement, or upstairs in the nursery with the children, or out in that old guest house nobody uses."

Marian walks away, disgusted.

April 15, 1973, morning: the Catalina Inn, Zihuatanejo. Marian, three of her new guests, two of whom are Lydia Anderson and Tony Mussante. We are eating breakfast—bacon, ham, eggs, orange juice, coffee, toast. Marian had come to my room to wake me up, asking me if I wanted to eat with them. She said she had to get out of the house.

"Don't you think Roberta is the most overbearing woman you ever met?" Marian is asking me.

"No," Lydia interrupts, "not overbearing; just goddam domineering, that's all."

I, of course, don't want to take sides. Why are they all forcing me to take sides, I wonder; is it because there are so few men around to make them all toe the line and behave?

Roberta can't stand Lydia. The day Lydia and Tony and Chrissy arrived, Roberta had an argument with both Lydia and Tony. They all sat in the gazebo looking out over the sea, exchanging veiled insults about bringing up children; of course, that was all any of us were interested in these days. I suppose if we had had our children when we were twenty instead of thirty we'd be acting normally by now.

Roberta had become so incensed, so outraged, that she had gotten up, walked across the terrace, and slammed into the house, the glass panes in the doors rattling behind her. Marian's house, aside from the house of the mayor of Acapulco, was the only modern one on the beach. All the others (*palapyas*, they were called) had thatch roofs, no walls, and hammocks suspended from the rafters for sleeping. Everything was suspended from the scorpions. The kitchens were all in separate huts, as was Marian's, with wood-burning adobe fireplaces for cooking.

I had been leaning on the edge of the gazebo, my arms around one of the supports, listening. On that particular occasion, I remember, I had agreed with Roberta, whatever the subject was, but said nothing, not wanting to antagonize Lydia, who bore any rejection silently, bowing her head even further over her chest, bearing her latest cross just as stoically as she had borne the desertion of her husband two years before. Since then, I believed, she had been chronically depressed. In the playground that day, the day of Timmy's nude climbing, Lydia had suddenly stopped, transfixed. She had grabbed my arm, her fingernails digging into my flesh, while she whispered, "See that woman? That woman over there?"

"Yeah? What about her?" I had asked, expecting to hear some scandalous tale at least.

"She looks exactly like the woman my husband left me for." That was the first and last time Lydia ever mentioned to me the fact that her husband had left her for another woman.

"Yes," Lydia repeated at the Catalina Inn "domineering. She's the most aggressive woman I've ever met. In fact she's the most aggressive *person* I've ever met."

"And her children," added Marian, "they're whining all the time. And do you know what the worst thing is?"

"What?" Everyone was all ears.

"She's always telling me things I don't want to hear. About her own bodily functions. Like the other day, for instance, she told me that she couldn't go out of the house in the morning without having a *bowel move-ment* first. I mean, who wants to know about those things?"

Marian was out in a boat, offshore, waiting for her children and her six guests to join her. They couldn't take it any more, the civil war that was raging in the house. They were going for a picnic on La Isla. Some-how I had been forced to take sides, and I'd landed in the minority group, that of Roberta and her children. Ingrid had miraculously remained im-mune, *virgo intacta*; she was speaking to everybody, including the newly arrived rather stuffy English couple and their son, Chip, who, upon meet-ing me, sputtered out, *"You're stupid!"*

Bonnie was carrying a screaming Philip out to the boat; it wasn't clear whether he was screaming because he wanted to go or didn't want to go. It became clear what the screaming was about when Marian, stern and cranky, sitting with her back straight and rigid on a plank in the middle of the boat, screeched out at her youngest son, "Stop that crying or you won't come with me at all," then reached out her arms and took him from Bonnie. Philip began trembling then with the effort to arrest his sobs. Big teardrops were quivering on the edge of his plump cheeks.

"Bye, see you later," Marian called out to me in a crimped voice. I stood there, ankle deep in warm green salt water, my toes digging into the fine white sand, appalled at the situation I was finding myself in.

"Come on, eat this!" Roberta was prodding me. "It's such a tiny bit!" She was holding out to me a minute piece of blotter impregnated with LSD.

"No," I kept telling her, "I don't want to!"

"Oh, come on, you'll have so much fun with Emma. You mean you've never taken it since you've had her? Oh, Augustine, you don't know what you're missing! You can really get on their trip with them this way, come on."

I resolved that I wasn't going to let Roberta talk me into anything. She had been coming into my room regularly for the past four days, hanging up my clothes, washing out my underwear, washing Emma's dresses, doing everything she could for me, and, at the same time, complaining that she was just a slave. "That's all I'm good for," she kept saying, "taking care of kids and doing laundry."

I relented. She completely overpowered me. Now that I was high she wouldn't let me go for a walk alone. "Why?" she bored into me, "why do you want to go off alone, by yourself? Don't you like us? I don't understand." I bowed to her demands on me. I didn't have the strength to resist her. My skin was beginning to feel as though it was caked with dried egg-white again. I could feel all my aches and pains. We all took a walk together.

We were making our way to the Catalina Inn swimming pool by way of the edge of the beach. Throwing shadows from the huerta along our right were banana, lime, coconut, and bamboo trees, mangos, ciruelas (plums), bougainvillea, and *vela de noce* (like jasmine). Through the foliage further down the beach, the native-owned hotel squatted, its 1930s socialist architecture a bizarre note against the straw *palapyas* and exotic fruits. Roberta pointed out a huge Banyon tree and told us that an Italian sailor had seduced her under it while she was on acid, that the experience had been cosmic, and that she was sure she was pregnant. Where was the Roberta of yesteryear, I was asking myself; where was the middle-class make-up expert? How had Rayanne Quackenbush gotten into the body of Roberta Haussman?

At the edge of the lawn of the mayor's house the children stopped, transfixed by the water spigots poking up out of the green grass. They all raced to the nearest spigot, Emma insisting that I turn it on. I turned it on and sat down on the grass, waiting for them to finish playing in the water.

Roberta's face hardened and turned to stone, only her eyes alive, dark brown and accusing. "Hurry up!" she demanded. "Let's go! I want to get to the pool!"

"You go," I told her, "and we'll meet you there. I'll stay here and watch the children."

"No!" She was adamant. The entourage had to proceed together or not at all.

"How do you feel?" she asked me, peering into my face. "Are you high?"

"Not really."

"Let's take some more then, I could take some more. Ingrid, go back to the house and get some more of that blotter." Ingrid trotted obediently away.

"I don't want any more," I told Roberta, "really!"

"Oh, come on! We just took a teeny bit. I don't feel it at all. Come on, take some more."

"I know, I'm sure I've had enough. It takes longer than this to start working. You don't know, you've never seen me on acid; I can have some real bummers!"

"But you just told me that you don't feel high; don't you want to get high? What's the matter? Don't you want to have fun? You think I'm going to put you on a bummer? Me? I love you; I just want you to relax!"

Ingrid returned with some more. I let Roberta put it on my tongue. She did it like a priest, giving out communion.

A strange communion. We're at the swimming pool, a manmade stone grotto, with a waterfall, an underwater passage, a Japanese house hanging over one end used for changing and eating, and all kinds of ferns, flowers, and trees. Emma just took a shit near the pool and I scooped it up with a banana leaf, hiding it under a mango tree, with one of the caretakers watching me from behind a fence. There's a life ring floating in the pool and I'm waiting for Emma to tell me that she wants to jump into it.

"Mama, see?" She's pointing to it, wanting to jump in. I put her in and leave her there, alone, floating without me. This is the first time she's done that since arriving here. In La Jolla she always wanted to jump into the deep end of the pool and I slapped her once, hard, on the bottom, making her cry, to discourage her. I knew then that I was doing the wrong thing; that she would end up afraid of water, and I was right. I tried to reverse myself then, by making her swim underwater. I would toss her up in the air a few times, catching her before she went under, and then after about five tosses I would tell her, "Now I'm going to let you go!" and I would let her go, underwater, going under with her, my eyes open, watching her, her eyes bugged out, terrified, her mouth closed tight, frantically swimming toward me. I knew that that was a mistake too.

She's very happy now, floating around by herself. She seems to have forgotten the days of La Jolla.

Ingrid is jumping in and out of the water at the shallow end, leaping up and down like a porpoise, or, depending on your point of view, a Greek goddess; the clear water streaming off her white-blond head, down her pink and white face, over her full, carved lips, over her tiny breasts. Her face is completely transparent, like a fine crystal goblet filled with nothing, sitting in the sun, sparkling. I'm stunned by her beauty and can't take my eyes off her.

By the side of the pool Roberta is sitting cross-legged, taking a wet bathing suit off of Noonoo. Roberta's belly juts out a little, and, combined with her long frizzy ash-blond hair and her dark, tanned skin, she looks like a Bulgarian peasant woman, slightly wizened, haggard, and tired. She's acting the part, constantly wringing out clothes, picking things up, putting them down, taking a child, letting it go, always busy, a worried frown on her face. Her damp ash-blond hair is hanging down on either side, over her bikini top. ("I stopped straightening my hair, finally," she said to me the other day, "but do you know that it won't grow any longer than this?")

"You look very tired, Roberta," I'm telling her. "Why don't you take a vacation away from the kids?"

She looks up at me, anger beginning to dawn in her face. "Do you really think I look tired?"

I'm sure she's angry because she can see in my face that I'm now looking at her as I would look at a statue, dispassionately, freed at last from her influence. She can't make me do anything more; I think she looks rather mad, as though she's about to have a nervous breakdown. The children are clinging to her while Ingrid frolics in the pool, unaware of her charges.

"Yes," I'm telling her, "I do."

"Well, I guess I am."

"You should get away."

"You don't look tired at all," Roberta states flatly, accusingly. "You look great!"

"I was very tired for six months, or nine months, I can't remember now," I tell her, guilty that I'm not suffering as much. I don't want her to be envious of me, I hate that. I would say anything to avoid it. When Emma was born, a woman who lived next door to us in the hotel, a woman from Curaçao with two children, girls, had given me a large, shiny, mahogany-colored bean.

"This is for Emma," she had told me. "It's to ward off evil spirits. She's such a beautiful child that people will keep telling you how beautiful she is and that's very bad luck for her. She should wear this all the time. In fact, you should put it under her mattress right now."

"Do I look really bad to you?" Roberta asks again.

"Not bad, Roberta, just tired."

We're on the path leading to the beach. Emma stops, so I stop, kneeling down beside her. She is smiling at me, her blue eyes enormous, her face transparent, her mouth in a huge grin, ear to ear, all six and a half teeth showing. There seems to be some secret hidden there, behind her eyes, hidden only because she can't really talk yet. I think the secret is that she knows everything already.

The love she is giving me, her eyes unwavering from mine, not blinking, is so intense and so beautiful that it scares me. The response welling up in me can't possibly match what she is giving out. We're still on the path, staring at each other. I'm afraid that if I could match her love it would kill me; I would be obliterated by feeling. She looks like a little goddess to me, a Buddha. Finally I snatch her up in my arms, to break the moment, and carry her to the beach.

She wants to go into the ocean. The sun is setting and the water is mauve, purple, pink, and violet. The surface looks like satin. We go in together, Emma wearing her water wings. I'm waiting for her to tell me she wants to get rid of them. I've acquired a perfect psychic communication with her mind.

"Mama, mama, off!" Emma is telling me, pulling on the wings. I take them off, not surprised that everything is running according to schedule, and throw them up onto the beach. Now I'm waiting for her to swim, unaided, without the wings. I put my hands under her arms and let go. She begins treading water, for the first time, uninstructed, laughing that beautiful husky laugh, deep in her throat. We tread water together, me pulling up my knees in water that is breast-deep, and telling her, "Good, Emma, great! Wonderful! You're treading water!" Then she begins to look blue to me; I can see all the veins under her skin (*"You kids are turning blue! Come on, out of the water! You're getting cold!"*) I hear a voice from my past, my mother's, telling my brothers and sisters and me to come ashore.

Afraid that she's getting cold I pull her out of the water and then, on the beach, I regret it. I probably could have taught her the doggy paddle at least, back there in the warm, satin, violet water.

Now we're at the clothesline back at the house. Emma's playing in the woodpile (scorpions!) while I hang up some clothes I've just washed. A window opens and Marian's head appears.

"How are you?" she's asking me.

"Me? I'm fine."

"Can I do anything for you?"

"Yes. I'm going to leave tomorrow at seven in the morning on the hydroplane. Will you make sure I get on that plane? Will you help me?"

"Of course I'll help you. But what's stopping you?" Marian laughs. "Gremlins?"

"Yes. Gremlins." I put my fingers on my lips, motioning for her to whisper. She comes out of the house, to the clothesline, an amused smile on her lips.

"What's the matter?"

"Come with me," I whisper, "we'll take a walk through the huerta and I'll tell you."

Emma was half asleep in my arms, sucking on my tit, as Marian and I walked through the dripping foliage. When we reached the giant bamboo tree Emma woke up, disturbed by its creaking, and said, "No, no, no, the tree!" (She'd been afraid of that tree from the first day; it sounded like twenty old rocking chairs, creaking in unison.) I told her it wasn't anything, just a tree. "Look." I pointed upward. "The branches are just moving in the wind, making that noise. It's like a rocking chair."

"Oh," said Emma, satisfied, and closed her eyes again, her mouth resuming its rhythmic sucking.

"Roberta," I told Marian, "she's been preventing me from leaving for the past five days. She wants me to stay here with her after you leave. You can't imagine how many reservations I've made and broken on that plane. I'm afraid I won't make it tomorrow and I really want to go home."

"What's the matter, Augustine? Are you afraid of her?"

"Yes."

"So am I."

"You invited me for a week and I've been here ten days."

"I know. That's okay. I enjoy having you; I didn't ask you to leave, but I'd really like to finish packing and get out of here. I'd really appreciate your leaving tomorrow."

"I feel sorry for Roberta, without a husband."

"Do you think she's flipping out?"

"Yes. Don't you?"

"Yes."

"We should help her then," I said, my eyes filling with tears. "What if it were me flipping out or you flipping out? Wouldn't we want to know that we could rely on each other?" I realized that I was beginning to sound maudlin.

"I have my own family to worry about," Marian stated flatly, "that's all I care about. Myself and my children." That ended that. I decided to change the subject.

"Why did you invite so many people when you're in the midst of packing and leaving?"

"I don't know. I just don't know."

"Maybe subconsciously you knew it would take your mind off the fact that you're leaving. After all, you've been here for five years, and now, with Brian dead and all, it must not be easy, to just pack up five years of your life and go someplace else."

"I know. I guess that's why I did it. I know that you and Roberta have been saying terrible things about me whenever I've turned my back," Marian continued in a surprisingly matter-of-fact voice that was just barely tinged with a certain force, as though she had to make herself do it. She sounded a lot the way my mother used to sound when reproaching my sisters and me for something similar. "But, I don't care. I want you to know that. I don't care."

"Yes," I confessed, "it's true. We have been saying terrible things about you."

"She's only staying here, you know, because you're staying. If you weren't here she'd never be able to stand it, with nobody else speaking to her."

"I know, I know, I promise I'll leave tomorrow morning."

When would I become an adult, I was wondering, and no longer get into these adolescent patterns of behavior? At least I was able to iron things out with Marian, but now I wouldn't be able to look Roberta in the face.

Whenever I left Frederick's side I got much worse. One of the reasons I fell in love with him and wanted to marry him was because his ideas sounded better to me than my own. I had always assimilated the ideas of whatever man I was with; and having made it a habit, I gradually came to regard my own ideas as only something to use when there weren't any others around. In other words, my brain was like a sponge, and in the absence of its current source of nourishment, my husband, the liquor it was lapping up was the heady mixture of those three wealthy jewesses, Roberta, Lydia, and Marian. At least when I was with my husband there was only one coffer of ideas to contend with; his.

I had thought that once you had children of your own you became an adult; that childbirth was like a primitive initiation rite; as soon as the baby was born you were mature, responsible, and wise. It had never occurred to me to examine the parents I knew—my own, for example.

In the dim light I could see all the lines grooved into Marian's tanned complexion, lines I had never seen before. Dark shadows were under her eyes and her neck was strained, the tendons sticking out, the skin around them like parchment, fine lines crisscrossing back and forth. I must look the same way, I thought.

"You look like hell," I told her.

"I feel like hell," she said, "but you; you look great."

"You must be exhausted."

"I am exhausted. And you're right. All of you being here, even with the fights and all, all of you have taken my mind off everything. I'm glad you came. But listen, Augustine, tell me something. How well did you know Roberta, ten years ago?"

"Not very well. She was working for a boyfriend of mine and she never liked me. I always used to have the feeling that she was in love with him herself and she resented me. We took a trip together, some job for some magazine, and she wanted me to sleep in another room. She said that it didn't look good to the hotel, that we were sleeping together and we weren't married."

"So, I'm more of a friend to you than she is."

"Yes. That's right. You were always more of a friend."

"What happened?"

"I don't know. I guess she's been manipulating me. That's the trouble with me. I need Frederick around to prevent me from going on someone else's trip. No matter what anybody said about him, not making money, he always saved me from myself. If I were with him this never would have happened. I think I'm missing something in my brain," I told Marian, "I'm so easily influenced."

"I'm the same way," Marian confided. "Brian, no matter how much of a hustler he was, always protected me. I always knew that I could never get into any serious trouble as long as he was around. I think that that's the best thing about men, the good ones, the ones that need women. They have a sort of balance about them that we lack, women like us. And that's what's wrong with Roberta. She needs Bill, that son-of-a-bitch. When you have little children and triplets at that . . . god . . . , you really need their fathers around. I mean, the kind of man who will give you a child and then stay with you and help you bring up the child isn't so bad."

"Look, look at Emma; doesn't she look blue to you?"

"She looks very happy and content."

"Not blue to you?"

172 "Well, she's very white. She doesn't have a tan, that's all. You're used to looking at the other kids, who've been here for a while."

"Maybe she looks blue to me because I'm on acid, but maybe she's cold; I'm not sure.

"You're on acid?"

"Yes, Roberta shoved it down my throat."

"We all took it then. *We* took it on the boat. My god, we're all on acid!"

> Real living is having friends that have acquired a reasonable intellectual attainment who like to fraternize with you and who you like to fraternize with and who speak highly of you and of whom you are able to speak highly and to enjoy the many things that raw nature offers.
>
> AUGUSTINE'S FATHER, MARCH 1972

Marian had telephoned me, before we left for Morocco, to tell me that Brian was dying, and would we come to the hospital, he wanted to see us.

Once we got there, she took me out into the hallway, grasped me by the arm, and told me that she couldn't stand it any longer.

"Brian has had a mistress since before he married me," she said. "This is the first I've known about it. Her parents threatened to cut her off if she married him so he married me for my money. When my father died and didn't leave me as much money as I thought he would, our marriage came to an end, virtually. He stayed more and more in New York with her, leaving me and the children in Mexico. I still didn't know. I thought they were friends. When I voiced my suspicions he told me that I was crazy, that he had been friends with her for ten years, and I was just a jealous, possessive woman. I went to England to find a nanny once, and when I came back Teddy told me that his father and Barbara Mierson both slept in my bed. When I asked Brian about it he told me that I was paranoid, that of course Barbara used to come into our room in the mornings and rap with him, sitting on the bed. She had come to Mexico while I was gone and I didn't think anything of it, because she often came down to visit us."

"Are you sure that they're lovers?"

"Sure? You're damn right I'm sure."

"But I've known Brian and Barbara longer even than I've known you and I've never heard a word about them being lovers."

"Then you and I were the only ones that didn't know. Harriet knew. She told me that she knew. And do you know who else told me?"

"Who?"

"Barbara herself. When I got the call to come to New York he was in her apartment. Later, here in the hospital, she told me how much she loved him and said that she hoped I wouldn't mind if she stayed in the room with me during the day. Can you imagine that? And on top of everything else I've got the children here, in our old apartment. I thought their father should see them again if he's going to die. I'm exhausted. I think I'm going crazy."

"*I walked down the beach once, with Brian, before he got sick,*" Roberta told me later, "*and he said he had a big decision to make. Should he stay with Marian for five million dollars, or leave her for Barbara, for twenty-five million dollars?*"

Back in the room, filled with holly and Christmas decorations, Brian asked Marian to call her uncle's restaurant and order pheasant under glass, wild rice, and *marrons glacés* for dinner. Marian didn't want to do it.

"Come on, Marian," I said, "I'll go to the phone with you."

We passed rows of rooms, filled with cancer patients, some nearly dead, others sitting up, talking with relatives, and, in front of the public telephone booth Marian told me that Brian refused any food that didn't come from her uncle's restaurant.

"He's just doing that to humiliate me," she insisted. "My family is furious, of course, now that they know about Barbara. He'll starve himself to death if I don't order food from *Le chat qui pêche*.

"He's dying anyway," I told her. "You might as well give him what he wants."

"All right, I'll do it if you and Frederick stay for dinner. Do you like pheasant under glass?"

The thought of pheasant, wild rice, and *marrons glacés* was making my mouth water and I knew that *marrons glacés* was Frederick's favorite dish, so I persuaded Marian to call the restaurant. Actually, I believed that Brian deserved to starve to death.

Now, a couple of months later, in the huerta under the influence of Roberta's acid-soaked blotter, I began thinking about that pheasant again.

"I'm getting hungry, Marian," I told her. "Let's go back to the house."

"What about Roberta?"

"Do you think you can handle her? Because I can't."

"Don't worry," Marian reassured me, "I'll protect you. At least Bonnie isn't on acid. She's the only straight one in the house. Maybe I can get her to make some dinner. Anyway, she can keep an eye on the children."

Marian led me back down the dirt path, back under the creaking bamboo tree, into the house. One of the Englishmen was making tea. Jason Price was his name, and he was the editor of *The Yellow Brick Road,* a semi-underground newspaper based in London. He had set the tea things out on the big table in the main room, the table where Roberta's children ate their pancakes every morning at sunrise. Now candles were lighting the room, music was playing, and the aroma of English tea filled the house. The English contingent seemed to be taking over.

Jason poured me a cup, asking, "How many sugars do you take?" just as Roberta walked in to announce that Bonnie was having a wonderful time; she had just taken acid for the first time in her life and she was out there, on the beach, communing with the moon.

"Who gave her the acid?" Marian demanded, her eyes blazing with fury.

"I did, why?" Roberta pretended to be puzzled.

"Why?" Marian screamed, "why? Because she was the only straight one in the house, that's why! And we have seven children under this roof all under five years old! I just can't believe that you gave her acid," she finished helplessly.

Roberta's eyes widened in surprised innocence. "I just thought that Bonnie should enjoy herself too. Everybody else is; why shouldn't she? She works hard."

As soon as I got over the shock that Roberta thought we were all having a good time I realized that she was playing the role of righteous benefactress to the core, and doing a good job of it besides. No matter what I thought, however, I wasn't going to be spared by my former mentor.

"And what's wrong with you?" Roberta burst out at me. "You look a little weird."

"I have a backache," I told her, "and I feel awful."

Roberta stepped right back into her role, as though she hadn't missed a beat, to ask me if there wasn't anything she could do for me.

"You've done enough for me. I don't want you to do any more for me," I told her, looking levelly at her, making it clear that my response wasn't dictated by social politeness, but by necessity. I wanted her to know that I meant it.

Marian, who had collapsed into a chair on the news of Bonnie's capitulation and was drinking her tea, listening to Roberta and me, roused herself enough to offer me a backrub in my room. Gregory, looking sad, trailed behind us.

I tried to go limp while Marian's long fingers kneaded my muscles, but, since Gregory kept questioning me about the events of the past week (like Brian before him, he spent most of his time in bed so was ignorant of the politics of the house), my muscles kept tensing up again. While Marian poured out generosity and friendship her lover remained aloof, determined to pinpoint the person or persons on which the blame could be fixed. For the first time I missed Brian. Brain would have laughed and scoffed at the quarrel; no, that's wrong—the quarrel never would have begun had Brian been there in the first place.

Roberta walked into my room, breaking off the interrogation to demand what was going on. She said she felt there was a conspiracy against her. Ridden with guilt, I told her that I was just tired. Would this never end?

Back at the main house, my digestive juices still working on the blotter, I found myself in the bathtub, drinking a rum and ciruela punch; apparently I had persuaded Jason Price to go to the bar for me. Ingrid was extolling the merits of *Dr. Bronner's Peppermint Soap,* a thick amber liquid that came in a plastic bottle whose label was covered with biblical quotations—all meant to convince the buyer that *Dr. Bronner's* is the path to salvation.

"Douche with it," she said, "you'll really love it; it feels so good!"

I rubbed it between my legs and the burning sensation was so strong that I began howling with pain. For a moment I thought Ingrid had done it on purpose. "Oh my god, I'm sorry," she apologized, "you must be very sensitive down there. It really feels good when I do it."

Suddenly the bathroom filled with people, all of them advising me on how to get rid of the burning. "Turn on the cold water tap and lift yourself up under it," counseled Jason Price. "No, not cold, lukewarm, here, I'll get the right temperature for you." He fiddled with the faucets while I elevated my pelvis to within a couple of inches of the spigot. Teddy walked in.

"Why are you leaving tomorrow?" he wanted to know, his blue eyes solemn, staring into mine. With his tanned skin and his curly blond hair he looked like a painting from either the Sistine Chapel or Sidney Renard's office ceiling. While the water cooled off my burning crotch I told him that Emma missed her father. His face fell, he looked as though he was about to cry. I realized my mistake; he was thinking about Brian. Before I could say anything else he fled from the bathroom. I suddenly remembered Emma, and my sense of time was still so fragmented, situations and scenes having taken on such a kaleidoscopic air, the house and the people in it becoming so surreal, that I was worried. "Where is Emma?" I asked Ingrid. "Is she still asleep?"

"Don't worry, Augustine, she's with the other kids in my room," Ingrid told me. "She's sound asleep." I put a towel around me and ran into Ingrid's room anyway. There she was, naked on the bed, sleeping peacefully. I got back into the tub.

"Don't worry about your daughter," Jason said, "we're all parents; nobody will let anything happen. If she wakes up someone will go and get her. Come back downstairs and have some dinner."

I lounged in the hot water a little longer; everything seemed resolved in a mellow glow. I finally knew what real living was—to have friends with whom I could trust my children.

CHAPTER XIV

Weaning I

> The first intimations of nonbeing may have been the breast or
> mother as absent. This seems to have been Freud's suggestion.
> Winnicott writes of "the hole," the creation of nothing by devouring
> the breast. Bion relates the origin of thought to the experience of
> no breast. The Human Being, in Sartre's idiom, does not create being
> but rather injects nonbeing into the world, into an original plenitude
> of being.
>
> R. D. LAING, *The Politics of Experience*

"This will make him come back!" Harriet shouted gleefully, as the
Polaroid picture popped out of the new SX-70. I looked at it. It was a
photograph of a glamorous woman, wearing a pink French tee-shirt that
was clinging to very large breasts. It was a photograph of me. I hadn't
nursed Emma for five days and nights. Once again, back at the Metro
Hotel, without money, without Frederick, I had become the passive, helpless, easily manipulated woman that was, I believed, the darker side of my
nature. I had fallen totally under the influence of Harriet Vanderlip, wasp
daughter of the military-industrial complex, having left behind, in Mexico,
that trio of warring jewesses.

Harriet, horrified to find that Emma was still sucking tit at fifteen and a half months—that I hadn't succeeded in weaning her in La Jolla, even with the help of Deedee and Lydia—had decided that she was going to do it herself.

"I'll come over here every night and sing her to sleep if you promise not to nurse her during the day." Harriet glared at me, almost defiant, daring me to break the rule. She pushed back the strand of brown hair that was constantly flopping into her left eye, dug into one of the voluminous leather bags she always carried with her, full of notes, photographs, tape recorders, and pills, and finally found what she was looking for—a rubber band.

"The coated ones are the best," she declared for the hundredth time, "they don't tear your hair!" Then she gathered up all the hair on top of her head, save for some short wispy bangs, and fastened the clump with the coated rubber band so that she looked like a fat Yorkshire terrier that had been groomed by a 1960s fashion model.

"Silent Night" was Emma's favorite lullaby. Harriet had taught her to love it.

"Listen, Emma darling," she said to my daughter, "I'm going to show you what I made for you today." Digging again into her satchel Harriet pulled out a cassette. She popped it into her Sony pocket recorder and, with a witchlike grin, pressed the "on" button. "Siiiii-alent, night . . . hoo . . . oly night . . . all is calm . . . all is bright . . ." It was Harriet's voice, singing, unaccompanied by any musical instrument. "See, I mean hear? Do you hear that, Emma? Now, I'm going to show you how to press the button and when you wake up in the night you can play it; it'll be just as though I were here beside you."

Gunter von Habsburg invited me to the screening of his rather brilliant movie. He had cast himself as the put-upon lover. Throughout the film Marie-Claude screamed and screamed at him—insulting him, abusing him, betraying him; it seemed that she truly hated him. Elkse Boserup had the last scene. She sat against the wall of a supermarket, smiling enigmatically at him. It was the kind of a smile that a woman can give only to a man she doesn't know; one to whom she's attracted but with whom she has never lived, hardly knows, but wants to attract. After living with the man to whom she has given this smile, after absorbing the insults, insecurities, uncertainties, arguments, disappointments, and, often, the blows, it is usually impossible to repeat the smile; those parts of the brain having been deadened to that particular man, the smile is waiting for a new object. Sometimes, often with the type of drugs that make it possible for the brain to forget, the smile returns again for its original object. This is an occasion to be grasped, and to be used intelligently by the woman.

After the smile the couple took a trip to an Indian pueblo in Taos. My interpretation of the scene was that, in the mind of Gunter von Habsburg, Elkse understood the Indian ruins, whereas Marie-Claude would have preferred to spend the time shopping for antique clothes.

Gunter's former psychiatrist was there at the screening—a woman doctor. His parents had sent him to her for treatment while he was between the ages of five and fourteen, five days a week, every week of the year, save for the times they took him to the ancestral German castle or down to Vero Beach. I supposed, since they were so rich, they figured they owed it to him. His mother, a very beautiful woman, had been converted to Catholicism, Freudianism, and modern art—in that order—during her marriage to Gunter's father. She was a world-renowned art collector, the benefactress of a Jesuit university in Miami, and the patron of many modern artists. She and her husband made it a practice to have their only son followed, wherever he went, to be sure that he wasn't spending the family fortune unwisely and also to be on hand should he suffer one of his "attacks."

"What are these attacks?" I asked a member of the family one day when she told me about the detective.

"Oh," she replied, "he goes crazy sometimes. We think he's a schizophrenic. He smashes walls, paintings, anything in the room. He has a regular fit."

"Is that all?"

"Well, my dear," she said, surprised, "isn't that enough?"

"If Gunter is schizophrenic, then I'm schizophrenic as well. I saw him do that once, when I was pregnant with Emma. I was staying at his brownstone and he got mad at Marie-Claude and he kicked a hole in a wall and smashed a priceless painting (probably a milestone in modern art). I didn't think that was so crazy. I've done much worse. I've caused much more damage in my own house, and I'm not even rich!"

"You don't think that's the product of an unbalanced mind?"

"No, just the opposite. I think that he exercised a lot of restraint, limiting his kicks to the wall and a painting when he really wanted to be kicking Marie-Claude. I only wish that the heads of governments had the same instincts."

"Well," she sighed, "maybe you're right; but he's caused his parents a lot of worry."

"Think of the worry he would have caused had he murdered someone. My only regret is that when I used to kick something in my parents' house, they didn't send me to a nice lady psychiatrist but, instead, beat the shit out of me!"

The nice lady psychiatrist seemed to be more beloved by Gunter than his own mother was. After the screening she told him that she would talk to him about the movie, "later." I felt rebuffed; I thought that Gunter should have said to her, "Oh, you can talk in front of Augustine; we're good friends; I don't have to hide anything from her."

Just to hear her talk, to see what she was like, I decided to ask her a question.

"My baby wakes up about ten times a night to be nursed," I told her. "What shall I do?"

"How old is she?"

"Sixteen months."

The doctor looked at me strangely. "Why don't you try rubbing her back instead?" she suggested. "All she wants is attention."

I wondered if she had ever given that advice to Gunter's mother.

"Cold turkey!" Dr. Fabin had told me when I complained about the pain in my breasts, "cold turkey . . . that's the only way to do it. Don't even *touch* your nipples!" When I told him that I couldn't stand it he gave me a prescription for Fiorinal, the aspirin and codeine combination that was my mother's favorite headache remedy—that is, since its invention. In the old days I remember "lying down" with her (*"let's lie down on my bed"*) on her double bed, under the covers, the eggshell-colored shades drawn against the late afternoon sun, both of us having taken a couple of Bayer aspirin for our recurrent headaches.

The third day was unbearable. My entire chest was in a steel vise, rhythmic waves of pain pounding against my ribs, drowning out the sound of my heartbeat. At two in the morning I telephoned Emma's pediatrician, Mario de Bomarzo, a cousin of my Uruguayan brother-in-law, Eduardo de Bomarzo. Their name, Bomarzo, came from Italy where the family, centuries ago, founded a village a hundred miles or so east of Rome, noted for its terraced garden built in the fifteenth century and filled with pornographic giant-sized stone sculptures carved by a Turk. The descendants of the original Bomarzos, four centuries later, were responsible for destroying most of the sculptures on the grounds that these works of art were fashioned by the devil. Frederick had used this garden in 1971 as a location for his movie *Cleopatra*; luckily several of the sculptures remained standing, though only few could still be classified as pornography.

Mario, unlike my progressive pro-Lamaze obstetrician, was a real old-guard, pro-AMA doctor. His second wife, a shy, virginal, fellow-Uruguayan, was going to give birth under drugs, since, Mario explained, it was her first time, and she was frightened. I had tried to convince her to do it without drugs, but both she and her doctor-husband had remained adamant. She was also going to bottle-feed her baby, and when she and Mario came to see me at the Metro Hotel just before we left for Morocco, to pick up Emma's old outgrown baby equipment, I had secreted among the baby clothes the La Leche handbook on breastfeeding. During that visit Mario had picked up Emma, tossing her into the air, and saying to her, "When are you going to stop nursing? You're going to ruin your mother's breasts!"

Later, after I left Morocco, I had taken Emma to his office, in Roosevelt Hospital, for another anti-measles shot. When we reached the hospital entrance, Emma threw herself down on the welcome mat and had a tantrum, refusing to go a step farther, apparently recognizing the building where she had undergone such torture in the name of disease prevention.

I picked her up off the welcome mat and once I had her inside the building and in his office, she settled down on my lap and reached her hand inside my tee-shirt to fondle my nipples. He stared at us for a while and finally burst out. "Obscene! That's what it is, obscene!"

Apparently this was a novel sight to him. I wondered if he had ever witnessed the peasant women of his homeland, nursing their toddlers (and their pigs, for that matter), or if they, like the French peasants, had given up this age-old custom and were firmly entrenched in the American bottle syndrome. Even the Moroccans had succumbed, it seemed, for, one day, having gone to a Berber house to buy kif, one of the mothers had led me down into her dank living quarters to show me her two-week-old baby. The infant's body was tightly wrapped in crisscrossed swaddling garments, a modern baby Jesus, and its head, like the heads of the drugged cobras that the magicians wrap around the necks of camera-wielding tourists, was the only thing that moved. It could also be likened to the toys that the sidewalk tradesmen sell on Times Square, those papier-mâché animals whose heads are the only things that move, being connected to their bodies with a device that sways with the air currents.

"Look!" she said to me, pointing to her bound breasts, "no more!" Then she held up a milk-encrusted bottle, grinned madly, and shoved it into the mouth of her babe in swaddling clothes (the swaddling, being the worst custom, was, predictably, the only one to survive). With sign language (being a woman and poor, she was uneducated and therefore spoke only Arabic) she made me understand that she had already borne several children and was only too happy to at last dispense with suckling.

Anyway, Mario, my reactionary Uruguayan pediatrician, was the only one to give me sound advice. (Albeit the soundest advice would have been to let her suck for another two years; the most "advanced" theories being that the human infant needs at least three years of breastfeeding.)

"Pump the milk out immediately," he told me, "or you'll have a terrible abscess!" Cursing my progressive Lamaze obstetrician, I went into the bathroom and took the breast pump out of the medicine chest (the beautiful glass pump made in France). It took me an hour to pump out enough milk to make the pain at least bearable. Then I swallowed two more Fiorinals, even though they made me sick to my stomach, being too exhausted and sore of nipple to continue with the pump, and went back to bed.

The next day was, again, sheer hell. My nipples felt as though they were thrusting out and down, begging for Emma's mouth. Or they felt as though they were penises, longing for a vagina to enter. Since I had been wondering what it would feel like to actually have a penis, thinking that I would like to step into a man's shoes for a day or so and try it out, I now felt as though I knew all about it, thanks to my nipples, overburdened

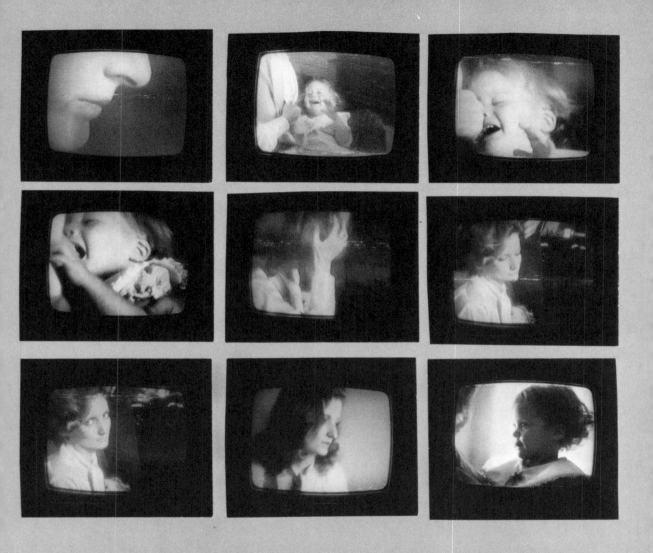

Emma looked longingly at the breast nearest her head and burst into tears. I felt like a ridiculous fool. There seemed to be no reason at all to wean her. . . . I decided to keep this defection a secret from Harriet.

as they were with a surplus of milk, just as a penis must from time to time be overburdened with too much sperm.

Big drops of milk were seeping out and soaking my white satin blouse, like a leaking septic tank. Emma looked longingly at the breast nearest her head and burst into tears. I felt like a ridiculous fool. There seemed to be no reason at all to wean her; why was I insisting? What if I never had another child and would never again experience a baby sucking milk at my breast? The thought was too tragic to bear; even more tragic than the fact of Emma's suffering. Knowing that about myself, that I was more concerned about the experience ending for me than for the baby, I felt guilty and selfish on top of everything else.

Now my breasts were burning with pain. The milk was pressing against every square inch of the upper portion of my chest. I thought I would die with pain. I lifted my blouse and raised Emma's head to my breast. She fixed her beautiful rose-colored lips to my rose-colored nipple like a clamp and drained out the pain. I decided to keep this defection a secret from Harriet.

That night she nursed twice again, tricking me into thinking she needed it to get to sleep. After the second session, just as I thought she would slumber off, she jumped up, full of energy, grabbed one of her plastic books, and tried to get me to read to her. I threw the book on the floor, exhausted, so she toddled into the kitchen where Harriet was foraging madly through the cupboards looking for something to eat. (I had taken advantage of her obsession with food to do the nursing, praying that she wouldn't walk into the bedroom and discover me. From time to time she would call out, "What are you doing in there?" "Just rubbing Emma's back," I would reply.)

After Harriet read the book to her Emma insisted on taking a bath with me. We spent an hour in the tub while she washed her hair three times and dental-flossed her eight teeth over and over again until she lost the container in the bottom of the tub. Laughing uproariously, she kept touching my nipples, saying, "Mama, mama." She went from one nipple to the other, seeming to discover that there were two for the first time. Finally she settled on naming the left nipple "Mama" and the right one "Nana." I tried to tell her that she was too big for that now, but she pretended not to understand, a sly grin on her face the whole time I explained the situation. I was dropping with fatigue and she was as fresh as a daisy. She lost the bathtub plug she had been playing with finally, and I thought, "At last; she'll give up the ghost and go to sleep," but then she found the extra plug and by the time she made me put it on her finger, as a ring, her eyes were practically closed with exhaustion.

She wouldn't let me dry her. The minute the towel touched her head she started whining. Usually, when she was that tired, I would give her a bath to tire her out even more and after it she would sink happily into the folds of a clean towel, curl up next to me on the bed, and, sucking on my tit, fall almost instantly to sleep. But this time she reacted to the touch of the towel as I had reacted to the touch of Frederick's hand on my brow while in labor. Why should she have been any different than me? Why couldn't a baby be irritable, just like an adult? At the time, however, I was too exhausted to reason, so I brought her to my bed and tried to give her a bottle instead of my breast; after all, she had already nursed for a good hour.

She threw the bottle on the floor, screaming, furious at me for presenting it to her. (Doctor Spock always calls it "presenting" the bottle.) I tried to diaper her and put a nightgown on her but she utterly refused to cooperate, screaming all the time and twisting away from me. I kept saying to her, "No more milk, Emma. Mama's breasts are empty . . . twice already . . . I'm tired, honey . . . I want to go to sleep." She took the bottle and stopped crying. Seemingly insatiable, she made incredibly loud slurping, gulping, sucking noises while I put my head down in my arms and collapsed on the bed

Thinking that she was concentrating on the bottle, I made the mistake of trying to diaper her after six ounces or so were gone. The screams started again.

If a baby is frustrated (and all babies are frustrated many times every day in the course of the usual handling) he will discharge the frustration and get it out of his system if he is allowed to do so. If someone will really listen he will discharge in what is usually condemned in our culture under the name of "tantrum." He will make violent physical movements and angry noises and will perspire from a warm skin. This is exactly what he needs to do.

HARVEY JENKINS, *The Human Side of Human Beings,*
the theory of re-evaluation counseling

I shrieked as loud as I could at her, "You stop crying this instant! I can't stand it!" My face trembling from the exertion of shouting, I ran into the living room and threw myself down on the couch. Not another sound from the bedroom.

Ten minutes later I went in and found her in the same position I had left her in. Her head on the pillow, she was lying on her back naked and asleep. I dressed her in her nightgown, kissed her lips, whispering, "I love you," and I thought she moved her lips a little against mine as I said that.

In the middle of the night I was actually hoping that she would wake up so I could take her in bed with me and make up for the terrible way I had screamed at her just before she fell asleep.

CHAPTER XV

*ADC**

* Government terminology for Welfare, meaning Aid to Families with
Dependent Children

Harriet decided that the only thing I could do to solve my desperate
financial situation was to ask Gunter for some money. It was either that
or Welfare, she told me, and I didn't want to go on Welfare, did I?

She settled her three hundred pounds down on the floor, gathered
her hair into a rubber band ("doesn't this look better?"), and dialed his
number.

"Shhh," she cautioned me, "I don't want him to know I'm over
here."

"Listen, Gunter, Augustine is desperate. She doesn't have a cent and
the baby needs food. . . . Yes, Frederick is still in Morocco. . . . No, if you
had produced that last idea of his. . . . I know you paid for a lot of tapes
but . . . yes, he wanted to make a movie out of them, you know that. . . .
No, I'm not casting judgment on you, I'm just worried about the baby. . . .
Do you want her to go on Welfare? . . . She doesn't know I'm asking you,

I'm at my hotel, I've just hung up the phone on her. . . . I promised I wouldn't ask you. . . . Listen, I'll play that part you wanted me for . . . the whore . . . if you loan her two hundred dollars. . . ."

Gunter agreed to give her the money. She took a taxi uptown and returned with the check. I put Emma in her portable Japanese stroller, the kind that folds up like an umbrella, and the three of us got into the elevator and headed for the lobby.

While Sidney cashed the check I took a look at Jasper Johns's painting of the American flag. It was badly in need of a cleaning. In the midst of my reverie Sidney informed me that he was subtracting one hundred dollars out of my check for back rent. Then Harriet counted out seventy-five dollars for herself, saying, "You owe me fifty and I need twenty-five to pay my phone bill."

While Sidney dusted off the tops of the television sets that were always lined up there in the lobby, waiting to be rented, I studied the remaining bills in the palm of my hand. Twenty-five dollars. My pent-up fury at my husband (for allowing me to get into this fix), at my landlord, for extracting his tithe, and most of all at Harriet (this wasn't the first time she had tried my patience), exploded in a hypoglycemic, dopamine-ridden rage. I looked at her, my adrenalin boiling to the surface.

"Junkie!" I screamed at her, "you just need the money to buy some more amphetamine! Get out of my sight! Here! Take the other twenty-five too!" I held out my hand, the money still in my palm, offering it to her. She looked at me in horror, and then looked around the lobby to see if anyone else had heard me. Sidney stopped dusting, the feather duster poised in mid-air, to tell me to calm down.

"Shuddup!" I screamed at him, "you slumlord!" Then I threw the twenty-five remaining dollars on the floor in Harriet's direction and started for the street, pushing the stroller in front of me. In the middle of the block, before I even got as far as the drugstore (where I owed a lot of money), I began to cry uncontrollably. I turned around and went back into the hotel, pushing the stroller rapidly toward the elevator where I pressed the button for the ninth floor, sobbing all the while.

Sidney stopped dusting, came over to me, put his arm around my shoulder, and told me that he was a family man too. I cried harder. He led me into his office and through it to the tiny storage room at the rear of the office where he had a little sink, installed there by him for the purposes of taking codeine for his constant headaches and applying cold compresses to his forehead. (*"My wife is worried about me, I've been to six doctors, no one can get rid of my headaches."*) An old pro at this, he soaked the ever-present towel with cold water and put it against my forehead. I decided on hysteria. Crouched on the floor under his sink, sobbing, I watched Emma staring at me from her stroller out in the office underneath the ceiling mural of Roman goddesses and their babies; her eyes, like those of the babies above her, very wide and blue. She wasn't making a sound; she just looked frightened.

Having decided on hysteria, I now found that I couldn't stop crying. I could hear Sidney, back out in his office, with Emma, on the telephone. He was calling Bellevue.

Within minutes both the police and three white-coated men arrived with a stretcher; shoving a piece of paper under my runny nose, they asked me to sign it.

"My father the lawyer," I told them, rapidly drying my tears, "told me never to sign anything without reading it."

While I read the papers I remembered that I had just written a chapter where the heroine is carted off to Bellevue, her child crying in the background. I wondered if I had made it all happen by writing about it before it happened. I refused to go. I told them that I wouldn't sign the paper and that I was all right now.

"We can't take her unless she signs that paper or unless a doctor deems it necessary," one of the attendants told Sidney.

"Who will take care of my baby if I go to the nuthouse"? I asked.

"That's a good question," one of the men replied. "Don't you have any sisters?"

"No," I told them, "I'm an orphan and an only child, and, anyway, I don't see any doctor here, deeming it necessary." They all left, eventually, without me.

"Close youah legs! . . . *Air pollution!*" shrieked the voice that had been blowing smoke in Emma's face as I held her in my arms in the crush of clients waiting to get up to the Welfare Office.

"You! . . . *You!* . . . Youah *Caucasian*, ain't you?" the voice sneered.

"You slut! You white Caucasian slut! Did you hearh what ah said? I said close youah legs! . . . *Air pollution!*"

My companion, Sarafina Brocani, edged up to me, whispering in my ear, "For god's sake, keep your mouth shut! That's a lesbian on methadone! Last week a woman was knifed in here!"

Sarafina volunteered to go to the Welfare Department with me, since she was very familiar with the place, being on Welfare herself as a Permanent Psychiatric Disability Case (APD, or Aid to the Permanently Disabled). Whereas I was applying for local money, she was receiving federal money, and would for the rest of her life, having been judged a permanent psychotic, or, in more precisely clinical terms, a classical schizophrenic. She had already spent a good deal of her life in the wards of Bellevue.

In Punta del Este, where the de Bomarzos spent their summers, Sarafina had been the next-door neighbor of Alexandra's husband, Eduardo. When Sarafina was seven years old her mother left her father there, supposedly sunbathing by the pool, and "ran off" to the United States with her lover, Eduardo's youngest brother, Franco. She left all her children behind except Sarafina, the youngest. Sarafina's oldest sister, Madelaine, resolved the conflicts brought about by her mother's desertion of her by going to Cuba at age eighteen, where, it was whispered by the rest of the family, she not only was without a refrigerator, but also had to cut sugar cane on weekends. Sarafina, on the other hand, had never recovered from being separated from her father and her country. She was subject to visions and sudden inexplicable violence (hypoglycemia? dopamine?) and on her last voyage into inner space had perceived herself as the Holy Ghost.

During the period of her transmutation into the third person of the Holy Trinity, a famous feminist lesbian writer had chronicled the episode (having been with her) in a New York newspaper. Half of the family was shocked that the writer didn't immediately take steps to have Sarafina incarcerated again rather than follow in her footsteps, avidly taking notes, and the other half of the family, being fans of R. D. Laing, considered the episode a laudatory attempt at scientific illumination.

I looked again at the lesbian on methadone; I still thought she was a man. She was tall, thin, and black, leaning against the shoulder of a woman who could have been her twin. She blew some more smoke in our direction. "Mama," Emma whispered, "man blowing 'moke in my eyes."

Actually, I had started the whole commotion, since I had announced a few moments earlier, "Would everyone who is smoking please stop? The air is so close in here, and it's about ninety degrees. My child is choking." That's when the black lesbian on methadone told me to close my legs.

I was there because the dealer's wife on the fifth floor of the Metro Hotel, Camilla Aponte, told me that *she* was on Welfare and since I had a child and no husband I could be on Welfare too. She warned me that it would be humiliating but made me promise to stand up under it.

"They'll probably break you down," she told me. "I don't think you're eligible for Welfare unless you break down and cry. They put me in an isolated room with two guards carrying guns, because I was screaming so much."

A policeman arrived on the elevator when it descended to the main floor, to prod the steerage into some semblance of order. Then an elderly man pulled out his prick and began taking a pee in the corner, the stream of urine pouring into the crack between the elevator floor and the hallway. Another man who was haranguing the crowd about Rockefeller and about how "he don't care about us common folk" was shoved in the ribs with the policeman's nightstick, pushed back a few paces, and allowed to continue his monologue as the urine from the corner trickled around his feet, momentarily deflected from its natural course down the elevator shaft.

The cop stood, arms spread out, guarding the empty elevator. The crowd shoved closer and closer to him until he shouted an order: *"Okay, keep two steps back!"* Finally, after what seemed like ages to the perspiring, cursing crowd, he gave the magic word: "The first twelve people can get on the elevator now . . . STEP BACK . . . TO THE BACK! Okay . . . THAT'S IT!" Then, after pushing the elevator button to close the doors and send it speeding upwards, he resumed his position of guard. Those who were lucky enough to get onto the elevator first, thereby being first in the upstairs offices, were the first ones to be taken care of in the morning; they were given cards with numbers on them, and the earliest arrivals got the lowest numbers. The farther down you were in the line, the higher was your number. Emma, Sarafina, and I were still waiting in front of the elevator, having been neither able nor willing to squeeze our way up to the front next to the urinating welfare recipient, only urinating there because he didn't want to lose his place at the head of the crowd.

Behind me a woman crouched in the corner, a two-year-old girl whining in her arms, a boy about four hanging onto her shoulders, and another of six or so guarding the three ratty-looking suitcases that stood in front of them. The mother had dyed blond hair, a metallic color, with black roots showing; she wore bright-orange lipstick, and her face, though it looked young, was deeply lined with two grooves running from the corners of her nostrils to the lower corners of her mouth.

Sarafina held my hand. A button stamped "Lesbian Power" was pinned to her shirt.

"If you think this is bad," she muttered, "wait'll you see the sixth floor."

"What's on the sixth floor?"

"That's my floor. All the nut cases are up there—and the junkies."

Sarafina had three copies of her autobiographical novel with her as reading matter for me while we waited for my number to come up. She had pledged herself to stand by me throughout the entire ordeal. "It's better to go with somebody who knows the ropes," she told me. "Those caseworkers won't tell you anything."

The elevator came down. All eyes were riveted to the numbers lighting up—6 . . . 5 . . . 4 . . . 3 . . . 2 . . . and, finally, the magic 1! The doors opened. The cop yelled the STEP BACK order. We were the first on the elevator and rushed to the back as he yelled "TO THE BACK! TO THE BACK!" The family of four with their three suitcases were right behind us, the little girl crying. Emma was silent, grabbing me around the neck. I had to ask her to stop choking me, her grip was so tight.

On the third floor a young, beautifully groomed black woman, nails and lips painted a bright red, hair straightened into a page boy, snarled at me: "Whaddaya want?"

"I want to go on Welfare."

"Why?"

"Because I don't have any more money."

"You married?"

"Yes."

"What's yer name?" I told her my name.

"Siddown," she yapped, "until I call yer name."

Sarafina and I settled into a couple of wooden chairs, Emma between us. The walls of the room and the corridors were covered with obscene graffiti. Sarafina pulled out her book and we discussed its merits. I told her I would liked to have edited it.

"Kate Millet told me it's the best thing that's come out of the women's movement," she retorted defensively.

"Oh, shit," I thought, "now I've done it. She's angry at me already and the fact is I love the book!"

"Oh, Sarafina, I agree with her. I think it's the best thing to come out of the women's movement too. It's the only thing with any poetry in it, the only thing with any humor." Why humor was necessary at this point I didn't know. I decided that that reaction of mine was purely reactionary. I personally had lost all humor down there in the ugly lobby of the Social Services building.

"Mrs. Marat!" the black woman called out. I trotted up to her desk, Sarafina behind me, Emma in my arms. "Who's she?" the black woman demanded, pointing a red-lacquered nail at my Urguayan ally.

"I'm her cousin," Sarafina said, stretching the point a bit.

"Well, go siddown. We don't need you here. And you can take the kid with you."

"She won't go to anybody but me," I answered, as meekly as possible, lowering my voice, bowing my head, and all but scraping my feet. If they wanted me to play Ole Black Joe I was going to play it—anything to get it over with as quickly as possible.

My interrogator handed me an application blank, finally, and told me to come back tomorrow with four documents. I told her that I already had all the documents in my purse. That was irrelevant, she told me; I had to make an appointment and come back tomorrow.

The next day Sarafina sent her girlfriend, Cynthia, to meet me at the center. I had never seen her before. She was wearing a yellow pants suit with a navy-blue-and-white polka-dotted blouse, short, curly, blond hair, and glasses. She appeared to be about twenty-four, was slightly plump, and quite pretty. She told me that she had a job at a public relations firm and that she'd have to leave me at ten o'clock but that Sarafina would come and take the second shift. She also told me that her aim in life was to get as many lesbians as possible on Welfare.

This time, on the third floor, I was directed to an older black woman, who was merely well-groomed; in contrast to the super stone-fox "receptionist" of the day before. I showed her my four documents—marriage license, birth certificate, Emma's birth certificate, and my Metro Hotel rent receipts. One look at the rent receipts and all hell broke loose. How could Welfare pay four hundred and fifty dollars a month rent? Out of the question. As advised by Cynthia, I remained silent. Next order. Bring back eight more documents. Meanwhile Sarafina showed up and Cynthia left. Emma was running around the room playing with other babies in between making demands for gum.

The woman wrote me a list.

1. Go to both of your unions and get insurance statements.
2. Get a new social security card.
3. Go to Family Court and file a warrant against your husband.
4. Get a health statement from baby's doctor.
5. Bring back all your royalty statements.
6. Bring back a bank statement.
7. A letter from your agent.
8. Income tax records.

". . . you don't have a bank balance? Get a statement anyway. . . . Look at this, Edith, look at this . . . four hundred and fifty dollars a month rent. . . . Now, Miz Marat," she continued, directing her gaze back at me, "how long do you think that will take you?"

"I'll be finished this afternoon," I said, rashly.

"This afternoon? You're going to do all that this afternoon? Good luck!"

Outside in the street Sarafina looked at me in amazement. "You're going to do all that this afternoon? It's a good thing Alexandra's going to take Emma to the country. I think you're crazy."

I went to every agency on the list, waiting sometimes in long files. For instance, at the Social Security office, there are banks of wooden chairs arranged like a schoolroom, all facing the government worker sitting at a desk, with telephone and typewriter, up in the front of each section. The people wait, sitting in these chairs, sometimes hundreds of them, waiting for their name to be called, all the while staring at the worker in front of them. Hundreds of pairs of eyes staring at at one person constantly.

A yellow butterfly was flying around our section. It landed on the green linoleum floor for a second and then took flight again, zigzagging between the shoulders of the waiting clients. No one paid any attention to it. The butterfly landed on the floor once more, and then I never saw it again.

At Family Court four black men stood in a single large cell, waiting. One of them was talking on the phone. The policeman had dragged the receiver through the bars and the telephone wire snaked out of the cell, between the bars, to the telephone on the policeman's desk in the opposite corner. On the landing a white man was being led down the stairs, his hands behind his back, the metal of the handcuffs glinting in the late afternoon sun, which streamed in a single ray through the bars of the window on the landing above him. I supposed they were all behind in their child support payments and alimony.

At the Federation of Television and Radio Artists, the secretary typing out my statement of health insurance told me that Welfare refused her when both she and her husband were in the hospital, sick and without money. Finally, getting up before the doctors advised, after a serious abdominal operation, she went back to work to support her husband and pay the hospital bills. Five months ago, this was, and her husband was still sick. I told her she should fight harder and insist on Welfare.

I ate a quick dinner and took a taxi to Hunter College to show some videotapes to a class called aptly "The Family." I had decided to show tapes of Frederick and me fighting. A female psychiatrist got up in the middle of the first tape, from her school desk in the first row, and walked out the back door; she didn't return. After the class was over I piled the hundred and fifty pounds of equipment into another cab and took the taxi to Mario de Bomarzo's apartment house. His doorman handed me a xerox copy of Emma's health statement and I took it home and read it.

There was a handwritten section in there, xeroxed along with the rest of the page, listing all the drugs I had taken during my pregnancy. Heroin, mescaline, marijuana, hashish, and cocaine. I had forgotten all about that. When I paid Mario my first visit with the baby, he had asked me what drugs I had taken during pregnancy and I had made a big scene over the anti-nausea pills I had been given by my first obstetrician, asking would they cause a deformity like thalidomide? When he said "no" I laid the bomb on him of every hard and hallucinogenic drug I could think of, just to see if I could shock him. He was from the anti-Laing part of the family, always sadly shaking his head over Sarafina, saying that she was "incurable."

The doctor hadn't blinked an eyelid over heroin, cocaine, etc. He had just calmly written it all down. And now, here it all was, popping up again to haunt me, just when I needed a clean record.

If they saw those drug references at the Department of Social Services I knew they would force me to go on methadone to get Welfare, even though I had only sniffed heroin three times in my life.

I ran up the ten flights of steps to our apartment, not bothering to wait for the elevator, went to my desk, and got out a bottle of liquid paper. I erased half of the drug statement and then ran out of liquid paper. I found some masking tape, cut it into narrow strips, and covered up the rest of the statement. The stationery store, the one with a xerox machine, closed at nine.

My next appointment was on Monday. Time enough to go up and get Emma from the country. The next interrogator on the list might not even believe I had a child.

I got off the plane in Syracuse, having borrowed the money for the fare from the always-solvent dealer on the fifth floor (whose wife was on Welfare) and hitch-hiked to Grenadier Island. A redneck picked me up. After telling me his sexual history he took me all along the back roads, avoiding the new freeway *"so the cops won't stop us for having opened beer in the car."* (He had made it a point to buy some beer and open it even though he didn't take a sip.) I was terrified and believed that I was certain to be raped. I planned out my attack. First go for the eyes with my fingernails and then kick him in the balls. Then run like hell. *Where's the nearest farmhouse? Is anybody there?*

"Let's get out here. I want to show you this waterfall." I got out of the car and looked around. Ah! Thank god! Some people over there on the other edge of the waterfall . . .

Back in the car, sightseeing over, no incidents; I had made it. He only *told* me that his intention was to fuck me. We discussed it philosophically. Actually, it was my mother who saved me.

"Did ya think I was gonna try somethin' there . . . back at the waterfall?"

"Well, to be perfectly honest with you, yes, I did."

"I'll be honest with you, too, is that okay?"

"Of course, I wish you would."

"I had the idea to try somethin' with ya, when I saw ya there, on the road . . . I mean . . . the kinda girl who hitch-hikes . . ."

". . . I'd never done it before. I missed the last plane to Watertown . . ."

". . . yeah, I know . . . but, if ya know what I mean . . . the way yer dressed and all . . . I mean . . . haha . . . not exactly like a respectable upstate housewife . . . ya know what I mean?"

I looked at my clothes. I had left the city wearing what I had on when I xeroxed the documents. I looked like a down-and-out hippie, which was, come to think of it, exactly what I was. My thin, semi-transparent Indian shirt was covered with liquid paper spots, I wasn't wearing a brassiere, and I had on bluejeans, no make-up, and uncombed hair.

I looked at his hands. Red, rough, calloused. His hair short, slicked back with grease. He was wearing a plaid cotton short-sleeved shirt with his undershirt showing at the neck and gray gabardine trousers. He had on black socks and was wearing brown loafers. He told me he was a farmer who worked for an airline company, sorting out baggage. He said that he had been married for two years, was the father of a three-month-old baby, and that his wife and he weren't getting along sexually.

"Would you go back to the freeway so I can call my mother and tell her I'm on my way? My publisher from New York is expecting a call from me and my mother expects me any minute. She thought I'd be on that last plane, the one I missed."

"You a writer?"

"Yes."

"You publish your books?"

"Yes."

"What kinda stuff do ya write?"

"Oh, just boring novels."

"Oh, yeah, sure . . . here . . . the turn-off is right up the road. Hate ta travel on that three-way though . . . sure ya gotta be back right away?"

"Oh yes, my mother will be waiting. She has the guest house all ready for me."

I told him he could take a swim and I invited him for dinner. When he saw the house he asked if it was a private house or a hotel. My father shook hands with him, also inviting him for dinner. He said he had to get back to his wife and baby, that he didn't like to sleep alone; that in fact he never had slept alone since his marriage, and yah, why not? he would like to take a swim.

"Doncha ever swim nude here?"

"Not in the daytime, with the boats going by," I lied.

"Oh . . . say, you know what?"

"What?" (We were both in bathing suits, wet, and a little cold.)

"I'd like to make love to you, right here on this dock."

"My father might discover us. Married women are supposed to be faithful in our family."

"Jesus . . . I've really got the urge."

We went into the boathouse.

"Ahhhh . . . this is great . . ."

"Hmmmmm . . . don't move."

"Oh, baby . . . does it hurt?"

"No. It feels good."

"I've only got the tip inside, only the tip . . ."

"Hmmmm . . . feels wonderful."

"It's just the tip now . . . and I don't want to hurt you. I'll put the rest in slowly . . . Jesus, I can't believe how excited you are . . . feel it, baby, feel that it's just the tip."

I reached down and felt for the rest of his penis. It was about two inches long.

"You can put the rest in if you want to. But slowly. Don't move too much."

"I know, baby, I know, baby, but I'm a man . . . and a man needs to move sometimes. A man needs to thrust sometimes. Goddammit you're hot. That's it, baby, oh . . . I can't believe it . . . this is heaven . . . that's it, baby . . . oh, baby . . . I feel ten years younger . . . I haven't had anything like this happen to me in years . . . god you're tight . . . What happened? Why did you stop? You didn't come, did you? Already?"

"Yes . . . I came."

Emma and I flew back to New York, to the Welfare offices, on Monday morning. The older black woman spread my documents in front of her, adjusted her horn-rimmed glasses, and frowned seriously into the nest of papers.

"Two thousand dollars. You made two thousand dollars two months ago. What did you do with it?"

"Food . . . and rent," I told her.

She got up from her straight-backed chair and took a few steps behind her cubicle and I could hear her saying to one of her black co-workers, "Look at this, Edith, look at this . . . two thousand dollars two months ago . . . and she says that she spent it on *food* . . . on *food!*"

"And rent," I reminded her.

A middle-aged gray-haired white woman sitting under a large sign saying ELIGIBILITY AND INVESTIGATION put my papers in front of her on the desk.

"Yes," she said, "we know that you really need the money. You went through the mill on Friday; that proves it . . . You know, I've been working for social agencies, within the system for forty years, trying to change things, and I'm not alone. There's a lot of us here who all started at the same time, in the Thirties, working against the system. Let's see . . . hmmmm . . . you're a writer . . . not much we can do there . . . you can't do any freelance work and stay on Welfare . . . let's see . . . hmmmm . . . you used to be an actress . . . good . . . you could do a little part-time off-Broadway play . . . make forty dollars a week and stay on Welfare . . . you know, if you get a part-time job Welfare will pay a dollar an hour for a babysitter . . ."

"They cost two dollars an hour now . . ."

"Oh, my goodness, I suppose times have changed . . . it's so long since my children were little . . ."

"Can't I just write magazine articles instead of doing an off-Broadway play? I hate the theater."

"Oh no, dear, no . . . they don't allow that . . . nothing freelance, you know . . . you have to pick up a paycheck at the end of the week . . . how old is your child? Cute little thing, isn't she . . . Two? Not two yet? . . . When she's two you can take her to The Hudson Guild, day-care center . . . it's free for Welfare mothers . . . then you don't need a babysitter . . . you'll be okay, with a nice little part-time job . . . once you get settled . . . let's see . . . your husband's French . . . where do you think he might be?"

"I think he may have gone back to France," I lied. She began writing "husband gone back to France . . ."

"Oh no!" I was suddenly upset. "Don't write that down, I'm not sure . . ."

"Dear," she said gravely, pushing her horn-rimmed glasses above her eyebrows, "nobody's going to pay the slightest bit of attention to what I write down. This is just a formality."

I decided to risk something, hoping to gain some sympathy. After three days of interrogations and accusations I had begun to feel like a social leper, and this toiler in the vineyards of poverty, dispensing her crumbs of human kindness, which were magnified through my now-myopic eyes into veritable loaves, appeared not only as the Christ of the loaves and fishes, but, more importantly, as the Christ who kissed the leper's cheek.

"Please don't write this down," I told her, "but I think my husband is on heroin."

"Dear, it isn't his fault. What choice does an artist have these days? What choice does *anybody* have? The government wants *all* our young men on drugs. That's why they have the methadone program. There's so much unemployment . . . Of course they don't publish the real figures . . . that the government is afraid of an armed uprising . . . if everybody is on drugs they won't complain."

Having gone this far I decided to go further. I could feel my leper's sores already beginning to heal.

"I suspect him of being a homosexual," I told her, "but please don't write that down either."

She smiled at me, a benevolent co-conspirator, and said, "It isn't his fault, dear. What choice does a man have these days, he can't feel like a man with this unemployment . . . The system is against them . . . that's why they turn to homosexuality . . . it's a form of rebellion against the government, that's all . . . Do you know what?"

"No. What?"

"Nixon . . . There's a phony organization called the National Caucus for Labor Relations . . . everyone who is a member is a paid informer . . . they get fifty dollars a day . . . fifty dollars . . . Can you imagine? . . . and anybody else who signs up is put on a list . . . Nixon gets the list. What do you expect under a system like this? Most self-respecting men turn to homosexuality these days . . . listen, there's another thing . . . Welfare won't pay four hundred and fifty dollars a month for your apartment . . .

Lindsay cracked down when we put those families in the Waldorf Astoria . . . too much publicity, the people went wild . . . but you can move into one of those housing projects near your street when they're finished . . . they're not so bad . . . Here, take these papers and go next door, the next cubicle, the housing department; they'll help you."

". . . and if you know anybody who owns a house and you can say that you're living there . . . they'll get your checks there . . ." A plump woman about thirty years old with red hair hanging to her waist, wearing no make-up, was questioning me. Her face was plain but it dimpled a lot as she told me the various ways and means of getting around the rules. I had just been to look at two filthy hovels (complete with twenty-four-inch color T.V. sets in perfect working order) that Welfare wanted me to rent. I told the redhead that I couldn't possibly live on the ground floor on East Sixth Street with no bars on the windows.

". . . don't tell anybody I told you about this," she continued. "It'll cost me my job. The only reason any of us are working here is because it's the only job we can get." She laughed. "But, if you think of anybody who owns a house so you can pretend you're living there . . otherwise we'll have to go through this ridiculous apartment search and you'll have to say 'yes' to something . . . and believe me those two apartments you looked at were the cream of the crop . . . You'll have to say 'yes' before they'll give you any money."

"Mario owns a house," Sarafina spoke up, "and not only that but he has a ground floor apartment that's going up for rent in two months."

"Great!" The redhead smiled. "Why don't you telephone him right now and ask him if it's okay?"

"He's on a vacation, but write it down anyway. He won't mind." I knew that Mario de Bomarzo would mind a lot, but I said nothing, happy to get the whole thing over with, at any price.

"What's his address?" the redhead wanted to know, pencil poised over the ubiquitous papers.

"Ninety-seven Horatio Street."

"Great! We'll say that I got you the house. Don't tell anybody you're not living there. You can get your checks there . . ." She picked up her telephone and spoke to one of the other workers, the black woman who was the second person to interview me.

"Haha!" the redhead laughed, "they can't *believe* that you actually *accepted* one of our apartments . . . they're so surprised! Do you have any furniture? . . . no? . . . if you go up to the Bronx and register in this hotel . . . you don't have to sleep there . . . just pick up the key and leave . . . bring back the receipt . . . then Welfare will give you thirty dollars more for furniture."

The ordeal was finally over, I thought (I had declined to go to the Bronx in order to be eligible for thirty more dollars; I told the worker that the subway ride wasn't worth thirty dollars to me), but I thought wrong. I was now ushered into a totally new cubicle, under a sign saying SPECIAL RESOURCES, where I was greeted by a white man about forty-five years old, wearing a bristly black mustache, white shirtsleeves, black tie and pants. I shouldn't say "greeted"; rather, he shouted at the woman who brought me in, "What! Another client! Forget it! I'm going home! It's a quarter to four!"

I flung my body across the door of his cubicle and, like the cop downstairs, spread my arms out to guard the entrance, and began screaming: "You can't go home! It's a quarter to four for me too! I've been all over this city getting the right papers and I don't have a penny and I'm not going to leave until you take care of me!" He refused. I continued ranting and raving, and then suddenly began sobbing hysterically; immediately the whole atmosphere changed. I had finally become truly "eligible" by breaking down emotionally. He led me to a chair and turned to the bevy of assistants who had been lounging at the door, listening, and asked them to bring me a glass of water. Then, turning to me, he asked, "Do you smoke?"

"Yes."

"What brand?"

"It doesn't matter."

"Get her a pack of cigarettes!" he ordered the eavesdroppers. Within minutes a package of Kools was placed in front of me—you might know, the only brand I really hate.

Meanwhile, from the cubicle on the right, behind the wall that I was facing, I could hear another worker on the telephone.

"Can you imagine . . ." he was saying ". . . Augustine Marat is in here, says she doesn't have a penny . . . applying for Welfare. . . . Yes, the writer!"

"Is that a reporter in the next room?" I asked the man from SPECIAL RESOURCES.

"Of course not!" he told me. "What makes you think that?"

"He's on the phone, talking about me to someone."

"What? On the phone talking about you? Nonsense! Everything that goes on in here stays within these four walls!"

"It'll probably be in all the newspapers tomorrow."

He continued scanning the pile of papers on his desk, only slightly raising his head to give me a quizzical expression, trying to make me believe that the conversation I had just heard in the next cubicle was a product of my own imagination, that, like Sarafina, I was a classical paranoid schizophrenic. I decided to let it drop; what was more important was the as yet unanswered question: What was I doing in this cubicle; what did SPECIAL RESOURCES mean?

He raised his head again, a cloying smile on his face, a smile that led me to believe that he was about to try and pull something over on me. I was right.

"We'd like you to sign these papers," he said, still smiling.

"What are they?" I asked him.

"Oh, it's just a formality," he told me. "It's a statement saying that you'll sign over all your future royalties to the government."

"Why should I sign over my royalties to the government?"

"Well, because . . . you see . . . the government has to protect itself!"

"Protect itself against what?"

"Protect itself against . . . (he didn't want to say the obvious, "protect itself against *you*") against . . . protect it's *investment!*"

"Do you mean to say," I asked him, incredulous, "that the government considers the measly three hundred and forty dollars a month, including rent, that it's going to give me, an investment? What about all the taxes I've paid? They won't give me unemployment because I never had a *salary*; I always worked for myself."

"That doesn't matter. If you make a lot of money then the government is being cheated."

"I won't sign it."

"Well, then, there's nothing I can do." He began to gather the papers together. I began shouting again. "You can't go home! I have to eat! I have a child to feed!"

"Then," he said triumphantly, "you'll just have to sign these papers. Look, if you make a small amount of money, you give it to us, but if you make a great deal of money, say a thousand dollars, then you can petition us to take you off Welfare and give you back your thousand dollars. Anyway, all I want you to do is say, 'Yes, I'm willing to sign the papers.' Then a lawyer has to look them over. That will take two months at least. In the meantime you'll be collecting Welfare. Then, if you say, 'No, I don't want to sign them,' we take you off Welfare. Believe me, this step is just a formality. You can have two months to think it over."

"Yes," I said to him, "I'm willing to sign the papers in two months."

"Good," he said, rubbing his hands together, satisfied (now he could go home), "I'll just write that down." He concentrated on the papers again, as though unsure of how to spell everything, and presumably wrote, while reciting aloud, slowly, "client willing to sign over possible future royalties to the Department of Social Services, New York City."

CHAPTER XVI

A Female
Chauvinist Idea

The idea that a mother misses her children more than a father is a
female chauvinist idea. I don't see why you think Emma is better off
with you, flying from Agadir to Paris to New York to California to
Mexico; when she could be with me in clean air, the wheat ripening
on the stems, the food . . .

FREDERICK MARAT, LETTER FROM MOROCCO, SPRING 1973

While in Zihuatanejo I had asked Gregory to make a tape of Emma
and me at the mayor's house. The mayor's nephew, a gourmet cook, was living there, and he agreed to pretend that he was madly in love with me and
wanted to marry me. I directed Gregory from my perch in one of the hammocks on the terrace. I asked him to make a video-tour of the interior of
the house while I provided the narration—telling Frederick what a rich
man he was, showing him the house, the paintings, the gardens, all the
while suckling Emma on the terrace hammock. Then I went into a bedroom, changed into a silk caftan, put on some make-up, brushed my hair,
and settled myself and Emma on the bed with its Indian canopy.

"If you don't come back, Frederick," I said, looking into the lens,
"Emma and I are going to stay here, in the mayor's house on Playa la

206

I directed Gregory from my perch in one of the hammocks on the terrace.

"If you don't come back, Frederick," I said, looking into the lens,
"Emma and I are going to stay here, in the mayor's house on Playa la Ropa.
His nephew is such a good cook."

Ropa. His nephew is such a good cook." Then I took the camera, went into the kitchen, and filmed all the gourmet utensils. "You see," I continued, "here are the utensils; tonight he is going to make a fabulous meal."

"Why don't you put on just your bikini bottoms," Gregory asked me, "and I'll film you nude on the front terrace, overlooking the bay." I did as Gregory suggested, and told Frederick that the pressure on me to be everything to everybody in New York was too much, and that he was only interested in smoking dope and working on his tapes while I cooked and cleaned. I told him that the apartment in the Metro Hotel was always a mess, even with a maid, that Emma loves the beach, that I hate cities and the people in them and that I guess he wants freedom. "For me," I continued, "there will never be freedom again. I guess that's the price of being a woman. I have given up hope of ever having any kind of happiness. The mess doesn't bother you because you can always leave and visit somebody . . ." I continued in that vein.

Then I sent the tape to his sister's house in Paris, knowing that he would end up there. I labeled it "Mother's Day."

On the day my first Welfare check arrived I received a letter from him:

> Augustine:
>   Your tape was very beautiful except for a few technical problems. There was a lot of drop-out. As for the Mayor's nephew, I don't give a damn. I think you should marry him. He makes a monthly salary.

The rest of the letter was divided into two columns—the column on the left enumerating my points and the column on the right rebutting them.

Mother's Day	has been invented by shopkeepers so they get a higher salary that very day.
you are only interested in working on your tapes	Ha, ha, that's my job!
The mess. I had to hire a maid. Still a mess	There is always a mess. The earth is a mess. It is not because you

I guess you want freedom. For me
there will never be freedom
again. I guess that's the price of
of being a woman.

I have given up hope of ever
having any kind of happiness

The mess in 914 didn't bother
you because you could always
leave and visit somebody

Just look. You get the peace and
the beauty and I am left with the
responsibilities all alone.

You drove me away

or me or a maid is going to pile
up le shit in two drawers and one
closet that the mess will be
evaporated. I and you are messie
forever. Even if you get a castle on
the beach it will be a mess The
mess is in our our brain. We got
to clean the mess in our brain
first a maid *can't* do it. Only us.

You guess wrong. I do not want
freedom, there is no freedom It's
not the price of being a woman,
it's the price of being on earth
and being humans

You are not the only one.
Happiness. Happiness is a fool
word. Happiness is use by the
political forces in the world so
everybody can go to work slave
away and hope happiness until
they dies

But you couldn't I wonder why

Ha Ha

You provoked me every day in
Maroc while I was trying to find a
spot for a house to stay for a
time and when I found it you didn't
like it. We have different taste I
guess

You beat me. You said terrible things to me all in front of the child whose screams I will never forget

If you do not want forget, it's your problime Emma and I has forgotten all ready and you were quite horrible too!

I have considered your career above mine your comfort above mine No wonder you hate me

No. *You were wrong* I always thought we had natural relasionships I never knew you were making efforts for me That's certainly why we have so much problems together. You are right! !

Please try to show some elementary politeness to me at least

I wouldn't do that to you. Politness is a trick to dissimulate your real caractere you use politness in ~~business bussess~~ buisness not in human natural relations.

My mother said that all the neighbors say to her I hear Augustine is getting a divorce The Cosmopolitan article being kill because of rumors

I told none to your *mother*, *Cosmopolitan*, to the *neighbors* of your mother . . .

Don't you remember you asked me to leave Tiznit?

Yes I asked you to leave Tiznit because you were complaining all the day and didn't like Maroc.

I spent all those nights putting her to sleep while you fucked Nan, Linda, Nancy, Geraldine, Bulle, Susan, Mary Ellen, Leontine, Angela . . . (*last three names added by him*)

I spend as much night as you did taking care of Emma since the day she is born to the day you left Maroc and taking care of you while you were pregnant

I won't discuss that anymore

Between you and I the only
difference for Emma was the breast
I DO NOT HAVE BREAST
therefore I couldn't breastfeed
her! ! ! ! !

As for fucking around while you
were putting her to sleep I never
did such a thing. I did fuck around
some time because you and I do
not fuck—but never had a love
affair but with you It's not a big
deal and there is no betraying.

I haven't had any other man

You should May be you will ~~felle better~~ feel better

You're a father and a husband,
Frederick,
you're not a hermit

I am not a father, not a husband,
not a hermit I do not know what
I am, thanks to god, I have still
something to learn (who I am)

of course we could go on forever like this, you answering to
the right column and me again and you again again again
again. You are the first personne i have such arguments
for so long Female or Male. Coming back to New York for
having the same scene between you and I again again
again   again   again—my mother and father didn't
beat me up—I am not use to beat up   I can't stand it
I do not beat you up   I am far less violent than you are
I do not throw glass bottle or knock you with my shoes
and fist   you always have blood in your mind when we have
an argument because you drive me crazy and pushing you
around you *took a knife, not me*, you said I want to murder
you—you are crazy and dangerous   you lost conscious
mind.   You are far more violent than I am—you
understand that if I was violent that would be very pain
full and leave marks and blood—I am *so much stronger*

than you are that its ridiculous to have physical argument
with you but you want it so I push you around like a
brother to his sister and you each time you are fighting
for kill   at least in your eyes   in your words   in your acts
Frederick

After I read the letter I telephoned Frederick's sister in Paris and left a message for him.

"Tell him," I said, "that the baby is with my parents, that I'm very ill and that I don't know when I'll be well enough to take care of her myself. I'm having a mental collapse." Then I waited by the telephone. Three hours later he called me and told me that he was returning as soon as his passport was in order. He was very upset about Emma. How could I send her away? he wanted to know. He said he had had a hard time getting out of Spain and that he was now in Paris. He should be home the following Monday. Today was Thursday.

I can't get Emma to wear shoes, ever since we came back from Mexico. We do all our shopping and walking to the park with Emma in bare feet. That's the only time I leave the hotel now, to go shopping for food or to go to the park. I can't stand the city, especially at night. The fluorescent lights give me a peculiar kind of headache; I feel as though there was something between my eyes, pressing against my forehead.

Today, in the street, an old man, walking with great difficulty, using a cane, came up to me saying, "What's the matter with you? Why don't you put shoes on her? You're wearing shoes, aren't you? My mother always put shoes on me when I was a little boy!"

"Is that why you can't walk, now that you're an old man?" I asked him. He shook his cane at me and muttered something. A few blocks away, a woman in the Puerto Rican district, sitting on a stoop, wanted to know why Emma wasn't wearing any shoes. "She might step on a piece of glass," the woman said. Minutes later a piece of glass pierced the sole of my rubber tong. I went back to the woman on the stoop and asked her where she bought the shoes for her little girl, who was sitting next to her. She directed me to a store on Eighth Avenue.

In the store a clerk, a middle-aged woman, asked me what I wanted. I had come in and sat down on a chair, exhausted from the heat and the cement pavements. My feet were burning.

"You can't try shoes on her without socks!" the woman insisted, so I asked her to bring me a pair of socks and I said I'd buy them.

"What size does she wear?" the clerk yelled from the sock counter.

"I don't know!" I yelled back.

"What do you mean you don't know! I can't bring you a pair of socks unless you know the size."

"Well, why don't you measure her feet?" I asked. "Isn't this a shoe store?"

"You'll have to come over here and find those socks yourself; I'm not going to measure her feet."

I had been hoping it would take a long time to fit Emma with a pair of shoes, so that I could recoup my strength sitting there, and let my own feet cool off before hitting the pavements again, but I decided that if they didn't want my Welfare money badly enough to find Emma a pair of socks without my help, well, fuck them. I stormed out of the store with Emma.

While I was soaking in the bathtub, a washrag on my forehead, wishing the bedroom window was open to blow in some air, Duñel came in to clean. Seeing me in the bathtub, she put the carpet sweeper down, leaning the handle against the wall, and came into the bathroom, sitting down on the toilet seat.

"Augustine," she said, "you wan know how to get Frederick back?"

"Yes, Duñel, I do. Tell me." I didn't want her to know he was coming that night; in case he didn't show up, I thought, a little magic wouldn't hurt. She had already proved efficacious in voodooing the policeman out of the eighteenth precinct—the one who had arrested Magda and me for filming on Twenty-sixth Street.

"You write 'Frederick' seven times on sheet of white paper. Then you sit down on paper." She pointed under her buttocks; I could see the top of her nylons and her white nylon slip under the green uniform. "Then you get candle. You take candle every night at eleven o'clock and you go like this"; she pumped the imaginary candle in and out between her legs, "like Frederick does, same rhythm. Then you say, 'Frederick, you come back to me, you be ready for me.' You do that one half hour each night, thinking only about how he do it to you. He be back tonight."

I wondered if the hotel grapevine had somehow gotten hold of the news that he was returning, even though I hadn't told anyone.

"Does it work, Duñel?" I asked her.

"You know where I'm from?"

"Yeah, Haiti," I answered. She cackled wildly.

"Listen, I tell you other things, what you do for him. But, you no tell nobody, understand?"

I knew I could never keep it a secret but I said "okay" anyway. I was wondering if she had put a curse on me for yelling at her a few days before.

"You eat two peanuts. Then you go toilet. You pick out peanuts and wash them. Then you ground them to powder. You put it in his food. He do anything for you after that. You know what else?"

I asked what else even though I was having trouble deciphering her English—I had to have her repeat the instructions four or five times before I understood them.

"You wash youah right foot," she said, pointing to her left foot.

"You mean your left foot?"

"Right foot," she repeated, pointing again to her left foot.

"Duñel," I told her, "that's your left foot you're pointing at. Here," I put my hand on her knee, "This is your left leg."

"Right foot," she repeated, "and then you wash youah right cheek." She pointed to her left cheek. "And then you wash here." She put her hand between her legs again. "You make him tea but you be sure and drink youah own tea first with clean water."

"Well, what do you do? Wring out the sponge that you wash yourself with in the teapot?"

"No, no, no. You make youah own tea first and then you make his with the water you wash yourself in."

"Okay, I get it. I'll do it."

"You no tell nobody?"

"No."

"Good. I tell you something else. You go splat!" She spit on the floor over her shoulder. "In everything you serve him, just splat! like that in the food. He do everything for you. Then, somethin' else you can do. You take off youah panties and you wipe the plates he eat on with them. Dirty panties. You no wash them."

I told her that I would do it all that night—everything I could do without him—and that I would get the candle that day.

"Augustine? You know what? You gi me white glass and white cloth and I do somethin for you at home."

"Something like you did for that cop?"

Duñel cackled again. "Augustine, I tell you; one woman isn't enough for any man. My husband, you know what he do? I gi him money; all my pay; I gi him fi thousand dollars. He spend it on woman. I say, 'Lissen, I know how you spend that money!' I put money now in a bank. I buy him shoes. I buy him socks. He happy. Augustine, you good woman. I see you. I come in here and I never see you wi a man. You good woman. Youah husband, he lucky."

Duñel reached over into the tub, embraced me, then went back out into the bedroom, picked up the carpet sweeper and began cleaning the rug.

PART THREE

THE FAMILY

CHAPTER XVII

As Fugitive, Alas, as the Years

All the longings that had possessed me as a child, inspired by *The Little Colonel* series, to wear long bell-skirted silk dresses, to linger "under a bower of flowering trees" while a tall, slim, handsome, blond-haired young man came up to where I was sitting on a marble bench, took my hand in his, looked longingly into my eyes and kissed me chastely on the lips, were to be partially realized in Gif-sur-Yvette. Although the blond hair on this mythical young man came from old photographs of my own father whose hair was arranged in that style, peculiar to young men of the Thirties—who wet their natural curls and combed them trying to flatten them to the point where their hair looked like a marcelled wig—the ambiance of the rendezvous spot was one that would be foreign to my experience until I encountered it twenty years later in my mother-in-law's family.

The realization of this recurrent daydream did not encompass the bell-shaped skirts or the marble benches. Nor did it encompass wavy blond hair, since Frederick had inherited the silky chestnut locks of his half-Russian mother and wore them, when I met him, in a page boy acquired by matting down the newly shampooed locks with a silk scarf tied under his chin in the style of a 1950s schoolgirl. It was only just before our marriage, when he asked me to cut his hair, and I liberated his curls by scissoring the hair in layers and blowing it dry under my salon hair dryer, that Frederick's hair resembled in any way that of the lover of my eight-year-old daydreams. Yet his maternal family did observe those nineteenth-century niceties that included four o'clock tea, set under a bower of hawthorn and bougainvillea blossoms, on a wooden table loaded down with china teapots, French marmalade, *brioches*, and fruit preserves.

Even grander than the fact that these details of my daydreams were realized was the fact that I married into a family rich in tradition and history. Still standing, in the back garden in Gif-sur-Yvette, was the laboratory in which my husband's grandparents had worked with the Curies to discover and make use of the properties of radium. Old pamphlets, full of instructions on applying radium treatments to cancer patients, now covered with cobwebs and dust, torn and yellowed, lay like autumn leaves that have drifted, over the years, through the paneless windows, and have been left to decay on those very stairs once trod by white-coated doctors and scientists.

"It wasn't Marie who did all the work, God knows!" Grandmère told me, her lips pursed together in disapproval, the tiny wrinkles on her upper lip all coming together like the folds of an accordian; "it was Pierre . . . even though Marie took all the credit!"

"But, Grandmère, I didn't know you spoke English!" (Her accent was flawless British.)

"Hmmmhpmm, there's a lot of things you don't know!"

"But I've known you for two years! Why didn't you ever speak to me in English before?"

She refused to answer.

"Snobbism," Minette told me, "she refused to let you know that she spoke English because of snobbism."

These rituals of lime-blossom tea and *madelaines*, Sunday visits, walks in the Bois, afternoon naps and snobbism, filled me with nostalgia, as though they were rituals that I was remembering from my childhood rather than the rituals I had merely read about as a child. I congratulated myself on finding at last a lineage, though borrowed, which I could fit into history, making the "nouveau riche" a class into which I no longer belonged.

The first time I visited Frederick's grandmother, the only one of her generation to escape radiation poisoning (except for Pierre Curie who died as a result of a bicycle accident), I sat at a distance from her watching the two bright-red spots that splashed the withered skin of her high, prominent cheekbones—spots not put there by anything so vulgar as rouge, but by the rigorous existence of a woman who still lived in a house without central heating, and in an area uncontaminated as yet by industrial smog. Spots that cried out: *"I belong to a woman who takes daily walks, who bathes in cold water, who feels the sting of wind and rain upon her face!"*

I found everything about her fascinating—from the spots to the stories she had to tell me about the Curies, about Frederick's misbehavior as a boy (*"We never thought he'd amount to much"*), to her mass of snow-white hair, piled high on her head in the style of a Gibson girl. She was born in Russia, the daughter of "intellectuals," and as a young woman emigrated to France with one of the groups who were walking from Moscow to Berlin and from there to Paris, during the Bolshevik uprising. Then she settled down with her new husband, in Gif-sur-Yvette, and once again enjoyed money as she had as a child in Russia, her family having been a part of the Court. The French money was to come from the radium, and they were the first family in France to have a swimming pool, a pool so large that as a child Frederick had rowed a boat on it, iceskated on it in the winter, and helped to drain it by carrying buckets of water away from it to pour on the surrounding gardens, where the roots of cherry, apple, rose, bougainvillea, hawthorn, and honeysuckle lapped it up hungrily. Now the pool was but a swamp, its concrete sides split in hundreds of places, weeds and vines snaking through the cracks and frogs croaking in a stagnant puddle at the bottom.

The house is filled with mementos of the past—photographs, scrapbooks, antimacassars, lace tablecloths, fading Persian rugs, plumbing nearly a century old, Tiffany lamps, and a treacherous, banisterless, spiral staircase. Nothing has been changed, nothing new has been bought, in seventy years. Grandmère, her husband, and her children spent the money very quickly on yachts, race cars, and parties, inviting everyone in Paris to come out to Gif and drink vodka, eat caviar, take photographs, drive the race cars, swim in the pool, and go cruising with them on the Mediterranean. I am allowed to look at the photographs now (carefully edited by Grandmère, so that I can only see those in which she looks beautiful), through the stereoscopic viewfinder made in 1910, and I see those graceful, elegant ladies and their top-hatted companions, posing languorously with white parasols filtering the sun upon their faces, in a light so soft as to make Richard Avedon, with his parasol-covered studio lights, green with envy.

Seen through the stereoscopic viewer, in black and white, the three-dimensional, perfectly modulated gray tones of the plates are more elegant, more beautiful than any reconstruction of the period by a Griffith, a Visconti, or a Peter Bogdanovich. There they are, beside the pool, atop a rocky knoll, or under a brace of chestnut trees, enveloped in billowing white lawn dresses, navy-blue cloaks and hoods, their hair arranged in rolls, chignons, and fuzzy wisps around their pre-Raphaelite faces; sublimely unconcerned about editors' deadlines, dirty dishes, bills from the Sony Corporation, xerox machines gone awry, and as yet unaware of the mutant, radiation-seeped genes coursing through their bloodstreams.

The places Grandmère has known belong now only to the little world of transparent plates, on which she maps them for her own convenience. None of them was ever more than a thin slice of glass, held between the claws of a stereoscopic viewfinder, the remembrance of a certain image is nothing but regret for a particular moment; the houses, roads, avenues, and the laboratory are as fugitive, alas, as the years.

Just as that tea-soaked *madelaine*, when I tasted it, brought to mind the atomically mutated genes of my husband (Is that why Emma's left eye strays?) so now the marijuana I am smoking recalls the same feelings that I experienced giving birth to my daughter, as her little body wound its way out of my vagina—terror and acute anxiety. What if her father never comes back? What if I've alienated him forever and he decides to stay there, in Gif-sur-Yvette, tasting the freedom he knew as a boy, under his grandmother's pink hawthorn bushes? Perhaps I'm exaggerating the fear I have of being left alone; I know I'm not exaggerating the exhaustion I feel, every day, alone with a small child. It seems that the very act of giving birth has left me vulnerable to words, gestures, and actions from others that in the past wouldn't have bothered me at all, but that now grate on a set of sensibilities so finely honed they seem too fragile to survive the onslaughts of civilization.

A boy I once knew said that women shouldn't take drugs; that they're high enough already. I suspected that he had a point, although he, like I, didn't know what it was then. The thing about women that he probably wasn't aware of, since he hadn't stuck around long after his wife gave birth to twins, and that I wasn't aware of at the time either, is that once you've given birth and experienced that life and death struggle of a foreign body fighting to get out of your own, then, when smoking mari-juana you're likely to go back into those moments that gave you so much anguish, those moments when the other little body seemed so big, so merciless in its fight toward the exit.

Trying further to analyze my feelings of isolation and acute anxiety, I am forced to conclude that it has nothing at all to do with the absence of Frederick. Because, despite being with him and Emma in the desert, the feeling struck me on the road to Tan-Tan beach, after two puffs of kif, that I was the only living being in an old, dusty stage-set, sparsely decor-ated with John Chamberlain's crushed-car sculptures. The mythical desert, towards which I had longed, was a disappointment: there were carcasses of old cars side by side with the carcasses of camels (one with his entrails being devoured by dogs as they spilled out of his rectum), and sheep, and, worst of all, the layer of dust over every square inch of sand, flora, and fauna gave me the same feeling I am experiencing now: utter terror. (Like a cosmic joke, the night I returned home from Morocco, without Frederick, I turned on the television to see the last scene in *Morocco*, where Marlene Dietrich goes off, without her shoes, into the desert, to follow her lover.)

And, in Mexico, on two dabs of an acid-soaked blotter, I remember how the sea looked like a giant toilet bowl, full of warm piss and rotting fragments of animals and kelp. When I stepped into it I felt as though my ankles were surrounded by newly released urine. Yet moments before, when my daughter appeared to me as a goddess, I knew she was seeing nature in a light that was fresh and sparkling, not in hideously inappropri-ate symbols of twentieth-century plumbing.

Now, in Central Park, where I wait with Emma until it's time to go home and get the mail (hoping that there won't be news of Frederick's retirement into his Proustian past), I find myself staring at a rock that resembles a bleached-out camel's skull that's been lying there for centuries. Ghosts of long-dead animals and plants hover, both in the immediate and the far-flung atmosphere, overtaxing the oxygen supply. I have trouble filling my lungs with enough air. Looking at Emma, her eyes sparkling with curiosity, her skin transparent and new, I remember what it was like to be a child and to experience that feeling of bliss upon rounding a corner that had never been rounded before. I remember riding a horse on Grenadier Island and coming upon a pond glittering in the sun—how exhilarated I felt; it was a feeling that's been lost to me ever since. I could always depend on nature to make me happy. The sight of anything I hadn't seen before, or of something familiar seen in a new way, the sun hitting it at a different angle, was akin to mystical transport. A thrill would run through my body, a premonition of an exhilarating future.

I see Emma in that same light now. She makes me happy because she always looks new to me. In fact she's the only thing I can look at without seeing a mounting layer of dust settling on the surfaces.

With this vision of life the irony of housekeeping mounts in intensity. No matter what I do to keep things clean there's always a shabby corner of the sofa, a permanent spot of grease somewhere, a fingerprint on a wall, a crack on the ceiling, a stain on a rug. I remember Frederick's letter, "the mess is in our brain," and now that I've seen the desert and even the sea as a mess, I suppose he's right.

And so, I struggle, I struggle to remain as unaffected by disorder as strenuously as I struggled in my college days, under the direction of Father Schroeder, to attain mystical union with God. Father Schroeder was introduced to me by Mrs. Ryan; he was her fellow-mystic and spiritual adviser and he used to pass out to his classes mimeographed copies of "Five short steps to mysticism, condensed from St. John of the Cross." "Mysticism for the masses," we called it. Instead of union with God, the Supreme Good seems to me now to be able to write without first cleaning the house. Otherwise, by the time it's clean I'm too tired to do anything but sit by the fire, sipping a Jack Daniels, reading *Cosmopolitan*, *Newsweek*, *Vogue*, or *Psychology Today*. These are the magazines I choose so that I can feel like a superior writer when I read the articles in them. It's only the human species that has this problem of disorder. In the animal kingdom there is no such thing as a messy house; only in the zoo do the poor beasts encounter that problem.

Today I read in the paper that there is a body of scientific thought that believes man was put on this planet originally in the form of a germ sowed from a spaceship and left to evolve and to be passively observed.

"Like a zoo," they said. Otherwise, these scientists reasoned, why don't the pilots of flying saucers make themselves known? If this is true, then it is the laissez-faire policy of the saucer men that keeps this zoo at a much lower level of cleanliness than that of either the San Diego zoo or the Los Angeles zoo.

Ma'am, how do you know the animals are unhappy? We feed them a balanced diet. Their cages are cleaned every day. It's only the elephants that are a bit melancholy . . . they're used to a lot of space to roam around in. We're going to solve that problem by not buying any more elephants.

KEEPER, L.A. ZOO, FEBRUARY 1974

CHAPTER XVIII

People Who Take Separate Planes

If anything ever happened to your father, I always wanted to go with him. For example a plane crash: I could never understand people who took separate planes so one of them would be left for their children. I wouldn't want to live without your father . . . no, not even to stay behind to bring up you children.

AUGUSTINE'S MOTHER, MOTHER'S DAY, 1973

The day Frederick came back I was very tired, so I decided to try and spruce myself up a bit both to disguise my exhaustion and to look seductive. I wanted to set my hair in Kindness curlers (the ones that Harriet insisted that I buy *"Sometimes you can look so ugly!"*) and make up my face. I expected him to walk in the door any minute.

I started by tweezing my eyebrows, and since I hadn't tweezed them in three months it was going to be a long job. Emma toddled over to where I was standing, in front of the full-length mirror on the inside of the bathroom door (the door being opened out into the bedroom), and pulled on my legs, grunting and making noises, begging me to tweeze her eyebrows too. I stretched the skin above her right eye and pulled out an almost invisible blond hair. She didn't experience it as pain; she wanted me to do it

226

again. Laughing, I pulled on the skin over her left eye as Frederick came into the bedroom.

He watched as I pulled out another of Emma's eyebrow hairs and then said sternly, "What are you doing to her?" I looked up. His skin was slightly green, he badly needed a shave, and he looked as though he was wearing someone else's clothing. He didn't look happy to see me. I knew right away that he had only come back because of Emma. By the set of his face as he questioned me I knew as well that he thought I had gone crazy during his absence. I stood there staring at his hair, which was hanging in greasy curls to his shoulders, thinking that he really needed a shampoo right away. By concentrating on his appearance I figured that I would draw my attention away from listening to his words, à la Lamaze, thereby averting a fight that we were sure to have if I allowed myself to listen to him. I still hadn't set my hair in the Kindness curlers, nor had I put on any make-up. I was standing there, in my underpants, my hair dripping wet.

"The lobby is crawling with cameras," he said next.

"Why?"

"Edith Irving is having a painting exhibition."

"Oh, that's right. I never told you . . . She was fined ten thousand dollars and two months in prison."

"That's only the beginning."

As I put in the curlers I knew that Frederick thought I was doing it for the benefit of the cameras in the lobby.

I gave Emma some rouge to play with and I smeared some brown eye shadow on her face in marks, like a Hollywood Indian.

"Augustine!" Frederick was shouting, "she looks like a Vietnamese victim! No, worse, she looks like she has chocolate smeared all over her face." I didn't tell him that I always let her play with my make-up, that I thought that if I was going to use it then she ought to be able to use it too. I knew he wouldn't approve of that theory. He thought she should know that there are things she shouldn't touch. The thing was that I couldn't make myself up unless I let her do it too. Otherwise, she cried and pulled on me the whole time. I was too embarrassed to tell him that I was putting the make-up on for him.

Now she was smearing rouge all over her face.

"She's *eating* it!" Frederick shouted. Emma was running her tongue over her lips.

I was too embarrassed to tell him that I was putting the make-up on for him.

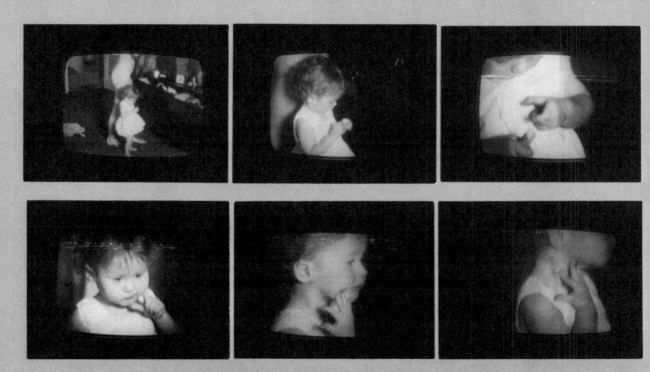

Now she was smearing rouge all over her face. "She's eating it!" Frederick shouted.

"So what? It doesn't have cyclamates in it!"

"Take it off her face! You're crazy!"

I grabbed a towel off the bathroom rack, ran it under some warm water, and washed the rouge off her face while she screamed.

"I'm taking her down to the lobby with me," I told him. "I have to buy cigarettes."

"Without her shoes?" He was incredulous.

"Why not? She hates her shoes."

"You're wearing shoes."

I thought about the crippled man who said the same thing to me on Eighth Avenue. I sat Emma down on the black and white linoleum of the kitchen floor, in front of the door, and started to put her shoes on her.

Frederick grabbed her away from me, gave me a dark look from underneath his sparse chestnut eyebrows, began cooing to her, "This is the way we put on your shoes, Emma," in a voice totally divorced from the voice he used when addressing me, took her into the living room, and sat her down on the bed (I had moved it into the living room while he was away).

"This is the way you put shoes on her," he instructed me, back in his normal tone of voice, "you don't sit her down on the *dirty* linoleum! We're going 'bye 'bye, Emma, 'bye 'bye, and we're going to put your shoes on you." He was back into the white dove call.

I thought how freaked out he'd be if he could see her sitting on the stoops on Twenty-third Street, imitating the winos. By now I knew every stoop in the neighborhood. Between Seventh and Eighth Avenues on Twenty-third Street, on the south side, the stoops were made of cast iron and were all very high to accommodate the high ceilings of the storefronts on the ground floor. On Twenty-second Street there were no storefronts, so the stoops were correspondingly lower and made of cement. On Twenty-first Street, between Eighth and Ninth Avenues the stoops were of stone and the houses were of a little better class—mostly brick or brownstone. The Twenty-third Street stoops were never without at least two or three winos sitting there, usually drinking a bottle of cheap muscatel. My favorite bum was a man of about fifty-five or sixty, always sporting a two- or three-day growth of gray beard, who was very loquacious and, to the unwary passerby, argumentative and pugnacious. That is, if they didn't appreciate his conversation and stop to chat, he would abuse and insult them. He was Emma's particular friend. She liked to sit next to him best of all.

Pease siddown, she would say to me, pointing to the step she wanted me to sit on. Then she would sit next to me or next to him, surrounded by empty wine bottles, cigarette butts, lottery tickets, and puddles of urine and vomit, depending on the hour. By evening the vomit began to accumulate, as the men had been drinking all day, usually on empty stomachs it seemed. I never saw any food other than an occasional slice of pizza. Emma could spend quite a bit of time chatting with the bums on those iron stairs, her hands calmly folded in her lap as she watched the sun go down.

It was sometimes difficult to maneuver her past the pizza parlor the bums used, since she liked to go in, put a quarter in the jukebox, and listen to the Spanish music while eating a pizza and talking to whoever was sitting near her. Then, her stomach full of canned tomato paste, she would dance around the tiny area between the tables and the counter, spinning wildly, sometimes carrying her routine out into the street. If I remained inside at the table a passerby was sure to stop and inquire of her, "Where is your mother, little girl? Are you lost?"

Frederick put the left shoe on Emma and as I watched him tenderly tying the laces I said, "I always put her shoes on her while she's sitting down in front of the door on the kitchen floor." He threw the remaining shoe at me and came toward me, his upper lip trembling. With his upper lip quivering like that he reminded me of my father, who was afflicted with the same symptom when in a rage or when babytalking to Emma. I reasoned that it was the emotions of both love and anger that called forth that minor epileptic fit from my father and to see it in my husband as well made me think that Freud was right—that we marry our fathers.

All the signs being there that Frederick was going to hit me, I grabbed the key off the kitchen table and walked out without Emma. I hadn't even finished putting on my make-up.

*My favorite bum was a man . . . very loquacious and, to the
unwary passerby, argumentative and pugnacious.
He was Emma's particular friend. . . .*

"You'd think that he'd never been away . . . you'd wonder how I ever managed to take care of her without him . . . God! what's so terrible about sitting her down on the kitchen floor? It gets mopped every day . . . it's probably cleaner than the sheet on her bed . . . he's just trying to drive me crazy . . . can't wait to criticize . . . sits crosslegged on that bed waiting for me to do something he can complain about. I hate him. I'm going to stay with him until I find somebody else . . . somebody with money who likes sex . . . then I'm splitting with Emma. Can I have another vodka gimlet?"

I was in the bar downstairs off the lobby, sitting next to a pregnant woman who lived in the hotel. She was complaining to me why she didn't have the abortion after the third appointment had been made. I had been talking to myself while reading the New York *Post* on the Irving case. The pregnant woman, whose name I had never known, told me that each time she made an appointment she got sick. This time she had bronchitis. She had gone to the hospital that morning and while there decided that she couldn't possibly have an abortion while she had such a terrible case of bronchitis.

"They keep telling me to make up my mind," she said, "but I have until the sixth month, don't I . . . under the new laws?"

"You're not really going to abort a six-month-old fetus, are you?"

"I don't know . . . I can't seem to make up my mind. If only the baby's father would come back . . ."

I looked at her stomach. She was a good six months pregnant already.

"How many months are you now?" I asked her.

"I don't know," she said, "I think it's about four months."

She had a terrible ugly scab forming on her left eyelid, where, she told me, Dominick, the father of the fetus, had crushed out a lit cigarette while fighting with her the last time she'd seen him.

"*You don't remember what he looks like?*" Frederick asked me later. "*He looks just like a character out of Dostoevski!*"

"If only I could get hold of my land in Florida," she lamented, "the land my ex-husband is living on."

"Why can't you?"

"Because he's a photographer, and that's where his darkroom is, and we need the money he makes to pay for the taxes on the land."

"Why don't you go down there and live in the house anyway?"

"His new wife won't have me," she said, by now rather drunk, "and he hates me too. They don't want me around."

"But if it's *your* house!"

She shrugged, told me about some other schemes she had for making money and about how she was going to get her boyfriend back.

"Which one?"

"You know . . . the baby's father . . . the one who put his cigarette out on my left eyelid."

Last night, at Gunter von Habsburg's, Emma wanted to undress all of Elkse's antique dolls. For the past three days she's been obsessed with dressing and undressing dolls. She likes them to wear a lot of layers. In this heat I can't bear to look at them. It finally occurred to me last night that she wants to see the sex of the dolls. I undid the pants of the boy doll, pulled them down, and raised his shirt. Being an antique doll, he had no penis of course; his wooden torso continued into a hairpin curve between his legs, completely smooth, not a bump in sight, and he was wearing a pair of white underpants, securely fastened with a pin.

"Penis," I told her, pointing to his crotch. "That's all she wants," I said to Frederick and Elkse (Gunter was in the kitchen, cooking dinner and complaining about the price of food), "to see what's under their pants!"

"It's *you*, not *her*," Elkse murmured, in her Icelandic accent.

"Yes!" Frederick agreed. "It's you!"

Straightening my back and taking a deep breath (battle preparation), I accused them both of mouthing Freudian inanities. "Neither one of you is a mother!" I complained, once again seemingly enraged beyond reason. "Stop ganging up on me!" Elkse was taken aback by my reaction but Frederick was smiling at me.

"After three days of going crazy, with her dressing and undressing dolls, I finally figured it out!" I was so triumphant about it all. "All I have to do is pull their pants down and she's happy, and you're telling me that it's all my idea!" They both had to agree with me, or at least they pretended to.

The next day I put all of Emma's outgrown clothes in a bag for her dolls. Without my telling her anything about it she caught on as soon as she saw the bag. Every day now she carries the doll in one hand and the bag in the other, asking me constantly to dress and undress the doll and then wrap it in a blanket (so much for my theory of the night before). While she eats she feeds the wrapped doll and then walks over to the edge of her special rubber-foam John Chamberlain sculpture-bed (constructed to make the nursing-nap more comfortable), sits down, and gives the doll her breast. I think about buying her a truck, to try and defuse the sexual stereotype she's cast herself in—but it seems a pity to try to wean her from her dolls; she loves them so much.

Emma was crying because I took her away from my breast. She woke up saying, "I wanna suck the mama! I'm a baby!"

"You're really crazy," Frederick complained, "nursing her to sleep; she's been going to sleep without it for three weeks! I'm leaving!"

I was so furious at him for that that I decided not to repress my anger and screamed at him, "Then *leave*, you motherfucker, *leave!*"

Emma cried harder, reaching for him. "And take Emma with you!" I added. I would think that a grown man would realize that the two of them tugging at me in different directions would be enough to drive me crazy (*If I weren't already crazy,* as my father says). I told them they could stay where they were; I'd leave instead. I didn't leave, though; I had no place to go. I just went into the bathroom and sat on the toilet seat.

Minutes later I went back into the bedroom to find them both lying in the bed together; Emma with the pacifier in her mouth, saying, "No-'ceam [scream], Mama."

"You like to see us fighting, don't you?" I asked her.

"Yef!" she answered, a big smile on her face.

"You like to see me scream at papa."

"Yef," again, this time with a giggle.

"Why do you want to sleep with papa?"

"Tickee, tickee," she answered, "where's Papa's pee-pee?" Then, reaching over to Frederick, she began playing with his penis, picking it up, dropping it, lifting the foreskin, watching it swell. I suddenly realized that she was treating it like a pet animal, trying to get a reaction out of it.

The entire winter was punctuated by arguments. I reproached Frederick for his Moroccan odyssey. I told him that the twenty-five-year-old Arab, Mustapha, who had been coming around daily to our house, supposedly to help us buy blankets and rugs and vegetables for the right price, was in reality a fag who was in love with Frederick and hated me for being his wife. The fact that he moved into our house after I left proved it, I said.

"He would fuck anything," Frederick said, "a chicken, a dog, a donkey."

"Right, like an animal. All those men were like animals. They hated me for being a woman first, for being American second, and thirdly for making money."

"The ones who weren't animals were the worst, that's where you're wrong. High society in Morocco was even worse than the rednecks—that Moroccan trip was your fault. You didn't want to go to Nepal and Nepal would have been the best place. 'Go to Nepal?' all the Americans said to you, 'with a baby?' By listening to them you missed the best scene. They have houses in Nepal for the cold, with fireplaces and wood; it wouldn't have been as bad as Morocco, even with snow!"

"I still say that it was having Mustapha around all the time that drove me crazy."

"If he bother you," Frederick said, "you just throw him a dirham."

We're arguing again about Morocco. Frederick says that when I called the police to complain about the cold house it just showed what kind of a mind I have, the mind of a cop.

"I didn't call him. The landlord called him. I went to the landlord's shop and complained."

"You were screaming."

"So what? They scream, don't they? I didn't ask him to call the police."

"You always manage to get the police into everything."

It's true. When in a state of panic I do tend to call the police. However, that day in Tiznit it wasn't me who called the police. I'm remembering the conversation I had with the Moroccan cop after I told him to put his palm against the wall and feel how cold it was:

"*We can't discuss this with you, Madam; we don't discuss things with women.*" (*On discute pas avec les femmes.*)

"*But I pay the bills. You can discuss it with me!*"

"*On discute pas avec les femmes! Où est votre mari?*"

"*My husband has nothing to do with it. He doesn't care about the cold. I pay the bills. I'm not a slave woman.*"

"*I didn't say you were a slave; but you're a woman. We discuss with husbands; it's the custom.*"

After that episode Frederick tried to send me back to New York but I got off the plane in the wrong city, thinking that Marrakech was Casablanca and by the time I made it to Casablanca, with Emma, three men tried to rape me—an American marine (while I was nursing Emma) and two Arab desk clerks; therefore I was only too happy to change my mind and go right back to Tiznit. I hadn't wanted to leave anyway and Frederick had been crying at the airport (probably because he was going to miss Emma, not me). When I saw him crying, sitting on the edge of the car seat, his legs dangling out the open door (he thought I was inside the waiting room), I said, "I'm not leaving, Frederick."

"Oh, yes you are," he told me, and then, to make sure that I would really leave he escorted me onto the plane, carrying my bags and asking me if I was sure that I didn't want to leave Emma with him. Little did he know we'd be back in four days (to find the house overflowing with Arab musicians, playing instruments and smoking kif).

CHAPTER XIX

Nursery School

Frederick and I separated in December because we couldn't stop arguing and I moved in with Alexandra and her husband, Eduardo. They had decided to spend the winter in New York because, I think, they were afraid of the political situation in Uruguay. The Tupamaros had set off a bomb in the family palace in Montevideo which succeeded only in blowing off the front door. However, since the door was a heavy medieval oak and iron affair, it was clear that the force of the explosion could easily have killed someone. When it got to the point where they had to take out kidnapping insurance my brother-in-law decided that they had better leave.

Although Alexandra was her usual sweet and generous self, I dragged through the days, depressed as hell, but trying to seem cheerful for Emma's sake. Living without Frederick was, as usual, worse than living with him. It was becoming clear to me that marriage is like a drug; once dependent on it it's nearly impossible to live without it. Damned if you do and damned if you don't.

I tried to find a nursery school for Emma (after telling Frederick's sister that I'd never put a child of *mine* in anything so horrible as a school) and walked the streets of New York looking at schools and getting more and more depressed at each one.

One school had a teacher whose personal grooming and appearance were so disgusting that I didn't want to subject a child of mine to such an unesthetic vision every day. His pants hung so low over his bulging ass that from the rear a two-year-old's eyes could only see, looking up, a mass of fat between his waistband and his shirt that consisted of the upper half of his buttocks, the dividing cleft perfectly visible, the cheeks on either side compressed into a series of ripples caused by the pressure of his waistband cutting into the flesh. Besides, he was German and sounded like Hitler when he gave orders to the depressed-looking little kids, who were usually crowded together in a tiny space between a dirty cot and a wall, listening to him read sadistic fairy tales. They didn't seem to be permitted to run around the enormous room, the basement of a gay activist church, nor did they seem permitted to go outdoors. Their faces were all pale gray.

The second school I visited kept the children "resting" on lines of foldaway cots while a group of harassed, anxious, neurotic-sounding young women explained to me that I would have to assure them that Emma would stay in the school for a solid year; otherwise they wouldn't take her. While I talked to them my throat felt as though a metal band was tightening around it. I left, speedily, before bursting into tears.

I visited the third school on a rainy day, carrying Emma in my arms because her shoes had given her blisters and she couldn't walk through the cold rain barefoot. By the time we arrived at the door I was exhausted and looking forward to releasing my load on the nursery school floor and sitting down. Since the school cost fifty dollars a week I figured they'd at least be polite, if not happy to see another potential two hundred dollars a month at their doorstep.

I opened the door on three young girls playing ring-around-the-rosy with their charges. One of them turned on me, furious, and said, "How dare you interrupt us like this? We're busy! Go out and have a cup of coffee and come back in half an hour. You should have telephoned first!"

"I tried to telephone but I couldn't find your number."

"It's listed!"

"But I asked for the Gingerbread House and they didn't have a listing."

"We're not called the Gingerbread House. We're called the Teeny-Weeny House."

"Then that's why I couldn't telephone. I didn't know your name."

"That doesn't matter. You should have telephoned. Go on out and come back later."

239

"It's raining."

"Will you please get out of here?"

Back at Alexandra's I told my sister I thought there was something wrong with me. "Why do I get so upset over such a minor thing as that," I asked her, "some stupid girl bitching at me in a nursery school?"

"It's because you're so sensitive," Alexandra told me.

"How can I desensitize myself?" I asked her, thinking that since she was so calm, cool, and collected, she must have some answers.

"By having a lobotomy," she said.

CHAPTER XX

Weaning II

The week before Christmas Welfare gave me a present. They cut off my payments because I didn't show up for a "face-to-face confrontation to determine your continued eligibility." I also didn't sign the papers authorizing the government to appropriate my royalties so they could protect themselves. Miraculously, however, I sold a book. Thankful that I had enough faith in myself to give up my three hundred and forty dollars a month for the sake of the possible thousands I was now about to earn, I let Frederick, who was coming by every day or so to pick up Emma, persuade me to take a vacation. On Christmas Eve I went to Paris, alone. Since my last book was successful over there, in French translation, I was going to kill two birds with one stone by doing some publicity as well.

Alexandra had decided to take Emma to her grandparents for the holidays. I was consoled by the thought that at least she'd get to see a Christmas tree.

My last sight of her was in Alexandra's bathtub, where she was playing with some rubber toys. I didn't say goodbye to her; Alexandra was afraid she would start crying. I had prepared her for her visit upstate an hour before, telling her she was going to see Grandpa and Grandma; then I slipped out the door leaving her then in the tub. She still wasn't weaned.

All the way to the airport I was depressed, seeing in my mind the sight of her alone, moist and rosy, in the bathtub. Losing a nursing child, even for a few weeks, was going to turn out to be as bad as losing her by death. That's how terribly I grieved for her. I told myself that I was going through a hormonal change similar to menopause, but, like a menopausal woman, physiological knowledge alone was no consolation. Rather than enjoying sleeping late, or no longer having to pull out a tit at any moment, I longed for her little body, snug against mine, her mouth clamped to one of my nipples. Like marriage, nursing was turning out to be one of those painful addictions; damned if you do, damned if you don't.

My hostess, a French actress named Sabine De Forest, laughed at me and told me I was just suffering from guilt. A newly converted feminist, she was of the opinion that the maternal instinct was merely a product of brainwashing, and, though the mother of two children herself, she filled my bedside table with books on the subject every night. The latest was by Shulamith Firestone. As I pored over a passage about test-tube babies and the horror of pregnancy and breastfeeding, the book had the opposite effect on me as the one intended by Sabine. Recalling my past life every night as I tried in vain to sleep, I decided that my happiest moments had been those when I was suckling Emma. I regarded my breasts each day, diminishing inch by inch, with as much repulsion as I would have regarded them had they been decaying with leprosy. Out in the streets of the sixteenth arrondissement I obsessively examined every breast that passed, trying to determine its state of functioning. Was it lactating or milkless, pregnant or childless, multipara or nullipara, sagging or firm? I didn't see faces, I only saw breasts. Finally I came to abhor a nonfunctioning breast and I tried to imagine Emma, surrounded by adoring relatives, the Christmas tree, her presents, and my mother's semi-annual turkey. I hoped these pleasures would compensate her for the loss of her mother's tits.

If Sabine's theories about motherhood were lost on me, her theories about politics were not. Primed with her lectures I went to my first television interview as fired up with rage as the Tupamaros. Forgetting all about my book, I raged on and on about Pompidou, Nixon, Vietnam, and female oppression. At the end of the first sixteen-millimeter magazine, in the garden of a famous dead writer, I raised my fist to the camera and said, in French, "Who is going to demolish these outmoded politicians? *C'est à vous, citoyens, c'est à vous!*"

"Wonderful," the camera crew clapped, "wonderful; now let's go down to the subway. We want to pretend that you've just gotten off the metro, and we want you to say a few words into the camera."

We took up our stations at one of the metro exits. I went down into the bowels of the staircase and the crew set the camera up at the top. "Okay," they shouted, "come on up the stairs!"

It was seven o'clock, the hour all the workers were coming home. I trudged up the stairs with dozens of them, stopped in front of the camera, and shouted, *"C'est l'enfers là bas* (It's hell down there), worse than Dante's inferno! Slaves! All of these people are slaves to the rich! Slaves to the giant corporations! To the Rockefellers, to the Rothschilds, traveling like poor dogs on that horrible metro from eight in the morning till seven at night. So the rich can fill their coffers and eat caviar and drink champagne! Look at them!" I pointed at the workers, mystified by my outburst, "pale and gray, they never see the sun from day to day! All for the rich!"

The crew was upset. They asked me, politely, to do it over again. I did the same thing a second time. That night I sat in front of the eleven o'clock news, waiting in vain for the film on the new American author to be aired. Finally it was clear that it would never be shown; I hadn't made the grade. The eleven o'clock news would never see my face nor hear my voice. In fact, out of the six or eight interviews I gave, not one was printed, aired, or televised.

Rather than bemoan my fate as an aborted revolutionary, I left town with Louise Arayo, a Philippine woman who was married to Fernando Arayo, a Spanish actor not only considered a genius but beautiful to look at as well. He had one problem. He was a schizophrenic.

Louise is one of the most beautiful women I have ever seen. She has almond-shaped eyes, a perfect white complexion, a round, moonlike face, and, astonishingly, a mantle of luxurious shining long red hair that causes endless comment, juxtaposed as it is with those oriental features. They have one child, a girl.

Louise, it was confided to me by one of her lovers, loves sex so much that she keeps her entire body, including her pubic area, shaved. I never thought of asking him what the connection was between sex and shaving; I couldn't understand it myself.

Louise and I were going to Tours to see her husband, who was in a mental institution, having just been released from a jail in Madrid, where he had spent eighteen months for possession of one half of a gram of hashish. The police knew that the case would get a lot of coverage, since Fernando was one of the most respected avant-garde actors in Europe and they wanted to "make an example" of him.

Louise herself wasn't any too stable a personality. She had spent a good share of her own life behind the bars of mental institutions. Right now, though, she seemed to be in good spirits. She had just discovered the art of pottery and spent four hours every day in a pottery establishment, learning the craft.

Fernando met us at the train station in Tours with an entourage of adoring fellow inmates. One of the group was the wife (an ex-patient) of the director of the establishment. He was a M. Guery, the R. D. Laing of France.

From the moment we arrived on the platform it was clear that the director's wife, Babette, was madly, adoringly, in love with Louise's husband. In fact everyone there was in love with Louise's husband.

We repaired to a local café. Fernando asked his wife for the mail. When he opened a bill for taxes he went crazy with anger, shouting at Louise and accusing her of being stupid and a vegetable, among other things, for not having opened the envelope herself and paying the bill.

"But you told me not to open your mail," she sobbed. "I was just obeying orders!"

Babette and entourage clucked and clucked, a Greek chorus, while Fernando continued to berate his wife, telling her that she wasn't a wife, that the least she could do while he was in the hospital was to pay his bills.

"The baby had a cold," Louise told him, "and I had to take her to the doctor's. I didn't have the money to pay your bills anyway."

It was a strange time to be talking about bills, I thought, especially with the talk coming from Fernando, an actor who, whenever he made any money, spent it on whoever was catching his fancy at the time. This category included tourists, beggars, hippies, concièrges, girlfriends, and fellow-madmen. He almost never spent it on bills. They still lived in a tiny one-room hovel in Montmartre. To go to the toilet they had to go out into the hall and squat over a nineteenth-century hole with porcelain footprints on either side. With the money he made they could have been living in a duplex in the sixteenth arrondissement.

In silence we drove to the nuthouse, where Fernando at once closeted himself with a couple of fellow-patients, to discuss the script they were writing for a movie to be made on the grounds.

I led Louise out to the highway, telling her that she needed some air. She couldn't seem to stop crying.

"What shall I do, oh . . ." she cried, her beautiful round baby face streaming with tears, ". . . tell me what to do. I'm so unhappy."

I pulled at her wrist. "Come on, Louise," I said, "let's walk farther up the road." I wanted to get her into the field, where the black soil of the Loire valley had just been turned over. I could smell it, rich and heavy, and I thought if we could just get close to the black mud we'd be able to solve these domestic difficulties. There was a sign posted; *Propriété Privée* it said. We stopped on the shoulder of the road.

"Listen, Louise," I said, while wiping her tears with a scarf and resisting the desire I had to embrace her and kiss her full on her lips, which were moist and plump, almost mauve in color, "you've got to take a stand."

"You're right," she sobbed, "you're so right."

"You tell him that you have a child to take care of, your pottery classes to go to, that you have the responsibility of the child since he's in the nuthouse, and just because you didn't pay one piddling bill for him it's no reason to humiliate you in public. If you want to be a vegetable you have every right to be a vegetable. What does he think mysticism is? With all his talk about it. It led him to the nuthouse and it can lead you to be a vegetable. That's what it is, anyway . . . the state of being a vegetable. A real mystic doesn't act in movies and write screenplays about it; he vegetates, like you. Just because you're not a hypocrite you're being persecuted. Tell him he can find another wife if he humiliates you any more. Tell him, 'I'm young and beautiful and I can get any man I want.

I'll just leave you for a man with money, a man who isn't crazy and who can take care of me and the baby!' "

"I got along all right without him while he was in prison," Louise choked out, her resolve to leave him growing again, remembering all the things she had said to me on the train about how she wasn't a wife to him anyway, he wasn't a husband to her; the marriage was finished. ". . . I was very happy while he was in prison. I was a lot better off as a matter of fact . . . I want to say (*je veux dire*), I want to say," she repeated, this phrase recurring in her speech constantly, like an American saying, "I mean," or "you know," all the time, or more precisely like a Frenchman saying (Frederick, for example, as I pointed out in the first chapter), *"Tu vois?"* . . . *"Je veux dire,"* Louise continued, "that I don't need him!"

"Of course you don't need him. Let him know that. Don't sit there crying when he abuses you. Just tell him you don't need him and if he doesn't shape up you'll get another husband."

Her round face became brilliant with smiles—the moon coming out from behind a heavy fog. She hugged me and thanked me and told me that I was right.

We walked back to the asylum. Fernando, having apparently received an illumination in our absence, met us at the door, all smiles, and tenderly took his wife's arm (a gesture she shrugged off impatiently, eager as she was to get on with the speech I had just put into her mouth).

"Fernando," she burst out, "you know I don't need you, I can get along without you. I was perfectly happy without you while you were in prison and I have plenty of admirers who would be only too happy to marry me . . . *je veux dire, je veux dire* . . . that you're impossible and I really don't need you!"

Fernando was more amazed than I was by this premature outburst, because I recognized it as being a part of my own character as well; whenever a woman friend told me anything about my husband or gave me any advice about my marriage I couldn't contain it at all; I had to burst out with it the minute I saw Frederick. Watching Louise was like watching a piece of my own brain that had detached itself and was acting independently of its other parts.

Fernando was in turn desolate and then angry. They had another argument wherein both decided that the marriage was finished. Then the three of us sat, like depressed children, in the dining room, watching the sun set on the fields. I was amazed that none of the patients was out

walking, a fact I later discovered was directly attributable to drugs. This modern, progressive, liberal establishment, so closely based (in its director's eyes) on R. D. Laing's philosophy that schizophrenia doesn't exist, that it's a necessary reaction to the madness prevalent in the patient's family, and that if the patient didn't react that way he would really be unhealthy, had so doped up its patients that they stayed in the stuffy, smoky room, puffing on cigarettes and watching television with a manic absorption rather than going out into those beautiful meadows, in a countryside that has been extolled in literature for centuries for its stunning beauty.

Before I left I stopped in Montmartre to see Louise and Fernando. He had been released for the weekend and they were both in their tiny apartment on Rue Blanche. I opened the door, finding it unlocked, to see that they were making love on the bed.

We made arrangements to meet later for dinner and I left.

At the appointed hour I arrived at the Brasserie Lipp, to find Louise with such a look of satisfaction on her face that not only did she not in any way resemble the woman I had spent the weekend with, but there was something mysterious in her face as well—something that could only be described as "Oriental inscrutability." She looked like a cat, eyes narrowed, purring on a windowsill in the sunlight or a fat, smiling Chinese Buddha. Anyone unacquainted with orthodox psychology would have said that the only trouble with that marriage had been that Louise didn't get fucked enough.

CHAPTER XXI

The Womens Have a Much Better Life Than the Mens

"I don't know what womens are complaining about," Frederick told me when I arrived home. "The womens have a much better life than the mens."

He had built up a routine in my absence of going to the laundromat once a day. I pointed out to him that it was easier to do larger loads on fewer days—he had never thought of that. He had also never thought of leaving it there to be done by an attendant and picked up later. (In the days that followed I realized how much he loved washing machines and dryers.)

"I wasn't able to do any work," he told me, "because I had to take care of the baby."

I began to set the table for dinner. "No!" Frederick shouted urgently, "don't do that! We can all eat out of the pot, with our fingers, the way they do in Morocco. The trouble with you is you make too much work. Everybody nowadays is trying to imitate Louis the Fourteenth, as though they had servants. That's where the idea of setting a table with glass and silverware and all those plates comes from."

Since our separation, Frederick had moved to one small room in the hotel, on the fifth floor, with a tiny kitchenette right in the room. Work had been started on the construction of a building right behind the hotel.

When I telephoned from Paris I could hear the drilling over the phone. It was deafening. Living in the room was the same as living in the construction site itself. Enormous cranes passed directly in front of the only window and the entire room shook whenever a dynamite blast went off. Frederick had Emma sleeping in the bathtub in an effort to get her away from the noise.

"We had to get up every morning at seven o'clock," Frederick told me. "That's when the drilling starts. I took her out right away, to the park. When she had to take a nap I put her in the bathtub."

"BOOM BOOM BOOM!" Another blast of dynamite.

"Boom!" Emma shouted, laughing.

"Why didn't you move to a room in the front of the building?" I asked Frederick.

"Because Sidney doesn't want us in the hotel any more; I had to pretend that this room was for Gunter von Habsburg. If I start complaining and change the room Sidney will kick us out. He says he can't stand our fighting. Besides, we owe him a couple thousand dollars."

"Do you mean that he doesn't see you leave the building every day with Emma? That he doesn't know you're living here?"

"Augustine, he like me. It's *you* that he doesn't want here. He knows that you're hysterical."

While I was away, Frederick had apparently become very friendly with a homosexual composer who lived on the eleventh floor. His name was Max. Emma sneaked out the door the first day I was home and by the time I found her she had traveled from the fifth floor to the ninth floor on that treacherous staircase with its nineteenth-century banister. Supporting the banister was a wrought-iron trellis that had at its base regularly spaced holes of about eighteen inches square. I had once seen, on the tenth floor, a three-year-old boy sitting on the left edge of a step, his entire body framed by one of those holes, and his legs dangling down into the stairwell.

Emma was advancing very rapidly up those stairs on her hands and knees and when she heard my voice calling her she yelled, "Go home, I wanna thee Macth!"

"Okay," I told her when I found her (all smudged with dirt from the filthy stairs), "you can see Max. But let me take you up there so you won't hurt yourself."

"Go home, Mama," she repeated, "I wanna see Macth!" Finally I convinced her that I wouldn't encroach on her privacy and that as soon as I dropped her off at Max's I would leave her there and go home. At Max's door, however, she changed her mind, and when he opened it, his heavy thatch of long black curls touseled from sleep, his rabbinical beard tangled and matted, she said she wanted to go back home.

"I'll come downstairs with you," Max said, "I want to see Frederick." We all started for the fifth floor. Emma began whining.

"Don't you want to see Papa?" I asked her.

"No Papa," she said.

"No Papa?" I repeated.

"No," she said, "no Papa."

Max gave me a strange look. "I've never heard her say that before," he told me.

"Do you want to see Alexandra?" I asked Emma next. "She's coming to take you for a walk."

"No," Emma repeated, "no Asanda."

Once down in the room Frederick shot me a dirty look for what I presumed was my indiscretion in bringing Max to our room. Frederick had a peculiar relationship with his own friends, those friends that he didn't share with me. He wanted to be able to see them in their own environment, without me, and without inviting them to his own apartment. It was the same with Malcolm the dealer who had cleaned the apartment for me the night before Emma was born. I suppose he looked on them as a series of oases to which he could escape whenever he wanted and be assured that he would be left alone. That was the way he dealt with living in a hotel, while I couldn't really deal with it at all.

Alexandra arrived to pick up Emma. Bedlam broke loose in the tiny room. Everyone started arguing and talking and crying at once. Max was in a corner drinking beer from a bottle, pretending that everything was fine, that there was no tension in the tiny room. I escaped to the bathroom, where I sat on the toilet, arms on the sink, my head in my arms, suffering from a hypoglycemia-dopamine attack. I was going to come out after everyone had left.

Alexandra and Emma left for their walk, after which Emma was going to spend the night at Alexandra's. As soon as the door closed on them I heard Max say to Frederick, "You shouldn't leave Emma with all those women. She shouldn't be alone with them. They're trying to turn her against you." I felt as though someone had thrown a brick into my chest. I could hardly breathe I was so angry. I decided to wait there, in the bathroom, until he left. I was afraid I'd kill him if I looked at him. I was also waiting to hear the rest of the conversation.

Frederick said nothing. Then Max came into the bathroom, saw me, and said, "Well, it's a small world." I remained silent, my head in my arms, hoping that he'd leave. He didn't. He sat down on the edge of the bathtub, staring at me. Finally I got up, said to him, "I think that what you've just done is the most despicable thing I've ever heard of in my life. Get out of here."

He tried to mollify me. "I can't understand," I said to him, "how anyone could deliberately try to break up a family like that."

"Now Augustine . . ." he began.

I grabbed the front of his shirt collar, the way a bouncer does in the movies, saying to him, "How dare you, a stranger, interfere in my family life? Now get out of here and stay out!" I pushed him out the door, shoving him in the chest after I released his shirt collar, and slammed the door after him. Then I turned my attention to Frederick.

"How could you have a friend like that?" I asked him.

"You're the one who invited him down here," Frederick told me. "He was never in this room while you were away."

"What the hell difference does that make? How dare he say a thing like that to you about me and my sisters?"

"Augustine, did you hear me agreeing with him? I know you're not trying to turn Emma against me. I don't pay any attention to what he says. Do you think I'm stupid?"

"It hurts me to think that you would have a friend like that."

"He helped me take care of Emma while you were away. He was really nice to her."

"You're the one who wanted me to leave. Don't use that as an excuse."

"Besides, he has good dope."

"That's more like it."

"And I'm doing some tapes for him. He's paying me. You're always asking me to get a job; well, I've got one."

"The only reason that you didn't answer him was that you knew I was in the bathroom."

Frederick laughed. "Of course I knew you were in the bathroom," he said. "I knew you were spying on us." After that the discussion became a full-fledged argument, which ended with Frederick slapping me in the face. I collapsed on the kitchenette floor, crying, until he said, "I'll make you some camomile tea; that will calm you down."

Later that evening, still fuming, I decided to call Max, to tell him how angry I still was with him. When I reached him he told me that he was just about to telephone me. That he had been trying all afternoon but the line had been busy.

"I just want you to know," I told him, "how furious I still am with you."

"And I want to explain to you, Augustine, why I said that to Frederick. I had never heard her say 'No Papa' before; and it was you who started it."

"What are you talking about?"

"On the stairs, when you said 'No Papa?' to her."

"You didn't hear her say it first?"

"No."

"Well, you see, that just goes to show how your mind works. Emma said 'No Papa' to me, and to make sure that I heard her right I repeated it. She always says 'no' something or somebody when she doesn't want to do something. She's two years old, you know; her vocabulary isn't very extensive. I've lived with her now for two years. I *am* her mother. I *do* understand her language—after all, I taught it to her. You just met her five weeks ago. Anyway, that's beside the point. Even if I *did* try to turn her against her own father, which is something I'd never do even if I hated her father, which I don't—I love him, you would have no business interfering. She's not your child. You didn't breastfeed her for two years, clean up her shit, wipe up her vomit, get up with her every three hours for six months . . . and then have some stranger try to turn her father against you. I think your problem is that you're in love with Frederick."

"Well, if you're talking about sexual love, then I must tell you that

I was sexually in love with him at one time but I gave it up because it didn't get me anywhere. It wasn't reciprocated."

I was becoming more and more determined to get out of the hotel and the city as well. I felt that the inhabitants were driving me mad.

"You're a match for him," Camilla Aponte, the dealer's wife, said to me. "You're the first wife to challenge him. Do you know that he told Tony that he was blowing his scene at the Metro Hotel by bringing me there to live with him?"

"Whose scene?" I asked. "His or Tony's?"

"Tony's," she explained. "Max hates me because I'm Tony's wife, and I never go upstairs when Tony's up there. Max won't even speak to me; he doesn't like women."

"Do you mean to tell me that Max expected Tony to move from Queens into the Metro Hotel without you?"

"Yes. Can you believe it?"

"No. I can't."

"We were going to get a divorce because we were so bored in Queens, leading the life of a straight married couple. When we moved here to the Metro Hotel it saved our marriage. I began having lovers for the first time in my marriage."

"Tony doesn't mind?"

"He loves it. You know that couple on the third floor, the Cacciolis? Well, Ed Caccioli became my lover and Ed's wife became Tony's lover. It saved our marriage. Now Max is trying to destroy it again, our marriage."

"Why does Tony see so much of him if he feels that way about you?"

"Because Max is the only person in the hotel with a brain. Besides, he's a brilliant musician. Did you know that Tony used to be gay? I was the first woman he'd ever fucked. That's what I told his mother and father when they complained that I have lovers. I'll show it to you; we made a video tape about it. We made a tape of the conversation between me and Tony and his parents. 'I'm going to tell your mother, Camilla,' she said, 'I'm going to tell her that you're unfaithful to my son. I know she brought you up to be a good girl.' 'Do you know that your son was having an affair with one of the Jesuits who was teaching him at college?' I asked her, 'and that I was the first woman he ever fucked? That I saved him?' "

"What did she say?"

"Oh, you'll have to see the tape. It's fabulous. Her husband just sits there, with a disgusted look on his face, telling her not to be so loud while she rants and raves at us, Tony and me, telling us that she's going to vomit any minute she's so disgusted, asking how can we even talk about such things in front of the baby. The baby, who's a year old . . . I didn't tell her that the baby nurses while Tony and I fuck. She'd probably think that that was more degenerate than Tony fucking the Jesuit."

"You're insane, Augustine," my husband said later that night, "insane to be jealous of Max. He's one of your biggest fans. He moved into the hotel because you were here. He loves you and admires you. Ha! Little do they know, your fans, how horrible you are to live with."

"Ow! Frederick, your hand is freezing! Take it away. Take it out from between my legs. How did you get so cold anyway?" (The radiator isn't working.)

"I put an ice cube in your cunt, so you'll die from it."

"An ice cube! You've put icicles in my cunt!"

"Don't worry, darling, I won't ever do it again. You'll never have to worry about me touching you again."

"You've put the Arctic Circle in my cunt."

"And you! You've put ice in my heart."

"Ice in your heart! Now that really is a straight cliché," I told him.

"Augustine, you're so straight that I can only explain it to you like that! Oh, the videotape machine," he went on, "what's it doing all set up like that? Here, let me push the on button. I want to record this argument."

"*I* was going to push the button; *I* set it up!"

"Well, my little darling, you weren't fast enough. Now, it's *my* tape, because *I* pushed the button! Did any of my girlfriends call tonight?"

"No, not tonight."

"No? What happened?"

"I probably scared them off last night, every time they called. They won't be bothering me any more."

"Right," Frederick sighed, with a mock-tragic air, rolling his eyes toward the camera, "terrible to be bothered!"

"How can they have such bad taste?" I asked him, ignoring the way he was posing for the camera.

"You have bad taste," he said, "not them."

"I don't mean they have bad taste to like you, I mean they have bad taste to call you when they know I'm here."

"They're not my girlfriends. We just . . . you know . . . fuck. Why shouldn't they call me here? See how straight you are?"

"Well, they could at least be friendly to me when they call."

"Why should they be?" Frederick laughed, "when you're just like a creep on the phone."

"I have to be a creep on the phone; I don't have anybody to screen my calls. If I had a secretary like Sabine does, on Avenue Paul Daumer, then I wouldn't have to talk to them," I told him, arranging my legs in a more glamorous pose and changing my profile toward the camera from the right to left, the side I thought was the more attractive and symmetrical.

"You're better off without one, dummy. Who want a secretary? All your straight things come up again. She drive you crazy, a secretary. You'd be bored to death, you'd be calling your doctor every five minutes. Look! You have the best life there is in the world! You're living with *me*! You can't expect *better*! You don't know that? You don't understand? I mean—really!—if you understood the system a little bit, you would be happy, much more happy. But, like everyone else, you just stay on the bed and get depressed . . . because you look at the typewriter and you lost all your faith."

"What does the typewriter have to do with it?" I asked him.

"It's an image, dummy," he replied.

"Well," I told him, "when I was at Sabine's house a peasant woman came to get an abortion. She'd never been in Paris before and she said, 'No wonder all the people are so unhappy in Paris; there aren't any trees!'"

"You've taken a bad example, Augustine. That woman was wrong. You can't have any other life than the one you have right now, because it's the most free and you can never do anything else. Anybody you're going to meet will get you in all kinds of troubles. You know that yourself. You're just crazy, you know. You *can't* live a straight life! You're such a *slob*! You forget everything like everybody else."

"Well, Frederick, I just wish you would take care of the baby sometimes."

That made him mad. He jumped out of camera range and began pacing the room, shouting at me. "Look, Augustine, I'm taking care of the baby whenever you want!"

"OOOOOH!" I shouted back, "you get up, you run out . . ."

"When was that?"

". . . and you're gone!"

"When was that?" he repeated, getting himself back into the frame.

"Ever since I've been back from Paris."

"That's not true! You're a liar! That's why I'm not going to do anything! You just *flip* everytime you take care of her. You don't recognize anything! When you take care of her for an hour you think it's been five days, because you have no patience. What are you going to end up? You're going to end up a fucking . . . cunt! And . . . you just *insist*! You're going to take care of the baby alone because that's what you really want! You know what your problem is? You complain about the wrong things. That's why we always fight."

"You never accept criticism," I told him. "You're just like my sister Alexandra; you hate to be criticized. You think you're a god . . . or a genius . . . don't you?"

"I think I'm a prick. A ridiculous prick. It's because of my father. You say everything is because of your husband. If I leave you it's because I'm taking my father as an image. He left my mother long before I was born. Then he only came home on Sundays, to criticize my report card. I was conceived on a Sunday night. But, you don't understand that everything you say is wrong . . . it's my fault that you don't understand that . . . you're so crazy . . . Augustine . . . look, I'm going to tape you for a few more days."

"*It's my tape!*"

"It's my tape! Who push on the button?"

Watching the tape, a month later, Frederick said to me, "You drive me crazy. You started beating me up! Over the tape! Hahahaha. You didn't understand that I was drunk and on top of that I took some pills! The guy who was living next to us, you drive him crazy too. You made him turn off his T.V. one night at eleven o'clock, remember? And this was at five in the morning! Hahaha, listen to you struggling with me! Look at you! You think you can win over me, with your little body?

Back on the videotape, Frederick is saying, "Augustine, get me a drink!"

"No."

"Get me a drink!"

"No, no, no, a thousand times, no!"

"I don't give a shit!"

"Okay."

"Get me a drink. That's my tape, anyway!"

"Okay, I'll get you a drink for the tape."

"Thanks a lot, Augustine."

"Frederick?"

"What?"

"How come your feet smell so terrible?"

"I tell you it's because you didn't buy me a new pair of shoes for the past two years. Kiss me, dummy."

"Okay."

"You don't show any passion. You don't go . . . you never make a sound. You don't go 'uuuuuum' like other girls."

"Frederick, the last time I went 'uuuuum' you rejected me. I'll never forget that night, before I went to Paris and I was so turned on by you, and I went 'uuuuuuuum' and my fingernails were trembling and you pulled away from me and said, 'You can't fool me! You're acting!' "

"You reject me too!" he said. "You used to tell me all the time that I have a small prick, that I couldn't get a hard-on!"

"I never told you you had a small prick!"

"Yeah, you used to say that all the time!"

"Never!"

"For years . . . for years I left my sexual powers, because you repress me so much . . . I have witnesses!"

"I never told you that, because it isn't true! If you could see some of the small pricks I've known!"

"You put me down all the time for my sexual things. That's how you lost me. Let's be straight with you. I had to find out. That's why I have other women. I had to. Remember? Really! you impressed me too much, you know, because you keep telling me I was really bad and I couldn't make love and everything and I didn't know how to make love and everything like that."

"You don't know how to make love."

"Well, that's why; who wants to make love with somebody who doesn't like the way you do it? I never had any problems like that before and then I say, 'Well, I should quit, because she doesn't like the way I do it.' "

"Well, I'm not everybody."

"I quit! And I quit forever!"

"I have higher standards."

"That's what I mean. I mean, I say to myself, 'She has higher standards and I don't think I should destroy her . . . you know . . . her feelings! That's why I better not fuck with you any more."

"Well . . . you could have thought about . . ."

"I'm not kidding! It's true!"

". . . raising your standards!"

"You can't raise your standards when you depend on your prick. I'm not American. I haven't been psychoanalyzed since I was born, you know."

"Neither was I!"

"Yes you were, but you didn't realize it. You were . . . from television and everything . . . The whole idea of America is a whole psychoanalyst."

"Shit!" I exploded, "if I told you that you were like the average French taxicab driver . . ."

"I am! You just don't realize it!"

"I've lost the point," I said. "What are we talking about?"

"We're talking about you," Frederick told me. "Me—I'm completely fulfilled."

"Sure," I said, "the great Western phallus is always fulfilled. All it has to do is masturbate."

"*What?*"

"Masturbate!"

"Right! What's wrong with that? I think you think that there's something wrong with it; since I saw the way you act with Emma when she masturbates, I think there's something *weird* between masturbation and you . . . because you had that kind of laugh . . . and your attitude changes as soon as she does that. You gotta be *cool* . . . when she does that . . . just be cool . . ."

"But I was just laughing!"

"Don't make any humor, because it's just . . ."

"You criticize everything I do."

"Not everything, because you . . ."

"Talk about something else!"

". . . because I keep telling you what a great mother you are."

"That's just a smoke screen to camouflage what you're really saying."

As we continue to watch the tape Emma is in the bedroom, masturbating, as though on cue. She's humping her teddy bear, while lying on top of him. Five minutes later she's up again. Meanwhile I've gone to the typewriter to transcribe the tape and she's climbing onto my lap, saying, "Is my work, Mommy, is my work," while trying to hit the typewriter keys.

"It's mine!" Frederick is yelling from the kitchen.

"No!" Emma shouts.

"Yes!" Frederick answers.

"I no big girl," Emma tells me next. "I baby. I wanna suck the mama!"

On the videotape Frederick is telling me not to interrupt the things he says.

"You should be happy," I tell him, "that I'm taking all this time to raise the level of your consciousness."

"Well, forget it. My consciousness is too low."

Emma has gone into the kitchen, where she's sitting on Frederick's lap. Rocking her back and forth, he's singing what sounds like African chants to her. She's singing along with him, just as high as he is, from breathing in the air around him, loaded as it is with marijuana from Dakar.

The lack of space in the tiny room that we were living in finally drove me so crazy that, one day when I couldn't get a connection to the switchboard I ripped the phone out of the wall and marched into Sidney Renard's office with it, slamming it down on his desk.

"Why'd ya do a thing like that?" he asked me, looking at the phone in disbelief.

"Because nobody would answer it."

"You're probably clickin' on the button too much. You know that drives her nuts."

"Why don't you hire two girls?"

"You know what it's like to get help these days?"

"Yeah, especially when you pay them starvation wages."

"I was gonna tell ya to use my phone, Augustine, but you're makin' my migraine headache worse."

"Take two Excedrin."

"Ya owe me a lotta money," he said, ignoring my medical advice.

"I know that," I told him, "but I haven't even paid my obstetrician yet, though god knows why I should pay him, he sewed me up too tight."

"Whaddaya mean he sewed ya up too tight? That couldn't happen in this day and age."

"He told me that it would loosen up with use but it hasn't had any."

"Whaddaya tellin' me, Augustine? That your husband doesn't make love to ya?"

"Yeah, that's what I'm tellin' ya."

"A young man like him? I woulda thought he was a regulah prince, a regulah prince! Whatsa mattah with him?"

"He says I don't excite him."

"That doesn't mattah. It's his duty as a husband ta satisfy ya. Doesn't he know that?"

"He isn't Jewish."

"I'm gonna ignore what ya just said, ignore it, but since ya told me, ya know what?"

"No. What?"

"That's yer problem, that's why you're so irritable."

"I'm irritable because I need a bigger apartment. If you don't give me one I'm moving."

"Augustine," Sidney said, "if you leave the Metro Hotel you'll find out what the real world is like. You'll end up by kissin' the ground the Hotel is standin' on. But you know what?"

"What?" I asked.

"I'm gonna give ya a new apartment. Why I'm doin' it I don't know. I'm a schmuck, I guess. But . . . don't tell anybody how much ya owe me because I don't want 'em to know just how much of a schmuck I am."

"Thanks, Sidney," I said, "that's really nice of you." Then I started to leave the office.

"Wait a minute, Augustine, wait a minute," he called out. I stopped at the door. "Why'd ya break off the cord so near the phone?" he asked me. "If you'd just pulled it out of the wall maybe I could've had it fixed!"

The new apartment is on the eleventh floor with a separate kitchen and a view of the Statue of Liberty. However, being on the eleventh floor, we also have a new maid. I really miss Duñel. I keep thinking about the bath she was going to give me, in banana peels, so I would make some money.

CHAPTER XXII

Her Rival Introduced

I used to feel that Mother was jealous of her daughters because Daddy used to pay so much attention to us and seemed to prefer being with us rather than her. Now I'm beginning to feel the same way about Frederick. I know that he prefers Emma's company to mine. I don't blame him; she's so much more fun than I am. I used to tell him that if he would take care of her I could do some work. Now that he is taking care of her so that I can work, I'd rather be doing what he's doing. When I say goodbye to them, as they go off to the park, or to another room to get stoned, I feel a pang of jealousy. Sometimes I'm jealous of Emma, being so much with Frederick, and other times I'm jealous of him for being so much with Emma.

Today I'm jealous of Elkse. She came into the apartment with Gunter von Habsburg while I was nursing Emma to sleep in the bedroom.

Her eyes were made up and her outfit had been carefully put together, although to the casual observer it would seem that she had just thrown her clothes on without any thought. That was one of the characteristics of the European women I knew. They could dress so well that they seemed to have been born wearing the clothes they had on. Everything they wore seemed to be part of their bodies—an ecological miracle.

I could see them, Elkse and Gunter, from the bedroom, through the crack between the double doors. I hadn't yet dressed, combed my hair, bathed, or put on any make-up that day. Not that I ever did, any more. After I abnegated housewifery it was but a short step to abnegating good grooming. If I didn't have to go to a business meeting I threw on anything in sight—thermal underwear, old pajamas, a towel—splashed some cold water on my face, topped by a layer of olive oil (I hadn't remembered in months to buy my favorite moisturizer, Elizabeth Arden's Velva Moisture Film), and put my hair in a rubber band. Elkse was so beautiful and self-possessed that whenever I was with her I worried about how I looked.

When Emma fell asleep I rummaged in my closet for something to wear. Everything was dirty and wrinkled, most of it on the floor. Finally I pulled a black jersey blouse out of the pillow case that served as a laundry bag, decided that it could go for one more wearing, and dragged a blue velvet skirt out of the pile on the closet floor. I sneaked into the bathroom by way of the kitchen and arranged my hair; pulling it back from my face on each side in two clumps, fastening it tightly with two rubber bands to stretch the skin around my eyes, obliterating the crows' feet, and surveyed the effect by using a hand mirror plus the medicine cabinet mirror, to get a good sideview. It wasn't bad. The crows' feet were but a few tiny faint lines, a tentative pencil sketch.

I fluffed out my hair, including the two rubber-banded clumps, backcombing it to make it look thicker, and searched for the kohl. The kohl stick was lost, so I whittled a Q-Tip down, put some kohl in my eyes, found some old cheap brown eye shadow and some mascara, and then worried about my red nose. The skin on my nose never seemed to lose a sunburn; six months later, out of the sun for all that time, it was still pink. Finally I located an old Max Factor pancake make-up patty, minus the top, and sponged some of it over my nose and under my eyes. Then I rouged my cheeks and put some vaseline on my lips.

I didn't want anyone to think I had just made myself up, so I sidled into the living room, keeping my face down, and headed for the telephone. I figured that if I talked on the phone a while, keeping my head down, then by the time I hung up no one would notice my make-up, having already become used to my presence in the room. I had found that it was only if you entered a room unexpectedly, after everyone else had been seated and talking a while, that your appearance was minutely scrutinized.

It was always better to first make your presence felt, subconsciously—that is, if you weren't really up to par appearance-wise—so that the other inhabitants of the room would be used to your vibrations before being forced to take cognizance of you. In this case, I didn't want them to scrutinize me right away, since I had just come from the bathroom and they would know that I had spent an elaborate fifteen minutes on my face. It didn't occur to me to go from the bathroom back into the bedroom and come into the living room from there, so that no one would know that I had been in the bathroom in the first place. That's one of the advantages of having money—to live in a big house, full of corridors, so that no one knows from which room you've come. I knew a painter once, from Latvia, who told me that a woman has to have money to be sexy. "I've been thinking about you all week," he said to me one day, upon finding me in an old dress, scrubbing the floor, "having erotic visions of you. And here I come to see you and you're a mess, scrubbing the kitchen floor!"

While on the phone with Harriet Vanderlip, who had, despite her amphetamine addiction, put on thirty more pounds since that incident in the hotel lobby (we had reconciled since then), I studied Elkse out of the corner of my eye. ("Keep your eye on the ball," I would say to Emma while playing catch, and, laughing at me, she would put the rubber ball against her eyelid.) Elkse was wearing a tight white cotton Victorian corset-cover, which, rather than emphasizing the flatness of her chest, made her whole upper torso look elegant and tiny, like that of a Japanese woman. I figured that she must have spent hours stitching it just so, so that it would give that effect.

She was also wearing a white Victorian petticoat, ankle length, and underneath the petticoat a pair of pale-green silk pajama bottoms peeked out. Around her waist was a silk, fringed, embroidered shawl, from the Art Nouveau period, elaborately arranged to accentuate her tiny waist and narrow hips. On her feet were a pair of sandals, and around her wrists and her neck were masses of turquoise and silver Navajo jewelry—not the new kind, but the very expensive old kind.

Let's face it. It really didn't matter what she wore; she could have been wearing a polyester pants suit with vinyl boots and she still would have been just as beautiful. Her silky, platinum hair hung in a perfect mass of nonsplit ends to her delicately pointed chin. Above her delicately pointed chin a pair of luscious, full, deep rose-colored lips framed a set of perfect, even, milk-white teeth. Her nose was in just the right proportion to the rest of her face—long, narrow, elegant, the nostrils set close to the sides, like slits in a Japanese paper lantern. Her eyes were smoky and mysterious, and even her eyebrows were sensuous, each fine hair springing separately from a clear, perfectly modeled brow.

Her gray eye shadow was only a suggestion, subtly pointing out the veiled, mysterious quality of her gray eyes. I was acutely aware of my thirty-two years—of each line in my face, of each vein in my hands, which, looking at them, reminded me exactly of my mother's hands, as seen by my eight-year-old eyes. The only difference between my hands and my mother's at that age was the fact that my mother always wore red nail polish, allowing the half moons to remain unpolished, with her nails cut off in a square shape. My nails are ragged, split, and dirty and I'm trying to clean them right now, while talking on the phone to Harriet, by using the edge of one of the nails on the other hand as I think about my mother with her ten children and perfect nails.

"I was afraid of you, Augustine. I didn't know what to say to you. You seemed so sure of yourself, so successful. I thought that Gunter liked you better than me . . . because you do things . . . you never talked to me . . . when I used to go over to see you, you never said anything to me . . . I thought you didn't like me."

". . . I was afraid of you . . . of your beauty . . . you never talked to me . . ."

"Oh, Augustine!"

Elkse and I six months later.

CHAPTER XXIII

Weaning III

Both Mary-Agnes and Alexandra were at home, on the island, for Mother's Day. We had decided to surprise Mother with a giant family reunion. All of my sisters took turns nursing Emma on their empty breasts (no child is ever weaned; it's all a propaganda conspiracy by the Gerber Company, the Evenflo Company, and the AMA). They had to be surreptitious about it because of Mother and Daddy and their constant stream of friends who were always monitoring everyone's behavior to be sure that it conformed with Roman Catholic rules and regulations. Pre-Ecumenical Council, they prided themselves on their conservatism and now felt they could behave like orthodox Jews—a minority group confident of its superiority. *"When the church bows and scrapes to the fads and fashions of the day,"* Daddy said, *"it's finished!"*

My sisters usually managed to perform the functions of dry wet nurses behind closed doors. One day, however, Daddy's retarded handyman, Mike, opened a door without knocking, as was his habit. (He was absolved of all breaches of modesty because of his mental retardation and he could always be counted on to take advantage of this situation.)

Emma was on Mary-Agnes's tit this time, and, while sucking, was rhythmically rubbing her pelvis against the edge of the bed. Mary-Agnes was sitting on the bed and Emma was standing, leaning forward to suckle and rub at the same time.

"She was practically having an orgasm," Mary-Agnes told me, laughing, "and just as she was about to come, Mike opened the door. I pulled her away, too abruptly, because I knew it would freak him out. Well, Emma let out a howl, poor little thing, she was so frustrated, and she cried for about twenty minutes."

Now Emma was calling Mary-Agnes "No-Agnes" instead of "Mary-Agnes." "Hi, No-Agnes," she would say, and go over to her, first pretending anger, by hitting her on a leg or arm and then, using the new appellation as a game, she would break into giggles as she repeated it to Mary-Agnes.

Alexandra was also discovered nursing Emma, but by Daddy. "He came in," she said, "looked at me in horror, as if he couldn't believe what he was seeing, and walked out again, without saying a word."

"Do you know," Mother said, "that in Buckeye, Arizona, when I was a child, there was a seven-year-old boy who used to come into the house and whistle for it? 'Mom,' he'd say, 'I'm home!' Your grandmother used to tell that story all the time."

"Well, Augustine," Mother's friend Helen Dick told me, "my daughter Lucy is still nursing her three-year-old. And she's going to have another baby. One will get one side and the other one will get the other side. The doctors told her that they'll have to stay consistently on their own sides; otherwise the new baby will be contaminated by her sister's mouth. I think it's obscene, but I've decided to stop talking about it. She won't listen to me; I'm just her *mother*!"

"Augustine," Lucy told me, "I try to do everything in my power to distract her, to get her mind on something besides nursing" (she said this in a singsong voice, almost a chant, as though it had been often repeated) "but I threw her sister Josie's bottle away when *she* was three, or rather Tony did; he made me throw it away . . ."

"Who's Tony?"

"Oh, I forgot, you've never met him. He's my husband. Well, anyway, he made me throw it away and now I regret it. I think when you do that you're depriving them of something they need, of love . . . if I had it to do over again . . . you know *some people* don't like it, they think we're dirty, don't they, Tina?" she asked her three-year-old, "but we're not dirty, are we, Tina? And we're going to nurse as long as you want to, aren't we? We don't care what *some people* say!"

Lucy was always a very serious girl. She was Mary-Agnes's age and we had all grown up together. She had five sadistic brothers who called her "piglet" when she was a teenager since she was on the plump side.

"Augustine," she was asking me, "how do you stay so thin? Are you on a special diet?"

"No, I just worry so much that it keeps me thin. Free-floating anxiety they call it."

"Oh, gee, free-floating anxiety? I've never heard of that."

"I don't think I've seen you, Lucy, since before you became a nun."

"Oh yes you have. Don't you remember that you visited us when we moved to Main Street? Thirteen fourteen Main Street in Watertown? I was out of the convent then. Then I went to nursing school. I didn't know what I wanted to do, I was a mess, wasn't I, Tina? I was so confused and so mixed up, but then I settled down, didn't I, Tina? And I got married. Now I'm very happy . . . How are you, Mrs. McDermott? That's a pretty nightgown you're wearing. You look pretty!"

"Thank you," my grandmother's voice quavered. We were in her bedroom; I was videotaping her. Grandma hadn't come out of her bedroom for the past ten years. She couldn't remember anything past the time she left Buckeye, Arizona, in 1928.

"Why don't you get a picture of my stomach?" Lucy asked me.

"Okay, Lucy, lift up your shirt."

"Oh nooo . . ." Lucy was embarrassed. "Do you know, Mrs. McDermott, that we're going to see a film on childbirth tonight at our Lamaze class?"

"Oh, dear," Grandma wailed.

"Oh no, it's nice, Mrs. McDermott. They teach you how to relax so you won't feel any pain."

"I should videotape your childbirth, Lucy."

"Oh, that would be so nice. I could call you when the baby's coming and you could come to the hospital . . . oh, here's Tony," she said as a man who looked like a pizza parlor chef came into the room. "Tony, this is Augustine and she wants to film the baby's birth."

"I don't see the point of that," he grumbled, "there's nothin' so special about havin' a baby. It's natural. Everybody does it. It happens all the time. It's like eatin' or sleepin'. Don't see the point at all."

"Right, Tony," my mother echoed.

"But, Tony," Lucy pleaded, her voice rising, "it's for the baby. She'd enjoy it later. Augustine's baby watches herself being born all the time. It's her favorite film."

"Jist don't see how you can make such a big thing out of it," Tony insisted, unimpressed, "it's a natural thing."

"I don't understand why you let her think she has a baby in her tummy when you wouldn't let her believe other things that aren't true," Mother was saying to me as she washed the dishes. The cook had gone to bed, as usual; she wasn't allowed to wash the dishes—too much work.

"What other things, Mother?" I was honestly puzzled.

"Oh, Augustine, you know what I mean!"

"No, really, I don't! Give me an example."

"Santa Claus, for example! You'd never for a moment let her believe in Santa Claus!"

Emma had been walking around lately, her stomach pushed out, holding onto it with both hands, announcing, "I have a baby in my tummy!" And then, once she had your attention, she'd reach both of her hands out, in a cupping motion, inquiring, "Do you wanna see my newborn baby?"

She was imitating Dr. Fabin, in the videotape of her birth, which she watched about three times a day. For several weeks she'd been demanding, as soon as she woke up: "I wanna see Emma born!" Then she would get out of bed, go to the television set, and try to turn it on. Frederick and I both made versions of Emma watching herself being born, so that now we had two tapes of her watching her own birth on the monitor. She had all the dialogue memorized. "It's a girl baby," she would shout, at exactly the right moment, after having bitten her fingernails during the preceding ten minutes of tape.

"No one's told her about Santa Claus," I reassured Mother, "but if they do I don't care if she believes it or not." (It turned out that she did.)

"*I wanna see Emma born!*"

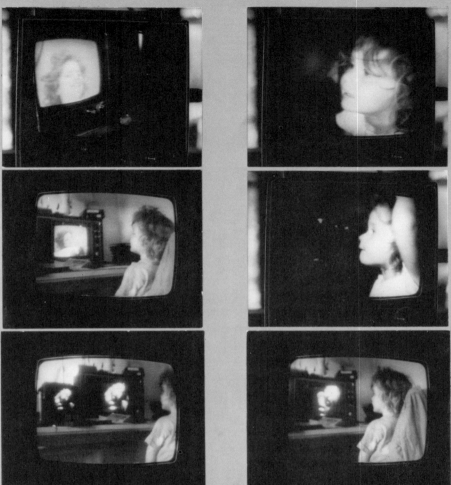

"*It's a girl baby,*" *she would shout, at exactly the right moment, after*

having bitten her fingernails. . . .

"I never heard of giving a two-year-old a choice," Mother was fond of saying to Emma, "but that's the way they do it with you. So I'll ask you: 'What do you want to wear?' "

I felt sorry for Mother. I felt that I knew just what she was doing—reassessing her whole life now that she was a grandmother; thinking "maybe if I had brought them up differently, like they're doing with their children, then they wouldn't have turned out like they did." And I'm sure she was right, even in ways she might not have considered. Emma is becoming a little reactionary: she loves nail polish, hair ribbons, dresses, and order. She's exactly the opposite of me. In other words, she's just like my mother. If Mother had let us go to bed whenever we wanted, not forced us to go to church, allowed us to masturbate, go to bars at night, see any movie we wanted, eat whenever we felt like it, sleep with her and Daddy, then I'm sure we'd now be exactly the way she had hoped us to be. Emma, for example, loves to go to mass with her; and if Mother won't wait for her to decide what dress she wants to wear (which sometimes takes up to twenty minutes) and leaves without her, Emma sobs and sobs with frustration and disappointment.

Back at the Metro Hotel, Emma's imaginary family has increased. I suppose that, seeing the extra room we have, she's decided that she can afford to have more children. Now not only does she have "Bigadalah and my friends" and "my newborn baby in my tummy" but she also has "my two girls." Yesterday, on the floor, she made a bed for "my two girls and my newborn baby." I was warned not to step on any of them as I went into the bathroom. It always seems so hard to get into the bathroom. In apartment 914 there were Frederick's cables in the way, and now in 1116 there are Emma's babies. They have their own pillows; there are three of them arranged along the edge of a quilt on the floor. Emma reads to her babies at night, and when she stops to sit on a stoop with the bums, she tells me that the stairs are the stairs to Bigadalah's house; she climbs up them, knocks on the door, calls out, "Bigadalah and my friends!" as loud as she can shout, and then, from the top step she looks down at me gravely where I'm standing on the sidewalk and tells me, "Bigadalah's not home, Mama."

When I look at her standing on those stairs, her blond curls lit by the sun, forming a halo around her head, her eyes so big, the whites so white, her skin so clear, and her little body so frail, I am overcome with feeling for her, so much so that I want to grab her and kiss her, almost devour her so that I can somehow merge with her. For the first time I understand Father Schroeder (Mrs. Ryan's friend) who urged me to blank out my mind by meditation so that I could merge with God. To me, Emma is God.

Do you remember those adults when you were a child who used to say, "I could just eat you up"? Or those adults who used to playfully take a bite out of your leg or arm or cheek? There is a woman at the Metro Hotel with two grown-up children who says to me, "I could just eat Emma up. When my children were little I used to bite into their thighs . . . ooooow . . .!"

CHAPTER XXIV

Just Look at Her Mother

Daddy became so enamored of Emma that he would telephone me to ask if he could come to New York by plane and take her back with him to Watertown, or to Grenadier Island, wherever he was living at the time. Frederick was always hesitant about this arrangement, saying that she would receive a bad education at the hands of my parents, and that every time we let her go any place she acted weird for three days after she returned home. The other mothers we knew reassured him that all children react that way to a different environment and it takes them all at least three days to get back to their former selves after returning home. Finally he rationalized that we couldn't protect her from the outside world indefinitely anyway, and the sooner she realized that there were all kinds of people in the world ("straight people," in his words), the better it would be for her future launching into "real" life. We never for a moment believed that what she experienced with us was "real." We were far too solicitous of her desires, too intent on keeping her from boredom, and too free of rules to be "real" parents. Besides, her father spent at least four-fifths of his time with her. This was never looked on by either one of us as "real." So whenever Emma's grandparents wanted her we came to see her as an astronaut, and made elaborate preparations for both her journey to the moon and her re-entry descent.

One time while she was away (we finally let her go only because Alexandra would be with her and thus deflect any too zealous attempts on my parents' part to re-educate her) Frederick and I reverted to the habits of our preparental life. I resumed my long lost habit of flirting, not only with other men but with Frederick as well. He, thank god, didn't follow my lead by flirting with other women, but confined his sexual advances to me and began treating me once again as a woman rather than as a mother—a creature who exists only to be criticized. (This criticism always left me very vulnerable vis-à-vis Emma, for, after all, Frederick's a good father and therefore his instincts must be at least as sound as mine.)

The night she returned, while Frederick was giving her a bath and I was making dinner, I stopped cutting the ends off the string beans and went to the doorway of the bathroom to tell him, "Make sure she doesn't get ahold of that razor sitting on the edge of the bathtub. Pick it up and put it in the medicine cabinet." Suddenly I heard my own voice and realized that I was saying something my mother would have said, in the same tone and with the same words.

> "Augustine, would you *run upstairs* and get me a needle. I think you'll find one either in my top right-hand drawer or pinned in the shower curtain or on the bathroom shelf. Look around; you'll find it."
>
> "Now, *Henry*, don't tell her that! Really honey, you know better than that!"
>
> "Alexandra, you're younger than I am, your legs are stronger, *run next door* and borrow a cup of sugar for me."
>
> "Mary-Agnes, put something warmer on the baby, she'll catch cold, it's chilly out, *run in the house* and find her sweater."

Mother, as I've explained before, existed as a Divine Right, a feudal queen, empowered by God to give orders, make arbitrary rules, and expect instant obedience. I think that even my father thought she was a bit excessive in this respect. We were never allowed to forget for a moment that she had reproduced six, seven, eight, nine, ten, or whatever the current score, with the implication that she had reproduced them against her will, that hardly any other women we knew were as dutiful in this matter as she was, and that, in return for her obedience under God, we were obliged to make life as easy for her as possible. About housekeeping, though, she was in conflict with herself. Because no matter how many maids she had she always did most of the work herself, as though it were her duty, like Sunday Mass or the Stations of the Cross on Fridays. I understood her predicament, though; I knew a boy once (the same one who said women shouldn't take drugs) who complained that his wife kept a messy house just so she would have to spend all her time cleaning and wouldn't have to think about weightier subjects; such as her career. He said that in this respect I reminded him of his wife.

Hearing myself speak as she would have spoken, against my will, the utter futility of life became apparent, as in a flash, an illumination, a streak of lightning; I felt like St. Paul of Tarsus. What a shock this was for me (a former hedonist), this transmutation into my mother —an Irish-Catholic-Jansenist-obsessional-religious-capitalist-puritanical-colleen. It was as miraculous and as inexplicable (it is necessary only to have faith) as the transformation of the bread and wine into the body and blood of Christ. *"When I get bigger,"* Emma would later say, *"can I have one of those white things in my mouth, like Grandma does?"*

I looked into the bathroom mirror to see if I could see my mother's face there; I felt so much like her that I was sure it must be her own features behind those words. It wasn't her face but it was a face that looked even more harassed than my mother's had ever looked. Framing it was a head of hair that looked like an unwatered California lawn in the summer. A lot of the faded red strands were so dry that they were actually stiff, falling in front of my face in spikes. For the first time I saw myself as what I was—a thirty-two-year-old mother.

In the past few years, whenever I examined my face in the mirror and saw lines, loose skin, or the tiny beginnings of future folds, wrinkles, and extra areas, I would tell myself that I was just tired, that the light was bad, or that I was exaggerating the effects of my age. Now I tried to be an objective observer and, armed with the memory of my mother's voice, tone, and words, I looked at myself as I used to look at my mother. I counted back, realized that when she was thirty-two I was eight, and tried to imagine myself as eight years old, looking at a thirty-two-year-old woman's face.

Happily playing with Emma in the bathtub, where she was showing him her latest T'ai-Chi exercises (which she had learned from watching Alexandra practice at her house), Frederick was unaware of the courageous thing I was doing. Beyond seeing myself as a thirty-two-year-old mother I saw that my own mother, at that age and having had at the time six children, had actually looked a lot younger and better than I did. (But how do I know I'm not imagining that, that because she was my mother she looked flawless to me. *"My mother is prettier than your mother,"* we used to tell each other . . . "Summertime . . . yo' daddy's rich, an' yo' ma is good-lookin' . . .")

Then I turned my attention to my husband, five years younger than I and, it must be confessed, I tried to exaggerate his few signs of age. I examined his fine-pored skin, the consistency of his facial coloring (the nose the same color as the rest of the face—in fact, the whole face exactly even in color, a creamy pale olive), and then, unsuccessful at picturing him five years older, I turned my attention back to the lines at the corners of my nostrils that continued beyond the corners of my mouth ("Charming parentheses," a journalist had called them. "Instead of pointing out her age, they serve merely to accentuate the curve of her lips, the size of her eyes."), and noticed that there was a double line already forming, parallel to each of those "charming parentheses." It seemed to me that despite every effort at outdoing every mother I knew, both in my present and in my past, all my efforts at never assimilating the signs of bitterness, boredom, fatigue, and constant parental vigilance into the very skin of my face, I was doomed to repeat, line by line, every permanent expression I had ever seen on every face of a mother over thirty years old. I remembered the nuns, of whom it was said and repeated as often as a cliché, "You can never tell their age; it's celibacy that preserves their looks."

"I'm repeating my mother," I told Frederick. "As soon as Emma gets back not only do I sound like my mother, but I actually look like her, too!"

"Of course!" he told me, "that's what I've been telling you!"

"But *you!*" I complained, "don't you think that maybe you sound like your father?"

"Of course I sound like my father, how could I have a choice? The mistake you make is you think that you're unique, that I'm different from you, but I'm human too, and I must sound just like my father."

"Isn't it funny? As soon as Emma is here, I become my mother . . . I can't help it . . . I even feel that I'm repeating her gestures. It's as though she were already inside me, her soul . . . reincarnation . . ."

CHAPTER XXV

Her Rival Revisited

My curiosity about who was going to take over our old apartment on the ninth floor was satisfied when Elkse was seen on Twenty-third Street, in front of the hotel entrance, carrying huge armloads of cardboard boxes; Frederick was behind her, lugging her video equipment. They were on their way to 914.

Her reasons for moving in were vague. I couldn't understand what had happened between her and Gunter, because when I asked her she shrugged and said things like, "Oh . . . I don't know. He is so strange. I need to be alone . . ."

Apparently being with Frederick was the same thing as being alone because he was constantly with her. "I'm helping her with her video equipment," he would tell me. Or, "She's lonely, she misses Gunter." The hotel grapevine had a different story. They said that she and Frederick had a drug relationship; that she was on heroin.

Adding to my suspicions was the fact that she made the apartment look much better than it had ever looked when Frederick and I lived there. She painted the window casements a deep blue, hung fabrics on the walls, refinished the furniture, and draped antique lace over the bedroom window. She reorganized the space so that not only did it look twice as big but it looked like a leisurely afternoon love bower as well. Frederick seemed to love it down there; he was never at home.

One evening I went down the two flights of stairs to look for him and met him on the staircase. He was carrying a glass.

"Here," he said, "a Margarita for you. Elkse made it." The drink was half gone. Sudden longing for a whole Margarita overcame me.

"I think I'll go down and ask her for another one," I told him.

"Yes," he said with a weird enthusiasm, "you should!"

Elkse came to the door wearing a coral-colored chenille bathrobe with nothing on underneath. I was sure they had been making love on what used to be our bed (now rearranged so that it stood in the middle of the room with the bureau, covered by a vicuña rug, behind it as a head-board). The mystery behind Frederick's weird enthusiasm on the staircase seemed to be solved. He must have been covering up his feelings of guilt, I thought, yet I affected the air of a casual neighbor as I looked around at the latest changes in the apartment. She seemed flustered as I settled down on what had been our old brown plaid couch with the scratchy fabric and asked her for a drink.

"It's all gone," she told me, "I'm sorry." I asked her for a Marlboro, so she lit one for me and sat there, silent, not knowing what to say. I stayed a while longer, both to make her suffer and to search for clues. I could see her beginning to fidget but I wouldn't move off the brown couch. I began to tell her stories and then I asked her for a joint; I wanted to get high, so that my stories would become longer and more labyrinthine; I hoped to make her as uncomfortable as possible. Just looking at her in that chenille bathrobe made my blood boil.

I had begun a terrible habit, while pregnant, of luring some unsuspecting woman, usually one I knew but slightly, into my apartment for a cup of tea or coffee, or wine if they happened to be drinkers (which was all the better, for drinkers are the most loquacious), and once I had them sitting comfortably, drinking their preferred beverage, I'd catalogue Frederick's sins to them. As I spun my tale I would become more and more incensed, to the point where I doubted my own intelligence and judgment —for how could I have married someone like that unless I was irremediably stupid? Or, worse yet, I would become convinced of my own superiority over him, thus feeling that the only reason for our marriage was a hopeless masochism on my part. Why get married unless the man is superior?

The reason I invited only women I knew slightly was that those women who were truly friends (who loved me) would either seriously analyze the points I brought up, and in the analyzing render them either more understandable or more insignificant, or, best of all (from the point of view of true friendship), point out to me my own failures and shortcomings as a mate.

I performed this ritual, both before and after Emma's birth, only with women who were not pregnant, who had never had children, and who were not, and never had been, married. Before Emma was born, I saw myself and my husband as two free souls, having a love affair, and behaving accordingly. Even after Emma was born, and until she was about two years old, I still had not assimilated into my idea of myself and Frederick the fact that we were in the process of becoming different people from those we had been when we first met. Just as, when the doctor first held Emma up, immediately after her birth I looked at her without being able to summon up the feeling that I was related to her in any way, so it was only after two or three years of parenthood that I could look upon my marriage as one that joined a mother and a father.

It was in this spirit of unconsciousness that I viewed all of Frederick's actions toward me. While giving allowance to the fact that my own time was totally taken up with my motherhood, I had yet to perceive that Frederick's time was similarly rerouted. Even when pregnant I saw myself as a different person and realized that I no longer viewed my husband in the same light as before, but when it came to him, I couldn't see that my pregnancy made, or should make, any difference in his relationship to me.

Like a prima donna losing her public, I complained and agonized over the fact that my husband was no longer the starstruck lover he had once been, even though the image of a starstruck lover may have been from the beginning simply a product of my own mind.

These unsuspecting women, grateful for the attention I showered upon them (formerly I had merely greeted them in the lobby, or spoken to them briefly at parties), were only too happy to listen to me and console me, assuring me that my husband was indeed a renegade, an ingrate, a drug addict of the worst sort, totally incurable, and, worse, unappreciative of the gem of a wife that he was lucky enough to have. They regaled me with tales of their own lovers, of the beastliness of men in general, unaware of the fact that I couldn't have been more susceptible to influence, that I immediately put myself in the place of the person talking to me, appropriated to myself all of their own traits, saw Frederick in the same light as they saw their lovers. In a word, I became those women.

These episodes further estranged me from Frederick, since occasionally one of my confidantes would let slip (seemingly by accident) a fact that she alone knew about him, and I would stew and fret over it, unable to drive it from my mind, searching for the appropriate moment to let him have it, between the eyes. Or after having enumerated his faults, exaggerated them, dramatized them, finding a voice to amplify my own, I would feel later—for instance, lying companionably with him in bed— that if I let him touch me I was betraying the woman to whom I had just spent two hours vilifying him. If he said something affectionate to me, instead of replying affectionately which I would have done had I not just spent those two hours gossiping about him, I would say something to him in an icy tone, being still in a vengeful mood and feeling guilty besides for having been disloyal to him. Horribly, those who knew him well told me that he "never has anything but good things to say about you; he adores you."

The situation was not unlike one I had experienced as a college student, when, returning home after a year in France, I was pounced upon by my sisters, who told me repeatedly how horrible our parents had been in my absence. After firing up my anger, they would leave me alone to stew with it, so that during the next family tiff, I would be unable to overcome my fury and would scream at Mother and Daddy that they could no longer blame me for the household dissension. My sisters had just told me, I would tattle, that during my absence they had behaved just as abominably as they had always behaved before my departure, proving that I wasn't the black sheep at all but that Mother and Daddy themselves were the original sins in the family.

I had thought then that it was unfair and manipulative of my sisters to fill me with such stories when they themselves were so emotionally disciplined that they would never let one word of criticism pass from their lips to our parents. At the time I never thought my sisters did this to me purposefully, just as later, after a horrible argument with Frederick, I never thought that these women "friends" had deliberately aroused my wrath against *him*. Yet after having had such a "tea" with one of my newfound friends, and after culminating it by an argument with Frederick, I would avoid the "friend" as much as possible, wondering what could have led me to talk that way to her about him, and bitterly regretting that I had instigated such a humiliating episode. Furthermore, I would then maintain that anyone who let herself be led into speaking against some- one else's spouse, even at the instigation of that "someone else," was a person to be avoided, a person with no taste and no discrimination. "I would never speak against a woman's husband to her, even if she begged me to," I was fond of saying at the time. "It's always a mistake, no matter what you think of him. That woman is sure to turn against you, eventu- ally." Smug in my self-righteousness, I was certain that those women in whom I had confided were fully aware of my reasons for no longer as- sociating with them.

Now, with Marie-Claude and her baby girl, Carry-Nation, in New York (ostensibly to be with Louis-François, the father, who is here trying to get a job), I have someone new to complain to. Not that Marie-Claude isn't a real friend and therefore ineligible to listen to my complaints; it's just that I have abandoned that former practice of complaining to mere acquaintances.

She's sitting here, at my kitchen table, having left Carry-Nation at the Irving Hotel with Louis-François. I've gone through my litany of complaints only to be told by Marie-Claude (once again), "But you are so lucky, you don't realize it! You have a man who stays with you, who's *there*, who takes care of the baby—look at me! The father of my baby doesn't even want to live with us!" Then she told me that she's living with a rich junkie in Paris and that she doesn't care that he's a junkie because he's so nice to her and "it's so nice, for a change, to live with somebody who's nice to you!"

"During my entire pregnancy," she told me, "Louis-François never *once* made love to me!"

"Not you too!" I squealed, delighted to find that my husband's avoidance of me apparently had been due to a defect in the contemporary French male, not in myself. Then I told her about Elkse and Frederick.

"OOOOOoh . . . not you too!" Marie-Claude laughed.

"What do you mean 'not me too'?"

"Didn't you know?"

"Know what?"

"When we were making that movie with Gunter, in New Mexico, I was so jealous of Elkse that I slept in her room just to keep her away from him!"

"But why weren't you sleeping with Gunter yourself?"

"Ooooooh . . . we were fighting all the time. I 'ated 'im, 'e 'ated me. But, you see, I didn't want Elkse to 'ave 'im." Excitement made her drop her *h*s. "You didn't know about Fernando Arayo either?"

"No," I told her, "I didn't know. What about Fernando?"

"Well, Louise was so jealous of Elkse that she went mad. She actually had to be committed."

"But Louise is always going mad."

"So what? What does that have to do with it? Elkse drove her to the looney bin again. My god, that happened two years ago! I can't believe you don't know about it. Louise had to send the baby to her parents while she recuperated."

"But Louise is so beautiful. Why should she be jealous?" It made me feel better to know that even Louise, one of the most beautiful women in the world, was jealous of Elkse. I wished she had told me about this when I last saw her, I might have been able to pick up some pointers.

"*Chérie,*" Marie-Claude explained, "Elkse Boserup is a very, very beautiful woman."

My worst fears were confirmed. Even the supercritical Marie-Claude thought that Elkse was a devastating beauty.

"I don't know what it is," Marie-Claude continued, "but Elkse Boserup has something about her . . . can you imagine? All of us so jealous of her? Spending hours worrying about her . . . analyzing her effect on our men? Aren't we crazy? Why does she pick on us . . . does she think that we 'ave such good taste in men? Those bums! We should 'ave given them to 'er!"

We began laughing and continued until we had built ourselves up into a state of hysteria. Holding her stomach, Marie-Claude kept interrupting her laughter to tell me more details. "Do you know," she sputtered, "that one day, in the desert, I walked into Gunter's room and Elkse was sitting there, in a chair. He was in the bathroom shaving. I put my finger to my lips to warn Elkse not to let him know that I was there . . . I wanted to hear what he was saying to her before I walked in . . . that's how jealous I was . . ."

We were still gasping for breath when Frederick walked into the kitchen. He had just come from Elkse's, we knew, because he was carrying a Panasonic Portopak. His was a Sony. We both took one look at the Panasonic and burst into howling screams again.

"What's so funny?" Frederick wanted to know.

I shook my head at Marie-Claude, motioning for her not to tell him. That made us laugh harder. Frederick left, disgusted with us. I was sure he was going back down to the ninth floor and Elkse Boserup.

The next day Frederick, Emma, and I went over to see Marie-Claude, Louis-François, and the baby in the dreadfully dirty Irving Hotel. It's so decrepit that the Metro Hotel looks like a Holiday Inn in comparison. Louis-François, while tenderly playing with his baby, kept telling me over and over again that he doesn't have any use for babies, that he never wanted a baby, and why does Marie-Claude burden him with this child.

"Her whole family and everyone associated with them is crazy," he said next. "Do you know what her mother's maid did?"

"To her baby, you mean?"

"Yes, that story. She murdered it." Marie-Claude had already told me the story. Her mother's maid had a two-week-old baby, and the baby cried so much that she put it on the bathroom floor in the Neuilly apartment on what they described as a "soft" mattress. Then she shut the bathroom door, the hallway door, and her bedroom door, to drown out the baby's cries. Eventually the baby stopped crying and after about two hours had passed, the maid went into the bathroom to find that the baby had died of suffocation because his face got trapped in the "soft" mattress. It was only in Europe that I had ever heard stories about soft mattresses and babies. Death by a soft mattress seemed as French as death by cirrhosis of the liver. Marie-Claude's tale of the death of the baby consisted mainly of Louis-François's reaction to it. He was living with her in her mother's overstuffed pink apartment at the time the baby died, and he refused to go to the funeral, saying the baby had been murdered. That was the day he moved out.

Emma is ecstatic to be around a baby. She keeps picking the baby's pacifier up off the floor and putting it back in her mouth, singing to her and trying to pick her up.

"Have a baby, Mama," she keeps telling me.

Marie-Claude says that the doctors in Paris advised her not to nurse the baby. They said her breasts were too small. Like all true French housewives, she has utter confidence in the medical profession, or at least pretends to; she knew very well how small my breasts were before I was pregnant with Emma; after all, it was she who said I should have the baby, on the grounds that pregnancy made my breasts look so good.

The next day Marie-Claude moved into our apartment in the Metro Hotel, saying she couldn't stand Louis-François and his friend, a beautiful Algerian musician who was living with him.

"Together," she said, "they are so oppressive." It was true. The two men were both in a state of severe depression and neither of them had the sense to hide out until it was over. Marie-Claude said that she also needed a rest. "Let him take care of his daughter for a while," she laughed, "it's good for him."

The dealer and his wife, downstairs on the fifth floor, seduced Marie-Claude into taking acid and a bath in their apartment. When she saw the lit candles, forming a circle around the tub, and smelled the incense, she freaked out and came running upstairs to me, wrapped only in a towel. Then she wrote up the experience and left it in my typewriter. It read: "Augustine is so beautiful, both inside and out; she made me a delicious spaghetti dinner; she is so wonderful; everything she does is perfect . . ." I was uncertain whether she had written this sincerely or whether she had left it as a sort of thank you note, since she had stayed in my apartment for so many days. I had no idea whether or not I was really beautiful (outside, that is; the inside I was sure of) or not, but if Marie-Claude thought so, I would try to take it as objective fact. I only wished I knew for sure.

The mantelpiece above the fireplace is littered with photographs of Emma. Frederick and Elkse have apparently gone to the seminary park with her, taking along Elkse's Polaroid. This evidence hurts me even more than the chenille bathrobe. I was the one who discovered that park, an enclosed courtyard full of fruit trees, flowering in the springtime, and surrounded by nineteenth-century brownstones, now inhabited by the seminarians and their families. The church was beautiful, full of stained-glass windows, and at six o'clock in the evening the tower bells chimed out Episcopalian hymns. I had been begging Frederick, for two years, to go there with me and videotape the church. He had always refused. Now I have to look at these photographs of Emma, taken by Elkse, playing among the fruit trees, under the stained-glass windows. I'm ready to cry I'm so wounded.

CHAPTER XXVI

"*Not Mutilation but Cultivation*"

Maori were taught that it was their sacred duty to insure the female orgasm; if ejaculation occurred prior to this, intercourse should be resumed with the woman in the superior position until she reached climax. Not mutilation but cultivation insured satisfaction.

ETTIE ROUT, *Maori Symbolism*

The three of us stepped out into the dirty hallway. I was barefoot and the grit under my feet (Why doesn't Emma feel it when she runs around in bare feet?) made me go back inside and get my shoes. It was too bad, because the marble floor of the corridor was truly noble. It was an austere black and white, making me think of an ancient Roman house. Once again I resolved to leave the Metro Hotel.

Gunter von Habsburg put his arm around my shoulder as Frederick pushed the elevator button. The woman with the scab on her eye was in the elevator with her new baby, a girl with a very large head. She was living with her baby girl in a tiny room in the hotel, along with four rabbits.

When I went to see the baby a week before, there was rabbit shit all over the floor, since she never picked up a thing. Moldy globs of Philadelphia cream cheese were lying about in their squares of silver paper, and there were paper containers from the delicatessen, their pink plastic forks still inside and coated with old food, sitting on every available surface. An enormous ashtray, filled to the brim with cigarette stubs, ashes, and roaches, stood in the center of the room. Against one wall a narrow pipe had been attached and hanging from it, on little satin quilted hangers, were about fifty new, clean, ironed, and starched baby dresses. There were pink cotton dresses with organdy aprons, dotted swiss with lace collars, hand-smocked gingham with red piping on the white linen collars, and lavender voile trimmed with embroidery.

The baby herself was lying on a pile of pee-soaked newspapers, her clothes wet; even the ludicrous wool bonnet on her head was wet. Since the room was stifling hot I tried to remove the bonnet.

"No!" her mother warned me, "don't take it off! She likes to have something around her ears."

I asked her how she was doing.

"Oh, I'm fine now," she said, smiling, "Dominick comes now and then to see the baby and she's so pretty that I'm real happy I had her." At the lobby the woman got out of the elevator, pushing her broken stroller ahead of her. One of the hinges had collapsed so in order to keep the stroller from caving in completely she had to exert constant upward pressure on the handle. It was one of those Japanese umbrella-type strollers, and the tiny baby was sort of wedged into it, a future case of curvature of the spine. Her head was lolling back and forth; she was awake but wasn't making a sound.

Gunter, Frederick, and I went into the bar. One of them sat on either side of me, on stools right at the bar. Gunter put his hand on my knee and the entire left side of my body began to warm up. At the time I didn't know about the telephone call between the two of them a week before.

"*Are you sure, Frederick?*"

"*Of course I'm sure. She need someone. We don't fuck anymore and she need it.*"

"*You won't be jealous?*"

"I'm not the type, Gunter."

"Don't you love her anymore?"

"Of course I love her. She's my wife."

We each ordered a double shot of Jack Daniels and a beer.

While the two men discussed business I stared at my reflection in the mirror over the bar. I tilted my head at its most flattering angle and kept it there. Gunter ordered another round of drinks and moved his hand up higher on my thigh. I put my glass to my lips, not moving my head, so that staring at myself in the mirror I could remain confident of my beauty. That way I could relax in the knowledge that Gunter found me desirable. For if I found myself desirable then I never had any doubts that any man would find me less so.

I have always felt my best in the company of two men (with no other women there). Tonight was no exception. I had been making overtures to Gunter all week on the telephone, unaware that the die had already been cast.

"Don't worry," Frederick had told me, "Gunter is going to take care of you!"

Gunter lit a cigarette and passed it to me. We all ordered another double. Gunter's hand moved higher. The Spanish bartender looked at us disapprovingly as I listened to the two men discuss Henri Langlois, the *éminence gris* of French cinema. Gunter was hoping to be invited to show his film at Langlois's *cinémathèque* (Frederick had already shown two of his there) but the fact that Gunter's mother was a heavy supporter of the *cinémathèque* didn't seem to help at all; in fact, Gunter was doubly damned, for if Langlois did show his film then it could be said that it was only because Mrs. von Habsburg had contributed so much money. What a dilemma!

After downing his third double and his fourth beer Gunter got off his stool and stood behind me, his arms around my waist. I remained immobile, not only to preserve the reflection of my arranged beauty in the mirror but also to better enjoy the sexual currents now flowing through my body from the waist down. I had learned, while pregnant, not to reject an experience that held real promise. I had told Frederick about the one experience I had resisted while pregnant—about the powerful physical attraction I had had for a musician—because what good was it to remain chaste if no one knew about it? Frederick responded with, "I'd never pass up anything like that; you're really crazy!" Needless to say I then spent many sleepless nights chastising myself for not having consummated my attraction for the musician; it was worse than the sleepless nights I spent over the pink snowsuit.

Frederick said he was going back upstairs to wait for Emma. Alexandra had taken her for the day, teaching her, no doubt, things like "pink is my favorite color," "I wan nail polish on," "look at my ruffled panties," and "where's the lipix?"

"Go on," Frederick poked me, "go with Gunter. He'll take care of you!" Gunter was moving toward the street door and Frederick toward the door that connected the bar with the Metro Hotel lobby. I hesitated between the two, not because I had any doubts about what I wanted to do but because I was afraid that Frederick would use it against me later if I went with Gunter. I could just hear him mocking me during our next fight. "Why don't you go to your lover, huh?" he would sneer. "Doesn't he want you anymore, is that it?"

I decided to take the risk. I walked over to the lobby door, kissed Frederick hard on the lips, and then joined Gunter at the outer door. He still appeared to be a little embarrassed but seemingly determined to overcome his conservative German nature, he put his arm around my shoulders again and led me to the curb where the white Citroën with the Maserati engine was parked.

At the intersection of Fifth Avenue and Twenty-third Street, a Mercedes pulled abreast of us. The moment the light turned green Gunter slammed the gas pedal to the floor, passing him easily and going very fast. He continued speeding down to Lexington Avenue, where there was another red light, and as I braced myself for a crash he put his foot on the brake, smoothly stopping the car within inches of the Cadillac ahead of us. I had been sitting on the edge of the seat, my fingernails digging into the white leather upholstery under my knees, clenching my teeth. Gunter laughed. The whole interlude was very nostalgic; it reminded me of my father's driving, my father trying to pass a car on a hill with a blind curve, a big red truck coming at us in the opposite direction, my mother, heavily pregnant, screaming at him from the back seat, "Henry! Henry! I'm *pregnant!*"

Uptown, he let himself into his brownstone and switched on the hall light, illuminating the paintings that were hanging along the staircase. I saw that he had acquired a new Warhol. It was a pink-and-green portrait of Mao Tse-tung. Upstairs, in the bedroom, he switched on the hidden lights that illuminated the two Max Ernsts. One of them was a landscape, as seen through a window. A waterfall in the background poured over the windowsill and seen through the water was a full moon and the silhouette of an olive tree. The other Ernst was a painting of an abalone shell containing the sea and a group of islands with fish flying over everything. In the corner was an African ancestor totem, a wooden figure of a man, human hair dropping from every inch of his body. Hanging over the bed was a seventeenth-century *nature morte*, its colors brilliant in the light of a hidden lamp shining from its place in the ceiling molding across the room.

Gunter pulled off his gray felt Stetson from Vero Beach. The silver and turquoise Navajo pin he had affixed to its band clattered against the parquet floor when he tossed the hat across the room. Walking over to his Chinese desk, ebony inlaid with ivory, he pulled an Art Nouveau silver box out of a drawer. The box was in the shape of a tiny chest with four little curved Louis Quatorze legs. Up the legs crawled silver roses with their thorns intact. The inside of the box was lined with pale-blue silk. He took a chunk of hashish out of the box, warmed it with a match, and sprinkled some of it into a small pipe. He passed me the pipe, and while I smoked it he pulled a waxed envelope out of the box, sprinkled the white powder from the envelope onto a black leather-bound edition of *Philosophie dans le boudoir* (another de Sade fan!) divided it into four lines with a single-edged razor blade, rolled up a ten-dollar bill, and sniffed two lines. The powder shot up his nostrils like dust into a vacuum cleaner. Then he handed the book to me. The heroin had been heavily cut; I realized how badly he had been burned when the membranes of my nose began smarting.

"If it bothers you too much," he said as I sniffed, my eyes watering, "you can inhale some warm water up your nose."

"It isn't that bad," I told him. The idea of warm water up my nose was worse than the doctored heroin.

He moved slowly, as if in a trance, and I followed his choreography, feeling warm and glowing. It was as though a golden mist had enveloped our bodies and we had all the time in the world to linger there, under the paintings and the Navajo rugs, which were beginning to turn golden as

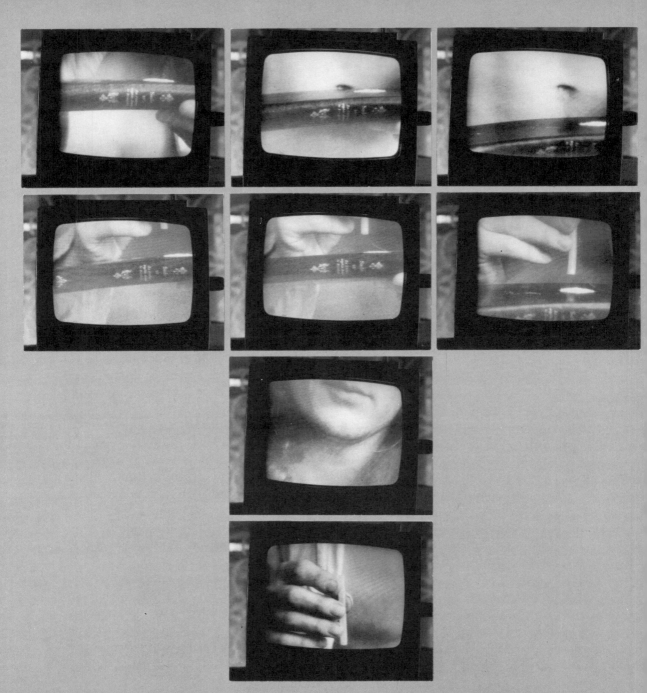

The powder shot up his nostrils like dust into a vacuum cleaner. Then he handed the book to me.

well. I closed my eyes and the skin on his bones was liquid gold against my body. I told my billionaire lover that he felt like a liquefied Inca statue, and as I laughed, he laughed with me. It was comforting to know that he understood both the symbolism and the history behind that image, as we began to leave our bodies together and to drift into space. I could no longer distinguish my own skin from his, my own body from his, my own mind from his. I was inside his body, inside his brain. Now the single organism that had been the two of us was shooting rapidly into the void. A part of my consciousness had, meanwhile, detached itself and was apart, watching and commenting, my own internal Sony Portopak. Often I had cursed this ability I had to watch myself like a television camera; it seemed to have developed as our videotape library piled up, and it wasn't like other talents—it couldn't be turned off. I hated it.

It was perfectly logical for me to both lose myself in someone else and to simultaneously watch it happen. It sounds impossible, but when it happens I'm never surprised. I suppose it could be described as the coitus interruptus of astral projection.

As we went into space I was wondering with that third eye what was going to happen next. A part of me said, "Wonderful, at last . . . the cosmic orgasm"; another part of me said, "It's too good to last; I don't deserve it; something will end it." A third part of me was blaming the whole third eye business on too much reading. I suspected that if I had been born before the *soi-disant* sexual revolution, I would have been able to approach sex with the simple gusto that I approached caviar, oysters from Normandy, or a bottle of Château Lafitte-Rothschild.

I hated to lay the blame on the Sony Portopak because that would mean that the life work of Frederick and me was making it impossible for me to actually live.

The second voice (*too good to last*) turned out to be the correct one. Gunter suddenly sprang away from me, hit the floor with a thud, looked at me with wild eyes, and said, "I can't stand it. This has never happened to me before." Shaking, he went over to his medieval oak dressing table and lit a Gauloise. The match flared up, illuminating his eyes. They were glittering, trembling, out in space; the blue irises no longer connected to his eyeballs. I linked into them, trying to bring him back to me, and saw him hesitate, freeze, as if thinking it over, calling his forces into play to debate this situation.

"No," he said finally, "don't do that to me." It was only then, watching him as he stood against that dressing-table, that I realized he was the very image, wavy blond hair and all, of the lover from my childhood daydreams.

At about four in the morning, lying beside him as he snored, restlessness drove me out of his bed into a taxi, across town, and into the bed of my husband. He was snoring too. I moved close to him, putting my arm around his hips. He woke up, very excited, and made love to me, violently, intensely, and passionately. I can understand that. Everyone wants to think that they own something that others consider of value. It excites them.

The next afternoon Elkse came upstairs to ask Frederick for some advice about her video equipment. They were huddled over the deck when Tony Aponte walked into the kitchen where I was feeding Emma her lunch and asked me, "Who's that chick in the living room?" When I told him it was Elkse Boserup he said, "Oh, so *that's* Elkse! Frederick told me that she *comes* a lot!" Though my heart was pounding, I continued pretending to be unconcerned over this latest revelation, and I waited until Elkse left to confront Frederick with it. He told me that he had only said that to Tony to make him jealous, that he had no knowledge of Elkse's orgasmic possibilities. Not satisfied with this explanation I went down to Elkse's and demanded the truth.

"How could you believe such a thing?" she cried. "How could you believe that I would fuck your husband, especially when I'm so depressed over Gunter, his best friend?"

"Easy," I responded, "I could do it myself. I could fuck Gunter no matter how depressed I could ever be over Frederick, his best friend. I find Gunter very attractive." I didn't see any point in telling her that I had already done it, the night before.

CHAPTER XXVII

"A Woman's Work..."

"It's a women's show, a women's show, Frederick," I kept telling him when he complained that I was using all "his" tapes for "my" video exhibition at the Women's Film Festival in Quebec. I had first planned to use only the tapes *I* had made of Emma, but as I studied the situation it became clear that I really needed several of Frederick's tapes to complete the picture. After all, I reasoned, when he made *Cleopatra* I was the one who found the cash, the cast, and the costumes. Did he give me credit as co-producer? No.

Finally he agreed to help me edit the tapes, only to tell me, as we argued over what images to use, that I was just like Gunter von Habsburg because I couldn't make up my mind. "That's a good lesson for you," he said, "on how hard it is to make films." Then he complained that one of the scenes I had edited was "heavy" and "corny." It was a scene where, as his penis pumps into my vagina, instead of showing it pumping back out I had cut to Emma's head being pulled out of it by Dr. Fabin. Dubbed over the sound track was a sentimental love song by a Frank Sinatra imitator that had been playing on the radio the night we taped the fuck scene. As Emma's head emerges the singer croons ". . . you'll never know how much I love you . . ." Frederick hated it.

As his coolness toward me accelerated and built up into near-repulsion the night before I left for Canada I never suspected that the real reason for this freeze had anything to do with my using his work; I thought he had reconciled himself to that. Instead, I believed that he had ceased completely to love me and must be in love with someone else (Elkse?), years of conditioning having led me to believe that one loses love only by its transferral to another.

After three grueling days and nights at the editing decks I suddenly couldn't stand it any more. Looking at my husband's inert body, pressed against the wall at the far side of the bed, apparently sleeping, I tried to put my arms around him. He pressed closer to the wall.

"You're driving me crazy," I whispered to him (whispered so as not to waken Emma), "I can't stand this lack of affection."

Sighing, he got up, naked, and went into the living room (so as not to awaken Emma), where he slumped into a chair.

"I'm exhausted," he told me, "I've been taking care of Emma for three days and nights. I want to sleep. You're crazy."

"Get out of here!" I screamed. "Go sleep with one of your girlfriends in the hotel; you've got enough of them."

"What's the matter with you?" he wanted to know, red-eyed with exhaustion.

"What about Max? Sleep with him. Surely he'll give you a bed."

Frederick flew at me, picked me up, and carried me through the redwood door into the corridor, saying, "This is my apartment, and I'm going to sleep in it. You're the one who's going to leave."

I kicked and screamed all the way to the corridor and, once there, dug my fingers into his hair and began rhythmically banging his head against the wall. Coming toward us, from the other end of the black-and-white marble corridor was Tony Aponte. Frederick was trying to slug me while I bashed his head and Tony pleaded, "Let her go! You're stronger than she is. Let her bang your head against the wall. It doesn't hurt!"

Earlier in the evening Camilla had slit her wrists because Tony wouldn't take the baby for a walk. She was now downstairs, nursing her stitches. They had videotaped the stitching.

"Let her go," he begged my husband, who, by now, had succeeded in landing a blow to my shoulder.

The noise woke Emma. I rushed to the heavy redwood door, not realizing she was behind it, and in my haste to reach her I slammed the door in her face, knocking her to the floor. I tried to pick her up to comfort her but found that I couldn't move; Frederick had almost knocked me out and my limbs were paralyzed.

When the blood rushed back into my head I cursed myself for not having been able to stop the fight sooner. I had tried to, when I first heard Emma's cries (remembering a scene from my own childhood, when, awakened by dim sounds I had gone to my bedroom window and seen my parents, out on the seawall, locked in a clinch, my father trying to stop my mother from throwing his briefcase into the river—silently, so as not to awaken us); but the adrenalin pumping into my blood wouldn't allow me to stop.

Within seconds the feeling came back into my arms and legs and I reached over and pulled Emma from her father, where he was cradling her in his arms next to me on the floor of the foyer. She turned away from me, sobbing, "I wan my poppa, I wan my poppa!"

While Emma slept it off the next morning, Frederick came up behind me as I worked on the last few details of the tapes (seeing me type, tape, or cook were the only things that turned him on), put his arms around me, kissed me, and, stroking my back, told me he was sorry. In the four years of our marriage it was the first time he had ever apologized to me. Then, releasing me he said, "Let me help you; I know you have to finish the tapes."

With Watergate in the background on the T.V. set he filmed the credits I had written out: *A tape by Augustine Marat—with the cooperation of her husband, Frederick Marat, her father, Henry Shannahan, and Gregory Waldon.* Unknown to my father, I was using some footage taped from his home movies as well as some of the segments Gregory had taped for me in Mexico (*Mother's Day*). I rewound the tape and reviewed my handiwork; having ripped almost all my material off the men in my family I thought how ironic it was that I had used it to draw such a comprehensive picture of the oppressed female.

"Look, Mama, Camilla's giving me the breastie-westie!"

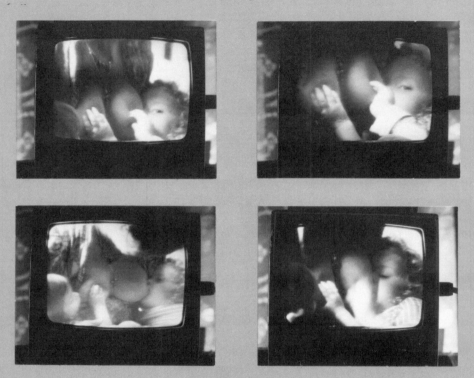

She was nursing two children, one hanging from each huge tit.

Frederick said it looked good, especially with the sound of Sam Ervin and John Dean in the background. Then, carrying Emma, he went down to the street with me, where I met Magda and her three hundred pounds of video equipment. He and Emma waved goodbye as the lady artists got into a taxi and headed for Kennedy.

"It was such a success, Frederick; they loved it! I played three tapes at once on three different monitors. It lasted for four hours and they wanted more. I promised to give another show tomorrow."

"Oh."

"What's the matter?"

"Nothing."

"Aren't you happy for me?"

"Look, I'm exhausted. I have to get Emma's breakfast."

"All right, I'll see you the day after tomorrow."

I felt horrible. I had been so excited by my success that I couldn't wait to tell Frederick, and now I was right back where I had started from two days before. I couldn't understand his attitude and came to the conclusion that it must be professional jealousy.

When I arrived at the hotel there wasn't a bellhop in sight. Magda stuffed herself on the elevator with her three hundred pounds of equipment, saying as the door closed, "Don't worry about it. He was probably just tired. I'm sure being a mother takes as much out of a man." While I waited for an empty elevator Max came into the lobby and told me that Frederick was angry because of what had happened with Emma. I was bewildered, because I thought we had been reconciled the day I left for Quebec. Getting onto an elevator alone I tried to figure it out. The apartment was as empty as the elevator had been so I dropped the bag on the floor, turned on the badly functioning air conditioner, and went back out into the hallways to look for my family.

I checked Elkse's. They weren't there.

When I opened Tony's door, down on the fifth floor, the first thing I saw was Camilla, looking like a reincarnation of Daumier's caricature of Delacroix's painting "The French Republic." Her dark hair falling onto their heads, she was nursing two children, one hanging from each huge tit. The child on the left looked up as I entered the room.

"Look, Mama," she bubbled out, "Camilla's giving me the breastie-westie!" There was my daughter, milk dribbling from her chin, with two black eyes. That fucking redwood door.

Frederick, lounging against the sink, was smoking a joint. He averted his eyes from me, threw the roach out the open window, and left the apartment without a word.

Camilla shrugged. "It was awful for him," she said, "watching her eyes turn black while you were being adulated in Quebec."

Things got worse. Frederick not only took Emma completely under his wing, as though afraid to trust me with her, but he also continued his verbal strike against me to the point where, if we found ourselves in the same room, anywhere in the hotel, he walked out rather than acknowledge my presence. Yet he was back in our bed each night, pressed against the far wall. After a week like this had passed, I asked him to leave.

The police are here. I called them to protect me from Frederick because when I tried to lock him out he ground my bare toes under his boot, right in front of Sidney Renard, whom he was mesmerizing at the time with a brilliant smile, so Sidney, not having seen him do it, couldn't understand why I called the police.

I know the police think I'm psychotic. Especially after Frederick told them I attacked him with a butcher knife (untrue). I just can't believe that the reason Frederick hates me so much is because Emma's eyes turned black. That's what everyone is saying—everyone who isn't telling me that it's a case of professional jealousy.

The police told me they don't understand why I'm afraid of my husband. He seems reasonable and calm, they said, and "he doesn't look like he's lying, lady."

"But he's a junkie," I told them, in retaliation for the false butcher knife story. "As policemen you ought to realize that junkies always lie."

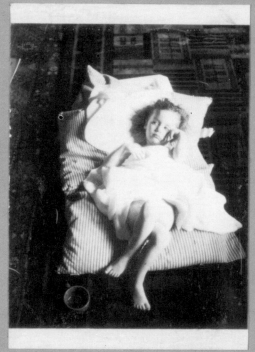

Frederick took Emma completely under his wing, as though afraid to trust me with her. . . .

Frederick pushed up his faded blue denim sleeves and held his spotless milk-white muscled forearms out to the cops. "Look," he said, "no track marks."

"That's because he takes it up the nose," I said.

"Under the law," they told him, "you'll have to leave; and all you can take with you is your clothes." Telling them he didn't have any clothes, Frederick picked up his three black notebooks and walked out with them, looking sad and vulnerable. The police took him to the window at the end of the corridor and, under the light, examined his nose for track marks.

According to Camilla and Tony, Frederick spent the rest of the day at their place, crying.

Three days later I returned home from the store with Emma, who was tired out and hanging around my neck, one of her hands inside my blouse twiddling my right nipple, to find Frederick peering around the corner of the hall. His face was covered with shaving foam and he was holding a brush. I realized that he was trying to sneak into our apartment to look for his razor and he wanted to be sure, before he did it, that he wouldn't run into me in the corridor. Someone had apparently alerted him that I had gone out—probably Mrs. Murray down at the switchboard. Everyone was on his side now since I had committed the unpardonable sin of calling the police.

Seeing me there, with Emma, Frederick ducked back around the corner.

"Oh, come on, Frederick," I called out, "I'm not going to bite you!"

"Somebody who would call the police," he yelled back, "is capable of anything."

Finally he agreed to a discussion. We decided that he would take Emma in the daytime, while I worked. This time I was trying to get a video grant from the government *"so that I can continue, for a while, my life's work in videotape—recording my daughter until she reaches the age of 21."* I had decided to confiscate the tapes and work on them myself. Somebody had to earn a living. We had already spent the advance on my book. Back rent.

"Mama, I bleeding, gimme a tampax," Emma is saying, her panties down around her knees.

"Okay, just be careful you don't drip it on the floor," I tell her, handing her a tampax whose cardboard plunger I've removed. She wedges it between the lips of her vagina (reminding me that that's how I thought they were worn when I was a teenager and afraid to ask my mother), and then she walks carefully into the living room, taking tiny steps so as not to dislodge the tampax.

Elkse is there, having become my closest friend—a feat she accomplished by appealing to my weakness for flattery.

"I was always depressed by you," she confessed. "Your beauty and your personality overwhelmed me so much that I felt insignificant beside you." Maybe I had been too harsh on my physical attributes, I allowed myself to believe; it could be I was more beautiful than my rival, although deep in my aesthetic sensibilities I had to admit that this wasn't so. Yet, on the other hand, it just may have been television brainwash that made me evaluate her looks as superior to my own. In ancient Greece, perhaps, I would have been the winner. As for my "personality," I knew that I was the winner, hands down. Moreover, she pointed out, we were in the same boat, both without a man. She still maintained that she loved Gunter, despite the mysterious rupture, which, he had told me, transpired because he was sick of her creative inactivity. And now, she insisted, she wasn't even seeing Frederick, as her loyalty to me precluded any continuation of her platonic friendship with my husband. My own deterioration into an afternoon soap opera wife made it easy for me to accept that last statement as perfectly reasonable.

I began to depend on her to bring me a beer whenever I called her, at any hour of the day or night, as I pushed buttons and pulled levers on the editing decks. She had, by this time, given up her career as an actress because she was unable to get out of bed in the mornings to make the rounds. I sympathized with her, because at her age I couldn't do it myself. It had taken the birth of Emma to get me out of bed before noon. Elkse was also severely depressed, a condition that leads naturally to clinging to a mattress in the mornings, hoping that if you sleep for another hour then by the time you open your eyes again the horrible mess called life will have gone away.

As I worked and drank and Elkse talked about her depression, I suspected her, at one point, of trying to foster my newly developing trend toward alcoholism so that she wouldn't be alone in her addiction. Frederick says that she's still on heroin, since she continues to call me at odd hours of the night asking for pain-killers for her toothaches. That's what he used to say when she called him at odd hours of the night, before he moved out. "She's a junkie," he'd say. "She doesn't have a toothache; she just doesn't have any heroin." Apparently when heroin is scarce all the junkies need pain-killers.

"We should take her to the country," Elkse said, as Emma's tampax finally plopped to the floor. "Look at her; she looks like a dirty Shirley Temple doll. She could use some sun." Emma was pale gray, her face covered with dirt from the hotel corridors. "How about Grenadier Island?" Elkse suggested. "I'm dying to sleep outdoors, under the northern lights. I haven't done that since I left Reykjavik. Don't you think it would help our depression?"

When I told her that I'd never in my life slept in the open she was horrified and succeeded in convincing me that I would find it a solution to all my problems. Emma, upon hearing the news, shouted, "Good! We gonna see Grandpa!"

CHAPTER XXVIII

The Northern Lights

My father picked us up at the airport, covered Emma's face with kisses, and packed us into the car. Halfway to the island Elkse asked him to get her Panasonic Portopak out of the trunk. She wanted to tape the sunset. After two minutes of taping Daddy said, "Isn't that enough? You're wasting tape. It's so expensive." She kept on taping while he muttered about the waste, the price, the foolishness of it all.

The taping completed, and Elkse sitting in the back seat with her camera and deck, Daddy took advantage of the sound of the air-conditioner to ask me, "She doesn't wear any paint, does she?" in a low voice, in his version of pig Latin, which goes "shitellee didelee idelee-idelzent widdelee-er idelenee pidelee-idelee-ent, dideleezent shidelee-y."

"No," I answered out loud.

After dinner Elkse was in such a hurry to get out on the river in a boat that I, always too eager to please, gathered up the windbreakers, Emma, and my brother Angus (who was already in love with Elkse), and, bypassing the living room, where Mother had coffee set up in front of a blazing fire, headed for the dock. Mother and Daddy were both hurt by our abrupt departure from the dinner table and I knew that that was going to be the beginning of our troubles. I hated to see them hurt like that but, always the victim of divided loyalties, I had to make some decision, so I resolutely

303

strode down the granite steps to the boathouse, feeling very guilty.

We went upriver, to Wellesly Island, where we docked the boat. Finding the cabin of some old friends of mine empty, we borrowed the two sleeping bags we found in a closet. When I saw that one of the bags was a double, I nursed the hope that Elkse would sleep in it with me, instead of Emma. I would try and put Emma in the single bag, I thought, and thus, under the northern lights, I would finally find the courage to approach the Icelandic beauty. I had realized weeks ago that my jealousy was fired by my own attraction for her—that if she had been just an ordinary girl I wouldn't have given a damn whether Frederick was sleeping with her or not; but to see them in my mind, her beautiful legs around him, her blue-red lips pressed against his (as she came over and over again) had been, all along, too much for my imagination to cope with. The idea that she preferred him to me, sexually, was a devastating blow; it must mean that she didn't find me as beautiful.

We spent about four hours out on the river, the motor turned off, drifting under the brilliant greenish glow of the northern lights, as several freighters passed us, their portholes and open doors sending streams of yellow light out onto the oily black water that swirled around their hulls. We returned about midnight and searched for a place to sleep outdoors. There were floodlights everywhere and I knew from past experience that extinguishing them would only cause an uproar; Daddy insisted on leaving them on all night so that the crews on the freighters would see his giant zinnias, glowing in the dark like a miracle. The only unilluminated spot was under the thirty-foot-high American flag, because there weren't any zinnias around it, only rocks. Rather than climb into the mosquito infested woods we climbed up the stairs to the bedrooms where Daddy waylaid me on the upstairs landing to complain: "Where were you? It's after midnight! We've been lying awake worrying about you all night, dammit; we haven't been able to get any sleep!"

"We just went upriver, to get some sleeping bags."

"Sleeping bags! Of all the damned foolishness I've ever heard! That tops the cake!"

"Why have you started staying up at night again waiting for us? You haven't done that since we were teenagers," I complained.

"What's the matter with you?" Daddy raged. "You know we've never gone to sleep while you were still out . . . on this dangerous river . . . with

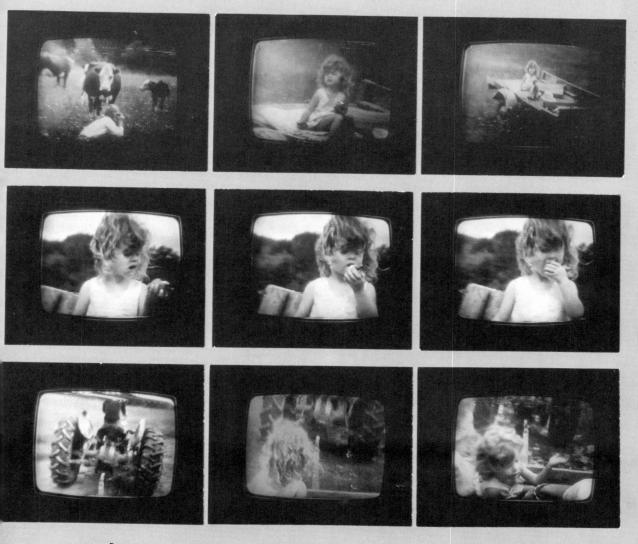

[My father] "You can't put a baby in that farmhouse. They don't have any indoor plumbing!"

a baby! Why, she should have been asleep in bed hours ago!" Actually, she was asleep, snuggled against my chest, until Daddy woke her up yelling at me.

Later in the night Angus jumped into Elkse's bed, asking, "Do you mind if I sleep with you? You're in my bed."

"No, no, no," Elkse protested, jumping out of the bed, "it's all right. I'll sleep in another room!"

We left the next morning. Angus took us, in the boat, down to the other end of Grenadier Island to the farm of Doug and Brigitte Redman, a hippie couple who lived with no running water. Before we left Daddy asked why we were leaving. "You can't put a baby in that farmhouse," he said to me. "They don't have any indoor plumbing!"

Once at the farm I never found the courage to suggest to Elkse that she sleep in the double bag with me. Instead, I got in with Emma while Elkse laid a whiskey bottle and a couple of Quaaludes on the grass between the two goosedown bags. We were both having trouble sleeping, despite the calming influence of the Milky Way. Meanwhile our host slept in the house with his wife, a constant reminder to me of the nights I had spent in his arms in the bottom of a boat out in the middle of the river.

To make matters worse, I hadn't been able to resist telling Elkse about Doug's endurance both in the fields and in the bed (boat, in this case). With a Priapan prick and an Olympian profile, my youngest brother's best friend had been hidden away all these years, a god amid the dusky pines of the Canadian border. Since he had never fallen in love with me, our affair remained as elusive as the exploits of the rum-runners back in the Thirties, who had cut such a narrow channel through the end of Wellesley Island that when the New York State Water Patrol (called "Prohios") tried to follow them their wider boats wracked up at the entrance. Doug's unfortunate capitulation, however, into the charms of the internationally famed and acclaimed beauty, Elkse Boserup, caused him to lose not only his discretion but his bearings as well, and like the boats of the "Prohios" in another era his marriage was nearly wrecked on the shoals of his desire.

Her long auburn locks tangled, her plump French Canadian cheeks rosier than usual due to prolonged crying, Doug's wife, Brigitte, trudged down the rickety stairs one chilly afternoon to apologize for having drunk so much the night before that she wasn't able to get out of bed all day. Since her drinking bout was directly attributable to the attention her husband had paid Elkse during a dinner party to celebrate the giant Great Northern pike he had just caught that day (winning the grand prize of the Labor Day fishing contest—a complete camping outfit, designed for the coldest temperatures, including goosedown sleeping bags, a kerosene stove, etc.), we decided, Elkse and I, to split.

Having exhausted all of our northern resources, we went back to the Metro Hotel, where in the following days Doug plagued me with telephone calls about how Elkse had left a sweater behind and how Brigitte had discovered him plunging his nose into it to inhale the "sweet scent of her perfume." I, being jealous, of course, tried to demystify the romanticism of it all by telling him that the perfume was from a bottle that belonged to one of my younger sisters; a bottle called Midnight in Paris, which was sold for three ninety-eight at the corner pharmacy. Elkse had asked to borrow it, I told him, because she had forgotten to bring along her can of Arrid spray deodorant.

Doug just telephoned again, this time from a public phone booth in the village at midnight, drunk. He and Brigitte were separating for a while, he said, because he wanted to come to New York to see *us* and Brigitte wanted to go to Montreal to see her friends. Now the story was that he couldn't make up his mind between Elkse and me. I couldn't believe that I'd brought it on myself, this surreal state of affairs. Elkse had said she didn't encourage him, that he had "followed her around," and that he wasn't her type. When Doug said goodbye he whispered into the receiver that his wife had just discovered him in the public phone booth of the parking lot next to the bar where they had been drinking and he had to hang up quick.

I went downstairs and relayed the message to Elkse, who sighed heavily, saying that she hoped Doug wasn't really coming to see her. She's now in love with a West Indian musician who has two wives and six children back in Jamaica. This is the first I've heard of him. I suspect that he is an invention of hers, that he doesn't really exist. I know she's in love with Frederick.

CHAPTER XXIX

The Violence Called Love

From the moment of birth, when the stone-age baby confronts the twentieth-century mother, the baby is subjected to these forces of violence called love, as it's mother and father, and their parents, and their parents before them have been. These forces are mainly concerned with destroying most of it potentialities, and on the whole this enterprise is successful. By the time the new human being is fifteen or so, we are left with a being like ourselves, a half-crazed creature more or less adjusted to a world. This is normality in our present age.

R. D. LAING, *The Politics of Experience*

Frederick is going around saying that I'm just mad because Doug Redman is in love with Elkse; that his own friendship with Elkse has nothing to do with it; and that all I need is a good fuck, which he isn't going to give me. I should go and see Gunter von Habsburg again, he says. In fact, why don't I marry him; he's so rich. Then he took Emma and went out into the hall, saying they were going to the park.

I ran after them to get in the last word, but both the corridor and the elevator were empty so I went down to Elkse's floor where one of the maids put her finger to her lips and pointed to the floor below. On the eighth floor I found them standing in front of a door, waiting to be let in. I slipped around a corner until I heard the lock click open and then I rushed to the door. A young blond deeply tanned Californienne with enormous breasts, wearing an Arab caftan, was standing there in the open doorway, about to usher my husband and daughter into her room.

I flew at her. "Is this where my husband has been sleeping?" I snapped.

"Well . . . sometimes, yes . . . he does sleep here," she said to me hesitantly.

I slammed my hand across her face and I was at her, pounding her head against the wall, tearing her hair out by its black roots. Emma was screaming, "No, Mama!" over and over again (I could see her out of the corner of my eye, near the door, tears streaming down her face) as I reached my fingers into the mass of bleached hair and tore at it. I tried to rip off the girl's caftan so I could expose her breasts, thereby, I thought, humiliating her in front of her lover and his child. I wanted to kick her in the crotch, too, but Frederick had gotten himself in front of her, had backed her into a corner, and was spreading his arms to protect her from me just as the policeman at the Welfare Department had protected the elevator from being inhabited by too many people.

The next few seconds are a blank. I only remember Emma's sobs and Frederick's voice telling her over and over, "Emma, your mother is crazy." Then the room was empty. I looked around. There was a rumpled mattress on the floor with a stereo player and two speakers next to it. Incense was burning on one of the shelves. *So this is the love nest*, I thought. *She treats him as I used to, before I had Emma; she plays music and burns incense. So easy to be sexy without children.* There was an antique Chinese lamp leaning against one wall. I took mental note of it and then I smashed the stereo set and went into the bathroom. The shelves were littered with jars of cream and make-up and perfume. I swept everything to the floor.

The kitchenette was full of dirty dishes. I smashed them all and then opened the cupboards and swept everything in them to the floor, where they crashed into the dirty dishes, already down there, broken to bits, egg and orange juice intermingled among the porcelain and glass. Then I went back upstairs.

I couldn't work or concentrate or think. My hands were itching for more destruction. I went back downstairs to my latest rival's floor, where the maids were all standing in front of her closed door, gossiping.

"I have to get into this apartment," I said. "My baby's clothes are all in here. I just want to get them out. Give me the key."

One of the maids put her finger to her lips, rolled the whites of her eyes toward me, and whispered, "Don' tell Sidney who gave ya the key!" Then she reached into her pocket and gave it to me.

Once inside the door I went to work again. First I smashed the silk shade of the Chinese lamp with the heels of my boots and then pried her Andy Warhol portrait (the only painting in the room) out the window, which took about ten minutes, since it was a tight squeeze. Leaning out over Twenty-first Street, I flung it like a frisbee. First it bounced off the fence of the tennis courts on the roof of the YMCA across the street and then it landed, seconds later, on the YMCA marquée.

In a drawer I found a portfolio of photographs; apparently she was a photographer. I tore them all up except for one shot of her own face, a big close-up that I put aside to take back upstairs with me for purposes of contemplation.

I went through all the rest of the drawers and then the closet, where I found two tape recorders, a tripod, and three cameras. I enlisted the help of the maids to carry them into the elevator, saying that they were mine. I didn't know what I was going to do with them.

Then I decided to go outside and look for Frederick and Emma. I was afraid he might be on his way to the airport to take her to France, a fear originally put in my head by my father, who, after our last fight, had said, *"You'd better watch out; he might just take her to France with him."* This idea, coming from my father, had been quite shocking to me at the time; it revealed the true feelings my father had for my husband. And all the time I had thought he liked him so much.

Out in front of the hotel Sidney was gossiping with the piano man from next door. I grabbed him by the tie, shouting, "Whoremonger, whoremonger, where's my baby?" A crowd gathered, most of them Emma's wino friends, but one of them was Sarafina, who had just been released from the psychiatric ward at Bellevue that morning. A week before her release Elkse and I had gone to see her, at the urging of Mario, who had described with horror the black and blue marks on her legs. The police had picked her up on Thompson Street, he said, where she had been found kicking perfectly strange men in the shins. Apparently, some of them had kicked back. We found Sarafina in a worn-out institutional dress, her hair a mess, holding her nicotine-stained fingers out to us and saying, "Look, I have an erection in my fingers. It's from being locked up in here and not being able to make love to June." June was the woman Mario had warned us about.

"Try to get her off the subject of June," he had begged us. "Tell her they won't let her out until she repudiates her affair with that woman. It's all imaginary." I repeated this speech to Sarafina, who assured me that she would follow my directions if I would just get her out of there. In order to accomplish that I would have to see her psychiatrist, whose office was just down the hall. Before I made the trip down the hall Sarafina turned to Elkse, demanded that she go out and buy her cigarettes and a Coke ("and make sure they're Tareytons"), and after Elkse left she asked me, "Who's that—your latest pretty little worshipper?"

Leaning against the wall near the psychiatrist's office was a lovely adolescent German girl who was crying. Her arms, two little flippers, about twelve inches long, ended in pink stubs, one of which she was unsuccessfully trying to use to wipe away the tears that were running down her cheeks. I averted my eyes, probably the worst thing I could have done to her, and knocked on the office door. An efficient-looking woman of about thirty-five, with a short brunette haircut, wearing a pair of yellow trousers and a blue shirt, opened the door to me, gave me a chair and told me that the only real and stable thing in Sarafina's life was her relationship with June. Mercifully for me, she said that she wouldn't allow Sarafina out of the institution yet.

Back in the common room Sarafina repudiated her affair with June, said it was all imaginary, and "now I'm ready to go home with you." Then Elkse walked in with four packs of Pall Malls.

"Goddammit!" Sarafina screamed at her. "You could at least have gotten me what I wanted! I said Tareytons, you bitch, Tareytons! June won't smoke Pall Malls!" Then all the other patients crowded around Eduardo's "adoptive" niece and former neighbor, taking every pack of cigarettes away from her.

Now here she was, in front of the hotel watching me try to strangle my landlord. With her was her newest girlfriend (June's replacement?), a thin and intense-looking creature, a button stating "Lesbian Power" pinned to her shirt. They were both wearing combat boots.

"Give it to him!" they were shouting. "Let him have it!" I broke my grip on Sidney's tie and begged Sarafina to go home, fearing that she would have another collapse if she witnessed any more violence. She refused to leave me, saying I had helped her, now she would help me.

Soon the police arrived, telling me that I couldn't do that, walk into someone's apartment and destroy it.

"You can't just walk into someone's family and destroy it, either!" I shouted at them. To my surprise they agreed, so I continued in my harangue, telling them that the Metro Hotel was no place for a child, with its junkies, pimps, dealers, and whores, that I had witnessed a murder on the fourth floor the year before, etc. They agreed again.

Sarafina, in the meantime, had been pushing me toward the front door, through the lobby and to the elevator; had pushed the button, gotten the elevator door open, and was shoving me on. As the doors closed in the policemen's faces she told me to get upstairs and lock myself in my room, where they couldn't come without a warrant.

We got into my apartment and Sarafina bolted the door, got a famous "movement" lawyer on the phone, and then settled down on the bed with her new lover. While the lawyer was telling me, "You'd better call the Legal Aid Society, I'm too busy, in fact I have to hang up right now," Sarafina was whispering to her lover, *"You're the sexiest thing I ever saw, yes you are, yes you are."*

When the fracas died down and my lawyer brother Anthony (named after the saint of Padua, and number four in the family line-up) promised Sidney that he would send him four hundred dollars if I wasn't prosecuted by the blond photographer, Harriet showed up with Emma. Frederick had dropped her off there at the end of his busy day (Harriet affected ignorance as to his present whereabouts). Emma seemed to have acquired a budding case of laryngitis, no doubt from screaming "no, Mama" over and over at the top of her lungs while I was beating up her father's lover.

As soon as my daughter saw me she jumped onto my lap and stuck her hands down my blouse.

"Cut it out, Emma," I told her, pushing her hands away.

"I'm just *warming up* my hands," she insisted, wide-eyed. "Does it bother you?"

"Yes."

"Well, take off your jacket, I wanna see your blouse."

"Why?"

"I wanna see your whole blouse. It's pretty."

"Okay, if you get me that pen over there on the desk."

She returned with an ashtray, giggling, and said, "Here's the pen."

"No! That's not a pen!"

After walking away five times and coming back with an ashtray, a crayon, a towel, saying all the time "Here's your pen," she finally returned with the pen, climbed back onto my lap, and plunged her hand back into my blouse, grabbing my left nipple and tweaking it back and forth.

"Does this bother you, Mama?"

"You *know* it bothers me!"

She released my nipple (which felt like a raw nerve) and laid her hand against the upper part of my breast, saying, "But I'm not *playing* with your mama! I'm just *holding* it! Now, lemme see Emma born again."

I put the tape of her birth on and at the end of it she looked up at me and said, "I wanna baby. A girl baby." She was croaking on the last sentence; I could see that her laryngitis was getting worse.

I put her to sleep by letting her suck her thumb and fondle my tit again, which by now felt like my clitoris feels when it's been handled too rapidly, and then, for the first time in my life, I called a babysitter.

She was a black student at N.Y.U., a fan of mine who in the past had said, "Forget about the fucking money, I just want to help you. If you don't get out of this fucking hotel you're going to go mad."

I told her I was going downstairs to the restaurant to have a farewell dinner with Alexandra and Eduardo, who were leaving for Uruguay the next day, and to telephone me if Emma's cough got worse. At the sound of her name Emma woke up whining, "I wanna go wiz you," her eyes still half-closed, so exhausted she was barely able to get out of bed, yet insisting on coming. I carried her downstairs to the restaurant booth where Alexandra and Eduardo were waiting and she alternated between my lap and Alexandra's. On her third shift to my lap her father's latest paramour and former owner of a Warhol original passed our table. Stopping her passage, I grabbed hold of her wrist and introduced her to the remnants of my family seated there in the Italian Mafia restaurant.

"Now," I said, my voice quavering, yet bitter, "in front of my sister, Alexandra, my brother-in-law Eduardo de Bomarzo, and my daughter, Emma Marat, I want you to tell me where my husband is hiding out."

"I don't know," she whined, "and what's more, I never slept with your husband. I just felt sorry for him because he said you threw him out and he didn't have anyplace to sleep. I feel sorry for you too, alone with a baby and all, and I don't really care what you did to my apartment. I want you to know that I really love Emma and I'll babysit for you whenever you want. She's like a daughter to me."

"I'll bet she is," I retorted, "she's spent so much time with you and her father in that love nest of yours upstairs."

Alexandra, the epitome of perfect femininity—tact, beauty, charm, generosity, and above all, *soothingness*—smiled winningly at the Californienne and asked her to sit down. She refused. Emma had crawled from my lap to the edge of the bench and was lying there on her back, her feet still in my lap, her busy fingers fondling the red velvet robe of her father's sleeping companion while she sucked the thumb of her other hand and made those maddening noises of satisfaction: "uhummmm . . . ummmmm . . . ahahah . . . uhummmmm."

The Californienne looked down on my daughter lovingly, dotingly, a surrogate mother. Emma then began stroking her velvet-encased thigh. This display of affection, friendship, and, worst of all, habit, on my daughter's part invigorated my waning rage and I demanded for the second time to know where Frederick was.

Eduardo, pained and embarrassed by my vulgarity, got up and walked away from the table, his aristocratic face twisted in distaste. I wondered where his self-righteousness came from; his own family was certainly far from being an example of refined sensibilities. In constant fear of the Tupamaros, his uncle ate with a revolver at the left side of his plate and had threatened Alexandra many times with a rifle as she drove into the driveway of the family palace in Montevideo.

"How do I know it's *you*?" he would demand, when she said that when he saw a blue Fiat he could be sure that it was his nephew's wife. "There's a *thousand* blue Fiats in this town; how do I know it's *your* blue Fiat?" His daughter had spent forty years locked in a bedroom with a trunkful of her collection of movie-star magazine photographs, in mourning over her inability to seek a career in the movies herself. Another uncle was a late sleeper; he never got up before five p.m. He slept with a revolver by his side and had threatened his wife with it many times if she dared leave the bedroom before he did, at five p.m. Any member of the family, no matter how close the blood tie, had to make an appointment to see him. He wouldn't answer the door otherwise. Eduardo's brother Monono had a collection of military helmets and spent hours before his mirror each day trying them on, one after the other, and admiring the effect. Then there was Sarafina . . .

"Please, Eduardo," I begged, "sit back down and finish your dinner. I'm sorry. I'll stop talking about my problems."

"He's just tired," said Alexandra, the eternal soother, "and he never admits that he's tired. Besides . . . you know, he hates dissension. It really bothers him."

"I never fucked your husband," the photographer blurted out in the midst of this discussion, and rapidly disentangling herself from Emma's probing fingers, she left the table, causing a burst of hysterical sobs to issue forth from my daughter.

"She seems very nice," Alexandra shouted above the sobs of Emma, "that girl. I think she's telling the truth. I feel sorry for her."

Eduardo, back at the table, glumly poked his fork into his broiled lobster, which had turned cold long ago, and said nothing.

Then a man in the booth behind us leaned over my shoulder (while looking lasciviously at Alexandra) and said, "Hi, Augustine, aren't you going to introduce me to the beautiful girl you're with?"

I turned around to see Jimmy Wilcox, the son of a filmmaker I knew in my younger days, a filmmaker who had said to me later, during my brief career as a famous actress, "Ah, Augustine, I keep saying to everyone, 'And there I had her, right under my nose, and I never knew what a great actress she was. To think I never used her in a film!'"

I introduced him to my sister and her husband (Emma was by now asleep in my lap).

"How's Elkse?" he asked me.

"Oh," I told him, "I didn't know that you knew her."

"Oh yes," he replied, "I met her a couple of weeks ago and then I

called her, just two nights ago, to ask her to go to the movies and she said she was too depressed to go out. What's the matter with her, anyway? Why is she so depressed? Is it really because of Frederick?"

"What do you mean, Frederick?"

"You didn't know? Oh, I'm so sorry that it had to come from me. I was certain that you knew about it."

"Are you sure?"

"Well, I asked her, I said, 'Why are you so depressed?' and she said that Frederick had just been there and that he had to leave to go upstairs to see you and Emma. 'Doesn't it make you feel weird and strange?' I asked her. 'Aren't you a friend of Augustine? Doesn't it make you feel funny to be like that with her husband? Especially when you live right downstairs?' She told me yes it did, it did make her feel weird and strange." I tried to cross-examine him about the meaning of "like that," but he remained steadfastly evasive. If only I had pretended that I knew all about it, then I could finally have gotten some accurate information.

Emma woke up in the lobby as I was saying goodbye to Alexandra and Eduardo; and, seeing that they were about to leave for Uruguay, she began sobbing, held her arms out to my sister, and said, "I wanna go wiz you." Alexandra held her for a while, soothing her and telling her that when she got a little older she could come to Punta del Este and "kiss horsies all day long." Then, sneaking fifty dollars into my hand and telling me not to get any more upset than I was—she was sure everything would work out and that she was sorry she had to leave, at a time like this especially—she went out the lobby door with her husband. I haven't seen her since. At last word she had taken out kidnapping insurance.

I dropped Emma off with the babysitter upstairs, telling her the latest gossip from the Italian restaurant, and said I was going downstairs to confront Elkse. The babysitter hugged me in sympathy (my only friend, now that Alexandra was gone) and said not to worry, she'd spend the night and it didn't matter when I got back. Tomorrow we'd *really* begin the packing, she said.

Downstairs on the ninth floor Elkse flew into a rage (which in her case is more like a mild tremor) and told me that Jimmy Wilcox was just jealous because she wouldn't fuck him that night when they met; besides, he was always drunk, and how could I listen to that shit. A veritable Leonardo da Vinci madonna, she lowered her divine eyelids, gave forth her usual sigh, and said, "Look me in the eye (for that she had to open it) and tell me that you believe I'm having an affair with Frederick."

It was getting harder and harder to look her in the eye (or anyplace else) because of my rapidly accelerating feelings for her. Whether these feelings were due to a real attraction toward her personally or because I was so starved for love that in the absence of anyone else I had chosen her as the receptacle for my passions I don't know; but in any case I did as I was bid: I looked into her soft gray eyes and said, "I believe you. You're not having an affair with Frederick."

I stayed with her for a couple of hours, getting drunk and stoned, until one of her admirers walked in, a bearded Italian artist with hyperthyroid eyeballs. In the course of the conversation he let it slip that he met Frederick in Elkse's apartment the night before. As I cross-examined him (lawyer's daughter that I am) Elkse tried to change the subject; blushing and stammering, she got him to say that he had made a mistake; it was out on Twenty-first Street that he had met Frederick.

I looked around the room, noticed some more Polaroids of Emma on the mantelpiece (clasped in the arms of Elkse, who was smiling meltingly into the lens), several of Frederick's latest videotapes stacked on a table, let my eyes wander back and forth between the Italian and Elkse, and said to him, "You're lying and I hate liars." Then I got up and went upstairs, my heart pounding, my head throbbing, a buzzing sound ringing in my ears.

A horrible rasping noise was coming from Emma's bed. I put my head on her chest to feel her lungs rattling and straining to breathe. When I lifted her head up off the pillow to try and relieve her breathing she woke up.

"Mama," she croaked, in a barely audible hoarse whisper, "I was crying for you."

"Oh, my poor baby, how could I have left you here like this? Why didn't you call me?" I asked the babysitter.

"Well, she woke up twice coughing, but then she went back to sleep so I didn't want to bother you."

Within five minutes we were on our way to the hospital in a police car, sirens screaming down Twenty-first Street, blazing through the red lights. Emma, wrapped in a blanket, was croaking confidences to me, so happy was she to see me, and talking about the siren. I kept telling her to save her voice but she wouldn't listen, just went on and on, telling me how she was crying for me and how she couldn't stand the noise of the siren. I put my hands over her ears.

Mario met us in the emergency room. It was three in the morning and I knew my breath smelled of alcohol; I was horribly aware of Emma's dirty feet, dirty face, and naked bottom. She was only wearing a tee-shirt. I could see clumps of dirt under her fingernails and her hair was a matted mess full of chewing gum. I knew what everyone was thinking—a neglectful alcoholic mother. That's what I would have thought if I'd been a nurse.

"Here," one of the nurses said, "we'll just put a diaper on her since we don't have any panties." Emma was very happy to be wearing a diaper; she loved the role of a baby. By watching herself on videotape so much lately she had become an expert on the gestures, vocabulary, and wardrobe of any baby between the ages of one week and two years.

Mario seemed a little angry that I had gotten him out of bed at that hour when it was only a case of the croup.

"The next time this happens," he said, "you should fill the bathroom up with steam and put her in it." I knew what he was thinking, too. That I had fallen apart because of Frederick. He knew all about the domestic battles at the Metro Hotel, since he was practically part of the family.

He drove us home. I put Emma in the double bed with me while the babysitter slept in the living room, among the packed trunks and boxes and string and brown paper. Emma woke up every two hours needing more cough medicine. I couldn't sleep myself, since I felt so guilty for what had happened.

Emma is asleep and I'm going through all of Frederick's videotapes, hoping to find evidence against Elkse. The first tape I looked at was a tape he had made of Emma while I was away.

"What beautiful long eyelashes you have," he was saying to her as she watched her own image in the monitor. He had hooked up the camera to the monitor and while he was recording her she was watching the process. The lens zoomed down on her eyelashes, splayed out over her round cheeks. The angle was from above. Then he switched to her profile.

"No," she said, "film my face." He switched the angle to a three-quarter view of her face and she smiled and began to make faces at herself. He reached out his free hand and held her mouth so that it looked like a fish's mouth. She began to make noises with her mouth held that way, and, fascinated by the sounds she was able to make, she continued to gurgle; they were both laughing. Then she became very inventive; imitating herself as a baby, as a one-year-old, as a two-year-old, saying, "Gaga, dada, mama, goo goo," with appropriate gestures. I had never seen such superb acting.

"Now lemme see T.V.," she said at the end. "I wanna see Emma." Apparently he then showed her the whole sequence, because there was a break in the tape. When they started to film again she asked, "Where's Mama?"

I was hooked; I had to find out what had happened every time I'd been away. I opened the locked trunks and went through the tapes. Finding one entitled *Dick Cavett and the P.O.W.'s*, I threaded it up on the machine. It turned out to be a tape of Frederick going down on a girl. I had never seen her before. She was very young and had enormous breasts. On the beginning of the tape Harriet was making macaroni for Frederick while telephoning me on Grenadier Island on Mother's Day. In the past, every time he had played this tape he had stopped it at the macaroni and gone into fast forward. I had never wondered what was in the middle before.

Now the girl was making obscene gestures toward my husband. She had a banana between her legs and kept rubbing it while licking her tongue toward the camera lens. In the background Harriet was asking, "Do you often come over here while Augustine is away?"

"You'll never leave," everyone kept telling me, as I continued packing, "you'll never get it all together. You don't really want to leave. You're just thinking up excuses to stay longer. Packing doesn't take that long." And: "Why don't you just leave everything here and split without it?" A woman I met on the elevator told me, "I tried to leave my husband once but I had so much trouble packing the pillows I had needlepointed that in the end I stayed with him."

Finally, one morning, Frederick showed up to take Emma to the park.

"I'm glad to see you're taking such good care of my tapes," he told me. "Max says that no matter how crazy you get, no matter how many dishes you break, you've never yet destroyed a tape."

Instead of asking him where he had been, I calmly told him that he couldn't take Emma until she had had her breakfast and then I went down to the street to buy some milk. In front of the deli I ran into Paul Campbell, a carpenter I had met while at Doug Redman's farm. He was from Nineteenth Street but he had been vacationing on Grenadier Island.

"You know," he said, "I think Elkse Boserup is very sneaky."

"What do you mean?"

"The last time I saw her she was over at Gunter's. She wanted to get something from him . . . something she had left behind—I don't know what it was . . . and I said to her, 'You know, Doug Redman is madly in love with you!'

" 'Oh, really!' she said to me, not looking at me. 'Oh, really'—that was all she had to say about it and I told her that he was a very serious boy and that he couldn't stop talking about her and that his wife was very upset and all . . . and she just didn't seem to care!"

"But," I asked him, "what do you mean by sneaky? I don't understand."

"Oh, just the way she sneaks around. Trying to get everybody to fall in love with her. Devious . . . that's what she is . . . devious."

"You know what? You're right!" I was suddenly furious again at Elkse. "And I'm sure she's been having an affair with Frederick!"

"I wouldn't put it past her."

"Why don't you come upstairs with me?" I asked him, happy for an ally and eager to hear more. "I'll make you a cup of coffee."

As we got on the elevator Moses Soyer was getting off. I was sputtering about Elkse and Frederick and Moses said to me, "What's the matter? You seem upset!"

"You'd be upset too!" I told him, "if your husband was fucking everybody in this hotel."

"Boy," he laughed, "you must really think a lot of your husband! To think that he's fucked everybody in this hotel! That's really a compliment for a man! Listen, when are you going to pose for your portrait? You keep putting it off."

I told him I was too mentally disturbed to be painted. Too bad, he died a year later.

In the kitchen Frederick and Emma showed up with a Panasonic Portopak.

"I suppose that's Elkse's machine," I said.

"Yeah," he laughed, "sure!"

"You can take Emma to the park but I don't want her down in that room, visiting your mistress!"

"I'm making a movie with her. She isn't my mistress."

"We know all about it, don't we, Paul?" I turned to my newfound ally, to confirm my suspicions.

"Look," he stammered, "I don't know anything about it."

It was only too clear that Paul Campbell was simply interested in making trouble and gossiping; when it came to following through, he was a dismal coward. I gave him a withering glance and asked Frederick what kind of a tape he was making, "a pornographic one?"

"You're crazy, Augustine," he replied, "and I can take my daughter wherever I want. You just try and prevent me."

Paul Campbell, having delicately leaked his information to me, was suddenly eager to remove himself from the fray. "I've got to split," he muttered, and ran out the door, leaving his coffee untouched on the kitchen table.

Hot on his heels, Frederick and Emma split for, I supposed, Elkse's apartment. I followed them. Racing down the stairs, I heard the elevator door open on the ninth floor; Frederick and Emma were getting out. (Frederick had taken the elevator in an attempt to foil me, to make me think he was going to the lobby; otherwise he would have walked the two flights down.) Our eyes met over the wrought-iron banister that connects the ninth floor to the tenth.

"Hi, Mama," Emma said, smiling, while Frederick rushed to his lover's door, shouting, "Watch out, Elkse, Augustine's on the warpath again!" It was becoming increasingly clear to me that my husband loved the whole scene; otherwise why would he bait me like this?

As Frederick tried to lock it, I pushed my way through the still-open door. Elkse was standing against the blue window casement, her elegant torso (the one I had so recently longed to enclose in my arms) encased in a matching blue-satin vest with leather ties crisscrossing across her bosom.

"Home wrecker!" I shouted. "Slut!" Then, turning to my husband, I commanded him to get my daughter out of there, that I didn't care how much time he spent with that whore but I didn't want my daughter contaminated. Elkse turned her back, sighed, and stared out onto Twentieth Street, too refined to be a party to my madness. Following her pained gaze, I noticed that a helicopter was landing again, on the Post Office roof.

"*Pretending that you loved Gunter von Habsburg,*" I screamed at her, "*when all you cared about was his money! I know all about you now! You drove Louise crazy, you drove Marie-Claude crazy, you drove Brigitte Redman crazy, and now you're driving me crazy! First you took away my apartment* (I knew this was illogical), *and then, not satisfied with that, you took away my husband! Now I suppose you want my daughter, too! Well, I've got news for you! You're not getting her!*"

During my outburst I was noticing that the apartment was immaculate; that tea was set out on a lacquered Chinese tray, and that, according to the labels on the mounting pile of videotapes that Frederick had been making with her, she had become not only my replacement in his affections but in his movies as well. I switched to French, thinking in my bombarded mind that my husband's native tongue would get the point across a little better. "*Elle n'a aucune responsibilités; c'est facile pour elle à rester tranquille. Elle n'a rien à perdre!*" Then I tried to wrench Emma from Frederick's arms. I succeeded in pulling her away from him and was standing in the entranceway to the kitchenette, holding her while weeping and raving in French about women who don't know what it's like to have children and an unfaithful husband without a job *en plus*.

Frederick lunged at me, twisted my arm behind my back, and I fell to the floor, the very same black-and-white linoleum floor that I had lathered with broken dishes over a year before, when we were living in that apartment. Emma fell on top of me, one of her arms pinioned under my back. As I screamed with pain Emma sobbed hysterically; her brilliant blue eyes bathed with tears and fixed on mine, she begged me, "Yet's go home, Mama, yet's go home!"

A bellhop, hearing the noise, rushed in and separated us (Elkse was remaining aloof from the struggle; she probably didn't want to tear her dress or, more likely, appear too human in the eyes of Frederick, thus losing her romantic appeal). Then he led Emma and me to the elevator. A new crop of Haitian maids were standing there, pretending to be shocked (I knew all about their own domestic explosions).

"*My wrist,*" I sobbed,"*my wrist! I think it's broken! Get me a doctor!*"

The maids turned away, silently shaking their heads, and went back to their duties.

Emma sat on the bed, the packed boxes and trunks around her, smiling at me, wanting to make everything all right.

"Funny?" she pleaded, "funny?"

"Yes," I tried to smile back, "funny." She had developed a technique to be used whenever she thought I was angry at her (for, whenever Frederick and I fought, she thought it was directed against her; on that subject, perhaps the only one, the psychology books don't lie). She wouldn't rest until I was smiling and agreeing with her that it was "funny" (or perhaps this obsession of hers was due to her mother's reputation as a "wit"). I hugged her and told her that I was going to rent a color television set so that she could watch it while I finished packing. She had rarely seen commercial television and was only used to watching herself on the tube.

The same bellhop who had rescued us moments before came up with the T.V. set. I plugged it in and turned to channel seven. Without noticing what was on the channel, I began sorting out clothes again. Suddenly Emma was screaming. It was a horror movie starring Ruth Gordon. A man carrying an ax loomed into view, his moon-illuminated face grotesque in a severe close-up. "*Mama,*" Emma, was screaming, "*turn it off! A monster, a monster!*"

"It's only a movie," I told her, hugging her again, "it isn't real, there's a camera there, and a whole lot of people behind a camera; it's just pretend." I snapped off the T.V. set and said to her, "Okay, forget about television; we're going out to buy some new suitcases."

In the sweltering sun we began walking down Ninth Avenue. Just as the heat waves were vibrating off the pavement, so my brain was vibrating with waves of rage against my husband and his mistress. At the first public phone booth I stopped and put a dime in the slot to call the Metro Hotel. I was glad that the sound of the traffic was going to mask my voice from Emma's ears. The dime rattled into the box and the phone began ringing. Mrs. Murray answered (my only friend on the switchboard, although I did overhear her complaining once that after all the time she had spent letting Emma play with the cords you'd think I would give her a bigger tip) and hearing my voice said, "It's a terrible thing! Men! They're all no good, let me tell you. Bums! Every one of them!" I asked for room nine fourteen after agreeing that yes, all men were bums.

"Yes?" Elkse's voice was faint in my ear, since the traffic was now in full swing, the light on the corner of Eighteenth and Ninth having turned green. Emma clung to my hand, docile and charming, as she always is after a major battle.

Left to itself, my voice would have shook, but I brought it out deeper from my throat, forcing it to remain steady; the result was close to the voice of my mother when she used to get into a rage against one of her children. It sounded like one of the lower strings on a violin as played by an amateur (like my father, for example, who has been taking violin lessons for the past fifty years and, as my mother says, "hasn't improved a bit").

I held Emma's hand tighter, my only ally. "It's me, Elkse," I told my rival. "I just want to tell you how much I hate you, how much I've always hated you—from the moment you moved into my old apartment in the hotel. In fact, I probably always will hate you, and if you want to get along in America you'd better change your tactics. That old-fashioned European coquetry just doesn't make it here (I ignored the fact that she had been enjoying a huge success with it so far). We're much straighter in America (I was forgetting *Cosmopolitan*'s advice to single girls); we don't practice that coyness you're so adept at, baby! *Get this straight. You're in America now and you know the old saying, 'When in Rome . . .'*"

Silence. Then, "I'm sorry you feel that way." Silence for two more minutes (I counted them by the clock above the pawn shop on Ninth Avenue).

"I never had anything like that with Frederick at all. I just don't know what to say."

"You don't have to say anything," I told her and hung up the receiver, grabbed Emma's hand tighter, and we made our way farther south to a cheapie luggage store on Fourteenth Street, where the manager offered me a job selling suitcases.

I put a tape on the machine.

"Is it a movie, Mama?" Emma asked me. "I don't wanna see any more movies."

"No," I told her, "it's just a tape."

By midnight she was asleep in front of the monitor, her thumb in her mouth (a habit she acquired from Normie the triplet, having fallen in love with him in Mexico), and everything but the monitor was packed. Then the zipper on the new suitcase broke. I went to bed cursing over the zipper and couldn't sleep; the lights on Twentieth Street were shining through the slits in the shutters and a rock group was banging away on the floor below me. I could feel the vibrations of everybody living above me, below me, on either side of me, an Egyptian pyramid full of live mummies. The only thing I hated more than New York by day was New York by night. The streetlights, hideous fluorescent slivers, creeping through the shutters, demanded my attention. I turned my back on them and still I saw them, dimly lighting up the room. I couldn't sleep.

I longed for Frederick but forced myself not to try and find him (for I knew that all I had to do was call almost anyone in the hotel and they would get in touch with him). I was going to be strong, leave him forever. I would never allow him to torment me again. And it was going to be his tough luck, his own fault that he'd never see his daughter again.

I fell asleep about four and dreamed that Frederick took me to a mental institution to visit Sarafina. He left me in a hallway talking to an attendant, and then disappeared. The attendant looked down at my feet, then up at my face, staring queerly at me. I noticed that I was wearing a pair of white wool socks, about two sizes too big, the toes hanging out over the edges of my feet. They were dirty and wrinkled and I wasn't wearing any shoes. I knew in an instant that she thought I was crazy, because I was without my shoes, and that she was going to lock me up. My white silk skirt began falling down around my hips; it was too big. I asked her for a safety pin. Instead, she led me through a room straight out of the "Big Freeze" scene in *Orlando*. Couples were dancing the tango in slow motion, enveloped in a beautiful blue-white icy mist. They were wearing blue-white furs around their necks and the ballroom floor was an ice-skating rink.

"Those people are all Thorazined up, aren't they?" I said to her, but she didn't respond; she just led me into the schizo ward and put me in a bed. Around the bed was a shelf lined with kidney-shaped pans, each one containing an aborted fetus. They were floating in pools of blood like shrimp and attached by fine cords to tomato placentas. Then a labor pain came over me, gripping me from neck to toe. "Oh, my god," I agonized, "now I remember the pain and I know I'll never be able to go through it again. I'll never be able to have another baby."

Along came a nun, dressed in white. She was carrying a wire coat hanger that she used to unlatch a hook, high above her head, on a big white door. The door swung open to reveal a big man, in bed, thrashing his legs (swathed in the white leggings so beloved by hospitals for childbirth) back and forth. Sitting at the foot of his bed was another white-veiled nun, her gray hair peeking out in bangs from underneath her coif. She was surveying her charge with a benign smile on her face, her hands folded in her lap. I knew he was in solitary confinement.

Lying on my back; my ears muffled by the pillow my head had sunken into, I began crying silently, tears streaming down my face in sympathy for the man in solitary confinement. Then I began calling for my husband. I wanted him to get me out of there; I felt the sadness of the world pressing me deeper into the pillow. "Frederick! Frederick!" I called, "Frederick, where are you?" Suddenly an alarm started ringing. I woke up, stumbled over to Emma's bed, and, taking her by the shoulders, I shook her awake.

"Emma," I whispered, "give me a kiss." Opening her eyes, she said, "Hi, Mama," in a quiet little voice, sat up in the bed, and, putting her arms around my neck, kissed me on the mouth. I was surprised that she kissed me on the mouth, because usually when I kissed her on the mouth she wiped it off with the back of her hand (as I remember doing myself when I was a child).

"I love you, Emma," I whispered to her.

"Sank you," she whispered back, "I love you too."

"Shall we go away tomorrow without Papa?"

"Yef."

I decided to test her. After all, she was only two and a half; how could I be sure that she understood the question? "Shall we take Papa with us?" I asked.

"Yef," she repeated.

I realized that the telephone was ringing (I had put it under a pillow in the kitchen) and had been, for quite some time. I went to answer it and found that it was Frederick.

"I want to see you," he said, "I have to talk to you." I told him that I wanted to see him too (how badly I didn't say) and then I got into Emma's bed. The sun was just coming up, hitting with its pink rays the helicopter on top of the Post Office on Ninth Avenue. I lay there, rubbing Emma's back, watching the helicopter change colors, and waited for my husband.

CHAPTER XXX

For the Sake of the Child

When the blades on the helicopter turned from cantelope to a dazzling silver I heard the door of the apartment open. Though I was telling myself that I ought to turn around to make sure it wasn't a marauding junkie looking for a T.V. set to rip-off, I just didn't have the force left in my body to move my head. I kept staring at the helicopter. Seconds later Frederick slid into bed behind me and put his arms around my waist.

"We know about the family, you and I," he said, "don't we? I can't help it. I never wanted a wife or a baby but now that I have both I can't live any other life. It makes me depressed to realize that I like it so much, that I'm stuck."

Newly energized by this revelation, I turned around to look at my husband. Never did he look more like my maternal grandfather. His hooded eyes were what I loved; the way his eyelids moved over them; Christ on Veronica's veil.

"Me too," I said to him, "me too."

"Won't you ever admit how awful you were to me?" he asked.

"You never fucked me," I told him.

"Don't you know why?"

"Yes," I admitted, "I remember. I remember that I wouldn't let you touch me when I was first pregnant. That I hated you, couldn't stand you in the same bed. That I pushed you away and said that a morning hard-on was just because you had to pee. I'm sorry."

We didn't say that we loved each other.

The next morning we rented a van to drive across the country. (I
was trying to follow in the footsteps of Great Grandma Simpson, Pioneer
and Daughter of the American Revolution, who had gone West in a covered
wagon.) As we carried the trunks and boxes to the elevator Emma kept
pestering me for things: "I wanna see my friends, I wanna glass of milk,
I wanna go out, where's my dolly . . ."

"Stop it, Emma," I said. "We're trying to pack up the van." So she
ran to her father, sitting on the floor locking a trunk, and said, "Papa, I
like you best!"

"Good!" I told her, "since you like Frederick best you can ask *him*
for anything you want!" Giggling, she climbed onto his lap, put her arms
around his neck, and asked, "Fed'rick, can I suck your mama?"

I went up to the penthouse to say goodbye to Magda. When I told her
about the events of the night before she warned me: "You've got to be careful about that," she said. "I asked Leni if I should leave her father for Jim
(Jim was Magda's jazz musician lover) when she was fourteen years old.
She said, 'Yes, Mother, I think you should leave him,' but she's resented
me for asking ever since. She feels that I treated her as the mother and
myself as the daughter. You shouldn't ask Emma for advice." Then,
laughing: "My god, she's only two and a half!"

Down on the street were the dealer and his wife, saying goodbye.
No one else had come downstairs, not one of those people whose lives had
been so entwined with ours for the five years we had lived there. We left
without fanfare, like tourists who were going home after a two-week
vacation in the Big City. Elkse and the blond photographer were closeted
upstairs, in room nine fourteen; *probably in each other's arms*, I thought
with a pang.

We stopped the van in front of the health food store on the corner
of Twenty-first Street and Seventh Avenue. The Greek who owned it, seeing
us in the van, Emma on her pile of blankets and quilts just behind the two
front seats and on top of a trunk, asked us where we were going. I stopped
drinking my carrot and apple juice combination, forty-five cents, and said,
"California."

"In that old truck?"

"Yes."

"Heroes, that's what you are," he pronounced in his heavily accented voice, "real heroes!"

In the van going across Pennsylvania, Emma gave us a demonstration of a new advancement in masturbatory techniques. Taking off her clothes with a coy smile, she crawled under a blanket on top of me. I was lying on the pallet. "My pee-pee won't come out," she said. "Where's your sharp bone?" Then she began grinding her pelvis into my ribs and hipbone. I tried to keep it from Frederick, afraid that he'd be angry at me, but hearing her breath come out in little pants he looked back, made a face, and continued driving.

Breathing a sigh of satisfaction, Emma finally said, "It's okay, you don't have to help me any more; my pee-pee's out now," and she discontinued her gyrations.

"You cold, Mama?"

"Yes."

"Here, put this on you," Emma said, grabbing a tee-shirt off the couch and putting it on my chest. "And this on your legs," she added, putting a sweater on my legs.

"You freezing?" she asked me.

"No," I told her, "not freezing, just cold. Get me your blanket. Out of your crib . . . no . . . don't try to climb into the crib. Just put your hand through the bars and pull it out."

"Oh," said Emma, "okay." She succeeded in that complicated maneuver and then said, "There, now you warm?"

"Yes. Thanks."

"Mom?" (This is a new expression, picked up in the Latigo Canyon nursery school, where she now goes each morning.)

"Yes?"

"I'm hungry," she said in a whisper, knowing that the subject was delicate, since she had refused to eat her dinner.

"I told you to eat your dinner and you refused," I said to her. "Now I'm too tired to get up."

"You know what I want?" she whispered again.

"What?" I asked her.

"Those little tiny things," she said, gesturing with her hands, making tiny parabolas in the air, "those teeny-tiny nuts, with the shells that you take off."

"Pistachios?"

"Yes, pitashos."

"We don't have any."

"Yes, we *do!*"

"When did you buy them?"

"Today," she said.

"Who were you with?"

"Frederick."

"Where are they?"

"In the car," she whispered.

"I can't get them. I'm too tired. Ask Frederick."

"He's *asleep!*" She had that tone in her voice implying, "How could you even think of waking him up?"

"Well," I said to her, "so am I!"

"But . . . Mama, he won't wake up!"

"Try him," I told her.

In the bedroom I could hear her saying, "Frederick! I want some a dose nuts!"

"They're on a shelf in the kitchen," he told her, apparently not really asleep.

Back in the living room she said, "Mom! He won't wake up!" I pretended to be asleep so she hesitated, looked for the nuts, couldn't find them, and then cautiously edged her leg up on the couch, under the blanket and fell asleep, next to me, sucking her thumb.

After a while I carried her to her crib (she had insisted on a crib, seeing that one of her friends had one) and went into the bedroom to get in bed with Frederick. At three in the morning she woke me up, calling, "Mom!" from her crib in the living room.

"What?" I yelled through the wall.

"I'm hungry!"

"Shit!" I complained to Frederick, "I *told* her to eat her dinner!"

"Give her a nut," he mumbled.

I got up, found the pistachios, and went into the living room. "Here," I said, "here's a nut."

"Thanks."

"Do you want a glass of milk too?"

"Yes. Thanks."

When I started back to bed she called out to me, "Mom! Hold my dolly like this, Mom! (she was holding her doll out to me, cradled in her arms). Otherwise she'll get cold!" She emphasized the "otherwise" to let me know that she had acquired a new word.

"Did you hear that, Frederick?" I yelled into the bedroom, knowing that you're not supposed to bring attention to their "cuteness" within ear-shot of your offspring, yet unable to resist. "She just said 'otherwise.' "

"Mom!"

"What?"

"Hold her . . . like this . . . *otherwise* she'll be cold, Mom!"

I got back into bed, only to hear five minutes later that little voice again. "Mom!"

"What!"

"I wanna see a tape, Mom!"

"Oh, my god, a tape! At this hour!"

"Why not?" Frederick groaned, "now that you woke me up, we might as well look at a tape."

He went into the living room and asked Emma what she wanted to see.

"The one we made today," she told him.

Frederick got her out of bed and put the tape on the monitor. It was a tape of Emma playing with her doll and teddy bear. First she has the teddy bear humping the doll and then the doll humping the teddy bear. Finally she gets on top of both of them and humps them herself, her little gray flannel skirt from Goodwill Industries bobbing up and down with the rhythm of her rear end.

After a close-up of her bobbing ass, the tape cuts to Emma, leaning out of the window of the car. I can hear Frederick saying, "Oh, fuck," as he tried to focus the lens.

"Fuck?" Emma giggles. "Fuck?"

"Yes," he says, "fuck!"

"Fuck!" Emma repeats. "Fuck you!" she shouts into the camera, asking next in an aside voice, "Am I too close?"

"No," Frederick tells her.

Laughing her head off, she yells, "Shit! Merde! Ca-ca! Pee-pee! Pussy!"

Having put in my day's work for the month at the Cooperative Nursery School in the canyon I know where the rest of the vocabulary comes from—the four-year-old boys who chant the words like a litany (daring any one of us "working mothers" to say, "Don't say that!") as they careen down the mountainside on pieces of cardboard.

My neighbor tells me, "If you think that's anything, you ought to go down to Malibu, where we used to live. All the eight-year-olds are smoking grass and sniffing cocaine!"

Across the street my other neighbor's nine-year-old daughter reports having watched her eight-year-old girlfriend "butt-fucking" a boy. She was outside, watching through the window, she says, because her mother forbids her to stay in any of her friends' houses when their parents aren't home. Her mother, no doubt, is the possessor of these charmingly old-fashioned set of values because of her background. Coming from Red Wing, Minnesota, she was a devout Irish Catholic mother of seven (at the age of thirty-seven) until her husband, after they moved West, convinced her that Buddhism was where it's at. He was converted by a local real-estate agent. On their kitchen wall hangs a tin-foil decorated shrine to Buddha, a kind of rice-paper Chinese scroll, hanging inside a disposable aluminum foil roasting pan, the scroll itself draped and hidden by a Liberty of London silk scarf. He gets up every morning at six o'clock and makes a long drive into north Los Angeles, where he works in a furniture factory that caters exclusively to the blacks of southern California.

"I wanna whisper something in your ear," Emma said to me one day after spending a couple of hours with Colin, their five-year-old son.

I leaned down and put my ear to her mouth. "I'm your lover," she whispered, giggling.

"Where did you learn that word?" I asked her.

"That's what Colin says to me," she told me.

I'm thinking about one of the first nights we spent in Latigo Canyon. Another neighbor took Emma and me out at midnight, under a full moon, to go horseback riding. Emma sat in front of me, trying to contain her fear as we galloped bareback up a hill, the moon casting shadows under the native white oak trees. At the top of the hill she said to me, "That was *fun*, Mama."

"How wonderful," I thought then, "that we're finally leading such a nice, wholesome life."

On the way to my sister Antoinette's house on Saddlepeak Ridge the next day, Emma said to stop the car, she had to pee. Frederick complied and we all got out, leaving the empty car with its front door open as we walked into the sagebrush to look at the view. Like a woman's leg, the toe at Palos Verdes, the thigh in Pomo, the entire area was encased in a pinkish beige nylon stocking of smog. Emma squatted down in the sagebrush, ass between her knees, and then looked up to say, "Close the car door before I pee."

"Jesus," I said to Frederick, "when she asked me to close the curtain in the bathroom yesterday, I said, 'It's okay, there's nobody here.' I didn't realize that, to her, as long as any available door is closed she thinks it's okay to pee; that it has nothing to do with modesty."

"You see!" my husband roared, "it's you who puts those ideas into her head, telling her 'it's okay, there's nobody here, you can pee.' She never would have made that association on her own; you're going to fuck her up for sure!"

Having learned my lesson back in New York, I let sleeping dogs lie and together we convinced Emma that she could pee even though the car door was open. Then we made our way along the ridge, high above the smog, to Antoinette's. (When I say "high above the smog" I fully realize that that's what everyone says about their domicile here in L.A.; but, as part of my self-imposed rehabilitation program, I've learned to incorporate into my being all of the native habits—thus learning, finally, to adjust.)

At Antoinette's everyone went out to search for herbs for the leg of lamb she was cooking, and while they were gone I told the children that it was so hot they ought to remove their clothes. As I was making a salad I realized that a heavy silence had suddenly descended over the house and, like all good mothers everywhere, knowing that silence is a sign of trouble I went on a search. In the master bedroom I found Emma and her cousin Gunnar, naked, on the double bed. Emma's fragile body was straddling that of her bigger cousin and she was urging him "Come on, Gunnar, give me just one little fuck!"

"What does fuck mean, Emma?" he asked, and she, apparently ig-

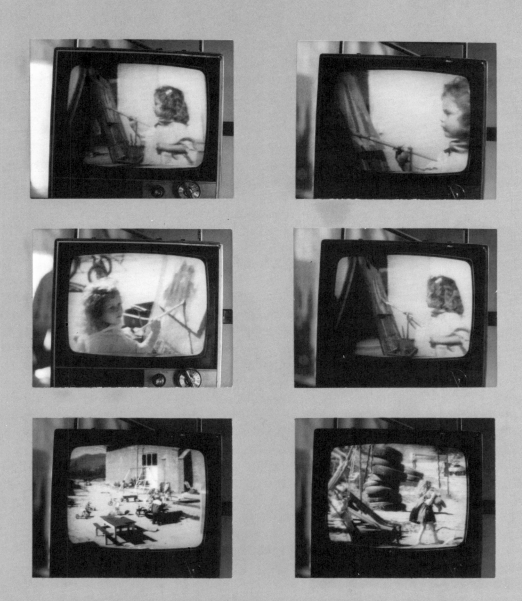

I decided that the truth must have come to her through the
nursery school in the canyon . . .
At School

norant, declined to answer. I searched my mind for where she could have witnessed the Primal Scene. It had been so unavailable in our apartment at the Metro Hotel that one day, seeing Camilla and Tony fucking, she had come running home crying, "Mama, Tony and Camilla are fighting!"

But that was so long ago I didn't think she'd remembered, and I decided that the truth must have come to her through the nursery school in the canyon, where, I was told, there was going to be a "sex education" course one day. Meditating on the often-heard cliché here in L.A., that "the nice thing about California is that there are so many different life styles coexisting side by side," I reflected that Latigo Canyon certainly is a far cry from Anaheim (that bastion of Disneyland, where the residents voted down sex education in the schools), and since there was no danger of pregnancy I left the babes to their innocent play and returned to my cucumber, onion, and tomato salad, a remembered staple on my mother's menu.

In the morning, the sun rising over the Santa Monica Mountains, Emma woke up with a demand that I write a letter for her, to her grandparents. I told her that I would have to have some coffee first and while it was brewing she kept insisting, "You're gonna write the letter, aren't you mama?"

"Goddammit," I finally screamed, "if you don't ask me five hundred times, yes, I'll write it. Didn't I say 'yes' once?"

She calmed down, telling me, "I wasn't asking you, I was singing a song to myself," then she chanted, "write a letter, write a letter," interrupting herself to say again, "see it's a song!"

While I drank the coffee she managed to find a ball-point pen and some paper. Then she dictated: This letter is for Grandpi, Grandpa:

> Up there the sun is out the water is o.k. This is what else is gonna be for a dress. A booful dress for me. Grandpi and Grandpa are gonna send me a pink dress, pink knee socks, pink shoes. And I can keep them—so booful and I can wear them. I can't wait.

I put a stamp on the envelope and went into the bathroom to wash my face. "Do you want to come in here with me?" I asked Emma.
"Why?"

"I just thought you might want to, that's all. Do you know why?"

"Doweedooeye," she laughed. I asked her "do you know why" just to give her a chance to try that joke on me again; I don't know where she picked it up, that "doweedooeye." She was standing out in the kitchen; I peeked around the curtain that passes for a door in this primitive cabin palmed off on us at an atrocious rent by the Buddhist real-estate agent before we realized that not only didn't it have a stove but it also didn't have any doors. She was peeking back at me, mouth closed, and ballooning over her tongue, which was pushed against the inside lining of her cheek, in an attempt to keep a straight face (so often, I've discovered, with small children, one learns that there is a real basis for expressions like "tongue in cheek"). Then she came into the bathroom and asked me to put some make-up on her. I choose Elizabeth Arden's "Pink Geranium" for her cheeks and Biba's "Blue-grey Stick" for her eyelids.

"Let me look in the mirror," she pleaded, so I gave her the mirror and she pulled down first one eyelid and then the other, smiled at the result, and said, "Okay, let's go." It was time for nursery school.

"Wait a minute," I told her, "I've got to get dressed."

"Okay," she said, following me into the bedroom. "I like your boots, Mama, they go all the way up." She was rubbing her hands up my snakeskin boots, feeling the scales.

"Do you want a pair of boots like that?"

"Oh yes."

"Okay, I'll get you some."

"You going to wear that sweater of Papa's?" she asked me.

"No," I told her, "it's too big. You ready to go now?"

"Yes, but first put something in my bottle."

I started to say, "All the kids will laugh at you if you bring a bottle to school, at your age (three)," and then realized that that's what my father would have said. I decided to try it anyway, just to see how she'd take it.

"Haha," she laughed, "that would be really funny! All the kids laughing at me!"

"You don't care?"

"No." She giggled.

I watched her as she hurried toward the car. Her eyeshadow was a little smeared. In one hand she was carrying her very first lunch box and in the other she was clutching her blue plastic Evenflo bottle. My baby.

A NOTE ABOUT THE AUTHOR

Before Viva turned author, she was a painter as well as an actress. For her roles in *Lonesome Cowboys, Nude Restaurant, Cisco Pike, Blue Movie,* and *Midnight Cowboy* she received an *Hommage* from the Paris Cinématique in 1970. She is married to the French filmmaker, Michel Auder, whose "Video Novel" of their daughter, Alexandra, has provided the illustrations for this book. They now live in southern California.

A NOTE ON THE TYPE

This book was set on the Linotype in a face called Primer, designed by Rudolph Ruzicka, who was earlier responsible for the design of Fairfield and Fairfield Medium, Linotype faces whose virtues have for some time now been accorded wide recognition.

The complete range of sizes of Primer was first made available in 1954, although the pilot size of 12-point was ready as early as 1951. The design of the face makes general reference to Linotype Century—long a serviceable type, totally lacking in manner or frills of any kind—but brilliantly corrects its characterless quality.

This book was composed by The Haddon Craftsmen, Scranton, Pa., printed by Halliday Lithograph Corp., West Hanover, Mass., and bound by The Book Press, Brattleboro, Vt. The typography and binding design are by Christine Aulicino.